Praise for *A Black and Endless Sky*

"Atmospheric and terrifying...readers won't be able to put [*A Black and Endless Sky*] down." —*Library Journal*

"In *A Black and Endless Sky*, Matthew Lyons has written a lush, unsettling, visceral story that is Lovecraftian and uncanny, yet touching and endearing. This is a powerful, immersive experience." —**Richard Thomas, Bram Stoker and Shirley Jackson Award nominee**

"A gripping read filled with tension and terror, the pacing is metered with otherworldly horrors and atmospheric haunts well acquainted with the unique isolation of the desert. A creepy and unsettling tale that gets under your skin and stays there." —**Kathleen Kaufman, author of the Diabhal trilogy, *Hag*, and *The Lairdbalor***

"Horror is at its best when hearts are broken alongside the things going bump in the night, and Matthew Lyons' *A Black and Endless Sky* delivers—prepare to be thrilled, touched, and scared shitless in this sprawling tale you'll wish was as endless as the ominous sky in the title." —**Fred Venturini, author of *The Heart Does Not Grow Back* and *To Dust You Shall Return***

"*A Black and Endless Sky* builds tension from the first page, delivers a powerful left hook, then pulls readers into the tumultuous lives of Nell and Jonah. From there it's a well-blended mix of action, noir, horror, and compelling humanity. Matthew Lyons is swiftly establishing himself as a master of gritty, dark noir, with his own brand of clear-eyed, effective character study. A talented author."—**Laurel Hightower, author of *Crossroads* and *Whispers in the Dark***

"Siblings Jonah and Nell take a terrifying journey that tests the bounds of family, loyalty, and reality. Thought provoking and scary. Read with the lights on!" —**Robert Rotstein,** *USA Today* **and** *New York Times* **bestselling author**

"An intense, gripping, innovative novel filled with a delicious panoply of horrors. Get ready for a wild, creepy, and high-octane ride." —**Daco Auffenorde, award-winning author of** *Cover Your Tracks*

A

BLACK

AND

ENDLESS

SKY

A BLACK AND ENDLESS SKY

By Matthew Lyons

Keylight Books
Nashville

Keylight Books
an imprint of Turner Publishing Company
Nashville, Tennessee

www.turnerpublishing.com

A Black and Endless Sky

Cover design by M.S. Corley
Book design by Misha Beletsky

Library of Congress Cataloging-in-Publication Data

Names: Lyons, Matthew (Short story writer), author.
Title: A black and endless sky / by Matthew Lyons.
Description: Nashville, Tennessee : Turner Publishing Company, [2022] | Identifiers: LCCN 2021025605 (print) | LCCN 2021025606 (ebook) | ISBN 9781684427093 (paperback) | ISBN 9781684427109 (hardcover) | ISBN 9781684427116 (ebook)
Subjects: LCSH: Brothers and sisters—Fiction. | Automobile travel--Southwest, New—Fiction. | GSAFD: Occult fiction. | LCGFT: Paranormal fiction. | Novels.
Classification: LCC PS3612.Y576 B57 2022 (print) | LCC PS3612.Y576 (ebook) | DDC 813/.6—dc23
LC record available at https://lccn.loc.gov/2021025605
LC ebook record available at https://lccn.loc.gov/2021025606

Printed in the United States of America

1 3 5 7 9 10 8 6 4 2

For Alice LeOra Merritt

One need not be a Chamber—to be Haunted—
One need not be a House—
The Brain has Corridors—surpassing
Material Place

Emily Dickinson

So, brother, raise another pint
Rev up the engine and drive off in the night
See you somewhere, some place, some time
I know there's better brothers, but you're the only
one that's mine.

Murder by Death

Prologue

THE MURMUR

From this far up, the desert looks like an ocean churning in the dark, the glowing worksite a galleon on black waves.

Down in the sandy scrub below, the workers use spotlights to stab holes in heaven, hunting the skies for helicopters, planes, drones, ultralights, anything, everything. They do not abide trespassers here. Not tonight. Not when they're so close. In between the lights and machines, jumpsuits and helmets scurry from trailer to trailer like nervous army ants, clutching clipboards and radios, trying to make sure everything hangs together the way it's supposed to. Tonight, something's different. Tonight, something's happening.

Word came from on high early the day before: they're finally going to breach.

They can't afford fuckups now.

They usually run a skeleton crew on the site, especially this late at night, but when the news broke that, after all their months of digging, they were actually going to break through and see what waited for them underneath the desert, the workers started showing up on their own. Not to try to log a few hours of overtime, not even to impress their supervisors—just to see. They've all been digging out here for so long that many of them forget what life was like before their shovels bit into dirt. This is what they've been working toward for months.

They wouldn't miss this for their lives.

Under the panopticon eye of the central tower, the gathered workers file through the chain-link gates, pushing past each other for a better view of the site proper, steam jetting from their noses and mouths in billowing white rushes. The desert gets cold at night, with snow on the way if the weather outlets are to be trusted. Working in the sand over winter can

3

be a nasty proposition—the snow sucks, but the cold is always worse. It leaves the ground hard as stone, soaks frost and ice into their bones, slows the work to a crawl. But almost none of them notice the freeze tonight; they can barely feel the chill past the electric anxiety that crackles between them, dancing across their collective skin in shallow blue arcs.

They crowd around the edges of what management's been calling the Well—the great hole that they all harrowed into the earth in pursuit of... well, what, exactly? Almost none of them know for sure, and the ones that do have been forbidden by frighteningly worded NDAs to say for certain. Security clearance and all that—a real bitch. No matter. They were sent here to dig, so they dug. Simple as that. Never mind the acousticians and sonar techs tracking their every movement and telling them where to excavate next, the tower overseers keeping their eyes narrowed behind plastic safety glasses, the strange static feedback like muffled screams fluttering their radios the deeper they plumb. They're company men and women to the last, and they know how to shut up and work when they're told.

Shoulder to shoulder, the workers flock to the edge of the Well and peer through the consuming darkness that fills it like black water, all the way down to the funnel's vertex, and the thing they found waiting for them there earlier this week, like a Christmas present left forgotten under the tree. The news traveled fast after they unearthed it. How could something like that not?

There's a door in the sand.

At first they hardly believed it. But then, one by one and group by group, they crept forward and saw it for themselves. It wasn't a door by any modern definition—a massive stone triangle pressed flat into the earth and buried deep under a thousand feet of frozen-solid Mojave Desert—but there wasn't any better word to describe it. For days after they uncovered it, they ran test after test to confirm what they already knew as the salient points spread among the workers like wildfire through dry grass: the door was ancient, its carvings remarkably intricate, and whatever hollow network that lay beneath it absolutely massive.

And now, tonight, after weeks and months of waiting, they're going to crack it open and see what's what.

Underneath the blades of light and the looming night sky, the crowd squeezes in around the chasm, a crown of jumpsuits and helmets and logos nervously shifting its weight back and forth until one breaks from its number: a demolitions engineer, satchel in hand, skidding down, down, down the sand and scree. Under the watch of all, she walks the full perimeter of the triangle door, tracing its labyrinthine patterns with her eyes as she plants the remote charges from her bag at each corner, coordinating over an open channel with the operators in the tower. It's so quiet down here in the black site's unburied heart, a natural anechoic chamber. Her pulse drums in her ears, and she has to force herself to breathe slowly as she attaches each charge to the stone, clicking them to life as she goes. The little red lights on the tops of the charges pulse arrhythmically, a strange crimson tremble bouncing from corner to corner. The third charge planted, she backs away from the door, unclipping the radio from her belt as she goes.

"Ordnance in place and active," she says into the walkie-talkie, her voice shaky. She watches her words snake around the crowd far above her like a vicious rumor, and when control finally radios back

"*Connection confirmed. Fall back and prepare for breach.*" She nearly collapses with relief. She hates being this close to the door. She's hated it since they first brought her down and ordered her to map the breaching charges to their sonar data. It feels bad, being this close to it—as if dread was a physical thing that could fill up your lungs and choke the life out of you. It feels like being trapped inside every nightmare she's ever had. Whatever lies beyond this door, they should not be going down there. But that's not her call. Not really.

Slinging the empty satchel over her shoulder, the engineer turns and scrabbles back up the funnel as fast as her hands and legs will carry her. Rejoining the crowd, she nestles herself beside two other engineers she's friendly with, crossing her arms over her chest as she turns to look back down at the door. It looks so small from up here. How'd they ever find it, buried all the way down there?

On her hip, her radio crackles and sputters again, static quickly resolving into familiar chatter.

"Confirm all clear, demolitions."

The engineer takes one more long, deliberate look down the Well, trying to keep the growing sense of vertigo at bay. *All clear.* Her last chance to back out, call it off, delay this some-how—if only for a little while. All around the crowd, faces turn her way, brimming with—what? Excitement? Anticipation? Fear? All three? Looking back at them, she understands that the time to call this off is long, long past. The decision's already been made, the die cast before the shovels ever hit the sand. If she doesn't do it, they'll find someone else who will.

No sense in prolonging the inevitable now.

She brings the radio to her lips again, her gaze still fixed on the triangular door. This time, when she speaks, her words are sure and strong, no shake to them at all.

"All clear confirmed."

"Understood. Breaching in ten, nine, eight, seven..."

The crowd braces as one. Nobody blinks, nobody breathes. The silence at the bottom of the funnel blooms and spreads like some invisible cancer, growing to infect every last one of them with its fearsome totality. They're not alive, in this moment— they're not anywhere, they're not anything. Together as fad-ing ghosts they watch, and they wait, and control counts them down from the safety of the central tower, each tallied second a miserable eternity. And then:

"...one. Breach."

At the bottom of the Well, the charges *thump* in a single, decisive concussion that the workers feel in their ankles, knees, lungs, and hearts. Sand cascades down the sides of the funnel in crumbling sheets, and for a moment nothing happens. The crowd holds its breath. Nobody speaks. Nobody blinks. And then they all start to hear it: a great brutal cracking, like some colossal tree falling in the distance, out of sight yet horrifyingly loud. The ground rumbles below their feet, as if the world is trying to split itself apart. The door at the bottom of the Well cracks, then tumbles away into the darkness below like it was designed to do exactly that. A second later, they hear the crash of the broken stone hitting the bottom of whatever chamber they've cracked open, and a whisper circles through the crowd as they ask themselves *Is that it? Is that all?*

They don't have to wait long to find out.

Not everyone notices it at the same time. It happens slowly, catching their attention and pulling them in one by one, holding them there, inexplicable, impossible.

Black smoke, rising in a diffuse column from the chamber below.

It floats up from the empty doorway in long dark curls that spiral ever inward, slowly coalescing as it spins in place, the patterns within growing more complex by the second. The wind pushes the twisting bulb of smoke back and forth, a misshapen head on a broken pivot, and for the span of a single breath the engineer is sure that she can see her dead mother's face in its coiling tongues, painted in inky grayscale against the headache-bright spotlights.

What the hell...?

Over their heads, the smoke swells and surges across the crowd, spreading wide like vultures' wings as it falls on them, swirling in between the workers, flooding mouths and nostrils and lungs in a noxious deluge. The engineer's quicker than most: clapping her hands over her nose and lips, she shoves for the gate, weaving through the hacking, sputtering bodies that surround her. Bile rises in the back of her throat, a bitter battery-acid tang that clings like aerosol. She chokes, she gags, she spits, she keeps pressing forward. Her eyes itch and blur red. Underneath her company-issue jumpsuit, her skin is starting to tingle and ache. Panic buzzes in her head like a fist of bees, and she knows she has to get out of here, right now, away from the smoke, the door, and whatever awaits below. This crowd isn't a safe place to be right now. Odds are she's only got seconds left before people start to—

Across the funnel, someone screams, a sound unlike any she's ever heard a human being make before. It's primal, almost animal in its desperation and horror. It shears through her, that sound—it leaves all other thoughts behind. Outside of herself, she turns and looks, and immediately wishes she hadn't.

Through the nervous, churning bodies pressing in on her, she can see someone thrashing on the far side of the Well, windmilling their arms in wild circles, thumping knotted fists against their own face as, all around them, other workers recoil and try to clamber away. Another scream rises from the thrashing jumpsuit—impossible to tell who it is from this far off—and then, clawing at their face and throat, they pitch forward, over the edge, into the funnel.

The crowd holds its breath as the thrashing worker plummets down the rough slope, somersaulting end over end, bouncing off the rocks, leaving bright red stains in their wake. The jumpsuit tears away in crimson ribbons as the worker's helmet snaps loose and goes skidding away across the uneven, jagged scree.

They all see it coming, but none of them can do anything about it. So, trapped in horrified silence, they watch.

The worker skids down the rocks, less a human body now and more a bleeding bag of flesh and bone, toward the gaping black hole at the bottom. For a second it looks like they're trying to keep themself from plummeting any further, digging their bare hands into the grit and sand as they tumble, but doing so only slashes their hands to tatters. More messy red added to the blur. When the screamer drops into the shadows below, the crowd stays quiet. Nobody cries out, nobody whispers or gasps or moans "oh, Christ!"—they just stand there, dumbfounded and terrified as they watch this person disappear into the earth.

Then they start to hear it.

At first it sounds like it's coming from below, a deep, far-off rumbling that resolves into a great churning mutter that rises and falls like speech, an incantation, a curse. But the murmur isn't coming from the cavern below. The murmur is inside their heads. Within seconds, none of the workers can hear the people beside them screaming for mercy, pleading, weeping, begging like frightened children. None of them notice when another column of black smoke jets from the bottom of the Well, thicker and darker than the first. It sweeps through the crowd in a horrid wave, pulling at their suits and masks, rock-ing them back on their heels as they clap their hands to their ears in a futile attempt to stopper back the sound coming from inside their skulls. Beside the engineer, someone shoves some-one else, and someone else shoves back. The panicked crowd turns animal, turns in on itself, terrified and furious. Fists start to fly. People start to scream. The roaring grows louder.

And then everything goes to hell.

Part One

THE CLACK

Walking a circuit through the bedroom, he went through the list in his head one more time, checking off boxes, making sure he had everything. He'd spent the last week packing all his things up, carefully filing them away in neatly labeled cardboard boxes to be shipped out to New Mexico, where they'd sit in his dad's third garage bay until Jonah figured out what the hell he was going to do now that his life had completely unraveled.

Molly had gone last Friday to stay the week at her sister's place up in Napa, a little place tucked away in the chilly early spring green of the valley. She'd wanted to give him the time and room to get his stuff together at his own pace; they'd already gone through the house at that point, stumbling their way through the awkward, stilted dance of *yours-or-mine*. Once that was over, Molly had squeezed Jonah's hand and left, heading north to work remotely and drink wine with Emily and deal with everything in her own way. She'd come back yesterday morning, eyes still as red and puffy as they'd been when she'd left. They hugged, they tried to comfort each other like they'd always used to, but it didn't work. Not anymore. They were two strangers under the same roof now. Their marriage was a dead furnace, the pilot light long gone out. All that was left to do was for Jonah to make sure he wasn't leaving anything behind.

Outside the house, he heard a car pull up to the curb, motor chugging and wheezing like an emphysematic in a hospital bed. He went to the window and looked down to the street to see a battered old blue Volvo station wagon idling by the front walk. As he watched, the Volvo's engine cut and the driver's-side door swung open to let a tall woman with choppy purple hair step out from behind the wheel, dark aviators fixed squarely over her face, a battered leather jacket draped snugly around slender shoulders.

Nell.

It had been a few months since Jonah had seen his older sister, and before that it had been, shit, years, he was pretty sure. This last Christmas, he'd finally bit the bullet, gone home, and broken the news to his dad and sister that things between him and Molly were, if not entirely over, at the very least rounding the last bend before the checkered flag. Dad—stubbornly single ever since Mom had died some twenty-odd years back—had taken it way harder than Jonah'd expected, but Nell hadn't bothered pretending to be surprised. She hadn't even blinked when he told her. She'd just studied him over the rim of her third Paloma for a long moment before speaking.

"You haven't seemed happy for a while, Jone," she'd said, careful to not set off another of their famous arguments. Seemed like they happened almost every time they talked, anymore. "You've been different, I guess. Not as happy as you used to be. I sort of figured it was either work, or it was stuff with Moll, but then you changed jobs and things didn't get any better, so...yeah. I guess I'm saying that sucks. And I'm sorry. Really."

"Yeah," Jonah said, tamping down the urge to take offense at her clumsy sympathy with the rest of his beer. "Me too."

The idea of taking a road trip had been idling in the back of Jonah's head for a couple of years by then, but it wasn't until things between him and Molly took a turn toward real, actual finality that he started seriously considering it. Maybe hitting the road was just what he needed right about now; avoid the interstates, take the scenic route back. It would add some miles to the trip, sure, but after everything that had happened, he figured it was probably better to give himself a real chance to try to decompress, clear his head some. Side roads were good for that sort of thing. Plus, if he was really being honest with himself, he wasn't going to complain about having a way to delay the inevitable for a little bit longer. He wasn't exactly proud of moving back to New Mexico, wasn't exactly looking forward to it either. For years he'd decried the people he knew who gave up and moved home from the Bay Area as washouts, unable to

hack it when the going got tough. But he didn't feel like a wash-
out; he didn't feel like he'd failed. He just felt hurt and broken
and sad, and he didn't have anywhere else to go but home.

It was Molly who suggested he invite Nell along. At first,
Jonah thought she was crazy or fucking with him—things
between him and his sister had been...well, *rocky* was putting it lightly, ever since he moved away. Even if they put on
a decent face for Dad whenever Jonah came home for the holidays, it never took long for shit to get weird and hostile again.
The two of them stuck in a car together for days on end? Forget
it. They'd spend the whole time fighting if they didn't manage
to kill each other first. Sure, Jonah and Nell used to be close, but
after all those intervening years, everything they used to have
was just ruins. Wreckage in the shape of a city.

Truth was, Jonah had never felt right about leaving Albuquerque like he did, up and vanishing without really telling
anyone, but it wasn't like he'd had much choice. Shit had gone
so wrong so fast, and he wasn't interested in hanging around to
get caught in the fallout. He needed a new life, a new him. He
needed to be gone, so he went. Need was funny like that.

Twelve years later, here they were.

Jonah thought he'd made his mind up about making the
trip back solo, but the more he thought about it, well, maybe
Molly was on to something. She usually was. Maybe some dedicated time together would do Jonah and Nell some good, help
them reconnect or something. When he finally got over himself
enough to call Nell and ask, he could actually hear her start to
smile. She loved the idea, she told him. Even offered to drive
out herself and pick him up so he wouldn't have to rent a car.
She could get the time off work, no problem; and besides, it was
going to be fun. Jonah was almost ashamed at how encouraging
it felt, hearing her say that, especially after everything that had
gone wrong between them. Maybe Albuquerque wouldn't be so
bad. Maybe his whole life wasn't over yet.

Down on the street, Nell caught him watching and
flashed her wide movie star grin, waving. Of the two Talbot
kids, she'd definitely gotten all the looks. Ever since they were
little, Jonah had been too tall, too skinny, his eyes too intense,

his hair too long, too dark, too greasy. With her big hazel-greens and expertly cut locks, Nell had always looked like she'd been plucked out of some TV show and dropped unceremoniously into real life. Jonah, on the other hand, looked like he was trespassing from some dimension where they only made junkie goth-rock clones of Bela Lugosi. Meeting his sister's gaze, Jonah raised a hand in return, then jabbed a finger at the floor: *I'm on my way down.* She gave him a thumbs-up and circled around the station wagon to sit on the front of the hood, lighting a bent Camel from a crumpled pack.

Downstairs, Jonah heard the front door creak open. Probably Molly stepping outside to say hi. Or, more likely, bye. After all, chances were this was probably the last time she and Nell were ever going to talk, at least for a really long time. There was a tiny little stab in Jonah's heart at that.

They'd always gotten along, Molly and Nell. Probably would have been really great friends if it hadn't been for Jonah. They liked the same movies, listened to the same bands, watched the same stupid TV shows. Back when things were good, Molly used to joke that the only thing keeping her and Nell from being best friends was Jonah's stubborn insistence on avoiding Albuquerque as forever as possible. Looking back on it now, he was embarrassed of how he'd gotten in the way of them really connecting, his baggage making things so much harder than they needed to be yet again. It was almost pathological at this point, like a curse or some cosmic joke, the universe showing off its sick sense of humor, except Jonah knew that last part was bullshit. The universe didn't have a sense of humor. The universe didn't care about you at all. The universe just *was*, and you thanked your lucky stars every day that it let you keep on living inside it, even when living inside it was fucking horrible.

Molly and Jonah didn't hate each other, far from it; they'd fallen out of love, and that was all. Looking back, things had started going wrong when they'd first bought the house, ready for some space where they could finally stretch out after years of cramped apartment living. Except after a while, the space had gotten to be too much, the distance too far. There was too much house in their house and not enough Jonah and Molly to bridge the space between. They didn't fight, they didn't argue—Jonah never let things go that far, even when Molly clearly wanted to. They barely even talked about it when he started sleeping in one of the spare bedrooms.

Taking one final look around, Jonah swallowed the crab-apple in his throat and went downstairs to wheel his suitcases out onto the front porch.

"Hey," Nell said, turning toward him as he stepped outside, proffering a sad, gentle smile. "Got everything?"

Jonah nodded. "Think so."

"Cool," Nell said. She pulled Molly into one last big hug, making it count; when they broke apart again, it was like watching a border being drawn down a map in thick, black marker. An impossible barrier, never to be crossed again. Reaching both hands out, Nell took Jonah's suitcases from him and stepped off the porch.

"I'm going to put these in the car," she said. "You guys . . . take your time. Molly, take care of yourself. Really."

"I will," Molly said. There were tears in her eyes already. "Drive safe."

Nell clucked her tongue and gave her new ex-sister-in-law a winking little salute. "Always do," she said. "I'll see you."

"Yeah, see you," said Molly.

They watched Nell wheel the suitcases down to the Volvo and load them in the back before climbing behind the wheel, leaving Molly and Jonah alone for the last time.

"I, uh," Jonah said, twisting his fingers into knots below his scarred-up knuckles, staring at his shoes.

"Yeah," Molly said. "Me too."

". . . You gonna be okay?"

She shrugged. "I guess so. Eventually, I think. Emily's coming down to stay for a while. That'll help, probably. Plus, I've got work to distract me, so that's something. What about you?"

Jonah glanced back at the station wagon, at Nell, at the long road in front of him.

"Yeah, probably." Between his ears, everything that he'd always meant to tell her, all his practiced goodbyes, it all turned to ash and blew away with the wind. "Yeah. I'll be all right. Couple of days off the grid. Probably do me some good."

"Supposed to be some weather later, I heard."

"Yeah, a little snow, I think," Jonah said. "Nothing we can't handle."

"And at least you're not doing it alone, right? Nice of Nell to volunteer. I bet you two'll have fun."

"Sure. If we can avoid killing each other."

"You'll be fine," Molly said. "I have faith in her. In you, too, for the record."

"That's a change," Jonah said, immediately regretting it.

Molly tore her gaze away from his. "Jonah..."

He was only dragging it out now; the moment that they'd both been ignoring ever since Molly got back from Napa. It was here; it was now. *This is as far as we go together.* They were standing atop a great divide, readying themselves to jump in opposite directions. This was the last time they'd be *them.* After twelve years, this was actually it. Not wanting to waste any more time, Jonah pulled Molly into a hug of his own, wrapping his long, ropy arms around her and squeezing her tight.

"I'm sorry, Moll," Jonah said, speaking softly into the crown of her head. The smell of her shampoo—and all the memories he associated with it—dug at his heart like an auger. "For everything. For all of it. For every—"

Pulling away, Molly put a hand on his elbow and squeezed. "I know," she said, the quaver in her voice telegraphing more tears to come—but only once he was gone. "Me too."

Jonah nodded. As if nodding would ever be enough.

"Let me know when you get h—" She caught herself mid-sentence. *Home.* That's what she was going to say. Jonah pretended not to notice the slip. He swallowed. Looked at his feet again. "—to your dad's place. Drive safe, and all that."

Her words were a dull blade twisting in his guts. Jonah chewed on the inside of his cheek until he had the courage to meet her eyes again. He wanted to tell her he loved her, how much she had meant to him, how wonderful she was. All their time together, it had to mean something. It couldn't all be for nothing. It couldn't.

But then the moment passed. And it was too late.

"Yeah," he said. "Will do."

Molly squeezed his arm one last time and let her hand fall away, crossing her skinny arms over her chest and looking past him, out toward the city they'd shared for so long. "Goodbye, Jonah."

"Yeah. Bye, Moll."

Pulling himself away from her orbit, Jonah turned and made for the car, leaving her there, alone in front of their house. Every step he took felt like wading through concrete—that awful black border on the map of his life, drawing itself wider and more impossible by the second. The walk to Nell's Volvo wasn't that far, but it felt like forever.

Pulling the passenger-side door open, he didn't climb in so much as fell into the seat, looking down into the footwell as he buckled himself in. He glanced up one last time. On the patio, Molly gave him a sad little wave, then turned and walked back into the house. Jonah waved back, but she didn't see. He watched her go; when the door closed behind her, he felt like he'd been flattened by a truck.

A second later, a small warm hand alighted on top of his own, giving it a gentle little squeeze.

"Hey," said Nell.

Jonah didn't look up. "What?"

"Hey, I said." She squeezed his hand again, harder this time.

"What?"

Jonah tore his attention away from his house—*the* house, he reminded himself; it wasn't his anymore—and looked over at his sister. Eleanor Leigh Talbot. One of the only constants in his entire life, not so constant lately. Sitting behind the wheel, Nell hinged her sunglasses up off her nose to look at him straight on.

"You good?"

He scratched at his scalp through his shock of thick black hair, then pinched his eyes shut until he saw stars. When he opened them again, Nell was still watching him, unblinking.

"No," he said, his voice drained of all life. "But at this

point what is there to do about it? It's done. It's over, messy and painful and useless as it is. No going back now. The end. Nothing more to talk about."

Nell's expression fell. "You know that it's okay to be upset about this, Jonah. It's okay if you need to talk about it," she said.

Resentment, childish and petty, fizzed in the back of his throat. Where did she get off, saying this shit to him right now? What gave her the right?

"Yeah, I know it is," he said. "I'm aware. Thanks."

"I mean, I know that you know—"

"No, I *get* what you're saying," he said, cutting across her like a straight razor flashing through a bare throat. "I understand. Thank you for your concern. Can we go now?"

"Sure," she said with a sigh. "No problem."

Nell turned the key in the ignition, kicking the Volvo's engine to life with a shrill mechanical whine. A second later, the old station wagon chugged away from the curb while, in the passenger seat, Jonah rested his head against the glass and, vision trained squarely on the sideview mirror, watched his old life slide slowly into the distance.

T hey passed out of the Bay Area lowlands soon enough, heading east just north of Hayward to cut through Pleas- anton and Livermore; before long, San Francisco was little more than a memory. Nell had never liked the city that much. It was too loud, too busy, too obsessed with its own image. Places were like people in that way—left unchecked, they could disap- pear right up their own assholes without anyone even noticing.

They'd been driving for an hour with the radio on low when Nell reached over and punched the Search button on the car ste- reo, cycling through the stations until she landed on something she wanted to listen to: The Cure, "Just Like Heaven." On the other side of the car, Jonah had tilted his seat all the way back to stare up at the roof of the car from behind his sunglasses. Was he seriously going to be like this the whole trip? She couldn't blame him for hurting, and understood that her brother had to heal, but . . . you could only lick your wounds for so long. Eventually you had to go back into the world and try again. Even if it ended up hurting you. Scars were only worthless if you didn't learn from them. Hank Williams had said it best: nobody ever got out of this world alive.

Still. Jonah wasn't alone, and he deserved to know that. She'd made an attempt when they were parked outside the house, but maybe it hadn't been the right time, or the right thing to say. Nell had always had a knack for saying the wrong thing at the wrong time, but she never let it stop her from try- ing. After all, it wasn't like Jonah had ever been great at under- standing his feelings, let alone talking about them. Maybe the best way through to him wasn't the straight path. Asking some- thing like "How are you doing with everything?" might work with other people, normal people, but Jonah hadn't ever been

21

normal people. That was okay. Maybe it was better to simply get him talking, and let the rest sort itself out. Besides, there were still plenty of things that Nell wanted to know.

Reaching over with one hand, she jostled one of her brother's knees.

"Hey. Hey, you awake over there?"

Jonah roused from his daze, turning his head to look at her.

"Yeah," he said. "I'm up. I'm good. What's up?"

"Something I've been meaning to ask you," Nell said. "Something I've been wondering."

"Yeah? What's that?"

"Did she ever see it?"

Jonah blinked slow at her.

"Did who ever see what?"

"Molly."

Jonah pulled his sunglasses off and rubbed at his face. "Right. Did Molly ever see what?"

"That side of you that you like to pretend isn't there. That side of you that drank a whole bottle of tequila with me one night at Carson's and then broke Tyler Malick's jaw and a handful of his teeth for talking shit."

Jonah's face darkened by a degree, then two, then three.

"I don't know what you're talking about," he said.

"Sure you don't. That must have been one of my other brothers," Nell jibed. "Because I have so many. Instead of just the one."

"Look, how about let's not, okay?" Jonah said, turning away again. "I'm really not interested in talking about ancient history right now."

He was never interested in talking about it. That was the problem. Back in the day, Jonah had been a hell-raiser supreme around Albuquerque, the kind of guy who grew up pissed off at the world, ready to meet trouble fist-first as soon as it reared its ugly head. And the thing was, he was good at it. There was no hesitation in him, no negotiation. He just handled shit, hell with the consequences. Maybe he had a natural talent for violence, or maybe he was just angrier than everyone else. Nell really couldn't say for sure. All she knew was once her brother started getting into scraps, word got around: when Jonah Talbot put you down, you stayed down.

And then, one day, out of nowhere, he just vanished.

An uneasy quiet settled between the two siblings, an impenetrable wall of nothing, the kind of stubborn, intentional emptiness that took years to fortify and harden. Only families ever got quiet like this at each other. Only families could sustain it. No one who wasn't stuck together with blood would put up with the cold, straining violence of it. Nobody weaponized silence like family.

"It wasn't his jaw," Jonah said after a moment that seemed to last a lifetime.

Nell kept her eyes on the road.

"I'm sorry?"

Swinging his seat back up, Jonah leaned forward to bury his face in his hands, then looked at her again.

"Tyler Malick. I didn't break his jaw. I broke his nose, and only because he wouldn't lay off you. You'd just broken up with that Bethany girl and you'd cut all your hair off, dyed what was left that really bright neon green. This was back before you started dating Andrew, remember?"

Right, okay. Nell remembered now. Tyler Malick had always been an asshole, ever since they were in high school—one of those shitheels who failed through life with a grin and ended up taking a job hustling used cars at his dad's dealership because it was easier than actually trying. He'd been a cunt since he was fourteen, and he'd only gotten worse with age, starting shit with anyone who looked at him sideways because he'd spent his whole life being told that "one day, Tyler, one day you're going to run this whole town," and the poor dumb bastard grew up actually believing it.

The memory of the night in question played like a silent picture show across the surface of Nell's aching brain: Her breakup with Beth had been coming for a long time by then, and on the day things finally fell apart for good, Jonah had taken Nell and her new fuck-you haircut out to Carson's bar to try and soothe the burns with some liquid therapy. They'd ended up staying there for hours, downing shot after shot and laughing and trying to forget what heartbreak felt like. A lot of the details eluded her now, almost a decade and a half after the fact; all she could say for sure was that at some point over the course of the evening, Malick was just *there*, taking up one of the empty seats at the table, uninvited. Classic townie douchebag move.

They'd tried to ignore him at first, they really had. Carson's was the kind of place that was always filled with friendly drunks sticking their noses where they didn't belong—it was part of the ambiance. You got used to it, or you found another watering hole. Simple as that. But there'd been something different about Malick that night. Eyes all rheumy, words mangled by the rotgut shots he'd been pounding, Nell could see that he was looking for trouble from the jump. Assholes like him always were, in one way or another.

She didn't know what had set the shithead off, only that when he had boiled over, he'd done it shouting and stomping around like Yosemite Sam, completely incoherent. Whatever it was, though, he'd seemed to think it was somehow Nell's fault. He kept pointing at her, getting louder and louder, until he leaned in to try and grab her by the wrist. That was a mistake.

Jonah had hit Malick like lightning striking a dead tree in an empty field. *Boom*. Malick floundered, only barely staying upright, and a second later, when the fool's senses came back to him, he'd actually tried to bum-rush them, eager to even the score. Jonah swung again. *Pow*. That time, Malick hit the floor so hard, he bounced. There was barely anything left of him after that second punch, just a mess of smashed face meat and awkward limbs laid out and yowling on the tile.

"Right, right, right," Nell said. "Okay, sure. So, who got the broken jaw? I'm pretty sure that somebody got one at some point, didn't they?"

"Yeah, same night," Jonah said. "One of Tyler's buddies. Parking lot, remember?"

The memory clicked into place inside her head. "Oh, shit, *right*," she said. "With the broken piece of pavement." She remembered now: after Jonah had thoroughly cleaned Malick's clock, the two of them had gotten out of there quick, in case anybody decided to be a dick and call the cops. Out in the parking lot, one of Tyler's crew, another entitled little incel freak that Nell didn't know, had come after them, swinging a jagged chunk of loose asphalt like a club or a shotput. Without missing a beat, Jonah had knocked the dude's legs out from under him and then field-goaled his head into the next time zone. After that, Tyler Malick and his shitbird friends never looked cross-eyed at either of them ever again.

Nell chuckled at the memory and rubbed at the bridge of her nose with her thumb and forefinger, trying to press away the dull headache that was growing steadily behind her eye sockets. It had been there for the past couple of days now, mostly low-level, simmering underneath the surface, threatening to eventually break through. Today, it seemed like it was finally making good on that promise. Wonderful.

"I mean, hey, fuck those guys, right? Malick and his goons. Play stupid games, win stupid prizes," she said.

Jonah sighed. "I guess."

"You ever miss it?"

"What, Carson's? It's still there, we were there over Christmas, remember? Same shithole bar it always was."

"No, not Carson's," Nell said. "I mean the other thing. Your life as a big bad street-fighting man, back before you went straight or whatever. Before Molly and all that."

"I don't know," Jonah said. Nell watched him hang his head the slightest bit. "In some ways, sure, I guess. I think everybody gets to a point where they miss being young and perfect and bulletproof, don't they? But that's how shit goes, right? We're in our thirties now. Gotta grow up sometime. Can't keep getting in shitfights over nothing forever."

"I guess."

"And, to answer your first question, no."

"No?"

"No, I never told Molly about all that."

"Any of it? Really?"

Jonah sighed. "I mean, some of it, I guess. As little as I could get away with. You can only dodge a question like 'How'd you get those scars on your hands?' so many times before it starts seeming sketchy." Out of the corner of her eye, Nell saw him cross his arms over his chest, tucking his hands, the knuckles crosshatched with white, into his armpits. "It's old news, anyway. Somebody I used to be. Somebody I don't really like that much. Never did, now that I think about it. I guess I thought keeping Moll in the dark about it was the better choice."

"Was it?"

Nell felt her brother withdraw the second the words were out of her mouth. It was a mistake to ask, and she knew it. She'd been toeing closer and closer to the line with him, bringing this up, but now she'd well and truly crossed it. After another second, he cleared his throat, shook his head.

"Look, I appreciate what you're trying to do, Nell; I really do. But honestly, it's a bit late for any sage advice on how to keep my marriage together."

With that, he turned his attention back out the window, watching the landscape whip by through the passenger-side window.

"All right," Nell said. "Sure. No problem."

She'd pushed him too far. But then again, hadn't Jonah always needed someone to push him out of his comfort zone? That had been true their entire lives. Probably she was just out of practice. It had been years since she'd been the one who had to do it, after all.

They drove on.

Passing into the pine-scattered California hills, Nell saw the sign first, rickety in rusted white-on-green, battered by time and weather and a handful of armed townies cruising by, hunting for target practice:

> *Broughton, CA*
> *Pop. 81,592*
> *Welcome*

She popped on her turn signal, easing down on the brake and veering the car toward the next exit. In the passenger seat, Jonah twisted in place, glancing back and forth, confused.

"What are we doing?"

Nell jutted her chin toward the exit. "Stopping for a drink."

"Why?"

"Because I'm thirsty?"

"Day drinking on a weekday? Really?"

"Okay, it's Friday, one; and two, thirst waits for no one, Jone. That's what makes it thirst," she said, piloting the car around the long exit loop. "Besides, it's just going to be the one. There's a schedule to keep, remember? Gotta get to Mowry by dark, check into our hotel, and get a full night's sleep so we can wake up bright-eyed and bushy-tailed. We have an itinerary here."

Jonah turned a questioning expression toward her. "Since when have you ever cared about itineraries?"

"Since now."

"Convenient," he grumbled.

"Relax," she said. "It's a road trip. It's supposed to be an adventure. We'll still get to Mowry with enough time for you to gamble some of your hard-earned savings away, don't you worry."

"I'm not worried about that at all," Jonah said, crossing his arms over his chest.

Nell patted him on the arm. "That's the spirit."

The town of Broughton was a scummy little place that, to Nell, didn't seem like much more than a wide spot stretched along the highway, filled with drive-throughs, gas stations, diners, and skeevy dive bars. Down every cross street, Nell could see a long stretch of boarded-up shops and storefronts, stooped apartment complexes, and empty, chained-off lots, but no people. Nobody walked around here. Probably didn't want to get mugged. Under the dead-gray sky, the whole town sagged and slumped, cracked and split from time and neglect. Up and down the main drag, eighteen-wheelers refueled under corrugated awnings while their zombie-eyed drivers cranked one out in the

backs of their cabs, sleeplessly chasing their next hit of sero-
tonin. Another nothing city lost to the American sprawl.

"Such a charming place you've picked out," Jonah said
sourly, watching the fractured little town pass by, fogging the
window with his breath.

"Oh, shut up," Nell said. "I think it's got character. Nothing a fresh coat of paint couldn't fix."

"Probably better to burn the whole thing down for the insur-
ance money," Jonah said. "I don't think anyone would miss it."

"You're a cynical asshole."

"Yeah, that's one way to put it. Seriously, though, why
here? I feel like I'm going to get black lung or hepatitis breathing
the air in this town."

Nell grinned. "You'll be fine. You've had your shots, hav-
en't you?"

"I don't think they immunize against getting robbed by a
fucking meth head."

"You worry too much."

Jonah shook his head.

"That's entirely not the point," he said.

They cruised through Broughton until they reached an
intersection at what seemed to be the far edge of town: straight
ahead was an on-ramp leading back onto the highway, while
left led to a dead end cluttered with old tangles of chicken wire
and scrap metal and cracked cement pylons. Nell took a right.
After a couple of minutes, they arrived at a ramshackle little
building with worn, splintered-wood siding and musty windows
that hadn't been cleaned for years. A short row of motorcycles
filled the parking spots underneath the welter of buzzing neon
beer signs that hung against the grimy glass: ST. PAULI GIRL,
COORS LIGHT, PABST BLUE RIBBON, MILLER LITE, FOSTER'S.

There was a hand-painted sign above the door that read
LOTTE'S TAVERN, and another one next to the window that
stated, beneath a crossed pair of cartoony six-shooters, 48 COF-
FIN: WE DON'T CALL 911, WE CALL FAMILY! Nell nosed the station wagon into an open parking space at the edge of the lot
and threw it in park, then killed the engine. Beside her, Jonah
pointed at the bar.

"There. You want to go in *there*," he said, incredulous. "You're kidding."

Nell took off her shades, folded them, and stowed them in her pocket. "What's wrong with *in there*?"

"Looks kind of rough, is all."

"Oh, come on. It's fine," Nell told him. "I mean, sure, it's not exactly Applebee's, but I think it'll do for a drink or two. Not like we're moving in next door or anything."

"That's probably for the best," Jonah said. "I think the only thing the next lot over's zoned for is a tire fire."

"Come on, give it a chance," Nell wheedled. "It might not be as bad as you think."

"Yeah, it might be worse," Jonah said. "Also, a drink *or two*? A few minutes ago, you said it was only going to be the one."

"What can I say? Plans change," she told him, smirking. Pulling on the handle, she stepped out of the Volvo.

Kicking the car door shut behind her, Nell craned her neck and breathed deep, relishing the faint sting of the cold inside her lungs. It was chillier out here; breezier, sharper, harder. Down along the coast, it was easy to ignore the fact that there were actual seasons in the world. Up in the hills, a few thousand feet above sea level, Nell could feel winter in the air, real and true — that same bitter, steel-hard cool she'd left behind a few days ago. Western winters were brutal and beautiful in their absoluteness, hanging on for months past the season's official end, stretching all across Wyoming and Montana down over the Four Corners and beyond. They were heading back into it now, and Nell couldn't have been happier. A few days driving through the cold would do them both a lot of good. Like coasting into another world. Another layer of separation from Jonah's old life and his new one. Just what the doctor ordered.

Rolling her neck back and forth between her shoulders, Nell rounded the car to cross the cracked parking lot, Jonah close on her heels. On the bar's front door, there hung another metal sign she hadn't seen before: sculpted in simple wrought iron, the number *48* framed inside a coffin. She'd seen the same logo drawn into the pistol grips on the sign in the window.

"Check it out. Local art," Nell said, pointing. "That's not nothing, right? Kind of like a boutique cocktail bar or some shit."

Jonah was nonplussed. "Sure," he said. "Real cool."

Nell turned to look at him.

"Okay, come on, this is supposed to be fun," she said, annoyed.

"I'm having fun," Jonah said. "Lots of fun." Deadpan, he flared his fingers and shook his hands like he was on stage. Jazz hands. "Check it out, I'm the Fun Machine, look at me go. See? Fun."

Nell raised an eyebrow. "Uh-huh."

Turning back, she curled a hand around the cold metal edge of the little sculpture and pulled the door open, leading them inside.

J onah had been in bars like this before.

Dingy old lights hung on rusty tracks overhead, casting the whole barroom in an anemic piss-yellow light that was only made worse by the chipped 1970s wood paneling that wrapped around the whole of the place. The bar itself, a long stretch of scarred old pine, was lined with vinyl-topped stools held together with clear stripes of packing tape. Behind it sat a full mirror wall, braced with dusty bottles and ropes of weakly glowing fairy lights that must have hung there for decades already, all but forgotten now. Beside the bottles was an old-timey cash register and another hand-painted sign, this one reading DON'T LIKE MY GUN? COME AND TAKE IT, HIPPIE!

The door creaked shut behind the Talbots as they stepped inside, the shrill whine of the hinges drawing every eye in the barroom. Jonah could feel his cheeks flushing hot apple-red as the scattered old-timers and shitkickers inside sized them up. He hadn't been under the microscope like this in a long, long time. It didn't feel good.

Over in the nearest corner, a group of grizzled men in battered black leather sat around a four-top, sipping beers and muttering among themselves. Glancing over, Jonah saw that the patch on the back of their leathers matched the design they'd seen mounted in iron on the bar's front door: the number 48 trapped inside a coffin. Okay, so this was definitely a biker bar. Great. That was just great. That didn't suck at all.

As Jonah followed Nell over to the bar, he could feel the bikers glaring at him, drilling holes through his back, getting a read. Jonah kept his eyes to himself. Nothing good ever came from starting shit with guys like that, especially on their home turf. It was plenty clear that 48 Coffin didn't abide strangers, and

that the Talbots—like every other fool tourist who mistakenly
wandered their ass in here—were entirely unwelcome. That
was fine. Jonah told himself it was fine. They weren't going to
be here long. They were going to have a drink, then they were
going to pay their tab, and then they were going to go. That was
all there was to it.

They took the first two open stools at the pine and waited
patiently for the bartender to make his way over. In the mirror
behind the bottles, Jonah could see the bikers in the corner still
watching them, especially the one nearest the wall, an old guy
with pale, intense eyes—serial killer eyes—and a tight salt-and-
pepper goatee grown over a messy scar that traveled the breadth
of his chin. Jonah tried to ignore him.

"Jesus," Nell said, rubbing at her temples with stiff fingers.
"Goddammit."

Jonah cocked his head at her. "What's going on?"

Nell moved her fingers to the hollows of her eyes, breathing slow.

"I'm fine," she said. "Head hurts, is all. I'll be all right."

"When'd it start?"

"Couple days ago, on the drive out to San Francisco. It's
kind of been fading in and out since, like I'm stuck between
stations."

Jonah kept his hands on the bar in front of him, looking
down at his hands. "Sucks. Sorry."

Nell pinched the bridge of her nose until the skin turned pale
and bloodless. "I'll be fine. Nothing a round or two won't fix."

Jonah had serious doubts about that, but he decided not to
push it. They had a long road ahead of them; there wasn't any
sense in causing any more static this early into the trip. If he
needed to drive after they got the hell out of here, it wouldn't
be a problem. It was only a handful of hours until they got to
Mowry, after all.

While Nell massaged her skull, Jonah pulled out his phone
and checked the route on his map app, stretching across the
Southwest like a crooked scar. They were already most of
the way to Yosemite National Park; they were making good
time. After they were done here, they'd head east on a cork-

screw path to eventually stay the night in Mowry, a cute little Nevada town that had never fully left the Old West behind, all saloons and dance halls retrofitted into theme hotels and casinos. Tomorrow morning, they'd shoot east-ish to Elbert, Utah, then down through Pecos, Colorado, and straight on till morning to Albuquerque. The whole trip wouldn't take more than two and a half days. If they kept to the schedule, they'd be at their dad's place in time for Sunday dinner.

After a minute, the barman, a crusty old bastard with a white handlebar mustache underneath a puffy purple-veined nose, made his way over to them, eyes beady and black. He had the look of somebody who'd been doing this job for way, way too long. Crossing a pair of thick slab arms over his chest, he nodded at the Talbots.

"Help you?"

"You know, I dearly hope so," Nell said. "Drinks for me and my brother here, if you don't mind."

"Gonna need an ID first," the bartender said.

Nell smiled wide. "What, we don't look over twenty-one to you?"

"Collateral for the tab," the old guy said, unamused. Jonah got the feeling he got that question a lot, like somebody asking a cashier if something's free because it didn't scan right. That shit never made you funny, it just made you an asshole. "ID, credit card, or pay cash as you go. It's your choice which, but it's gonna be one of 'em."

"Hey, fine by me," Nell said, producing her wallet from her coat pocket, laying her driver's license on the bar with a hard plastic *snap*. Sliding it off the pine, the bartender made a show of checking the photo against her face, then made a low *mm-hmm* in the pit of his throat, apparently satisfied.

"What'll it be?"

"Gin," Nell said. "Whatever's on the rail is fine. Make it a double too."

"Rocks?"

Nell shook her head. "Unnecessary."

"Fine." The bartender looked at Jonah. "You?"

"Seltzer," said Jonah.

"Seltzer?!" Nell sounded like somebody had slashed her tires.

Jonah kept his eyes on the bartender. "With a slice of lemon, if you've got it."

"You're fucking kidding me," Nell said. "You're making me drink alone?"

"Someone's gotta drive us the rest of the way to Mowry," he said. "If you're drinking doubles, it sure as hell isn't going to be you."

Nell touched a hand to her chest. "Why, Jonah, dear brother, I am *offended*," she mugged. "When have you ever known me to not hold my drink?"

Jonah threw her a look.

"Do you really want me to answer that?"

Nell sighed. "Fine, fine." She looked back at the bemused bartender. "You heard the man. Seltzer it is."

The bartender looked from her to Jonah and back again. "Double well gin and a soda with lemon. Fine by me."

He shuffled away, leaving the two siblings to consider their blurry reflections in the bottle-crowded mirror.

"So, what's the worst that could have happened?" Nell asked, after the bartender was well out of earshot.

Jonah looked at her. "What?"

"If Molly had found out who you used to be," she said. "If you'd said *fuck it* and told her everything."

A knot of tension pulsed at the base of Jonah's neck.

"I thought I said I didn't want to talk about this, Eleanor."

"Well, I do, *Jonah*. I actually think it might be kind of important. So come on, spit it out. What's the deal?"

Jonah sighed. "Have you ever let anything go in your entire life? Like, has anyone ever asked you to back off and you, y'know, actually did?"

"Hasn't happened yet," Nell said with a shrug.

Jonah shook his head. "I swear to god, you are the most stubborn person on the planet. Why do you even want to talk about this? Like, for real, what good is it going to do? It's not going to fix anything, it's not going to change anything. It's just going to make me feel like shit."

"Look, I'm trying to talk to you here," Nell said. "That's it. We haven't talked about anything real in forever. Just the weather and what TV shows suck and whatever else. I miss talking to you, the real you, underneath all this emotionally distant bullshit. I'm curious, that's all."

"This isn't you being curious, Nell," Jonah said. "This is you picking at scabs because that's what you do. You're fucking pathological."

"At least I'm honest about who I am," she said.

Jonah ground his teeth.

"The hell is that supposed to mean?"

"I mean, this isn't you," Nell blurted. "This meek, moody dude that you turned into, he isn't my brother. Not the brother I knew, at least. Honestly, I haven't seen you, my you, in *years*. I don't know what you did with him exactly, but whatever cage you locked him away in, I really wish you'd let him out once in a while."

"Nell, I just got *divorced*—"

"And I know that's been hard for you," she said, hanging her head. "I'm not saying it hasn't. But it's not about the divorce, Jonah. It's about everything else. It's about you, and this person you turned yourself into."

"I don't even know what that means—"

Nell fixed him with a hard look. "Except you kind of do, though. Come on, I know you do."

The bartender shuffled back over, set their drinks down on the pine in front of them, and walked off without another word. Jonah sipped his seltzer.

"You gave up so much of yourself when you fucked off to California and married Molly," Nell said. "So goddamn much that sometimes I have a hard time even recognizing you. I know that losing her hurts, but be honest, she's not the only thing that's gotten lost in the mix. There's this whole other part of your life that you up and walked away from one morning, and now you spend your days pretending that it never happened, that it doesn't exist, that you're not the same guy you used to be. You can't tell me you don't see that."

Jonah's shoulders fell as he searched for the right response.

"I'm still me, Nell. I am. Maybe I'm not exactly the same me that you remember from when I was twenty-one, starting fights and getting into shit with assholes, but I'm still me." He paused. Thought about the way to say it. "You're right, though. I am different, because I chose to be. The person you're talking about, I made a decision to leave him in the past, move on, try and be better. I don't know why you can't do the same."

"Because you're not *past* anything, Jonah. Not at all."

"Bullshit. You don't get to make that call."

"No, not bullshit," Nell said, shaking her head. "It's written all over your face. Come on, when was the last time you got in a fight? Like a real one, with fists and all. Not some shitty argument over email about who booked the wrong conference room or whatever."

Jonah blew air out of his mouth in a thin, sharp stream. "Years," he said. "Years and years. Been long enough that I don't really remember. Back before Molly ever even showed up, probably." Except there was nothing *probably* about it. Jonah knew exactly when the last fight he'd been in was. He might as well have had the date carved into his brain with a screwdriver.

"See, that's wild to me," Nell said, sipping her gin. "You don't even remember. That's absolutely bonkers."

"Why crazy?"

Turning her head, she gave him a look that was painfully, dangerously close to pity.

"Because I remember a time when you'd get into bloody scraps more often than you'd brush your teeth."

Jonah swirled a finger around the lip of his water glass, sending stray beads rolling down the side.

"I was a pissed-off guy, Nell. For a lot of years."

"*Was.* Sure," said Nell. She took another sip from her gin, swallowed hard enough for her brother to hear the gulp. "Jonah, you're the angriest person I've ever known. You were then, and you are now. At least back then you had the balls to own it. And what was so bad about that guy, anyway? He was honest about himself, what he wanted; shit, he was a lot of fun. He laughed all the time. When was the last time you did?"

"Come on, I laugh."

Nell shook her head, swirling her drink.

"It's been years since I heard you laugh, Jonah."

"Maybe you're just not that funny," Jonah said.

"And maybe you're avoiding things again," Nell told him.

Jonah felt the tiniest charge of flame catch in the pit of his stomach. He tried to ignore it, but that was easier said than done. He didn't want to do this; he'd given Nell every chance to stop, and she'd gone and dragged him into it anyway. Goddammit.

"Look, you want me to cop to it? Fine. I'll admit it, I did a lot of fucked-up things to a lot of fucked-up people back then, sure. But I worked really hard for a lot of years to get over that part of myself, because, news flash, I'm not exactly proud of it. I never was. That version of me that you're remembering so fondly? He was someone I stumbled my way into being by accident. That's all."

"Nobody's anything by accident," Nell said. "And people don't change."

Jonah shook his head. "You know, it's funny: the people who say that people don't change are usually the ones who are the most scared of it. Maybe you should turn that all-seeing spotlight back on yourself, Nell. Might not like what you find out, though."

"Stop trying to dodge the point. You're not different, and you know it. This version of you you've been trying to sell, it's a costume. It's bullshit. Nobody changes, not really. They can't. Especially not the worst parts of them, the stuff they don't like about themselves. They hang on to that shit like a worry stone. You can dig deep down inside yourself and pile it under miles of concrete, pretend like it was some fluke, something to be forgotten, but it's still there, waiting for its chance. Nothing—and I mean *nothing*—stays buried forever. Get right with yourself. That's the only way anyone ever really moves forward."

Anger, vulnerable and stinging, pricked at the corners of Jonah's eyes, threatening to spill over into tears or worse. He blinked it away, trying to keep his breathing steady.

"Easy for you to say," he said, setting his jaw. "*Move forward.* Fuck you. You never left home, never got serious with anyone, got a job at a bar so you could drink for free, shit, you still live three minutes away from Dad. Pretty sure it's his home address on your ID, isn't it? Still having a hard time getting a place that isn't a month-to-month shithole? Big surprise. You never tried to do anything real in your entire life. You took the easiest way out you could, decided to be a fucking townie. You're thirty-five years old, Nell. Tell me something, when are you going to get your shit together and grow up?"

"As if you know what you're talking about," Nell sneered back at him. "You left, remember? You're the one that decided he'd rather pretend to be someone else and married the first way out of Albuquerque he could find. And look at you now, heading right back to where you started. Good. Fucking. Job." She drained her gin, then raised a hand to snap her fingers at the bartender. "Hey, can I get a refill over here?"

Down at the far end of the bar, the grizzled old barman scowled and pulled the stoppered bottle of gin off the rail as he started toward the Talbots.

"You're such an asshole sometimes," Jonah said to his sister, trying to keep his voice steady, trying to ignore the way her words had cut him. "And a hypocrite."

"Fuck yourself," Nell snorted. "Just because you're scared to death of who you pretend you aren't doesn't mean everyone else has to do the same. Coward."

That last word hit him like a bullet to the heart. Shaking his head, Jonah pushed away from the bar, nearly toppling his stool over as he stood.

"This was such a mistake. I don't know why I thought you could be nice and normal for a couple of days."

He turned and started to walk away.

Still sitting at the bar, Nell called after him: "Where the hell are you going?"

"The bathroom," he said. "I have to take a piss. Is that okay with you?"

"Great," Nell scoffed as the barman poured her second double. "Go right ahead. Bailing out as soon as shit gets tough. At least you're consistent."

"Have another drink, Nell," Jonah said. "That's what

you're good at, right? Thanks for making one of the hardest days of my life way worse, by the way. Super considerate."

"Oh, poor you." Rolling her eyes and throwing him the middle finger, Nell went back to her gin. "You better hope I'm still here by the time you get back."

He didn't turn back to look at her. He didn't want to give her the satisfaction. Hands deep in his jeans pockets, he kept his shoulders stiff and square as he followed the signs for the men's room.

Shouldering the door open with a bang, Jonah went to the sink against the far wall and threw the faucet on full blast. He hung his head over the cracked porcelain and watched the water froth and swirl down the drain as he tried to breathe. Of course. Of course she'd turned it into this. Of course they couldn't go two hours without getting in some shitty little fight about one thing or another. He didn't know what he was thinking, inviting her along like this, especially now. Nell couldn't not pick at a scab, and she never, ever let go of shit. It was part of her nature, written into her genetics like freckles, green eyes, and clinical depression.

Then again, maybe they deserved each other. Two broken people who couldn't stop hurting people. What a fucking joke.

Jonah splashed handful after handful of cold water on his face, trying to breathe away the big dumb fist of nerves and anger that had settled in the hollow space below his heart. He was mad at Nell, mad at Molly, and, maybe most of all, mad at himself. It just figured. All of it. Above the mirror, the bare fluorescent light hummed and droned in its fixture, casting sallow light across his strong mismatched features.

The man looking back at him in the stained, streaky mirror was more unfamiliar than he should have been. Body too tall, too skinny. Cheeks socked-out and sallow where they hadn't been claimed by the blotchy red flush that had swept up his neck from below the collar of his shirt. Black hair shaggy and unkempt, even pushed back and away from the blade-tip of his widow's peak. Dark circles underneath both eyes. He looked like he hadn't slept in a week, or else had recently come off a legendary meth bender. Maybe both. He frowned at himself. It

was almost funny: right now, he looked on the outside exactly
how he felt inside. Broken, alone, adrift. Home was nowhere
now; home was no one. He'd gone too far and ended up far off
the edges of the map. He was a stray dog, lost in the rain.

Jonah filled his hands with water and slurped noisily from
them until his lips kissed his palms. The water tasted good, a
tangible counterpoint to the febrile heat filling his face. He
hated this. Still, maybe it was better for them to have it out now.
Maybe he'd get back to the bar and she'd have gotten the message; maybe she'd back off until they got to Albuquerque and
they could go back to comfortably ignoring each other again.

Yeah, and maybe Jonah would sprout wings and fly the
rest of the way home.

*You're the angriest person I've ever known. You were
then, and you are now.*

She was wrong about him. He had to believe that she was
wrong about him. They'd lived apart for years, hadn't spent any
quality time together outside of holidays since he moved away.
Her information was so far out of date, it was collecting dust.
She was just being Nell about it, as cruelly stubborn as ever. He
didn't think that she would really abandon him in some shit-
ball meth-lab town. Even for her, that would be too much. Dramatic. She'd always been so dramatic. Still, the fact remained:
the time for them to call this whole thing off was already long
past, and they both knew it. Nell talked a big game, but that was
all it was. Sound and fury. Truth was, they were stuck together,
no matter how much of an asshole either of them decided to be.

When Jonah looked in the mirror again, there was a young
man staring at him from one of the stalls.

Barely nineteen if he was a day, he was casually handsome, with razor-fine features and bright blue eyes. His skin
was gray and waxy, but the effect did little to erode his natural
good looks. He could have been a model or an actor with that
face. He was almost beautiful. Jonah ran the back of his hand
across his mouth, trying to will away the sudden dryness that
had swept across his tongue, and watched the boy in the streaky
glass.

"See something you like, fuckface?"

The kid's voice sent a weird icy chill dancing across the surface of Jonah's heart, freezing him from the inside out. All harsh and craggy, the sound didn't square with the kid's looks. Despite his delicate features, he sounded old, in his seventies or eighties. He sounded like his throat was rotting through.

Standing there, looking back at the kid, Jonah's lungs felt heavy, like it was impossible for him to draw a full breath. Like someone was sitting on his chest. Struggling against the pressure, Jonah exhaled, and his breath came in a steamy billow, as if he were standing outside in the dead of winter. His blood sang in his head while his stomach clenched and surged, threatening to empty its contents into the chipped, scummy old sink.

Not here, not now, not like this. Come on.

In the sallow bathroom light, Jonah could almost see all the way through the kid to the cracked, scribbled-up tile behind the toilet. There, but not really there. He blinked, and the kid's face shifted, sloughing down like a stretched-out Halloween mask, sprouting messy red splits beaten deep into the flesh, wrapped in grotesque purple-black bruises like lavender blooms. One eye cataracted and turned the color of spoiled milk, while the other, bright blue and bloodshot red, drooped in its socket like a loose bead of wax.

"See something you like, fuckface?" the kid asked again, broken teeth falling out of his mouth like bloody Chiclets.

Feeling dread creep up the back of his neck, Jonah met the kid's hideous scowl as long as he could, then looked down into the sink again, watching the water chuckling down the drain.

"You're not really here," Jonah said under his breath. "Go away, Alex. Please."

He closed his eyes and tried to focus on the white-noise hissing of the faucet, ignoring the sound of the boy's raggedy breath inside the stall. Jonah pressed at his temples with the heels of his hands, grinding circles of pressure into his brain until his own panicked breathing slowed, the stress receding into the static that whispered endlessly in the back of his mind. When Jonah looked again, the boy with his dead, gray face was gone. Had never been there to begin with. Just his imagination fucking with him. The argument and bad memories feeding off each other inside his head. That was all.

He wet his hands under the running tap and ran them through his hair, slicking a few loose locks away from his face. That's when he heard the yelling from the barroom.

"Hey, what the fuck is your problem? Huh? Hey, I'm talking to you, goddammit!"

He didn't recognize the guy's voice; but, even after years away, Jonah knew what it meant when someone sounded like that. There was only one person in the world who could piss somebody off that bad, that quick.

"No, excuse me, why don't you back the fuck up off me, asshole?!"

Nell.

Through the flimsy men's room door, Jonah heard glass shatter. Quickly drying his hands on his pants, Jonah threw the door open and stepped back into the barroom to find Nell standing nose-to-nose with one of the bikers from the corner table in a pool of broken glass and spilled beer.

Shit.

The dude was big, broad and burly, with a long blond beard and hair to match, standing easily a head and a half taller than Nell, probably a hundred and fifty pounds heavier, too, with thick, cabled arms covered in dark tattoos. He wore a battered leather kutte around broad portcullis shoulders, black jeans, heavy boots, with a folding knife on his belt that was closer to a machete than a Swiss Army. Jonah had noticed him before, watching him and Nell argue from the corner table. He'd seemed big then; but now, looming over Nell, he looked absolutely massive. When the guy saw Jonah coming, he extended a single finger from one ham-size fist, pointing at Nell's face, eyes narrow and furious.

"Man, is this your girlfriend?"

"My sister," Jonah said. "What's the problem?"

Nell glared at him. "Jonah, stay the fuck out of this."

"Hey, pump the brakes, okay? Tell me what's happening."

"Eat shit," she spat. "That's what's happening."

The biker looked back and forth between the two Talbots. "Jesus," he said. "Some relationship you two have."

Jonah let the little snipe pass. Wasn't going to do anybody any good, getting pissed off now.

"Help you with something, man?" Glancing back and forth from Nell to the big biker, Jonah could already tell that he was quickly running out of chances to defuse this situation, whatever *this situation* was, exactly. "What happened here?"

"Nothing," Nell said, too fast.

"Slapped the beer outta my hand," the biker said. "Broke a glass. Made a mess. You call that nothing?"

"Learn to take *no* for an answer," Nell said. "Maybe you won't lose so many drinks that way."

The biker scoffed. "Listen to this bitch," he said. "You need to learn some goddamn manners before that big mouth gets you in real trouble—"

"Hey, there's no trouble here," Jonah interjected. "Sorry. We're good. We'll go."

"No, we will *not* go," Nell said. "I'm a paying customer. I have as much a right to be here as anybody, without getting hassled by brainless shitfucks like you."

"You haven't paid for a goddamn thing yet," the grizzled old bartender barked from behind the pine. In response, Nell dug a wadded twenty from her pants pocket and threw it in his face.

"Here you go," she said to him, snatching her gin off the bar. "Keep the change and blow it out your ass."

The bartender's face pinched up tight and started to darken with rage. For a second, Jonah really thought he was going to take a swing at her, but the craggy old shit kept both his hands flat on the bar, glancing over toward the other bikers in the corner.

"Terry, anything you can do about this?"

The oldest of the bikers, the one with the goatee and the serial-killer stare that had been mad-dogging the Talbots since they'd walked in, perked up at the mention of his name, slitting his eyes.

"Vaughn," he said to the big guy, his voice deep and serious.

"It's fine," the big guy replied, keeping his glare fixed on Nell. "It's dealt with."

"*Vaughn,*" the old guy said again, his tone turning sharp.

The big guy didn't look away. "I said it's fine, Ter. Couple of asshole tourists. Nothing I can't handle."

Blowing air, Serial-Killer Eyes leaned back in his seat, raising his glass to his lips, saying nothing else, a deep scowl pressed deep into the lines of his face.

The bartender cleared his throat. "So why don't you handle it already and kick these assholes the fuck out of here, Vaughn?"

They were losing control of this situation, and fast. Goddammit. That blunt fist underneath Jonah's heart turned icy and screwed itself tighter and tighter, a familiar sensation, though he hadn't felt it in years, dragged screaming into the light by Nell and that gray, rotting face in the bathroom mirror. He knew what was going to happen next. No avoiding it now. It was just a question of who moved first.

He breathed out slow and curled his hands into loose fists, then stole another look over at the other three bikers in the corner. The one in the middle—Terry, that was Serial-Killer Eyes' name, Terry—was older, midfifties give or take a few years, but the other two were about Jonah's age. All three of them were dressed to match the big guy, draped in black leather and cheap, messy ink, radiating with nerves, ready to pop off at a moment's notice. Great. That was just fucking wonderful.

Rage fired like a forge in Jonah's chest. None of this should have happened at all—it was all so goddamn avoidable. All Nell had to do was sit quietly and drink her gin like a grownup and not do suicidal shit like picking a fight with the scary bikers in the scary biker bar. That was the bare minimum, and she couldn't even manage that. Jonah had to give her credit for one thing, though; she was right—some people never changed.

Vaughn took another step closer to Jonah's sister, knotting his hairy, thick-knuckled hands into hard, heavy clubs.

"You heard him," Vaughn said. "Get the fuck out or get thrown the fuck out. Both of you. Now."

Nell showed him every tooth in her head. "I don't think you're man enough to make me, princess."

"Fuck off with that," Vaughn said. "Crazy bitch."

"Oh, no, are you backing down already, big man?" Nell arched one eyebrow high and made a show of looking the biker up and down. "That's a shame. I would have liked to see how hard a pretty girl like you can swing those dainty little hands."

Vaughn sucked his teeth. Cracked his knuckles. "You really want to find out?"

"Nell, *don't*," Jonah said, his voice suddenly stony.

"Yeah," Nell hissed back at Vaughn, showing him every tooth in her mouth. "You know, I really do."

Without blinking, she raised her half-empty rocks glass as if she was toasting the man, fired back the rest of her gin, then whipped the glass at Vaughn's head.

S he saw the blood before she heard the glass break. In an instant, a crooked red spiderweb opened up in the greasy flesh above the big man's brow, pouring blood like a faucet. The sound of the rocks glass shattering into a thousand tiny knives across his thick skull was huge in the stuffy little barroom, enormous, impossible. It swallowed every other sound that dared challenge it. For a second, Vaughn stayed standing, his eyes spinning back into his skull like the reels on a slot machine. Then he swayed, and sputtered, and fell.

In the corner of the barroom, Terry screamed as if he'd been stabbed in the heart and bolted from the table toward the fallen man as his compatriots and the other gathered dirtbags leaped to their feet, a flurry of bodies scattering all at once. From behind her, Nell heard a hoarse growl—glancing over her shoulder, she saw the grizzled little bartender swing a sawed-off baseball bat at her head, the handle wrapped up with black electrical tape.

Ducking out of the way at the last second, Nell threw her body forward, clamping her hands around his wrist, slamming it against the scarred-up wood between them again and again and again until he let go, dropping the half-bat to the floor on Nell's side of the bar, yowling and clutching at his battered arm. Grabbing his head with both hands, Nell yanked down as hard as she could, smashing his face against the bar top with a wet, satisfying crunch, bouncing him to the floor in a daze, blood gushing from his nose and mouth.

Nell heard a cry from behind her and turned in time to see her brother lunge forward to meet two of the bikers as they closed in, while the third, Terry, sprinted to Vaughn's side, falling to his knees on the floor beside the fallen man, wailing *No, no, no, no, no—!*

Across the barroom, Jonah darted in and fired a vicious cross into the face of the first biker, a sturdy bearded type sporting a brush cut. The impact rang out with a hard, raw-boned *clack*. It was a familiar sound. The guy yelped like a kicked dog when Jonah drilled him, the noise a mess of disconnected syllables, and faltered back, spitting a mouthful of red. A second later, he squared up his fists and pressed back in, furious, distracted. Jonah let him.

Nell had seen her brother pull this move before. Poor bastard never stood a chance. Jonah dodged one swing, then another, creating an opening a mile wide. After that—well, after that it was only a matter of how hard Jonah was going to hit the guy.

Quick as a rattlesnake, Jonah flashed forward and hammered at Beardy twice more—first in the jaw, setting him off balance, then again in the belly, hard enough to turn his guts to paste. Beardy deflated in an instant, falling back and clutching at his ruined insides, gasping desperately for air as Jonah twisted in place like a dancer, turning his attention onto the other biker, the one with the combed hair and the glasses. Jonah fired a sharp kick into the guy's kneecap, stopping him in place, then clubbed him in the nose once, twice, three times a douchebag.

Glasses yelped in surprise and pain as his head snapped back from the impact, barking something in a language Nell didn't know but understood well enough. Jonah decked the guy again and again until Glasses finally dropped. It had been years since Nell had seen her brother hit anyone, but even after all this time it was like nothing had changed. He was older, sure, maybe a little more out of shape than he'd been in his twenties, but the core of him, the things that made him *him* were still there, still intact, immutable. He could still spin like a top; he could still lay someone out flat; he could still fuck shit up. This was what Jonah was always best at, what he was meant to do.

On the floor only a few feet away, Nell saw Terry rising

to his feet over Vaughn, shoulders hunched like a rabid wolf's, pale eyes full of murder.

"*Bitch*," he roared, standing to his full height. "You fucking *bitch!*"

Fast as she was able, Nell scooped up the bartender's half-bat and swung it at Terry's face in a wide, diagonal arc that he dodged nimbly, baring yellow teeth at her. She swung again, but this time the old man was waiting for her. Twisting sideways, he fired off a pair of quick jabs that caught her first in the jaw, then in the heart, dropping her to the ground beside Vaughn as she struggled to breathe. Curled on the floor in a pool of broken glass and blood, the big man was shaking and convulsing terribly, his eyelids fluttering, only the bloodshot whites visible underneath. His neck was strained and corded beneath a clenched rictus, a thin trickle of foamy drool pulsing unevenly from one corner of his mouth.

Holy shit, was he having a fucking seizure?

Circling around, Terry kicked a foot at Nell, tagging her hard in the ribs. Nell yelped and flung the half-bat at his head, but she was too slow. He ducked out of the way with ease. Hunched down, the old man lunged at her, reaching for her throat with a knobby, oversized hand. Without thinking, Nell launched a boot into his groin, snapping her leg out as hard as she could. The effect was immediate. Clutching at his smashed dick, Terry yowled and stumbled back, tangling his feet in the big man's still-convulsing form, then fell to the ground with a low, deep groan. Nell scrambled away, wincing from the pain and swiping the knife off Vaughn's belt as she braced against the bar and hauled herself back up to her feet.

On the other side of the barroom, Jonah was rounding the pool table, keeping distance between himself and Beardy and Glasses, both on their feet again, each wielding a pool cue and looking plenty the worse for wear. Beardy moved first, jabbing the cue at Jonah's ribs like a spear—catching the shaft with one hand, Jonah hauled the man in close and caught him with a savage uppercut to the jaw, then threw himself backward, putting all his weight into yanking the cue away as Beardy fell. Snatching one of the pool balls off the green felt, Jonah whipped it at Glasses's face, catching him high up on the cheek with a hollow THWOCK. Bye-bye, Glasses.

On the ground, Terry was coming around again, glowering at Nell, struggling to stand.

For a second, she actually considered using Vaughn's knife to try and keep him down, keep him away, but that was too much, and she knew it. She didn't want to kill anyone; she just wanted to get the fuck out of here. From the other side of the room, she heard her brother call her name. She looked up just in time to see Jonah toss her one of the pool cues—she caught it in one hand and, turning to face Terry, drew her arm back like she was setting up a tennis serve.

CRACK.

The lacquered wood caught the old man across the forehead, and he hit the floor like he'd been personally slapped down by God.

Nell looked back over at her brother. He stood slumped against the pool table, his hands bloody and shaking something terrible, wearing an expression that Nell hadn't seen on his face in years: a frenzied mix of anger, fear, and elation. Some part of him was actually enjoying this. Panting, Jonah crossed the barroom toward his sister, holding a hand out.

"Come on, we need to get out of here, right now," he wheezed.

On the ground, Nell could see that Terry was coming to, face painted with blood from where the pool cue had split him open, washing down his jaw, his neck, and his leathers in a wet red fan, the skin underneath already dappled with black and purple blotches. Blindly, he pawed at his own clothes, searching without finding, still in a daze. Nell stood there for a second and watched him fumble, unsure as to what he was doing.

"Motherfuckers," the old guy moaned. "Goddamn motherfuckers... hit my fucking brother..."

One of his hands disappeared underneath the back of his vest, then emerged again a second later clutching a shiny silver handgun. Nell's blood ran to ice at the sight. Without thinking, she kicked the gun out of the prick's fist, sending it skittering across the barroom floor, far out of anyone's reach. The old guy rolled his muddy, bloodshot eyes up to glare at her, burning with hate.

"Kill you," he mumbled at Nell. "Fucking kill you both . . ."

A giddy, terrified bolt of electricity shot up Nell's spine, telling her to run, run, run, but then Jonah was there, kneeling down over the bloody old biker. He curled a fist in the collar of Terry's shirt, then reared back and punched the guy in the face for good and all, dropping him flat.

"We need. To go. Now," Jonah said to Nell, his voice horribly calm.

Together, they made a break for the door, punching through into daylight with all the subtlety and grace of a brick through a plate-glass window. The air outside was cool and crisp and almost painful against Nell's sweaty skin; the cold (and that kick in the ribs) made it hard to breathe too deeply. Nell glanced back over her shoulder to see if anyone was coming after them, but there was no one there. Ahead of her, Jonah was already halfway to the Volvo. Twisting around, he clapped his hands at her.

"Keys! Keys, keys, keys!"

Without thinking, Nell pulled the car keys from her jacket pocket and tossed them to him. Effortlessly, Jonah plucked them out of the air and sprinted the rest of the way to the station wagon as Nell turned around one more time and considered the row of motorcycles parked out in front of Lotte's. Looking down at her hands, she saw that she was still holding Vaughn's knife, the blade tucked safely away in the grip. The reality of it all started to set in then. She froze. They'd fucked up so bad. *She'd* fucked up so bad.

They're not going to let this go. They're going to run you down like a pack of wolves, and they're going to kill you slow for what you did in there.

It didn't have to be like this.

"Nell, what the fuck are you doing? We have to go, come on!"

Jonah's voice was a hot spike launched through the icy floe of her thoughts. Returning to herself, she snapped the blade open and plunged the sharp tip into the nearest bike's front tire and twisted, dragging it halfway down the wheel, shredding the rubber. She did the same to the back tire, then kicked the bike over, toppling it and the other three to the ground like dominos, then tossed the knife into the gravel. Fuck them. Behind her, she heard Jonah blast the Volvo's horn once, twice, three times.

"Let's go! Come on!"

Inside the bar, she could hear someone shouting. Maybe a few someones. Her eyes went to the door. At any second, those black leather assholes would come spilling out, ready for round two, and Nell had a sneaking suspicion that if she and Jonah stuck around for it, this time someone was going to end up dead. She'd seen the gun in Terry's hands. She knew the score now. Turning around, she double-timed it for the waiting station wagon, hopping in the passenger seat as Jonah floored the gas pedal, the car thumping out of the parking lot before she'd even closed the door. They hung a left and careened wildly onto the street, back toward the highway that stretched out in front of them like a cracked black ribbon.

They drove for an hour or more, speeding along the Interstate, putting as many miles between themselves and Lotte's Tavern as they possibly could. They rode in silence, the only sound between them the unrelenting whir of the car's heater, the little glowing knob on the dashboard cranked all the way to MAX against the early April chill. Jonah stayed white-knuckled around the steering wheel until the dashboard fuel light clicked on with an electronic *ding*, then steered the station wagon into the parking lot of a scummy little gas station across the street from a derelict McDonald's and a check-cashing franchise. Through the musty windows in the front of the station shop, Nell could see a few people browsing the dusty aisles underneath the gaze of an exhausted-looking attendant in a green polyester vest. Without a word, Jonah threw the station wagon in park beside one of the pumps, then killed the engine and stepped outside to swipe his credit card and lean against the hatchback while he waited for the tank to fill.

Inside the Volvo, Nell sat and stewed, still feeling the flesh over her heart throbbing obstinately where Terry had tagged her. She idly rubbed at the sore spot with one hand, trying to massage the pain out. There'd be a bitch of a bruise there tomorrow; she was lucky he hadn't cracked her sternum or damaged her heart or something. Christ.

Nell plucked a Camel from her dwindling pack—three left—and jabbed it between her lips as she punched in the dashboard lighter. When it popped out again, she twisted the glowing coil against the end of her smoke, her face burning with embarrassment, a toxic ball of shame flopping back and forth in her stomach. She felt so stupid. Bikers. Fucking bikers? What the hell had she been thinking?

All she'd wanted was to get Jonah into a little scrap like old times, see if he could shake off the dust some. That was it. They'd gotten in a hundred bar fights before. But thinking back on it now, yeah, maybe she should have known better than to start shit in a place like that, with assholes like them. Except fucking *Jonah* though. He had to take everything so goddamn personal. He'd pissed her off, made her misjudge the situation, made her lose perspective. This shit was as much his fault as it was hers.

Still, nothing to do about it now. No way to unfuck the past. Best you could do was keep pushing forward, try to do better next time.

She took a slow, deep drag, then another, letting the nicotine buzz spread through her body in a warm, gentle flood, sanding all the sharp edges of her frayed nerves down to soft, manageable bends in the road. Now if only it could help with the pain behind her eyes, she'd be in business.

Keeping the burning Camel balanced between her chapped lips, she stepped out of the car. In the distance, she could still hear the hiss of cars speeding by on the highway as she circled around the car to lean next to her brother, the grit and asphalt crunching softly under her feet.

"Hey," she said.

Jonah didn't look up.

"Hey," she said again. "Jonah."

Still nothing.

"Okay, so I'm getting the silent treatment now," she said.

"You're not supposed to smoke out here," Jonah replied, pointedly not looking over.

Irritation crackled along the ridges of Nell's brain. "Oh, great. That's super helpful. Really mature, Jone. Thanks for that."

Leaning there, Jonah finally turned to look at her, fixing her with a furious glare.

"Are you kidding? You don't get to talk to me about mature, Nell. Not now, not ever, and especially not after that suicidal stunt you just pulled. You want to play *Who's the Asshole*? Look in a fucking mirror."

Nell set her jaw and tried to let the slight pass. "Look, I'm not trying to start shit here, okay? I'm trying to get you to talk to me. This trip is going to suck if we're silently pissed at each other the whole time."

"This trip sucks already," Jonah shot back. "And I *am* angry at you. Frankly, I have a right to be. So do me a favor, leave me the fuck alone and try not to make everything worse for a little while. Do you think you can manage that?"

Nell hung her head. "Look..." she trailed off. "Do you at least think we should call the cops or something?"

Jonah raised his face to the sky and shook his head, exasperated. "And tell them what, exactly? That we bumbled into a biker bar like a couple of shitheads and picked a fight? You glassed a guy, I broke somebody's face open with a three-ball? Yeah, that'll go over really well. I can already hear them laughing. I mean, shit, odds are the bikers own the cops in that town anyway. So, no. We're not calling the cops. We are getting as far away as we can, as fast as we can, and we are both hoping to high hell that that's the end of it."

"It is," Nell said. "It has to be."

"Yeah, maybe. I don't know. I hope so," Jonah said. "Things don't go away because you close your eyes, Nell. That's not how the world works."

"Said the man still trying like hell to be someone he's not," she said, suddenly angry.

"All right, you know what? No," Jonah shot back, his face twisted. "I'm not the one who fucked up here. So before you start up with that shit again, I'd really consider your own role in our current predicament. None of this is my fault."

"Takes two to tango, last I checked," Nell said. "I wasn't the only one fighting. Shit, your hands are still bloody. Or didn't you notice?"

Jonah glanced down, his face pinking at the rusty blotches smeared messily across his knuckles.

"We had to get out of there somehow," he said. "And it sure as shit wasn't going to be through diplomacy. Not after you glassed that dude."

"Oh, fuck him," Nell cried, incredulous. "Him and his

whole family and all of his friends too. It's on them as much as it's on me, Jone. And you too. You play all innocent, but I see you, little brother. I see you better than anyone. I saw the look on your face in there while you were oh-so-nobly smashing that guy's nose in with the pool ball. Admit it, Jonah. For one fucking second, you were that guy again, and *you actually liked it.*"

"Let it go, Nell," Jonah said, a cautionary tone in his voice.

"*Let it go,*" she sneered, digging her heels in. "Same old song, as if you're suddenly any kind of expert. Don't lie to me, Jonah. You're not that good at it. And anyway, I don't know what you're so bent out of shape about. It was a *bar fight.* They happen all the time, probably twice as often at that shithole. We walked away standing, and they get to sit and lick their wounds. Nothing more to it. It's over. End of story."

Jonah's eyes bugged out. "There's no way you actually believe that. Those weren't just drunk townies looking to flex, Nell. That was a *biker gang.* They make their whole living doing fucked-up shit to people who, more often than not, do not deserve it. You walked into their house and spat in their faces. You really think they're going to let that go?"

"We got away, Jone," Nell said. "Free and clear. In a couple of hours we'll be a bad memory, a story they never tell their friends. They'll dust themselves off and get on with their shitty lives, and that's the end of it. No harm, no foul. Like it never fucking happened."

"Okay, that, right there," Jonah said, jabbing a finger at her, his expression bent with contempt. "That is the thing I probably hate most about you."

"I'm not going to ask what you mean, so you might as well tell me," Nell said.

"You always seem to think you're the smartest person in the room, but you never are."

Nell felt a blade slide into her heart. He was so fucking mean sometimes. Standing there together, she felt a thick, awful silence pass between them, a powder keg just itching to explode.

"Fuck you," she said, wounded, her voice barely above a whisper. "Seriously, fuck you so much for that."

"Yeah, fuck you too," Jonah grunted. "You always do this, making your shit everyone else's problem. Try cleaning up your own messes once in a while, or at least don't drag me into them."

She wanted to rage at him, scream at him, but objectively, intellectually, she knew that he wasn't really wrong. She did this kind of thing more than she'd have liked to admit, put people in positions where they had to deal with her problems. Deep inside her heart, she felt something relent, the shackle of a rusty old padlock finally popping loose.

"...Look, I'm sorry," she said a moment later, her voice a little softer now. "I didn't think—"

"No, you didn't think," Jonah snapped at her. "You never stop and think, Nell. You never have. You just *do*, and let other people clean up the goddamn travesties you leave in your wake. We could have ended up dead in there, you do understand that, don't you? Both of us. That prick pulled a *gun*. If shit had gone another way, those assholes would have tied us to the bar and carved pieces off us until we died. They would have made it last for *days*." He shook his head. "Sometimes, I swear to god, it's like you were born without any forethought at all."

Nell swallowed against the lump in her throat, trying to stay calm. "But it didn't, Jone. It didn't go another way. We're okay. We're standing right here, aren't we? We got out of there, didn't we?"

"This time," Jonah said, raising a finger. "But how many more of those do you really think you've got in you? How many more times do you think you can go back to that well before your luck runs dry? We're not twenty-two anymore. We're not bulletproof. Nobody is. Eventually, shit goes wrong for everybody, and that goes double for them that keep putting themselves in the crosshairs."

On the side of the car, Nell heard the gas pump shut off with a pressurized thump. Standing still, she watched Jonah unsheath the nozzle from the tank and replace it in its cradle before twisting the cap back in place. His shoulders hung low, his eyelids were drooping. She could see that whatever fight had been left inside him was well and truly gone now. He looked like he had back in San Francisco: sad and tired and old. She barely recognized him like this.

"Jonah—"

"You know what, fuck this, you're driving," Jonah said, cutting across her. "You're the one who decided to kick a dragon in the teeth, you can play getaway driver. I'm done. I need a break." He tossed her the keys and stalked around the car, dropping himself into the passenger seat without another word. Pushing herself off the hatchback, Nell went to the driver's-side door, climbed in, and leaned forward to rest her head against the crest of the steering wheel.

"Jonah, I'm sorry," she said again, trying to force the embarrassing quaver out of her voice.

"I don't care," Jonah said, turning away, his voice clipped. "Just drive, okay? Get us the fuck out of here before we piss off any other killers or whatever."

The ball of toxic waste in Nell's gut did one final somersault, threatening once more to eat all the way through her before mercifully settling back into a comfortable shame. She wanted to yell at him, hit him with some cutting remark that would bleed him down to the bone, but she resisted the urge. Jonah might have been acting like a prize shithead, but he wasn't all the way wrong, either. She'd really fucked up this time, and despite all of her bluster, she knew it. She'd started some shit that she couldn't control, and the fact of the matter was that they were both lucky as hell that they'd gotten away with only bruises and split knuckles.

Eventually, shit goes wrong for everybody.

Nell ashed her cigarette out the window, then cranked the ignition to life as Jonah buckled himself in. A second later, she popped the car into drive, pulling away from the little gas station, heading back toward the highway as her brother dropped his seat all the way back, laying it flat like a cot and rolling onto his side, turning his back to her. The message was clear enough: *Don't talk to me, I'm not even here.* A few minutes later, she heard his breathing change as he drifted off to sleep. She kept her eyes on the road. Her headache was getting worse.

There was a light in the distance.

Every so often, she'd see it flash, an off-white glimmer pulsing in an irregular pattern at the edge of the afternoon sky. Sometimes it would flicker twice, sometimes four times, sometimes only once. It was like a lighthouse sitting just past the horizon, coaxing her ever forward, on and on and on. The cars and the highway and their lights dissolved into static as she drove toward it, the hills and trees reduced to twisted shadows painted on the backs of her eyelids.

As the sun started to drift down the dome of the sky, staining the clouds overhead a burnt orange, the glimmer persisted, beckoning Nell on. Feeling the hard, stubborn pain that had long been rooting deep in her skull start to contort and unfold into something far more intricate and terrible, she drove straight at the glimmer, pulled along by that persistent ache, a loose nail drawn inexorably toward a powerful magnet.

There were still so many miles to cover between where they were and where they were going.

Terry
Broughton, CA

The first time he'd stitched someone up for real, he'd been in Kuwait. First Gulf War. He'd joined up fresh out of college, didn't even think about finding another job. Degree or not, Terry wanted to serve his country, wanted to save people, wanted to earn the right to call himself a capital-C *Citizen.* His boots hit sand early on, right before Desert Shield tipped over into Desert Storm. He'd never been more excited for anything in his life. He honestly thought he was going over there to help.

Trained as a 91 Bravo—a combat medic—he'd soaked all the standard abuses of boot camp, then shipped off to Fort Sam in San Antonio to learn how to dress wounds, disinfect, stitch up skin, CPR, all of it. He was damn near the oldest in his class, too: all the others were just kids, most of them fresh out of high school or maybe a little younger, with the right lie. Terry liked to think that being older gave him an edge; it was obvious early on that he was the best out of all of them, and he'd simply figured age probably had something to do with it, rather than any kind of innate talent.

It happened on his first day over in the sand. The kid was named Carter, Ansel Carter, Private First Class. They'd been sent out on routine patrol with a scad of other guys, but when things got hot, Carter was the one that got it. Rotten luck for all of them, but for Carter more than the rest. One second everything was fine, then out of nowhere the air was swarmed with bullets. At first Terry didn't even see that Carter had been tagged, instead figured he'd been smart and hit the deck; it wasn't until he saw the blood that he realized he needed to go to work.

The bullet had slipped perfectly between the cracks in Carter's vest, a shit roll if ever there was one. Kid wouldn't stop

freaking out, asking for his mom, all the cliches. When they
got back to base, field medical was short-staffed, so Terry—
Corporal Verger back then—was tapped to jump in and help
stitch the boy up. A couple of days later, Carter was back on
his feet, ready and eager to get back into the shit. Terry was
amazed. Turned out, some people were just kind of invincible.
Others only thought they were.

He'd sewn people up plenty of times since then—including
himself more times than he cared to count—but Carter would
always be Terry's first. You only got one first. You only got one
lots of stuff. Like brothers. No matter what the army had spent
years drumming into him, all his life Terry only ever had one
brother.

Now he had none.

"You okay in here, Ter?"

Standing in front of the men's-room sink, Terry pulled
the sutures taut below his dwindling hairline and glanced
over to regard the muscular little mustachioed man standing
in the doorway. Harlan. The old bastard had been tending bar
at Lotte's for as long as Terry could remember. Folks who knew
said he used to be a safecracker or something back in the eighties, ended up in some nasty shit out in the Colorado dust that
he'd only survived by the skin of his nuts. Whatever it was, he
never talked about it, and Terry never asked. It was easier that
way. He stole another look at the little man. Harlan'd always
been a little rough around the edges, but the double black eyes
and the broken nose from where his face had met the bar made
him look like a corpse that had only recently clawed its way out
of the grave.

"Yeah, fine," Terry lied, going back to his stitches. He
looped the needle through again and tugged, pulling the gash
in his forehead another quarter-inch shut. "What's the stats out
there?"

"Nothing serious. Finished sweeping up the glass and shit,
got most of the blood out of the floor, but it's definitely going to
need another going-over." Harlan jerked a thumb toward the
barroom. "The guys are waiting to talk to you when you're done
in here."

Terry ran the curved needle through both sides of the wound once more and pulled, relishing the dull red sting as the medical nylon slid through his skin.

"Tell them I'll be out in a second. And give the floor another scrub. Place needs to be spotless."

Harlan nodded. "Yeah. Got it." He vanished back out the door.

Tying the last stitch off tight, Terry snipped the suture off with his multitool, then produced a little blue glass vial from his pocket. Uncapping it, he knocked out a heavy bump of white powder onto the back of his hand and snorted it back, rolling his head back and forth until he felt the coke start to spark his synapses. Wiping his nose, he stood looking at himself in the mirror for another minute, shifting his expression, making sure the stitches weren't going to pop loose or bleed any more than they should. Looked good enough. There'd be a nasty scar there when it healed over, but not even the best doctor in the world could help that. Terry washed the blood from his hands and, drying his palms on the legs of his jeans, stepped out into the barroom, crossing over to where Darko and Gillam sat, nursing beers and wounds in equal measure. As he approached, Gillam rose from his seat, running a hand over his cropped skull and down through his beard.

"Hey, Ter. You—"

Terry raised his hand, gesturing for him to sit his ass down again. "You two all right?"

"Yeah, fine," Gillam said. "You know. Little knocked around, but nothing we can't handle." Beside him, Darko nodded in assent, the glare off his glasses leaving his eyes dead white.

Gillam leaned forward in his seat. "So, when do we go after these assholes, man? They don't get to get away with this, Ter, you know that—"

"I know," Terry said, in a severe tone that told Gillam in no uncertain terms to shut the fuck up. He knew plenty well the cost. He didn't need soft-ass Gillam saying it again.

The sound of the glass bursting against Vaughn's head was the sound of the first phase of Terry's life coming to an abrupt, painful end, and the next being born bloody and screaming. For a single, desperate second before he hit the floor, Terry had thought Vaughn would be okay, that all the medication and years of experience would be enough to keep his little brother safe from the thing he'd lived his whole life afraid of. Ever since they were little kids and Vaughn's seizures were bad enough to scare Terry into pissing the bed from nightmares, Vaughn had always bounced back. Sometimes it took hours, sometimes it took days, but it always happened. He always bounced back. Until he didn't.

Terry's little brother died shaking and suffering, all knotted up on the floor of the barroom, foam leaking from his lips, his head split open where that nasty little bitch had glassed him.

Epilepsy was a real motherfucker.

They buried him while they were still bleeding, loaded him up in the back of the van and drove out to the hills to plant him where nobody would find him. It was the smart play, no matter how much it hurt—and it really fucking hurt. Better for Vaughn to disappear rather than be discovered by some civilian—or, worse, some cop. Vaughn wouldn't have wanted shit to go down like that. He was 48 Coffin to the bone, a true believer since day one.

After it was done, they marked the spot with an X cut in the closest tree, then headed back to Lotte's. The whole thing didn't take more than forty-five minutes; just like that, it was like Vaughn had never been there at all. An entire life washed away in the span of time it took for the oxygen in his blood to drop past the point of recovery. All because some fucking tourist decided she wanted to do things the hard way.

He deserved better, Terry's baby brother. But he wasn't ever going to get it. Not now, not ever.

The anger was a hole burning through the pit of Terry's throat, all acid and blood in extremity, a level of rage he'd never felt before. This wasn't *pissed*; pissed was a shadow that paled in comparison to the fury he felt right now. He was going to burn the world down looking for those assholes; and when he found them, he was going to pull them apart, inch by bloody inch. But right now, he had to stay in control.

"Hey, boss?"

Terry turned around to look. Harlan was standing behind the bar, down by the cash register.

"Might want to see this," the little man said, and skated a little piece of plastic down the pine. Peeling it off the bar, Terry held the little plastic rectangle up to the light to look. On the front was a shitty, grainy picture of the bitch that had killed Vaughn, and beside that, three lines:

TALBOT, ELEANOR LEIGH
5756 VISTA VERDE DRIVE
ALBUQUERQUE, NM 87107

"Left it as collateral for the tab," Harlan said. "Never bothered taking it back. Stupid. Heard the two of them talking about driving out to Mowry too. Before everything went to shit," he clarified.

Terry palmed the ID. "Mowry, Nevada?"

"Unless you know of a different one, yeah, probably."

"You get the other one's name? The brother?"

Harlan screwed his face up in thought. "I think it was Joe or something. Joseph, Jonah, maybe."

"Doesn't matter," Terry said. "He's dead anyway."

"So. What is plan?" Darko asked, his voice deep and guttural in his thick Serbian accent. A smile danced at the corners of his lips, anticipatory. Darko lived for this kind of shit.

Terry shot him and Gillam a look. "What do you think the plan is?"

Gillam rapped his fists against the chipped tabletop. "So that's it? We're going after them?"

Terry turned the license around in his fingers like a talisman and looked up at his guys.

"Like you said. They don't get to get away with this. They die bloody. I promise you that. Call the troops, get 'em here, now. They're going to hold down the fort while we're gone."

"Wait, we? You mean just us?" Gillam asked. "Nobody else?"

"Nobody else," Terry confirmed. "Any more than us

three and we'll draw too much attention. State cops take special notice of riders in kuttes, you know that well as I do. We make too much noise, get too public about shit, pigs'll start getting itchy, maybe call backup and try to pull something they shouldn't. I don't want anybody—and I mean *anybody*—fucking this up for us. Nobody gets in our way. Vaughn deserves better than that. We do this under the radar."

"Okay. You're the Prez. Consider it done," Gillam said.

"Good. Take the van," Terry said. "Me and Darko will ride out ahead, scout a route. We'll call you if whatever. Mowry ain't that far, probably make it by nightfall if we ride hard."

"So, we're heading out?"

"We're heading out," Terry said. "Probably be a couple of days before we're back, so do what you need to do to make it work. Get your guns, change of underwear, whatever else. We don't turn around until the job's done."

He pocketed the driver's license and turned around to walk out of the bar. He had to get ready. They needed to move, now.

Outside, the sun was already sinking close to the treetops, a chill in the wind pricking at the back of Terry's neck as he took one last look at what the Talbots had done to his bike. Kicked over, both tires shredded to fuck... these assholes. Gillam had mentioned that they'd gone after it, but Terry hadn't seen the extent of the damage until now.

No matter. He could take Vaughn's bike. Felt like the right thing to do anyway. Harlan could pay to have his towed and fixed up while they were gone.

Down the alley beside the bar, yellow headlights split the gloom as the unmarked black van rolled into the parking lot. From the driver's-side window, Gillam shot him a watchful look, then threw the van in park and let it idle, waiting for Terry and Darko to lead the way. Terry saw a small orange flare behind the glass, casting Gillam's face in low relief as he fired up a cigarette and blew smoke, the cherry a tiny firefly floating in the dark.

He patted himself down once more, making sure he had everything: under his kutte, his sawed-off over/under and his old silver .45 sat snugly inside their nylon holsters; one of the burner phones from their stock buttoned inside the left breast pocket of his coat while the right held his wallet, thick with cash. Vaughn's keys jingled loosely in his pocket. Seemed like he had it all. Might as well get this show on the road. They were already losing daylight.

Terry turned in place, back toward the bikes, and felt his boot scuff against something half-buried in the gravel. Kicking it loose, he knelt and picked it up: an oversized folding knife, the dull-silver blade long and razor sharp, the 48 Coffin logo subtly embossed in the dark micarta. Heat, feverish and unrelenting, flooded Terry's cheeks as he knelt there, cradling Vaughn's blade in his open palm. Jesus. Jesus fuck. He thumbed back the lock and eased the blade down to rest in the grip, then slid the knife into his pocket beside the driver's license and ran a thumb along the stitched-together gash in his forehead.

He was going to bury Vaughn's knife in both the Talbots' hearts if it was the last thing he ever did.

Ding-ding-ding-ding-ding-ding-ding-ding-ding-ding-ding-
ding-ding–

Jonah came to with a start, jolting awake from a dream that he couldn't remember but still felt in his chest and his arms. His lungs burned, as if he'd been trapped underwater, thrashing breathlessly toward the surface but never quite able to reach it. Pulse clanging in his temples, he drew air in great heaving gulps that upended his stomach, made him feel like he was going to vomit. Blinking against the muddy daylight, he pitched forward and laid both hands flat on the Volvo's dashboard, trying to force his body back under control.

Breathe. Just breathe slow.

The car wasn't moving anymore, he could feel that much. The engine wasn't even on. As he sat there, trying to shake off the remains of the nightmare, a dry, tepid breeze danced across his face and arms, making the feathery hair there stand at attention. He craned his head back and forth until the joints popped in the meat of his neck, and he breathed slowly, trying to get a read on the situation as his vision began to clear.

–ding-ding-ding-ding-ding-ding-ding-ding-ding-ding-ding-
ding-ding–

"Nell?" Jonah rubbed at his eyes with sore, swollen knuckles until he saw stars. "Nell, what the hell is...where are we? Nell?"

Slowly, the world fell into place around him, but it was a world that didn't make sense. They weren't parked on a road, they weren't...anywhere, really. Beyond the car windows, there were no roads, no power lines, no anything. Sky above and sand below. They were in the middle of the goddamn desert, off the edge of the map.

"Nell, stop fucking around. What the hell are we doing out here?"

Jonah glanced around the Volvo, waiting for her to answer, but there was nobody behind the wheel. Nobody in the back seat. Nobody standing outside.

Nell was gone.

Across the car, the driver's-side door hung wide open, the desert wind blowing through the car in weak gusts, Nell's keys hanging from the ignition. In the footwell, in front of the gas and brake pedals, his sister's last three coffin nails had tumbled into the seam between the mat and the door, the crumpled pack no doubt long blown away.

Jonah's guts burst into a tangle of cold ribbons, his pulse racing in his head to match the incessant, maddening chime reminding anyone within earshot that the keys were still in the ignition.

–ding-ding-ding-ding-ding-ding-ding-ding-ding-ding-ding-ding-ding–

Reaching over, Jonah snapped the keys from the steering column, cutting the grating noise off at the throat. The silence that rushed in to fill its place was monstrous in its totality, an unseen entity that came crashing out of the sky, trampling everything in its way. His head throbbed and his pulse grew louder in his ears, his heart rate jumping to a frantic machine-gun rat-a-tat. His breath took on a faint wet wheeze that he swore hadn't been there before. Yanking clumsily at the door handle, he spilled out of the passenger side of the Volvo and onto the bare ground with a crunch, the urge to puke surging in his throat again, stronger this time. Bending at the hip and bracing himself against the side of the car, he coughed and spat until the nauseous swell passed.

Jonah couldn't even see the road from here, stranded in the middle of this big empty. He was surrounded on all sides by rough, raw terrain. The only sign of which direction the road lay were the tire tracks pressed into the dirt behind the Volvo, arcing off into the distance. His back crawled. He felt exposed standing here like this, like he was being watched, scrutinized, studied. An ant underneath glass in a kid's bedroom.

The landscape out here was so strange, all craggy and barren—jagged rocks, scrubby plants, and gnarled, bone-dry trees dotted the choppy sandhills all around him, while overhead the waning afternoon sky hung too close to the earth, scattered with mottled purple clouds that looked like fresh contusions. There was no one else around for miles—so why did he feel like he was being watched? Walking around to the front of the car, Jonah drew a deep breath, cupped his hands to his lips, and shouted "Nell? Nell!"

His voice echoed off the empty hills, bouncing back and forth as he craned his head to one side, listening for any sign of people, other cars, anything at all; but there was nothing. He was totally alone. A frosty breeze whipped across the desert hills and hit Jonah full force in the chest as worry began to mount and transform into full-blown panic. Twisting in place, he looked over to the driver's side of the car and saw footprints—Nell's—leading away into the sand, cresting over the nearest hill and disappearing into the distance.

That anxious shake jumped through his chest again, but this time it wasn't because of the wind. This wasn't just weird, this was bad. This was very fucking bad. Experimentally, Jonah laid a hand on the Volvo's hood—it was cool to the touch. Wherever Nell was, she'd been gone for a while. Even though it was still light out, Jonah had to consider the possibility that the car could have been sitting out here for hours already.

Fuck.

His first thought was to call 911. Screw the barfight back in Broughton, screw the bikers and the shitstorm of trouble he and Nell were doubtlessly going to be in once the cops came calling, he needed help, now. Retrieving his phone from his pants pocket, he clicked it to life, the glare of the screen harsh and painful in the low desert light. But up at the top of the screen, the service indicator, next to a little antenna logo, just read X. No service. Probably wasn't a tower around for miles. Jonah was on his own.

Double fuck.

The anxiety and dread crashed over him in a tidal wave:

What if she's hurt out there? What if she's lost? What if she got attacked by something, bit by something, and she needs help? What if? What if? What if?

In that moment, none of their shit mattered anymore. The arguments, the distance, everything they'd never bothered talking about, none of it. The only thing that mattered to Jonah right now was making sure that Eleanor Leigh Talbot, one of the only constants in his whole stupid life, was safe. If he had to cross the desert on foot, walk the rest of the way to Mowry, fight the bikers again, he'd do it. Whatever it took. Because at the end of the day, no matter how fucked up things were between them, Jonah knew Nell would do it for him. She wouldn't even think twice.

Circling the rest of the way around the Volvo, Jonah kicked the driver's-side door shut and followed his sister into the desert.

Jonah walked.

Nell's boots and the big prints they left behind made her path easy to follow, straight as an arrow headlong into the wastes, never wavering or meandering off course. Had she been out this way before? The sureness of her path sure made it seem as if she knew where she was going—wherever the hell that was.

He stayed close to his sister's trail, passing by desiccated trees and spindly yucca, oversized anthills and misshapen cacti and more than a few sun-bleached animal skeletons half-buried in the sand. Hill after hill, deeper into the desert. Where even was this? It didn't look like California, so... Nevada? Probably Nevada.

Even in the stubborn early-spring chill, the walk wasn't exactly pleasant, the stubborn heat from the sun still radiating off the sand in sharp little waves, sucking more energy from his body with every step. His mouth dry and cracked like old plaster, Jonah had already sweated most of the way through his shirt; the sand in his shoes made his feet feel like they were

already blistering. With every step, he imagined his socks drooping down, soggy with pinkish, viscous fluid as the bulbous sores
on his soles ruptured and wept. But still he walked. He wasn't
going to stop until he found her.

Climbing another hillock, he came to a place where Nell's
path grew narrow and corkscrew, cutting between a copse of
near-dead trees as it wound up to a rocky hilltop that, from
where Jonah was standing, looked impassable. Had she climbed
over it? Sprouted wings and flown? As he drew closer to the
rocks, he saw more footsteps in the dust along the narrow ridge
that lined the hilltop, where Nell had hugged the craggy wall to
circle around to the other side. Steadying himself with a hand,
Jonah followed suit, keeping close to the rock , moving slowly,
carefully. As he cut his way around to the other side of the ridge,
his breath caught in his lungs like an arrow fired point-blank
into his chest. On the other side of the hill, far, far below, sat
a great, wide basin in the desert, buffeted on all sides by rocky
hills that hid it from view unless you were up high enough. But
it wasn't the sudden appearance of the basin that stole Jonah's
breath: that task was left to what lay in its center.

There were buildings down there.

Away from any road, any power line, any mile marker,
there was a whole complex down there. And Nell's footprints
led straight toward it.

The place was abandoned, that much was obvious. Still, Jonah
approached slowly, sliding down the side of the basin on his
heels, focusing on the buildings ahead as he approached. As
he drew closer, he could see discarded forklifts and industrial
shipping containers, spotlights and control stations and trucks
stamped with unfamiliar logos. Shredded tarps and weathered warning signs cautioning trespassers to keep out hung
from sagging chain-link fences that surrounded battered white
construction trailers. The biggest notice hung on the front gate
beside an almost cartoonishly oversized stop sign:

WARNING

NO TRESPASSING

PRIVATE LAND

PROPERTY OF BURKHOLDER

CONSTRUCTION AND CONSULTING.

IT IS UNLAWFUL TO ENTER THIS AREA

WITHOUT WRITTEN PERMISSION OF

THE ADMINISTRATOR ON DUTY.

WHILE ON THIS PROPERTY, ALL PERSONS

AND THE PROPERTY UNDER THEIR

CONTROL ARE SUBJECT TO SEARCH.

PHOTOGRAPHY OF THIS AREA

IS STRONGLY PROHIBITED

18 USC 795

NO DRONE ZONE

STRICTLY ENFORCED

Jonah read through it twice, glancing back and forth between the sign and the pair of brutalist concrete towers that sat a dozen feet back from the enormous gate. There was no movement in the towers that he could see, but that feeling of being watched still hadn't let up. If anything, it had only gotten worse.

Still. Nell's footprints led through the gate, so through the gate was where he was going.

He laced one hand through the rough chain-link and pulled hard, dragging it open with a shrill, grating *screeeee*. Throwing it wide, Jonah stepped through, ignoring the way his back still crept under his sweat-sodden shirt. Whatever the hell this worksite was, he wasn't keen on sticking around; the faster he found Nell, the faster they could get back to the car, back on the road.

This place must have been something, back before all the people had gone, leaving everything out here to rot and crumble, eaten by the desert. Jonah imagined the rows between the containers and the machinery bustling with people, but now there weren't any signs of life at all, beyond Nell's bootprints wending their way through the site, past the industrial generators and derelict office trailers. It was as if the people working here had just picked up and left one day, abandoning the site to the ravages of time and weather. He passed through the site silently, keeping his shoulders hunched up around his ears as he scanned his surroundings like a frightened dog. Stepping off the path and picking one of the trailers at random, Jonah tried the handle. The door swung open easily.

The air inside was stagnant and musty with stale sweat. In the corner of the room, a dusty little mini-fridge sat on the floor. Jonah toed it open: inside, bottles of water lay stacked between a few half-cans of Bud Light and some Tupperware'd leftovers that had long fouled and gone to waste. Bending down, Jonah grabbed one of the waters, cracked the cap, and drained it in one gulp. There were three or four workstations in here, all covered with scattered papers and office supplies and a fine layer of dust. Jonah leafed through some of the loose pages, but they were filled with weird corporate-speak about *specimen containment* and *updated breach protocols*. He couldn't make heads or tails of it. Tossing the pages back on the desk, he pocketed another bottle of water and let himself out of the little trailer again. He was wasting time. He had to find Nell.

Overhead, the sun had slipped behind the bruise-purple clouds, giving the whole sky the shimmering rainbow look of an oil spill. It was going to be dark soon. Jonah wanted to be out of here before then. Pausing beyond the trailer door, he thought to call out for his sister again, but he couldn't bring himself to raise his voice, or even speak. Back at the car, the quiet had felt oppressive, a crushing weight to be fought against, pushed away. Not so, here. The thought of disturbing the fragile, tremulous silence that had invaded this place was all but unfathomable to him.

As quietly as he could, he descended the little staircase and picked up his sister's footprints again, heading deeper into the abandoned worksite. All around him, concrete buildings reached for the sky, their windows dull and inert. He didn't want to be here, hidden away among the abandoned wreckage and the silence. Even the air here was uncomfortable; warm and soupy, it was as if the earth had opened up to breathe hotly into his face. He suppressed a gag, then another, and kept walking.

It was at the center of the worksite that he found the hole. A hundred feet across or more, it funneled down at an uneven angle to terminate in a triangular breach that had opened up deep in the sand. From where Jonah stood, it looked like an impact crater, like God had hauled off and sucker-punched the planet when Earth wasn't looking. All around its edge sat industrial digging machines, backhoes and excavators, loaders and dump trucks heavy with sand and soil, as still and devoid of life as the rest of the site. Jonah understood right away. Carving this pit out of the desert floor hadn't been some easy task, and it hadn't happened by accident. This—whatever *this* was—had been the point of this place; this hole in the earth was what all the rest of it was for. Feeling his back start to prickle again, Jonah got in closer to the pit and looked over the edge.

He could see where the rock and scree on the nearest slope had been punched in by Nell's footsteps, heading down toward that void at the bottom of the crater that leered back at him like a dead eye. Jonah chewed at the inside of his cheek until he tasted blood. Goddammit.

Arms out to keep himself balanced, Jonah stepped over the edge and started down the side of the crater, carefully stepping in Nell's tracks as he descended toward the empty triangle. Sand and grit slid from under his feet with each step, calving off the slope in loose cascades that spilled down into the shadows that lay beyond. When he reached the bottom, he knelt at the edge of the hole, squinting to try to see inside. Clicking on the flashlight function of his phone, he shone it down into the darkness; but beyond the dull triangle of daylight thrown by the afternoon sun, he couldn't see anything. No Nell. No anything. Just dark, infinite emptiness.

Well, wait. That wasn't entirely true. As he shifted the light back and forth, he could see that what he'd first taken for an endless nothing was in fact a wide tube of jet-black stone, reaching down and away from the strange, triangular hole, like a chute or a manhole leading deeper into the earth. It was steep, sure, but it wasn't a straight drop like Jonah had first thought. He could slide down it, if he needed to. Looked like Nell had.

Behind him, he heard more rocks sliding loose from the slope of the crater, disturbed by...what? Twisting around to look, Jonah searched fruitlessly for the source of the disturbance. There was nothing there. As he turned back, he felt the stones beneath his feet shift under his weight and he jerked to the side to keep his balance, only realizing half a second too late that he'd let go of his phone in the process. He watched it bumble awkwardly through his fingers and into the hole below, the light spinning in lazy circles as it bounced off the dark stone and vanished into the shadows. A second later, he heard the far-off sound of plastic and glass slapping the ground with a sharp *crack!*

"Fucking shit," Jonah said, as fear climbed his spine anew.

Clutching the edge of the hole with both hands, Jonah lowered himself into the chute feet-first, trying to summon up the courage to let himself drop. No way to judge how far it was from here to the bottom, not at this angle, and definitely not without the light on his phone. He clenched his teeth and counted down from five. On one, he let go. For a second, he was suspended in midair, falling for what felt like forever...then his ass hit stone and he was sliding down-down-down through the chute, all but blind, trying not to scream. A second later, he crashed out of the tube in an awkward heap, spilling onto the ground, heart hammering behind his ribs. Sprawled there, Jonah rolled over, straightening his body out to make sure he had his bearings before he got to his feet again. He was okay. He was fine.

A few feet away, his cell phone lay faceup on the stone floor, a spiderweb cracked deep into the glowing screen. Son of a bitch. When he picked it up, a painful white glare burst from its underside, the flashlight still shining resolutely. Small mercies, he supposed. Jonah turned the light around the stale chamber he'd landed in, trying to understand what he was seeing.

He was standing in the vestibule of an underground cave network, the stone walls banded and black in the shadows, darkened tunnels branching off in a dozen different directions.

Jonah had seen caves like this before, lava tubes underneath Hawai'i that he and Molly had toured on their honeymoon. But the caves underneath the Big Island were smooth and well-worn by countless feet over the years; what Jonah was standing in now was rough, almost primal. Nobody had set foot down here in a very long time. Nobody but Nell. And now him, too.

He turned back toward the hole that he'd come tumbling out of. Didn't seem like there was any other way out of this place, unless he wanted to go searching through the branching caves for another, which he already knew was a stupid idea. He was going to have to be careful not to get lost while he was down here. As he studied the end of the chute, he noticed a long, dark smear leading away from its mouth, messy and uneven. Was that... blood? It was long dry, but there was no mistaking it, now that he'd seen it. Christ. Jonah's stomach turned. He couldn't stay down here. He had to find Nell, and then they both had to get the hell out, right now. That was it. That was all.

"Nell? You down here?" he called, listening to his voice bounce away and disappear into the depths of the cave network. "Nell, it's me, it's, it's Jonah! Say something if you can hear me!"

Nothing.

Jonah looked around, tracing the flashlight beam along the stone for any sign of his sister, any sign of anything, and found that if he held the phone at just the right angle, he could make out faint markings on the cave floor, places where a pair of boots had disturbed the dust and grit. Moving slowly, he began to follow her tracks again, ducking down as the caverns grew cramped around his tall, lank frame.

As he moved deeper into the tunnel, he found that he could see marks carved into the stone walls; long, unbroken strings of glyphs unlike any language Jonah had ever seen before stretching from passage to passage, looping overhead and underfoot, all curves and hairpin angles that made his head swim. Line after line, the symbols were cut deep into the rock like scrimshaw, drawing in claustrophobically, almost mechanically close before exploding out in a completely different direction, two directions, three. Jonah looked back down, keeping the light on the ground: Nell's footsteps seemed to be following the glyph lines deeper into the caves.

What the hell had Nell led him into? And where the hell was she?

"Nell!" he called out again. "Nell, I'm here, say something if you can hear me, okay? Nell?"

Scuff, scuff.

Jonah paused, tilting his head to one side to listen. What was that? For a second, he had been sure that he could hear something moving in the darkness, not too far off. Probably in some adjacent cave he hadn't yet explored.

"Nell?...Nell, is that you?"

He shone his flashlight around in an uneven arc, the glare catching the edges of the strange carved glyphs, making them dance, as if they were seconds away from jumping off the walls and swarming him like a flood of spiders. But there was nothing there. No one. He was alone.

Scuff, scuff.

Jonah froze. Holding his breath, he slowly pressed the light to his sweaty chest, casting the labyrinthine caves into darkness again as he listened to the silence. He definitely heard it that time. It was close, too. Only feet away. Maybe less. He held his breath and stayed still as stone, begging his heart not to beat, afraid that the sound of his pulse would draw it—whatever it was—closer.

Scuff, scuff.

Something brushed against the back of his legs.

Jonah yelped and broke into a run, the light in his hand flickering and flashing in a mad jitter along the carved cave walls until he stumbled into a large open cavern, his frantic footsteps echoing loudly inside its vast expanse. This space was brighter than the corridors that had come before it, lit from within by a strange blue glow that Jonah couldn't quite pinpoint. At the far edge of the room, the floor seemed to just...drop away, giving way to a great empty chasm that seemed to go down and down forever. At its edge, atop a long slab of smooth stone, lay a pile of old rags. He turned his light around the great room and felt his breath come up short when the beam from the back of his phone passed over the telltale curve of a human skull, perched on top of a pile of moldering bones that sat slumped against one of the far walls. Jonah bit back another yelp and forced himself to look closer: draped in dust and cave mold, they'd been here for a long, long time. Whoever they were, they'd died trapped and alone in this desolate underground. Must have been horrible.

Glancing away from the ancient remains, Jonah turned his attention back toward the great chasm at the far side of the cavern and gasped. What he'd taken previously for a pile of rags on the stone slab was Nell, her body bent and twisted like a pretzel. Jonah launched himself forward to where his sister lay, climbing onto the stone beside her, careful not to move too fast lest he pitch forward over the edge and into the waiting chasm. Kneeling down, Jonah gingerly lifted Nell off the hard surface, unfolding her from herself, cradling her head in his lap, brushing short purple locks of hair away from her face.

"Nell? Nell, hey, it's Jonah. I'm here, okay? I'm right here. Nell, come on, you gotta wake up, come on—"

His sister's eyes trembled open briefly, but there was no recognition there. Her pupils were pinpricks in the dark, giving her eyes a blank, vacant look. That couldn't be good. As he held her, her eyes slid shut again, rolling back and forth underneath their lids like she was dreaming.

She didn't look like she was hurt: he couldn't see any blood or broken bones, as bent and twisted as she'd been, but Jonah wasn't a doctor, and it was dark as hell down here, even with the light from his phone. There was really no way to tell if she was okay or not. But he'd found her. That was enough for now.

Over the edge of the great slab, in the great empty below, something began to growl, a deep, damp rumbling that quickly grew and spread to fill the caves around them. Quickly grabbing his phone and gathering Nell in his arms (*she's so light*, Jonah thought, *no dead weight to her at all*), Jonah dashed back into the tunnels, away from the slab, those ancient bones and that horrible roar, twisting and turning, following his own footprints through the dark, nerves frayed to the seams.

Carrying his sister, he ran until he came to that very first chamber and the hole in the wall that led back up to the surface.

He nearly wept when he saw it. Balancing his phone in one hand, the pinhead LED set in its back lighting their way, Jonah paused in the middle of the room, adjusting his grip. The little glowing circle danced back and forth at his feet as darkness swarmed in around its edges, threatening to obliterate it. Down here, in a place like this, light was frail, as if the shadows might suddenly bite down and devour it whole. Jonah understood; places like this were darkness's home turf. Jonah and Nell and the light, they were all trespassers on the verge of being found out. Setting his sister on the ground, Jonah went to the chute and squatted down, trying to gauge the space the two of them would need to get out again.

It would work. This was going to work. All they had to do was get back up to the surface, and then they were home free.

Balancing Nell on his back, Jonah knelt down and started to duckwalk back up the tube, keeping his balance with one palm on the stone, closer and closer to daylight with each step. He kept a steady pace, shifting his center of gravity back and forth so Nell wouldn't slip off as the incline grew steeper. After another minute, it felt as if he were carrying her up the side of a wall. Jonah's legs burned, and his lungs strained for air that wouldn't come. It was too close in here, too small, but he had to keep going. It was only a few more steps. The car wasn't that far. They could probably make it before dark if he ran, and Jonah had every intention of running as fast as he could, even with Nell on his back. The second he was above ground, he was going to take off sprinting, and he wouldn't stop until they got to the Volvo; he didn't care if he had a heart attack doing it.

When he neared the top of the chute, Jonah carefully lifted his sister through the triangular hole, easing her up and through, making sure she wasn't going to tumble back down. Nell secured, Jonah reached for the edge to pull himself out after her. Only a few more steps—

Scuff, scuff.

It was so close behind him now. Biting back another scream, Jonah leaped for the chute's mouth and the low daylight beyond, and suddenly he was floating in midair, feeling his stomach pitch and roll as his hands scrambled wildly for anything to grab onto. Flashing both arms out, he caught himself on the edge of the hole, hanging on by his forearms, kicking wildly, trying to find some sort of purchase. He scrabbled past the edge of the hole with bare hands, feeling the rocks slice into his palms as he dragged himself the rest of the way up. Blood ran down his fingers while panic and fear rose in his chest, screaming for him to *Get out get out get out get the fuck out!* That consuming darkness had risen to meet him now. It was only a matter of time before it dragged him down again and ate him whole.

Inch by inch, Jonah dragged himself up and over the edge, flopping down next to his sister, wheezing for air, nausea churning his guts. Twisting to one side, he retched and loosed a thin cord of brown vomit into the darkness below, keeping his eyes shut. He didn't dare look in the hole again. He didn't want to see what was or wasn't down there, worming up through the chute with a razor-slash smile on its face.

All around them, the worksite was quiet as a tomb, the only sounds the rattle of Jonah's lungs and the crunch of the gravel under his feet. That was just as well. Pulling Nell into an unsteady fireman's carry, Jonah started to hike quickly out of the pit. He had to get them back to the car.

Over the hills, dark clouds were starting to gather.

Back at the Volvo, Jonah set his sister down across the back seat, then pulled the spare water bottle from his jacket and drained it, feeling his head swim and tilt against the exertion. He circled around the car and dropped himself behind the wheel, tossing the empty plastic in the passenger-side footwell, struggling to catch his breath. A second later, he slid the key into the ignition and cranked it until the engine turned over and the car hummed to life.

The clock on the Volvo's dashboard said 8:45 p.m. Later than he'd thought. In the rearview mirror, in the red glow of the taillights, he could still see the tire tracks they'd left in the dirt when they'd first arrived. It wasn't much, but it was better than nothing. Just needed to follow them out again. Soon enough, he'd hit a road, then a highway, and eventually Mowry. They couldn't be that far now. There'd be a hospital there, he was positive. He just needed get her there first. He checked his phone—still no service. He killed the phone's flashlight and cracked screen and pocketed the thing. Had to save what little battery he still had left.

Taking one last look at the strange terrain surrounding them, almost pitch-black now that the sun had slipped beneath the horizon, Jonah thought how lucky he'd been to have made it back at all, traveling through the dark like that. He hit the headlights: in their bright glow, he could still see the line of footprints he'd followed back, already fading in the wind blowing off the hills, so much stronger now than it had been when he'd first woke up. He crossed his arms on the steering wheel and leaned forward, resting his head and closing his eyes.

He still didn't know what the hell he'd seen out there. Had he seen anything, really? Sitting here now, he barely knew what was real and what was imaginary, the product of his own exhausted, anxiety-riddled mind. It all already seemed so foggy and strange, like something out of a dream. It was almost easier to think that he'd hallucinated all of it. But he wasn't crazy—at least, not any crazier than he'd been when he woke up this morning. Something had happened out there, just like something had driven the Burkholder company away. No denying that. It was real. He had the sand in his shoes and the cuts in his hands and arms to prove it. All that mattered now was putting as many miles between him and his sister and that fucking ghost town of a worksite as he possibly could.

Jonah threw the Volvo in drive and, feeling the tires bear down hard on the dirt, floored the gas until he hit asphalt.

t was long after dark when the three of them finally made it to
Mowry. The sunset had been a gorgeous thing, exploding the
sky into a wildfire of oranges and purples and reds and blacks,
and when it finally slipped out of sight, night rolled over the
desert hills like the tide, snuffing out everything but the beams
of their headlights slicing down the blacktop.

When the green city-limits sign whipped past on the roadside, Terry signaled to Darko to pull over, then slowed to a stop
along the highway's gravel edge, feeling the night air bluster
through his leathers, crisp and cold. It felt good. It felt like being
alive; a job he was doing for two now. A minute later, the van
rumbled up behind them and Terry stepped out in front of it,
twirling a finger: *turn around.* Inside the Econoline, Gillam did
as he was told, hooking a uey in the middle of the cracked two-
lane to park along the opposite shoulder.

Crossing the highway in the glare of the van's headlights,
his shadow a stretched spider dancing atop the asphalt, Terry
rapped his ringed knuckles against the driver's-side window and
waited for Gillam to roll it down.

"What's up, boss?" Gill's eyes were nervous, his fingers
drumming against the wheel.

"Kill the lights," Terry said.

Gill did as he was told.

"Need you to stay here," Terry said. "Keep watch. One
road in and out of this place. Me and Darko'll head into town,
see what's what. You keep your goddamned specs on, understand? They come in, they leave, anything, I don't care. You
call me if whatever. You know what they're driving, right?"

"Old station wagon. Blue. All beat to fuck."

"Good. Don't follow them, nothing stupid. I don't want them knowing we're here until I want them to know. Got it?"

Gill nodded. "Got it. What if they don't show?"

"They'll show."

"But what if they don't?"

"Then I'll see you in the morning," Terry said. "Try not to fall asleep."

Gillam ashed his smoke out of the open window.

"All right, I'm on it," he said.

"I know you are," Terry told him, and walked away.

On the other side of the road, Darko was sitting still on his bike, watching Terry intently.

"All good?" Darko asked.

"All good," Terry said, swinging one leg over his brother's bike. "C'mon, let's go."

Kicking Vaughn's motorcycle to life, he cranked the throttle, launching a roostertail of grit from under his back wheel, then launched off into the night, toward the distant lights of downtown Mowry. Behind him, Darko followed suit. Together they peeled off into the night, into town to wait for Gillam's call. One way or another, they were going to get these fucks.

Jonah
Mowry, NV
872 miles to Albuquerque

Rubbing the exhaustion out of his eyes for what felt like the hundredth time, Jonah looked down at the clock: almost midnight already. Jesus. Sailing past the city-limits sign, he tightened his deathgrip around the steering wheel and tried to focus on the scant town lights rising up out of the darkness in front of them. Not far now. Just a couple more minutes. He could last a couple more minutes. He was pretty sure.

Mowry was a relic, a little town near Nevada's eastern edge that had clung on to all the trappings of the Wild West long after the Wild West had gone the way of the dodo. Jonah had first been here years ago with Molly and their friends. They'd wanted to cut loose, gamble a little bit and have some fun, but none of them were interested in the acid trip of Vegas or the chintz of Reno, so Mowry was perfect for their needs. All bars and casinos along the main drag, lit by streetlights and marquees ripped straight out of the 1950s, it was chock-full of places where the uncaring and unwary could spend their money, far removed from reality. They all drank too much and spent too much money and went home hung over and broke and happy as they'd ever been. Jonah had been looking forward to coming back for a long time, but now found that he couldn't care less.

He pulled up outside the front of the Silver Dollar Hotel Casino and put the Volvo in park, taking a cautious glance back at his sister. Her eyes still wavered underneath their lids, but she seemed stable enough for now. Inside the hotel's front doors, he was clobbered by the sounds of electronic slot machines and the smell of cigars and air fresheners as he weaved between the waitresses who wandered the casino floor, shuttling drinks to gamblers who sat watching their savings slowly drip-drip-drip away. Jonah turned his attention to the front desk and the clerk

83

standing behind the computer: he was a young guy, maybe twenty-one at the outside, with a face full of teenage acne that still hadn't faded away entirely. Jonah proffered a perfunctory smile as he approached.

"Welcome to the Silver Dollar Hotel Casino," the kid said as Jonah drew in close. "How can I help you tonight?"

"Yeah, listen, is there a hospital around here? Anything like that?"

The clerk shook his head. "Sorry, no," he said. "Closest one's probably in West Wendover, but that's still a few hours north, probably more now with the storm rolling in. Why? Is it an emergency?"

"I don't think so?" Jonah said, his voice dreamy and bone-tired. "I honestly don't know. It's my sister. We were out along the highway and she, uh, she fell. Is there an urgent care, maybe? A doctor in town?"

"Sorry, not one you're going to see tonight," the kid said, his face flushing. "Doc Handey's got her office over on Pineview, but by now she's probably gone home for the night. She's old. It's late. Is it an emergency or something?"

Jonah turned back to look out the glass doors at the Volvo, unsure how he'd even begin to explain the last ten hours of his life to this kid.

"I don't know," he said again. "She's just... out. It's like she's sleeping. I don't know."

The clerk looked down at Jonah's hands, at the flaking blood and the scars piled high on his knuckles. When the kid saw that he'd been caught gawking, his face turned a brighter shade of pink, but he didn't look away.

"Do... do you need me to call the cops?" he asked, a nervous quaver shaking his voice.

"No," Jonah said, forcing his voice to be calmer and friendlier than he felt. The last thing he needed was for this kid to call 911. "Honestly, she's, uh, she's probably fine. Now that I think about it. Thanks. I'll just wait and see how she's feeling in the morning."

"...the morning?" the clerk asked, tearing his eyes from Jonah's scarred-up hands with visible effort.

Jonah sighed. "Yeah. Right, sorry. Reservation for Talbot." He produced a credit card from his wallet and slid it across the desk. Reading the numbers on the back, the kid clacked on his keyboard.

"All right, Mr. Talbot, I've got your reservation here. Looks like we've got you booked in room 707. Everything should be ready to go up there, so let me just get your keys for you." The kid produced two electronic keycards and handed them over. "Are you going to need help with your baggage, or...?"

Jonah shook his head. "No, thanks, I think I got it," he said.

The clerk looked relieved to hear that. He couldn't blame him. The kid seemed nervous enough as it was. No need to complicate shit further by making him help carry an unconscious woman up to a hotel room. Probably not the weirdest thing he'd ever be asked to do, working the graveyard shift in a gambling town, but Jonah had no interest in making the list.

The kid passed him a receipt to sign and a ballpoint pen with the words *The Silver Dollar Hotel Casino: Where Everyone's a Winner!* printed along the side. Jonah scribbled his name on the line and passed both back without making any more eye contact, afraid to spook him.

"This place have parking? Another elevator?" he asked.

The clerk pointed over his own shoulder. "Around back. You can't miss it."

"Thanks," Jonah said.

"...Have a nice evening."

"Sure, you too," he said, feeling the kid ogling him up and down as he walked back into the night.

Lurching into room 707 with Nell in his arms, Jonah set her down on the nearest bed. She was still well out and only stirred slightly when Jonah lifted her onto the mattress, her eyes floating open for a moment, looking without seeing. After he'd wheeled the luggage cart and the rest of their things into the room, Jonah let the door swing shut, threw the deadbolt, then sat down on the edge of the second bed and watched his sister until he heard her start to snore softly. Snoring was good. Snoring meant sleep. Now they just had to make it through the rest of the night.

He got a change of clothes from his suitcase and headed into the bathroom, shutting the door and dropping his things on the countertop. Disrobing, he cranked the shower on to full blast and stepped into the steaming spray, letting the heat sink into his skin as the sand and sweat and dirt rolled off him in runny sheets. He scrubbed himself raw with the grainy hotel soap, scouring his knuckles until those stubborn red stains finally came away, sluicing down his fingers to circle the drain.

He crossed his arms against the wall underneath the showerhead and hung his head, letting the scalding water hiss across his back, suddenly intensely aware of his own exhaustion. God, but he'd taken a fucking beating today. It wasn't just saying goodbye to Molly or the bruises from that shitshow at the bar, the walk back and forth across the desert, or what had happened—whatever had happened—underneath the worksite. It was everything, all of it, together. He'd been running on fumes for a while. At this point, it was a marvel he was still upright.

What a profoundly fucked-up day this had turned into.

Pushing himself off the wall, he ran a daub of shampoo through his hair, washed it, rinsed, then shut off the water and stepped out to dry himself with one of the stiff towels from the rack. Swishing a mouthful of water from the sink faucet from cheek to cheek, he spat, then stepped into his clean clothes— fresh underwear, a pair of basketball shorts, a ratty old Nick Cave and the Bad Seeds T-shirt—relishing the feeling of not wearing something sodden with filth and sweat for the first time in most of twenty-four hours.

Out in the main room, Nell had rolled over and curled into the fetal position, her ribcage rising and falling steadily. Jonah pulled the spare blanket over her shoulders, then turned out the light and climbed into his own bed, feeling his sore, heavy body creak and pop as he settled uneasily into the cool sheets.

He really hoped Nell was going to be all right. She wasn't dead at least, and he supposed that had to be enough for now.

Through the glass, between the blinds, he could see snow starting to fall outside, spilling from the sky in thick flakes that twisted and danced upwards through the air, seemingly immune to gravity's pull. The sky was dark against the flurries, making them look like stars that had come loose from the sky. Far below on the street, he could hear drunks crying out in surprise and delight as they stumbled through the snowfall, moving from casino to casino.

Tomorrow they'd make the drive up to West Wendover, get Nell checked out. After that, he had no idea. For a second, he thought about calling Molly, but nixed that idea right out of the gate. It was late. She wouldn't listen, probably wouldn't even answer, and even if she did, what could she do about it? Nope, forget that. He considered calling his dad next, just to let him know what had happened, but quickly banished that thought too. Calling now would only worry the old man, especially since Jonah still didn't know and couldn't explain what the hell had happened to Nell out in the desert. Dad had plenty of his own problems without Jonah calling in the middle of the night to dogpile onto them like an asshole.

Tomorrow. He'd call his dad tomorrow, after he got Nell to the hospital, after they knew more. He could try and explain things then.

Looking back on it now, what had happened underneath the worksite seemed so far away, almost unreal. But it had happened. He knew it had. Something had happened to Nell down there. Something had grazed the backs of his legs.

Hadn't it?

Jonah rubbed at his eyes again. What the hell had she been doing down there anyway? What had she been looking for, all the way out in the desert? Shit, how had she known that that place was even there?

Rolling over to look at his big sister, Jonah felt his breath catch in his chest.

There were curls of black smoke rising from Nell's lips.

Jonah's heart froze as his mind spun, trying to comprehend what he was seeing, but he could already feel sleep rising up to take him. He was having trouble holding on. He was so fucking tired. Fighting to stay awake for a few more seconds, Jonah watched the dark smoke coil and twist in the air above Nell's face, folding itself into different configurations, strange shapes he'd never imagined could exist. It was like a dream had slipped loose from his head, momentarily escaping into the real world to play. The idea occurred to him that maybe he was already asleep, maybe this was the dream. Watching the smoke drift out of Nell's mouth, Jonah's eyes began to tingle and itch and water. Tears rolled down his face to seep into the pillow.

Then he blinked, and the smoke was gone.

He was hallucinating. That had to be it. Exhaustion burning holes through his brain. He'd run his tank all the way down; if a bomb hit the side of the hotel tonight, odds were good he was going to sleep through it.

Lying still, he sank, feeling his body grow heavy as it pressed deeper into the mattress. Glancing back at Nell, he watched for another plume of smoke, some confirmation that he hadn't dreamt it, but there was nothing. She was asleep, and that was all. But in the moments before sleep dragged him the rest of the way down under its dead tide, Jonah swore that he could hear someone in the hallway outside their room, pacing back and forth.

Scuff, scuff.

S he was alone.

All around her, everything was damp and dark, drenched in shadows. She didn't know how long she'd been trapped underground, searching for a way out. She'd woken up shivering on the hard ground, shot through with agony, unable to remember what had brought her here in the first place. She'd lain there for the longest time, trying to will her body back to normal, away from the lingering sensation of being slowly pulled apart, then reassembled all wrong, her head and limbs sewn where they didn't belong. Now, hours (Hours? Minutes? Days? Time didn't seem to matter here) later, she still hurt, but the pain had become manageable, if not entirely ignorable.

Nell dragged her bare feet along the stone floor and moved through the caves, away from that stuffy, airless chamber she'd woken up inside of. It was strange down here, the caverns almost tubular, the air damp and fatty, clinging to her clothes and skin in a kind of sick gray film that covered her body in a chilly creep. How the fuck had she ended up down here?

Trudging on, she noticed after a while that the stone was beginning to shift and reform around her. The changes were small at first, barely perceptible, really—the faintest quiver of motion in the corners and the shadows—but it wasn't too long before they became obvious, the passages ahead sealing themselves off of their own accord, the black rock slithering shut as she drew near, the oily subterrane deciding her path for her. Eventually, every shaft had closed but one, where the jagged stone gave way to a kind of soft, dark rot that dripped and bled from the walls in foul clumps. Stopping where the rock met the muck, Nell squinted, trying to see how far down it went. She really didn't want to go stomping through that shit, but then, it didn't seem like she had much choice. Turning around and going back wasn't an option, and all the other ways forward had sealed themselves, closed up, healed over, not even a scar left behind in the rock to show that they'd ever been there.

Fuck it.

Nell took a deep breath and stepped one foot into the sludgeway, then the other, trying not to puke as her bare soles sank into the flesh-warm slime. The stench of it was horrendous, thick with rot and putrefaction, a dead body left to bloat and burst in the heat. Pressing on down the nauseating tunnel, Nell moved as quickly as she could until she came to another dead end. Another fucking dead end. She wanted to scream.

She hung her head and shut her eyes, only to realize a second later that somewhere far overhead, she could hear noise. Faint and uneven, but undeniably there. Were those voices? They were too muffled to make out clearly, but if she was hearing it, she figured that she couldn't be that far from the surface. With how soft the walls seemed, she figured that she could maybe make it through if she dug far enough. Something deep inside her, something animal, recoiled at the idea of touching that disgusting rot with her bare hands, let alone tunneling up into it, but she knew she couldn't stay buried down here forever. So there was nowhere to go but up.

Holding her breath, she reached up and plunged her arms into the low, rotten ceiling, the grime hot and greasy around her arms. Bile ballooned in the back of her throat, an oily slip dancing at the root of her tongue, but she gulped it back. She could puke all she wanted once she was through this shit. She just had to get through it first. Pushing her arms deeper, Nell dug at the warm decay with both hands, pulling putrid handfuls away until she'd cleared out enough space to climb up into and keep digging. Up and up and up she burrowed, breathing as little as she could, feeling the vile sludge soak into her clothes and her skin and her hair. She clawed past bones and roots and odd shapes she couldn't identify as her lungs struggled, desperate for air, but she wouldn't open her mouth. She couldn't. No way she was going to find out what this revolting shit tasted like. She'd suffocate first.

Then, as her lungs shuddered and threatened to burst from the pressure, she broke through.

Gasping for air, Nell dragged herself up and out of the hole she'd excavated, crawling away on hands and knees to collapse on her side as she fought to catch her breath. Still feeling the revolting scum creep across her body, she clung to the ground, clutching at the brittle grass with numb fingers, convinced she'd go tumbling into the sky if she let go for even a moment.

The sky, Jesus, the *sky*. Bright enough to scorch her eyes to cigarette burns, it was stained blood red from horizon to horizon, almost apocalyptic. Nell winced away from it as she beheld its crimson fury and the strange, horrible thing that sat high in its center.

At first she thought it was the sun, but the sun had never looked like that. Perfectly round and black as oblivion, a great ragged dead spot hung far overhead, pulsing and writhing and turning in place. It was so alien that it was almost offensive—it repelled Nell as much as it infuriated, a messy scorch mark pressed deep into the fabric of the sky. She lay there staring up at it through slitted eyelids, trying to understand what she was seeing, until at last it clicked.

It was a hole.

Something had burned a hole through the sky.

Unsteadily, Nell rose to her feet, wiping filthy hands on her jeans and tilting her head to stare at the scorched hollow above, deep in the blood sky's brute glare. From where she stood, she could see that the sky around the hole's edge had turned solid and fleshy, blackened by the heat and flaking away on the breeze. If she squinched her eyes, she could even make out the pulsing veins and trembling meat underneath that charred, ruined skin. Then a soft voice parted the air like a blade through flesh, holding her in place.

The hole was talking to her. She could hear that terrible wound *whispering* to her in some strange, inhuman language, telling her secrets and lies, muttering inside her brain as if she'd been hardwired into its abominable essence. Standing on the face of this unfamiliar earth, underneath that cruel firmament,

Nell listened to the words inside her head, and as she did, saw
something moving inside the void, just beyond the edges of
the sky's blistered skin. A pale, grasping hand with too many
fingers, a cracked and bleeding mouth, a knot of tangled bone
above an eyeless face.

Something inside was trying to escape.

In the red distance, Nell could see a tornado boiling on
the horizon, full of razor blades and teeth, drawing closer. She
felt her body start to bend again (Again? Had she bent before?),
warping out of joint as she began to float off the ground, lifted
toward that great dead lacuna by some invisible force. She could
taste smoke on the air now, clouding her brain, poisoning her,
remaking her into something else. The pain was everywhere
now; the pain was everything. Nell drifted up and up, twisting
and distorting into some new configuration, feeling the hole's
brutal, grotesque majesty take root in her heart and spread like
a plague as she screamed and screamed for no one to hear.

Part Two

THE

PASSENGER

Anna
Elko County, NV

She woke up well before sunrise, curled up in the back seat of her car under the long coat she'd pulled over her thin shoulders the night previous. Her hair, long and frizzy, hung about her head in a messy halo. She pushed it out of her face with sleepy hands as she licked at chapped lips with a dry tongue. Sleep had taken her quickly after she'd finally closed her eyes last night, dragging her down to the deepest depths and holding her there the whole night through.

Her skin buzzed with nerves while, behind her eyes, an insistent pressure pulled this way and that at an irregular tempo. The sensation wasn't unfamiliar, it was there most mornings anymore, but she could already tell it was going to be worse today than it had been in a while. No big deal. Probably just weird dreams aggravating things, coupled with the night's hard chill still tenaciously clinging to her bones. The windows had frosted over in the night; she could see snow collecting around the edges of the glass. She lay there a few minutes longer, letting the electricity coursing through her skin settle as her vision wandered around the dome light, the plastic trim, the cheap gray upholstery. There was a stain on the roof near the back window, something crusty and dry and dark, like spaghetti sauce. When had that happened? Had she ever eaten spaghetti back here? She couldn't remember now.

Anna rubbed her fingertips against her temples, trying to remember how long she'd been on the road. It seemed like forever. The last time she'd been back to her apartment felt like a hundred years ago and about a million miles away from where she was this morning, parked on a dirt road off some highway in nowhere, Nevada. Her latest sojourn had taken her from coast to coast and back again, and after driving for so long and going

95

so many days without a break, she was just tired. She'd been doing a lousy job of taking care of herself. Again. She supposed that was the thing about higher purposes—having one didn't make the day-to-day suck any less, it just made all your other problems seem so much smaller by comparison. So much easier to ignore.

Rolling up to a sitting position, Anna tossed her coat into the front seat and leaned forward to hit the headlights, then opened the door and stepped out into the cold, dark morning. Snow crunched under her boots as she emerged, the air slashing at her bare arms and the dozens of intricate tattoos there, turning every inch of exposed skin to gooseflesh. Down at the far end of the dirt road, a wrecked old pickup sat trapped in the glow of the headlights, buried under snow and sand, abandoned long ago.

She'd parked the car along a narrow hairpin just off the two-lane blacktop last night, a side road of a side road—Anna hadn't even noticed it until she was right on top of it, jamming on her brakes to make the turnoff, lucky that the highway hadn't iced over yet. She'd nosed the old Chevy down the dirt road a ways and parked close to an embankment where the ground rose high enough to keep her hidden the whole night through.

Standing still in the morning breeze, she listened—for other cars, for wildlife, for anything, but there was only silence. Between the dark above and the dead white of the snowy ground, she might as well have been standing on the moon. It was moments like this that she loved most, the small chances she got to luxuriate in her solitude, totally alone yet completely connected. They grounded her better than anything ever had, helped her gather strength enough to do what needed to be done. It was in these moments that she felt closest to God.

She breathed deeply, letting the frosty air claw at her lungs as she raised her hands to the sky. Turning her palms up, she laced her fingers together and rotated her arms back as far as they'd go, relishing the soft burn as she worked the sleep from her joints. Bending at the hip, she folded her lean figure in two, curling her inked-up arms around the backs of her knees while, all around her, the snowy desert whistled and blustered.

Unbending and standing straight again, Anna rubbed at her biceps, massaging her muscles back to life. Temperature last night must have dropped more than she thought—she'd woken up a lot stiffer than usual. Bedding down in your car wasn't exactly the most ergonomic way to sleep, but after so many nights, she'd mostly gotten used to it. Finding a quiet place to park for the evening was better than spending money she didn't have on hotel rooms anyway. Most highway cops were pretty understanding about that sort of thing, and the ones that weren't got dealt with. They were just men, after all. She answered to a far higher power than them.

Anna'd been rolling along the Great Basin Highway for a couple hours before she pulled over to stop for the night, heading south on Highway 93 after she'd finally finished up in Twin Falls. The job had been simple enough—couple of days at the house of a nice couple who were terrified both *for* and *of* their teenage son. Anna had thought the whole thing was probably BS until she saw the kid levitate a foot and a half off his bed and spin around like he'd been rotisserie'd. Whatever it was that had been hiding inside of him, it had perked right up after she got in close, splitting the boy's head wide open like an oleander made of blood and teeth. Like the floating, it was a neat trick, but Anna had seen better.

The thing had feigned grandeur at first, claiming some noble lineage, as if that would somehow impress her. *I am the Devil and I come to do the Devil's work.* Same boring line as always, just another imp pretending at the throne. But that was okay. Anna knew how to deal with imps and every other jabbering thing that had clawed its way out of perdition. The boy's parents had cried like children when she explained what had to happen, but they came to accept it, eventually. People like them always did. Better for their child to earn salvation with an instant of pain rather than an eternity of suffering. A quick stroke of the razor and a splash of blood and it was done—the boy and his possessor, sheared apart once again.

Another fiend bound to the Chain. Another lamb from God's flock, delivered into His loving hands.

Amen.

She went around to the back of the car and popped the trunk open, then started rummaging through her things, her duffel bag of clothes and essentials, the toolbox. From the duffel, she drew her toothbrush and a half-rolled tube of toothpaste, her deodorant, and a gallon jug of distilled water, half-frozen from the night. Splashing water on the bristles, she squeezed out a dab of Colgate and started scrubbing at her teeth.

Overhead, she could still see stars twinkling in the sky, distant and chilly. They were always so beautiful this time of morning.

Spitting foam onto the snow, she realized with no small amount of surprise that her skin was still humming, the Chain still spinning, still pulling. Like a compass at the base of her skull, twirling round and round to settle on its own True North. The things trapped inside the Chain, they weren't smart, but they had a certain gravity to them, drawn inexorably to their own kind. It was a handy advantage when she had to use it. Made it a lot easier to track down the strays, at least.

She scanned the horizon, the hills, the line of the empty highway spooling out into the distance. There wasn't anyone else around for miles, she was certain of that. There was no reason for the Chain to be yanking this hard right now. Focusing on the sensation, she turned in place, tracing the pressure, trying to get a sense of what it was pulling her toward. Whatever it was, it was right on top of her... or it was very, very big.

Most of the time, when something pinged that internal radar, it was a tiny little blip, a momentary flicker on a dark screen, but this? This was like strapping her face to a floodlight, and it was only getting brighter.

What the hell was going on here?

Anna closed her eyes and let the Chain pull a little harder, trying to get her bearings. South. Whatever it was, it was south of here. Taking a slug off the gallon jug, she rinsed and spat again, then wiped her lips with the back of her hand. She rolled a quick swipe of deodorant under each armpit, then put everything back where she'd found it, clapped the trunk shut, and went to the driver's-side door, bending down to climb in. Curling one tattooed hand around the wheel, she turned the key in the ignition, urging the old Chevy to life. She didn't know where the Chain was taking her this time, but that wasn't a problem; she'd let it pull until they got there. Just like always.

Over the hills, she could see the light of the sun starting to climb the horizon. She turned her attention inward once more, feeling the Chain and all those screaming atrocities trapped inside it buck and thrash against their bonds, desperate to get out, to escape, to be free.

Not today, not tomorrow. Sorry, boys.

Taking one last look at the rusty old wreck caught in her headlights, she dropped the car into reverse, then drive, and pulled back onto Great Basin, heading south.

Jonah
Mowry, NV
872 miles to Albuquerque

The shower was running.

That was the first thing that Jonah noticed as he slowly surfaced, like a submarine rising from the ocean floor. The shower was running. He opened his eyes. Light, huge and unforgiving, spilled in from the window on the far side of the hotel room as feeling inched back into his body, bit by painful bit. Christ, he was sore.

Rolling over beneath the blankets, he turned his head to listen to the sound pouring through the bathroom door—the soft, unmistakable hiss of water against tile. Yeah, that was definitely the shower.

Wait, the shower?

The details of the day before hit him in a rush, and an instant later Jonah was moving, thrashing out from under the covers, nearly throwing himself out of bed as terror thundered in his heart. What the fuck was happening? Who the fuck was in their bathroom? The water shut off abruptly, and a moment later the door swung open to reveal Nell in a fresh change of clothes, a towel turbaned tightly around her head.

"Morning," she said, giving him a questioning look. "What's going on? You okay?"

Jonah looked from his sister to the steam spilling out of the bathroom, a memory flashing across the surface of his mind— *black smoke rising from Nell's lips*—before vanishing again, lost to the cold mist of his sleep-addled brain. Standing there, barefoot in the middle of the hotel room, his vision swam and he felt himself swaying as Nell snapped her fingers in his face.

"Jonah, hey." Nell waved a hand at him. "Hey, earth to Jonah, come in, Jonah."

Jonah blinked and fell back into his body in a single, awful *shove.* He watched his sister carefully, a weird chill laddering up his back as she pulled the towel off her head. Nell took a step toward him; instinctively, Jonah took a step back, not knowing exactly why.

"Okay, for real, what's going on with you? Are you okay? You're freaking me out a little," Nell said.

Stumbling back to sit down on the edge of his bed, Jonah stared at his bare feet against the ruddy hotel carpet and rubbed at his unshaven cheeks, suddenly feeling both trapped and very, very exposed. This wasn't right. None of this was right.

"You..." he started, looking up at Nell again, searching for words that wouldn't come. "Are you all right?"

"Yeah, fine," Nell said, pulling the towel off her head and tossing it onto the mattress as she sat down across from him. "Why wouldn't I be?"

When Jonah looked up at her, he saw a dead, flat light flicker across her eyes, there and gone again.

"Uh," he said.

"Uh? What does *uh* mean?"

"Are you—are you sure you're feeling okay?"

A smile split Nell's face. "Jonah, I'm fine," she said. "Honestly. Slept great. I don't know what you're so worried about."

Jonah gawked at his sister, aghast. Was she being serious? After everything that had happened yesterday, after the bar fight and the bikers, the desert and the hole and whatever had happened to her underneath the ground, she was suddenly just fine? No. No, bullshit. He wasn't buying it. More than anything, the fact that she seemed okay right now was proof positive that things were absolutely not okay. His mind spun like tires trapped in mud, unable to find traction. He wanted to ask her what was going on, to understand, to get some kind of explanation, but then that empty light flashed in her eyes again, turning the words in his mouth to ash.

"...Yeah. Sorry. Bad dreams, I guess," he said, his voice subdued.

"You'll get over them." Nell patted him on the knee, then stood. "You hungry?"

Jonah's stomach growled at the thought of food, but he still couldn't manage to escape the dreadful orbit of everything that had gone wrong in the last twenty-four hours, least of them not being 48 Coffin. After the worksite and the hole in the desert, he'd managed to put his anxieties about the bikers aside, even forget about them for a little while, but the time for that was over now. If 48 Coffin was coming after them, they'd had plenty of time to catch up in the night. Shit, shit, shit.

"Honestly, I think we should probably just get back on the road," he said. "We still have a long way to go."

"Well, I'm starving, so I'm making an executive decision here. Breakfast first," Nell said. "So how about you put some clothes on, we'll pack up and go get some food before we hit it, yeah? Gotta be a diner somewhere around here. I think a small mountain of bacon and flapjacks is just what you need to banish those bad dreams for good. Coffee, too. Lots of coffee."

"Sure," Jonah said, deflating. He wasn't going to win this argument. "Sure, yeah, sounds great."

He dressed as quickly as he could while Nell gathered up all their things, repacking their suitcases and double-checking the room to make sure they weren't leaving anything behind. The hotel was unsilent around them; Jonah could hear the floors and walls creaking and groaning, the water in the pipes behind the walls, the whoosh of air in the ducts. God, he was still so tired. He felt like he hadn't slept at all. Vision still bleary, joints stiff and sore, he felt trapped in the borderlands between dreaming and waking, slogging through knee-deep waves that he couldn't seem to get free of.

Shuffling toward the door, he checked his watch: it was still early, not even 8 a.m. yet. Jesus. How was that possible? When had they gotten in last night? Everything had been blurring together since he'd come to yesterday in the desert. Sleep hadn't helped; it had only further smudged the ink around the margins. Reality no longer seemed concrete to Jonah; it had gone all soft and runny, as if it would come apart in his hands if he tried to hold on to it too tight.

He followed his sister out into the hallway and, standing aside to let Nell pull the door shut, saw a flicker of movement out of the corner of his eye, there and then not. He turned to look, but only saw their shadows on the wall, their edges rendered razor-sharp by the bright sunlight flooding in through the balcony doorway at the end of the hall. At first it seemed normal, but then, feeling his head lurch again, Jonah watched as Nell's shadow started to move on its own, turning to watch him from where it was cast, pressed against the gaudy old wallpaper.

"Nell, no . . ." he whimpered breathlessly.

Long and twisted, the shadow grew and stretched, consuming Jonah's own as it reached an arm out to touch him, grasp him, pull him into its terrible entirety. Jonah wanted to scream, wanted to run, but found himself unable to move, unable to breathe, unable to blink. Heart stopped in his chest, lungs frozen solid, he was at the shadow's mercy. Spreading to fill the wall, the shadow shivered in place, then started to warp and change, sprouting twisted branches from the top of its head like snarled, malformed antlers, coiling around themselves like snakes or tree roots—

"Jonah."

He jumped at the sound of his sister's voice, and when he looked again, her shadow had recoiled, squeezed back into the shape of his sister. As if nothing had happened at all.

"What?"

Nell looked over at him, her expression chilly and vacant.

"Did you see something?" she asked.

Jonah felt that terrible cold wash through him again. "Sorry, what?"

Nell cleared her throat. "Did you say something, I said."

Jonah shook his head, trying to clear the cobwebs. Against the wall, Nell's shadow was just a shadow again, perfectly unremarkable. Looking away from her, he nodded, afraid to see that flat, empty light in her gaze once more.

"No, no, I don't think so," he said.

"You sure? I could have sworn I heard you say something."

He shook his head again, still not looking over. "Wasn't me."

"Oh-*kay*," she said, though the way she said it made it sound more like she was saying "bullshit."

"What about you?" Jonah asked. "You sure you're doing all right?"

"For the seventy-third time this morning, yes, I'm fine," Nell said, heading down the hallway toward the elevators. "Now come on. I need breakfast."

Jonah didn't say anything else. He just followed her down to the lobby, keeping his eyes on her shadow the whole way.

Nell
Mowry, NV
872 miles to Albuquerque

After checking out at the front desk, Nell and Jonah wound their way through the casino floor to the back doors and the parking lot beyond. The morning outside was bright and blanketed in snow, a freezing wind blowing in across Mowry from the ghostly hills off past the far side of town. Zipping her leather jacket up to the hollow of her throat, Nell led her brother across the icy lot to where her station wagon sat waiting for them, piled over in powdery white. But as they approached, she could see that something was off. The car was off balance, sitting at a bad angle, way too low to the ground— *What the fuck?*

Quickening her pace, Nell weaved in between the parked cars, closing the distance, trying to get a better view; when she saw, she felt a nail of rage press deep into her brain.

"Oh, what the *fuck already*," she said, her voice trembling with fury.

At some point in the night, somebody had taken a blade to three of the tires, leaving them hanging in black rags around the hubcaps, less *slashed* and more *vivisected*, their innards dusted with snow. Catching up, Jonah wordlessly went to the other side of the car and knelt down, dropping out of sight.

"Christ," he said. "They really did a number on them, Nell."

"Fucking *god*," she barked, her anger growing like a bonfire. "Is there anything else over there? Any sign of who did this shit?"

Standing back up, Jonah gave her a wary look. "Yeah," he said. "I think so. Here."

He laid a fist atop the Volvo and cast it toward her, sliding something dark and angular across the roof of the car. Nell

105

caught it in one hand and held it up to examine it in the morning light: a long, wicked-looking folding knife with a coffined 48 mitered into the handle. She knew this knife. Holy shit, she knew this knife. She'd swiped it off that big douchebag back in Broughton, used it to slash the tires open on that motorcycle before she kicked it over.

"This was them?" she asked. "Those fucking biker assholes?"

Jonah's shoulders fell as he nodded at her. "It was stuck in the tire over here. Or what's left of it."

"Fucking fuck me," Nell shouted as anxiety ripped through her body. "Is there anything else? Any sign of them?"

"You mean did they leave a business card or something? Sign their work? I think they already did that."

Nell jabbed a finger at his face. "Okay, don't be an asshole right now. You know what I mean."

Jonah shook his head. "No, nothing," he said. "Some footprints in the snow, pretty much filled in already. Nothing useful. Looks like they came off the street, maybe, but it must have been hours ago."

"Goddammit. God fucking *dammit*," Nell said, slamming her empty hand on the Volvo's roof. "So what do we do?"

Jonah looked vexed. "I don't know," he said. "Nothing? Nothing right now, at least. Those psychos obviously know we're here, so if they were going to make their move, they probably would have already. Since they haven't . . . I'm not sure."

"Bullshit you're not sure, there's something," Nell said. "We can do something."

"I mean, get the tires fixed, probably. I can go inside and talk to the clerk," Jonah said, sighing. "I'm sure there's a garage in town, someplace that can get us a new set."

"Yeah? Tell me, who has money for that kind of shit, Jonah?"

"Well, it's not like we have a choice, unless you feel like spending the rest of your life in beautiful Mowry, Nevada. You can sling drinks at one of the casinos, maybe I can learn to deal cards or meth."

She shot him a severe look. "What did I say about not being shitty?"

Backing off, Jonah held a hand up. "Look, how about I split it with you, okay? It's no big deal. We just need to get the car fixed and get the fuck out of Dodge as soon as possible."

Nell paused. "You sure?"

"Yeah," he said, fidgeting in place. "It's fine. I'm going to go talk to the clerk, okay? We'll figure out everything else after that. It's not like we're going anywhere, so, yeah. Breakfast, I guess."

Nell glared at the ruined tires one last time, then dropped the knife into her coat pocket and pulled out her keys. "You go ahead," she said. "I'll be here with the bags. Probably need a couple of minutes to cool off, either way."

She unlocked the car and pulled open the driver's-side door, poking her head inside, looking for her cigarettes. Nobody should have had to deal with this kind of shit without nicotine. She stuck a crumpled Camel between her lips and lit it with the Bic from her jacket. Her brother's face appeared outside the passenger window a second later as he stooped down to look at her through the glass.

"You see anything, any sign of them, you come running, okay?"

She gave him a mocking little salute with two fingers to her forehead, sneering around her smoke.

"Aye-aye, cap'n."

Jonah stayed there for another minute, watching her with that same weird look he'd been wearing all morning. Sitting in the driver's seat with one foot on the snowy ground, Nell smoked and watched him cross back over the icy parking lot, back to the Silver Dollar, his shoulders hunched high. She took another drag, feeling the smoke sparkle her lungs as an unfamiliar voice snaked through her head.

There's something he's not telling you.

Twenty minutes later, they were sitting in Mowry's only diner, tucked away in a booth situated in the far corner of the dining room. They'd only had to wait a few minutes

before the tow truck pulled into the parking lot to wheel the
Volvo away. After that, they stashed their bags at the hotel's
front desk and made the short, cold walk to the diner at the
far end of Main Street, shoulders set against the wind as it
pushed them along, trapping them in the swirls and gusts
of snow that it kicked up from the sidewalk. The light outside was brilliant, almost blinding; even sitting here, now,
sheltered by the diner's big tinted window, the morning was
painfully bright, the sun glaring off the snow and stabbing at
Nell's eyes through her aviators. Irritated, she pulled them off
her face and tossed them on the table between them. Fucking
useless.

The diner was a busy place this morning, filled with folks
wolfing down plates of eggs and pancakes, chasing their break-
fasts with huge, steaming mugs of coffee. Dear god, coffee. She
felt her soul stir at the smell.

Nell stared out the window at the little gambling town
until the waitress, a pimple-faced twenty-something sporting a
nametag that read KATEY, walked over and handed them each
an oversized menu. Nell studied the girl's face, her practiced
smile and the dark circles under her eyes, and wondered how
long she'd been on shift.

"Can I get you two anything to drink while you decide on
breakfast?" Katey asked.

"I will have the largest coffee you're legally allowed to sell
me," Nell said. Looking over at her brother, she raised two fingers at the girl. "Actually, better make it two."

The girl laughed, the ice around her eyes sloughing off a
little bit. "I think I can make that happen for you, sure. Cream
and sugar?"

"Black's fine for me," Nell said. "Jone?"

"Cream and sugar would be great," Jonah said glumly.
"Thanks."

Without another word, the girl stashed her pen and pad
in her apron and whisked away, weaving through patrons and
tables to the big old coffee machine behind the counter, probably a fixture of the diner since the 1960s. Katey was cute, in a
plain-ish, townie sort of way. Probably grew up around here,

dreaming of the day she could get the hell out for good, leave the whole place in flames and move to New York or LA to be an actress or something. Nell couldn't blame her. She'd only been in town for a couple of hours and already knew that the place sucked.

Leaning in across the table, Nell looked at her brother and, keeping her voice down, asked, "Okay, for real though, what are we going to do about these fucking biker assholes?"

Jonah breathed out slowly and rolled his fingers against the tabletop.

"I honestly have no idea," he said. "They obviously know where we are, and since they left the knife, they wanted us to know it. But they haven't made their move yet, didn't kick the door down last night and kill us in our sleep, so . . . I don't know. Maybe they're waiting for something. The right opportunity, maybe."

"So, what's the plan? Because sitting here and waiting for the axe to fall isn't exactly my idea of fun, Jone."

"Waiting for the axe to fall is pretty much the only thing we've got right now. Sorry. When the car's fixed, we'll get the fuck out of here as fast as we can, but until that point, let's just have some food and try to stay calm. We're not going to fix anything by worrying ourselves to pieces."

Nell sighed. "I hate this plan."

"Yeah, well, let me know when you come up with a better one."

When she looked up again, Jonah was watching her over the top of his menu with that same weird look he'd been wearing all morning. Like she'd suddenly turned purple or sprouted a second head out of the side of her neck or something.

"Okay, seriously, what?"

Jonah shook his head. "Nothing. I don't know. It's nothing, forget it."

"No, it's obviously not nothing. If it was nothing, you wouldn't be looking at me like that. You'd be deciding what kind of skillet scramble you want. So come on, stop acting like a fucking freakazoid and just tell me what's up already."

Jonah looked away as Katey returned with their coffees

and a small basket of single-serving creams and sugars. Saying thanks, Nell told her they'd flag her down when they'd made up their minds about food. Once the girl was out of earshot again, Jonah doctored his coffee, then plunged his weathered spoon into his mug and started to stir.

"What do you remember about yesterday?" he asked unsteadily.

Nell took a sip of her own coffee. It was hot and bitter and caffeinated. It was perfect.

"I don't know," she said. "It was a day. Stuff happened."

"Right, but what stuff? Like, specifically, what do you remember?"

Nell rolled her eyes at him. "You're being real weird, man. It's not a good look."

Jonah held a hand out, placating her. "Look, you asked, so just, humor me here. Please."

Nell shook her head. "Okay, fine. Yesterday. I checked out of my motel in San Fran, I picked you up, we said goodbye to Molly, and then we drove out to Broughton," she said, counting off on her fingers. "I remember the argument we had at the bar. The fight, obviously, then getting into shit again when we stopped for gas. After that, you went to sleep all pissy—don't make that face at me, you know you did—and then...and then..."

Nell searched her memory, retracing her steps from the day before. Everything was so clear for the first half of the day, but after the argument at the gas station...after that...

There was nothing.

Her memory after that point was completely blank, the second half of the day scudded over by a gray, indifferent brume. It was as if she'd been speeding along a beautiful, winding highway, only to find that the blacktop suddenly ended, spitting her off the side of a cliff. She didn't know where the road had gone—all she knew was that she was falling without anything to hold on to.

"...I don't remember."

Jonah kept stirring his coffee, his expression serious and steady. "Nothing?"

"No," Nell said coldly. "Nothing."

"And that doesn't freak you out at all?"

"Yes, it freaks me out," Nell hissed. "Of course it freaks me out. There's a whole chunk of my memory that's apparently just gone, Jonah. Like, *gone*. What the fuck?!"

"I don't know, Nellie," he said, worry furrowing his brow. "I'm not sure, exactly."

"But you know something. You wouldn't have brought it up otherwise," Nell said, trying to keep her anxiety in check. Across the table, Jonah drew the spoon from his coffee and set it aside, then curled both hands around his cup, letting his gaze drift down to the battered formica tabletop.

"Something happened yesterday," he said.

Nell balked. "Something like what?"

Jonah breathed out in a thin stream. "After that argument at the gas station, I was pretty pissed still, so I closed my eyes, decided to try and sleep it off."

"I remember," Nell said.

"Yeah, well, when I woke up, it was, like, hours later, and we were in the desert, like parked in the desert. Not some side road or something, I mean, like, the middle of the desert. Totally off the highway. I guess you must have driven us out there, but you weren't around for me to ask. Time I woke up, you were gone. Like, gone. Left the keys in the ignition and wandered off into the sand."

"Fuck off."

"I'm being serious, Nell." Sitting there, he recounted the afternoon before to her, speaking very slowly, as if each word were a razor blade inside his mouth. It didn't make sense to her, and it sure wasn't familiar: Footprints in the desert. A worksite. A cave. An ancient body underground, and a long walk back to the car with her slung over his shoulders. The images were vivid and strange, some of them outright terrifying. Yet she remembered none of it.

"Holy shit," she said when he finished.

"Any of that sound familiar?" Jonah asked.

She shook her head. "No, nothing."

"Yeah, I didn't think so."

Nell screwed her eyes up tight, squeezing her lids shut until she saw stars. "Look, what if we went back there? To the worksite, I mean?"

Jonah's face drained.

"No," he said. "No, Nell. No. Hell no. I don't...I can't. I'm sorry, but no. Veto. Why would you want to go back there?"

"To see," Nell said, her voice wire-tight. "Maybe there's something there that was left behind or something. Maybe I'm not the first person this happened to. I don't, I don't know."

Jonah shook his head. "There's nothing there, Nell. No one. It's a fucking ghost town. It's dead."

"Yeah, well, maybe somebody from this Burkholder Construction left something behind that'll tell us what they were doing out there."

"They were digging, Nell."

"But digging for what, exactly?"

"I don't know. I don't care," Jonah said. "I'm telling you, it's not a good idea." His voice was lethally serious.

"Why? Because you're scared?"

"Yeah, I'm scared," he exclaimed, a little too loud. All around them, heads turned. Blushing, Jonah leaned in, lowering his voice. "No shit I'm scared, Nell," he said. "You weren't there; you didn't see what I saw. You didn't feel the air in that place. It was wrong. There was something sick about it, like the whole atmosphere had been poisoned or something."

"Except I *was* there," Nell reminded him. "Wasn't I?"

"Yeah, you were," he said, his tone resigned. "And whatever it was that led you out there, you blacked it all out. You were gone until this morning. That's not normal. Look, I don't know what the hell happened to you; I don't have any explanations. I'm just telling you what I saw, what I felt, and whatever it was, I'd rather turn around and head up to the hotel room to open a couple of veins in the bathtub than go back, all right? I'm pretty sure that if you remembered any of it, you'd want to get as far away from it as you could too."

"So what, we go hop in the Volvo and keep going? On the road again, back to Albuquerque? Act like nothing happened?"

"I don't want to act like nothing happened," Jonah said.

"It's just that I don't think either of us knows for sure *what* happened."

"Did you even look up this Burkholder Construction? See what else they're into? Anything like that?"

Jonah shook his head. "I was more concerned with getting you back to the car and making sure you were safe. Honestly, before I saw you step out of the bathroom this morning all bright-eyed and bushy-tailed, I was planning on getting you to an ER. The night clerk at the Silver Dollar said there's a hospital up in West Wendover. I think we can make it in a couple of hours, maybe a little less if we push it."

"I. Feel. Fine," Nell said, punching each word into his stupid fucking face. "How many times do I have to tell you that?"

Jonah threw up his hands.

"Fine, Nell. Fine. You're a big girl, you can make your choices. But if you don't want to see a doctor, then yeah, I think the best thing we can do right now is get back on the road and get home as fast as possible. When shit goes wrong again, I'd rather not deal with it out in the middle of nowhere. I've done that enough for one week, alright? Fucksake."

Nell hung her head and breathed out slowly, trying to get her mind around all of it.

"Look, I'm sorry," she said. "I know you're trying to help. I don't know, man. This is some heavy shit to drop on someone over breakfast. Kind of wish you hadn't."

"Not like you gave me much of a choice," he said, checking his phone. "Look, I'm going to go call the garage, see where we're at, okay? Maybe they've got the tires on already. It'd be really nice if we could get the fuck out of here."

"Yeah, make it two votes for *getting the fuck out of here*," Nell said, swirling the dregs around the bottom of her coffee cup. "Let me know what they say."

"You going to be all right here?"

"I'll be fine. You go ahead," Nell said, raising her cup. "I'm not going anywhere. Not going to go wandering off into the hills again."

Jonah stood up from the table, his expression pinched with worry.

"You know you look like Dad when you make that face,"
Nell told him. Her voice was laced with acid. "Go ahead. I'll get
the check and meet you outside. I need a smoke or something."
Just go already, please.

Then he was gone. When she looked up again, there was
someone who wasn't Jonah sitting across the table from her.

She had dark, frizzy hair tied back in a severe ponytail and
muscled arms covered in tangles of dark tattoos that reached all
the way down to her fingertips. In her lap lay a long gray coat,
and around her neck hung a plain gold cross suspended on a
simple thread-thin chain. She was pretty, and built like a brick
shithouse, but there was something nervous and calculating in
her eyes that Nell didn't like the look of.

"Hi, there," the woman said. "You've got royalty in you,
haven't you?"

Jonah
Mowry, NV
872 miles to Albuquerque

H i, yeah, this is Jonah Talbot. I'm calling to check on the Volvo that got brought in about an hour ago? Needed new tires."

"Yeah, I know the one you're talking about," the guy on the other end of the line said, not sounding particularly happy about it, though Jonah didn't know why. It wasn't as if he was the one who'd spent five minutes on hold, waiting to have this conversation. "You can head on over to pick it up, should be ready by the time you get here."

"Great, see you soon," Jonah said, and killed the call without waiting for a response.

Standing in the little hallway between the dining room and the restrooms, Jonah clicked his phone off, pocketed it, then held his hands out in front of him, examining the scabbed-over cuts in his knuckles. It had been years since he'd hit anyone. For the longest time, he'd honestly thought that he'd moved past it, all those shitty things he used to be. He'd put so much time and energy into locking it away . . . and all it took was one terrible decision from Nell to let the monster out of the cage.

He wanted to blame her for everything that had happened, as if she had some unique talent for summoning up the very worst in him; but he couldn't, because that wasn't the truth. It was him that had let go. It was him that had kicked the cage door off its hinges. Back in Broughton, Jonah could have turned tail and run, he could have stood there and taken the beating, he could have done anything other than what he did. But the truth was, Nell was right: it had felt good to let loose on those assholes. Shit, it felt *great*. For a second, he was that guy again, young and perfect and bulletproof, the guy he'd been back when none of it mattered. Back before he ran away and got married

115

and did everything he could to forget himself, the real him, the one that grew up so goddamned angry after his mom died sick and young, the one that hit like a fucking howitzer and tore into assholes like a rottweiler at the first sign of trouble. The one that was always more than happy to ignore the fact that his actions had consequences.

See something you like, fuckface?

He shoved the dead face back to the farthest corner of his mind, willing away the dread that was corkscrewing inside his belly. He had to get back to Nell. They needed to get out of Mowry.

Nell
Mowry, NV
872 miles to Albuquerque

E xcuse me?"
　　All around her, the diner had gone quiet. It had been bustling when she and Jonah had walked in here; now it was a ghost town. Where had everyone gone?

"Gosh, I'm sorry about that," the woman across the table said. "That was rude of me. I'm Anna Dechant." She extended one inked-up hand over the tabletop to shake. Nell didn't take it.

"Is that supposed to mean something to me? Do I know you?"

Across the table, the woman shook her head and smiled wide, showing off a mouthful of perfect white teeth. Nell felt an abrupt rush of fever, a swell of nausea, as if she might throw up or pass out or both. What the fuck was going on?

"No, you don't know me," Anna said. "At least, not yet. Sorry, I didn't catch your name."

Swallowing back her sudden sickness, Nell studied her. Tattoos covered the majority of her skin, all baroque designs and phrases in Latin and Greek and a handful of other languages Nell didn't speak or even recognize.

"It's Nell. Talbot," she said reluctantly.

"Huh. Never met a Nell before, or a Talbot, for that matter," Anna replied.

"Well, now you've met both," Nell said. "Lucky you."

The woman's smile grew. "You have no idea."

Nell didn't like the way she was looking at her. There was something strange about the glimmer in her eyes, something stony and remote. As if she were observing Nell under glass, a sample in a jar to be poked and prodded and examined. She played nice, but there was something off there, something Nell

117

couldn't put a name to just yet. It wasn't just the sudden sickness she'd felt a second ago, but that sure wasn't helping Anna's
case any.

"Is there something I can help you with, or is this, like, a
thing for you? Showing up at people's tables uninvited, I mean,"
Nell asked.

"No, not at all," Anna said. "I am sorry to disturb you like
this, it's just, you might not know it, but you're very special,
Nell. Far more special than you even know."

Nell ground her teeth. She was so not in the mood for this
weirdo shit.

"Okay, great. Glad we talked about this," she said, eager
to escape the conversation. She waved her hand at the table
between them. "Thanks for . . . whatever you think is happening
here. I'm going to go." She moved to stand up from the table.

"Saw that someone slashed your tires," Anna said.

Nell froze in place and looked at her.

"What did you just say?"

Anna jerked her head toward the window. "Back at the
hotel," she said.

Confusion and anger clattered behind Nell's eyes.

"What the shit, have you been watching us or something?"
she demanded, trying to stare bullet holes in the woman's face.

"Only for a little while," Anna said sheepishly. "Just since
this morning. If that helps any."

"No, it doesn't help any," Nell said, her voice drawn wire-
tight. "What the fuck are you watching us for?"

"Because I know what's happening to you," Anna said.

Nell shook her head.

"Right, sure. I don't know what you're talking about."

"You're missing some of your memory," Anna said. "Probably a pretty big chunk too. It's just gone, like someone went in
and scooped it clean out of your head. Right?"

Nell's belly ran cold when she said it. Everything that
Jonah had recounted about the day before raced through her
mind again, every insane little detail that she couldn't make
sense of, followed inexorably by the dead-channel static of
where the rest of her memories should have been. Across the

table, the woman was still smiling, the expression practiced and perfect underneath her basket-case gaze. Nell had known people who smiled like that before. Mostly it had been dealers, but there had been others too, people who wore sweetness like a costume, cloaking themselves in it to draw you in close enough to strike. People who smiled like that were always trouble.

"What the hell do you know about that?" Nell demanded, despite herself.

"Probably a lot more than you," Anna said. "That's why I wanted to talk."

Nell sighed. Hung her head. Curled her hands around her still-warm coffee cup.

"Fine," she said. "Talk."

"Tell me when you started losing your memories," Anna said.

"Yesterday," Nell said. "Yesterday afternoon. There's a whole stretch that should be there and just...isn't. It's like things were normal and fine, and then it's this wave of static. But the thing is, I woke up this morning feeling great. Wouldn't have even noticed that anything was missing until my brother pointed it out."

"No," the woman said. "You wouldn't have."

"Why not?"

"Because it doesn't want you to remember."

"*It?*"

"It," Anna said, nodding. "Look, I am sorry to be the one to tell you this, but you're not the only one inside your head anymore, Miss Talbot."

Pressing her back deep into the red vinyl booth seat, clutching her coffee cup so tightly she thought it might burst in her hands, Nell stared at her. She studied the sharp blade of the woman's jaw, the stillness of her hands, the lines of her tattoos.

What...?

"Tell me, Nell, do you believe in God?"

The question hit her like a bucket of ice water, snatching her from the half-trance she'd fallen into. Was this woman serious?

"I believe that people who ask that question out of

nowhere are generally fucking crazy," Nell said after a second. "Does that answer your question?"

Anna looked unsurprised, even amused. "Nell, you need to listen to me—"

"No, I think I'm done talking to you," Nell interrupted. "Whatever you're on about, whatever you're selling, I don't want any. Not now, not ever. So why don't you do us both a favor and fuck off, okay?"

With a little sigh, Anna produced a blue ballpoint from her pocket and slid a paper napkin from the top of the stack at the end of the table. Uncapping the pen, she scribbled something on the napkin and, folding it in half, slid it over to Nell. Nell didn't pick it up.

"That's a lifeline," Anna said. "If you're smart, you'll take it." She slid out of the booth, brushing herself off as she stood, looking down at Nell with an expression that was dangerously close to pity. "This is going to keep getting worse. The lost memories are just the beginning. I'm sorry. But I can help, if you want me to. I'm probably the only person who can. Just think about it, okay? Before it goes too far and things start happening that you can't take back."

Nell gave her the hardest death glare she could muster.

"Get the fuck away from me," she said, bringing her luke-warm coffee to her lips.

"It's your choice," Anna said. "As long as you're sure it's the right one."

Then she turned and walked out. Nell held her breath until she was all the way gone, then counted to a hundred before standing up from the table herself, tossing a ten-dollar bill down next to her empty mug. The folded napkin was still on the table where Anna had left it. Nell swept it off the table and opened it up. Inside, there was a phone number scribbled underneath a quick note: *Anna. Call me when you need help.*

Chewing on the inside of her cheek, Nell stuffed the napkin into her pocket and beelined for the door.

Outside, the wind pulled doggedly at Nell's clothes as she lit one of the loose cigarettes from her coat pocket, blowing a gray plume at the morning sun. Up and down Main Street, posters advertised the different casinos, enticing patrons with free drinks, free buffet, free show, free hotel rooms, free everything, free anything.

Breathing smoke, Nell looked around for any sign of Anna, thankfully finding none. Across the street, a stray dog trotted down the sidewalk, out for a morning jaunt. Nell imagined this was probably a good town for strays. Lots of friendly strangers to give you food, lots of warm places to sleep. But as Nell watched, the dog slowed, then stopped, and turned in place to watch her back. A second later, it took off like a shot down the nearest alley, weaving around a drab-black Econoline to disappear into the morning.

Fucking weird.

Everything today was so fucking weird.

Rolling the burning cigarette back and forth between her fingertips, Nell scratched at her scalp and replayed her conversation with Anna, going through it again and again, trying to make it make sense.

This is going to keep getting worse.

You've got royalty in you.

It doesn't want you to remember.

It would have been easy to dismiss the woman as crazy, but the thing was, Nell had dealt with crazy enough in her life to recognize it when she saw it. Despite everything she'd said, Anna wasn't crazy; or if she was, then she wasn't a liar. Whatever she was selling, it wasn't a delusion or some line she was trying to feed Nell. She believed it with her whole goddamned heart. Which was almost worse than crazy, now that Nell thought about it.

She ashed her cigarette onto the ground as another chilly breeze danced across the parking lot to shear through her jacket. Turning away from the wind, she pursed the Camel in her lips and cupped her hands, red and bone-raw from the cold, around its cherry, taking another slow, deep puff to keep it glowing until the bluster died down again. When it did, she pulled her

cell out and thumbed through her contacts, scrolling down to
the D's. She tapped the name she'd been looking for, then *Call*,
holding the phone to her ear while it rang once, twice—

Click. "Hello?"

"Dad, hey, it's me," Nell said.

"Well, hey yourself, Nellie Leigh," her dad said on the
other end of the line, his voice light and happy. "How's the road
trip going? How's your brother?"

"Yeah, I don't know, it's okay, I guess."

"Just okay?" Dad's voice took a down note. "Something
wrong?"

"I don't know," Nell said. "Things are a little weird, Dad.
It's kind of hard to explain."

"Is it stuff with Jonah? He doing all right?"

"I mean, it's hard to tell," Nell said honestly. "You know
how he is."

"Yeah, I know," Dad replied. "He plays his cards close to
the chest, but try and be patient with him, Nellie. Being on your
own after spending so long with somebody, I mean, something
like that takes time to get used to." Nell knew right away that
Dad wasn't really talking about Jonah and Molly. He was
talking about himself and Mom.

"I know, Dad. I'm trying."

"You get a chance to see Moll before you two hit the road?"

"Yeah," Nell said. "For a minute or two, just enough to
say bye."

"Mmm," the old man said thoughtfully. "Sure. She holding up okay?"

"I mean, I guess so. It was weird, being there. Weird and
sad."

"Fits," said Dad. "It really is a shame about them. I always
liked her."

"Yeah, me too."

On the other end of the line, Dad cleared his throat. "Did
you have a chance to talk to him about, you know, what happened to you?"

Nell ground her teeth, trying to think of an artful way to
dodge the question as another cold gust rocked her in place, slic-

ing through her whole body. She turned away from the wind, hunching her shoulders against it, trying to protect her cigarette. She didn't have that many left, and knew she was going to have to get more probably sooner rather than later. Did she still have cash for that, or was the ten she'd left inside the last of it? There was probably an ATM close by, but she didn't really feel like going hunting for it. She fished her wallet out of her pocket and fluttered the folds with the pad of her thumb. There was still a little cash left, but—wait.

Wait.

Her driver's license was gone.

Why the hell was her driver's license gone?

Then she remembered, and her chest went numb.

She'd left it back in Broughton. Put it down as collateral for the bar tab.

Which meant those biker assholes had it now.

Shit. *Shit.*

The wind died down again, and as it did, Nell heard a rough growling behind her. Slowly, she turned and froze in place. The stray was back, standing only a few feet away from her now, dark eyes wide and wild with rancor. As she watched it, it curled its lips back, baring every yellow tooth in its head as its growl grew louder.

Abruptly, Nell said, "Dad, I uh, I gotta go."

"Oh. Okay. No problem. Drive safe, now. Tell Jonah I'm excited to see him. I love you, bug. I'll see you soon."

"Yeah, love you too," she said, blindly killing the call and dropping her phone in her pocket, keeping her eyes on the dog. Legs planted wide, its shoulders were hunched up high, the fur on its back standing straight as cornstalks. Cautiously, Nell took a step backward, careful not to move too fast, not wanting to piss it off any more than it already was. The dog growled louder and started to advance on her.

"Hey, pooch," Nell said, pinching her cigarette between her knuckles. "Hey, it's okay, buddy. It's okay. I'm a friend, all right? No need to start anything here..."

With her empty hand, she reached out to try and calm the dog, eliciting a sharp bark as it gnashed its teeth at her, warning her away. Stupid. Was she trying to lose fingers? She knew better than that.

The dog drew closer, keeping low to the ground, its teeth like glistening saws underneath serrated black lips. It snapped its jaws at her again, and she felt an alien fury stir in her chest, something cold and cruel that told her to attack, pounce on it, close her hands around its throat and smash its head open on the ground. It would only take her a second, half a second if she was quick. Skulls were so much more fragile than they seemed. They broke apart so easily.

The dog, as if sensing the thought, barked louder, bristling with fear and fury, jaws glossy with drool. Taking another step back, Nell's heel caught the cement wheel stop, and she went windmilling onto her ass, dropping her cigarette as she hit the ground with a painful *crunch*. The dog lunged at her, and Nell opened her mouth to scream, cry for help, anything, but the wet, throaty noise that came ripping out of her was about as far from a scream as she'd ever heard. She heard herself growl—actually *growl*—at the poor stray, a vicious, animal retching that seemed to have shaken free from the deepest core of her body.

The stray's eyes went wide with confusion, and it recoiled, jumping back. Nell snarled again, and the dog spun and ran, tail tucked tightly between its legs. Nell watched it beat its retreat, brushing grit and dirty snow off herself as she rose from the frosty ground. Hands shaking, she knelt down to pluck her smoldering cigarette up off the asphalt and took a long, steadying drag as she heard the chime of the diner's front door. She looked back to see—Jonah.

"Hey," he said. "What's up?"

She searched for the right words but came up empty. What could she tell him? That she'd been cornered by some inked-up bible basher? That her voice wasn't her voice anymore? That she'd scared off a wild dog by barking in its face? No. She didn't want to give Jonah any more reason to treat her like a freak. He was already doing a great job of that on his own.

She blew smoke. "We good to go?"

"Yeah," Jonah said uneasily. "Just talked to the guy. Car's ready."

Nell took one last drag and pitched the guttering Camel into the nearest snowbank. In the diner windows, she could see a shadowed reflection of herself, clothes dancing and pulling in the wind.

"Great, let's," she said, then turned and walked away.

T he three of them sat in the van and watched.

"The hell was that?" Gillam's voice was strained.

"No clue," Terry replied, as the Talbots bundled up and went walking back down Main.

Behind the wheel, Gillam slumped down into his seat while Darko spun his butterfly knife open and shut in the back of the van. Terry followed Eleanor with his eyes, trying to read her expression. She looked worried. Good. He wanted her worried, wanted her scared. She deserved it, after what she'd done to Vaughn. That was why they hadn't followed them into the hotel last night to cut their throats in their sleep. That was why they were still watching them this morning. It had been Terry's idea to slash the tires, Terry's idea to leave the knife. He wanted these Talbot fucks to know they were coming. He wanted them to expect it; and when he finally reached into their hearts and tore the life from their ruined bodies, he wanted them to know that they'd done this shit to themselves.

He'd been up all night, keeping watch, keeping his senses sharp with key bumps from his little blue vial while his guys slept. He wasn't going to miss shit, if he could help it. He'd half expected that stray to fuck Eleanor up, maybe even rip her throat out. Shit, he'd actually been rooting for the dog there for a minute. Killing her himself was obviously his first choice, but he wasn't about to complain about fate dealing him a winning hand. Except then the dog had gone and turned tail and ran off like it had been shot. The hell was up with this chick?

Behind him, he heard Darko start to move toward the front of the van, sticking his head and skinny shoulders between the two front seats, watching the Talbots disappear up the road.

"You want to take them now?"

"Nah," Terry said, shaking his head. "Let's hang back. Wait until there's nobody around to help them."

A shell of gray clouds spilling fresh snow dragged itself across the dome of the sky as Nell and Jonah made their way out of Mowry on a new set of tires. Setting the windshield wipers to counteract the snow, Nell hit the headlights and pointed the station wagon east, heading for the far edge of town and the highway beyond.

"How are your hands?" Nell asked, nodding at the dark scabs scribbled across her little brother's crosshatched knuckles. "Looks like you fucked them up a little bit yesterday."

Turning red, Jonah tucked his hands into his pockets, hiding them from view. "They're fine. I'm fine."

"Been a while since you used 'em like that, huh?"

He glared at her. "Can we not, Nell? Please? I don't want to talk about it again, and especially not right now."

"Yeah, sure," Nell said, her voice clipped. "No problem. We can just have some quiet car time. You don't want to talk, we don't have to talk. Message received."

Jonah sighed. "It's not that I don't want to talk at all, I just don't want to talk about *that*. We've already argued enough for one trip. I just want things to be normal for a little while, okay? Even if we're just pretending, I want everything to not be fucking horrible for, like, a couple of minutes."

Looking over at her brother, it was as if Nell could see all the way through him, all the way down through the meat and blood and bone to the wretched, raw fear that sat like a rock inside his chest. She saw his life played backward and forward, a juddering, wretched picture show of pain and suffering, a pattern that reached like a fractal tree into his past, back as far as Jonah had been Jonah. She saw—and felt—every ounce of hurt he'd ever doled out or taken onto himself, his rages, his sorrows, that jagged stone behind his ribs growing bigger and heavier until it threatened to crush his heart outright. Frail, frightened, broken. Just another maggot like the rest of the selfish maggots filling up this planet, scrabbling around in the dirt and the muck as the world fell apart around them. Dead things eating dead things eating dead things. As if they wouldn't crumble like all the other ghosts that came before them, as if their mouths wouldn't fill with dirt and rot as their bodies softly collapsed into the yawning, waiting mouth of oblivion.

And then, as suddenly as that train of thought had come upon her, it was gone, snatched from her head, a balloon whisked away by the wind. Out of the corner of her eye, Nell could see Jonah watching her still. Had she said all of that out loud, or only thought it?

"What?" she asked, trying to sound casual.

Jonah shook his head and righted himself in the passenger seat, turning his attention back out toward the slushy winter drizzle.

"Nothing," he said. "Just forget about it."

Nell raised her fingers in surrender, keeping the heels of her hands on the steering wheel.

"Fine by me," she said. She turned the windshield wipers up a notch and sank her foot deeper on the gas pedal, speeding the station wagon down the highway. A second later, she turned up the stereo and let the road carry them away.

They were half an hour out of town by the time 48 Coffin caught up with them.

Checking her mirrors, Nell watched them approach from behind: two motorcycles and a dark Econoline, exhaust pipes pummeling the empty winter air, riders decked head to toe in black leather adorned with a familiar logo.

"Oh good, here comes the fun parade," Nell sneered, her voice suddenly shaking with rage. Beside her, Jonah twisted around in his seat to watch the bikers approach, scratching nervously at his neck, leaving red tracks in his skin.

The motorcycles screamed around the station wagon, screeching to a halt directly in their path. Nell stood on the brake, feeling the Volvo skid on the wet, freezing asphalt before rolling to a dead stop in the middle of the highway, drawn across the double yellow line like a single stitch pulled through a slit throat. For a single moment, everything—the bikes and their riders, the station wagon, the air in Nell's lungs—was quiet. Headlights rose in the rearview mirror as the Econoline rolled up behind them, the same one she'd seen parked across from the diner back in Mowry. Figured.

In the passenger seat, Jonah unbuckled his seatbelt and let his forehead hit the dashboard with a hollow thump. Outside, the first rider climbed off his bike and started toward the car, shucking his helmet off his head and tossing it aside. His eyes burned with a wild intensity beneath a long, sewn-shut split in his forehead, his blond-white goatee in disarray. Terry. Nell studied his face, remembering fondly what it had felt like to open his head up with the pool cue. On the bike further back, the other rider pulled off his helmet—Glasses. Probably meant that Beardy was the one in the van. Good to know.

Standing astride the double-yellows, Terry pulled a break-action sawed-off shotgun from inside his jacket and leveled it at their windshield, his aim steady and true.

"Put it in park and get the fuck out," he shouted. "*Now.*"

He got out of the car slowly, hands raised high like he'd seen in countless movies. Nell did the same. The air around them had gone stuffy and still, charged with a kind of bad electricity Jonah had felt only a few times before in his life. It never meant good things. Standing in the middle of the black-top, staring down the stacked barrels of Terry's sawed-off, Jonah started to seriously consider the idea that he might not live to see tomorrow.

"You killed my brother, you rotten bitch," Terry said as he stalked toward the Talbots, shotgun raised. "The only family I had left, and you took him from me."

"...What?" Nell said, her voice soft and timorous. "No, no, I just glassed him, I didn't..."

"He was fucking *epileptic*!" Terry roared.

"Oh god, oh fuck—" Nell stammered. "I didn't, I'm—!"

Terry's eyes flared. Without missing a beat, the old man shifted the shotgun to his other hand, balled up a fist, and fired a hard right hook to Nell's jaw, snapping her head back like it was spring-loaded. A hit like that was enough to lay anyone out flat.

But Nell stayed standing.

For a second, everything froze. Jonah, Terry, even the wind. It all went still. Then Nell slowly rolled her head back around to reveal a wide blood-streaked smile, that flat dull light hanging in her eyes again. Jonah's heart skipped a beat, then it skipped two. That ugly grin on Nell's face spread wider and wider as if it might split her head in half, then she reared back and spat a mouthful of blood into the old man's face.

Enraged, Terry made a strangled noise in his throat and wound up to hit her again, but Nell was quick—too quick. In one fluid movement, she caught his wrist and pulled, using his own fierce momentum to yank him forward as she drove a knee into his sternum, knocking him back as the other biker dismounted from his motorcycle and rushed her.

Jonah shot forward, meaning to help his sister, but someone hit him from behind, spearing a shoulder in the small of his back, tackling him to the ground, abrading his skin on the asphalt. Caught in an awkward tangle of limbs and wrists, Jonah thrashed back and forth to kick himself free, then clambered away and looked around into a familiar bearded visage, now red with fury. Of course.

Jonah fired a sharp kick into the guy's face, splitting his nose wide open, then threw himself on top of him to hammer at his balls and belly with knee after knee after knee. Dazed, Beardy rolled his head around, trying to see through the noseblood pooling in his eyes.

"Fuck you," he groaned through pulpy lips. "Fuck the botha you."

"Yeah," Jonah said. "Fuck me. Right."

Then he hit him with everything he had.

In all his many years away from himself, Jonah had almost forgotten what a perfect, malignant joy it was to just haul off and punch someone as hard as he could. He loved every part of it: the windup, the swing, the follow-through. The follow-through was the most important part, though. It was like hitting a ball; you didn't aim at the ball, you aimed six or seven inches behind the ball and let your arm do the rest of the work.

Boom. Jonah's fist collided with the biker's face like a wrecking ball blowing through a brick wall, the impact flinging blood and sweat and snot off the guy in a wild spray. The biker groaned again, then went limp. Leaving him there on the ground, Jonah twisted to look back toward his sister and felt his heartbeat catch in his throat.

Nell was moving faster than Jonah had ever seen in his life, spinning like a whirlwind, ducking out of the way of the other bikers' punches and kicks, goading them on, leaving them desperate and sloppy. Jonah was baffled. Nell had never moved like that before, never fought like that before, not ever. She'd always gone in for the cheap shots: eye pokes, fishhooks, throat punches, whatever was quick and effective. *No such thing as a fair fight*, she used to say, cackling over whatever shithead she'd last kicked in the balls. Even back in Broughton it had been like that, with her using every possible advantage just to make it out upright, but this...

Nell lunged in again and Terry feinted to the side, weaving around her to snake his forearm across her throat, locking her in a tight stranglehold. Nell's eyes bulged and her arms went wild, flapping like stork wings, trying to find purchase, trying to get loose from the old man's death grip.

Oh, fuck no.

Jumping to his feet, Jonah dashed over and drove an elbow into the old biker's spine to loosen his grip, then hauled him all the way off his sister and began to drag him away.

"You lousy little prick—"

Jonah's ribs exploded with pain and he stumbled back, clutching at his stomach as Terry wrenched himself free. The old biker had caught him with a sucker punch, a nasty little uppercut to the midsection that stole the breath right out of him. Terry hit him again, harder this time. Jonah barked with pain and swung blindly, trying to buy himself some space. Terry smirked.

"Here I was, thinking that you was some kind of badass after what happened yesterday, but you're not. You got lucky. That's all. Just another fucking wannabe."

Stepping in close, Terry peppered him with a flurry of quick jabs that Jonah managed to deflect just in time to get caught with a sneaky right cross that rang his head like a bell.

"See, luck counts for shit," Terry said, pressing his advantage. "At the end of the day, winning fights is all about who's better at hurting. Who's willing to soak the most pain and keep going, who's willing to do some shit they can't take back."

He fired off a slow roundhouse punch; Jonah knocked it off course with ease and realized a second too late that he'd taken the obvious bait like a sucker and left himself wide open again. Terry clouted him with a straight shot to the chest, and Jonah felt his heart flutter and spasm as he stumbled back, barely able to keep his arms up now.

"I mean, you got potential, sure." Terry feinted right and jabbed left, popping Jonah one in the cheekbone. "But I gotta be honest with you, kid." Punch. "End of the day, I don't think you have it in you." Punch. Punch. Punch.

Jonah wavered, reeling from the old man's onslaught, forcing himself to stay upright despite his every impulse to give out, hit the ground, lie down like a good boy, and take the beating. They deserved this, he and Nell. They did it to themselves. You lived your whole life running up a tab, never knowing when the bill would come due. Maybe this was their time.

Still. Deserve it or not, it didn't mean he had to play along.

Cracking his knuckles, Terry stepped in close and threw another punch; but this time, Jonah was ready for it. Quickstepping inside the old biker's wingspan, Jonah whipsawed his fist into Terry's teeth as hard as he could, connecting with a monstrous *crack!* Terry's eyes spun, then he dropped in a heap.

Out of breath, racked with pain, Jonah leaned to the side and threw up.

When he stood up straight again, he saw Nell on the other side of the car, bloody grin still fixed on her face, dancing around the last biker like Fred Astaire, baiting him in closer and closer until he crossed some invisible point of no return. Nell twirled in place and snatched Terry's discarded helmet off the ground, then smashed it into the poor bastard's face so hard, it was like she was expecting candy to come spilling out when she broke him open. Glasses went flying, spewing blood and teeth as he fell. Panting, Nell tossed the helmet aside and knelt down over the guy, pinning his arms to the ground with her knees. Her hand floated to her pocket. For a second, Jonah didn't understand what she was doing, and by the time he did, it was too late to stop her. The knife was already in her hand. The blade was already out.

No.

The knife flashed in Nell's fingers, and a deep stripe of red opened up along Glasses's cheek. The guy screamed. Nell didn't let up.

"Nell, what the fuck?!" Jonah shouted, running forward to intercede. Nell slashed at Glasses again, opening up a second gash beside the first. Jonah caught her arm before she could cut the guy a third time, and for a second it was like she didn't even notice that he was there. She just kept yanking down on the blade, confused why it wouldn't do what she told it to.

"Nell, stop, okay? Nell, you have to—Nell—Nell!"

Torn abruptly from whatever trance she'd fallen into, Nell twisted to look at her brother with that same horrible emptiness still brimming in her eyes, plain and obscene. As if she'd gone away from herself but forgotten to turn the lights off. Jonah held his breath and tried to not wilt in the face of the terrible void that had seemingly opened up inside her. As if he wasn't completely terrified of it swallowing him whole too.

"He's done," Jonah said, his voice a breathy gasp. "They're all done. Come on. We need to go."

Nell watched him for a moment that seemed to last a lifetime, and a second later, a dark shape rose up behind her, thin and bloody. At first Jonah thought it was Terry, ready for round three, but he was wrong: it was a young man, with blazing blue eyes and gray waxy skin that seemed to molder against the bright red blood that poured down his dead face. The ghost showed him a mouthful of broken teeth and bloody sockets, his cracked purple tongue hunting along swollen lips from corner to corner and back again.

See something you like, fuckface?

Jonah blinked, and he was gone.

Nell stood silently and circled around the car, stepping over Terry and the bearded asshole without another look. Jonah trailed her at a distance, wiping the blood from his reopened knuckles off on his jeans; when he looked again, he saw that Nell had knelt down to pick up Terry's shotgun. Jonah froze. She turned the gun over and over in her bloody hands, smearing it with red fingerprints as she stood, her expression still vacant. Blinking slowly, Nell raised the sawed-off and fired a shell into the engine of one bike, then turned and did the same to the other, blowing a pair of fist-size holes clean through the chrome. The gunshots were huge and obscene, twin thunderclaps that whipped at the sky above and echoed off the rocks and hills around them.

Then everything went silent again. Smoke hung in the air like a plague. Jonah watched his sister in terror as she crossed over to the Volvo and tossed the shotgun in the back, then climbed in drawing the open knife from her pocket, as that dreary light evaporated from her eyes. Jonah looked back at the highway around them, at the felled, bleeding men and their trashed motorcycles, trying to understand. He wanted to scream, to rage, to turn inward and get lost in his own resentment. It wasn't supposed to be like this, but they couldn't change it now. They'd gone too far, done too much damage already. They had to keep moving.

Climbing behind the wheel, Jonah kept his eyes straight ahead as he drove away, afraid to look at his sister but afraid to look anywhere else, convinced that if he did, he'd see that dead kid again, standing in the distance, smirking with a mouthful of blood and shattered bone.

Nell
Highway 50, NV
830 miles to Albuquerque

What the fuck were you thinking, Nell?! What the fuck was that?!"

Sitting in the passenger seat as they raced along the highway, Nell dug her fingers into her knees, trying to get a handle on everything that had just happened. The details were vague and elusive, as if a miry fog had suddenly flooded the inside of her head, clouding her thoughts and her senses, obscuring all the horrible, violent things that she'd just been party to. It had been her hands on the helmet and the knife, she knew that much, but she didn't think it was her that had done them. She'd watched them happen, but she hadn't been in control. It was as if her body had suddenly gone on autopilot and started fucking shit up all on its own.

"I don't know," she said, scared and frustrated. "I don't know, okay? I'm sorry, I didn't . . ."

"Sorry doesn't fix shit, okay? Honestly, I don't even know what to say to you right now. It's like you can't help but wreak havoc wherever you go. First the bar fight, then you get lost yesterday, and now this? I can't, Nell. I really cannot. You're going to get us fucking killed, you know that?"

"Getting lost was not my fault!" Nell snapped back, trying to cover her vulnerability with anger. It didn't work. "I don't know what happened out there, but I know it wasn't my fault, and fuck you for saying otherwise."

"How can you be sure, though?" Jonah asked. "I mean, really. If you don't remember what happened, how would you know? I mean, unless you've been lying to me all day—"

"I have *not* been lying to you, Jonah—"

"Then something else is going on here, okay? I don't know what it is, but it's not nothing," he said. "This is not okay. None

137

of this is okay. That wasn't just some fight. You cut that guy's face up, Nell. Why the fuck would you do something like that? Shit like that is not fucking normal. You have to see that; you can't tell me you don't."

Nell felt her face flush a deep red as she turned her attention to the folding knife in her lap, its sharp edge still wet with blood. With shaking hands, she thumbed the blade into the handle and shoved the thing into the glovebox, remembering how she'd yanked it off that biker's—Vaughn's—belt as he twitched and foamed on the barroom floor. She felt sick to her stomach again.

"He said his brother died," she said, her voice small and frail. "Back at the bar, the guy I glassed. Vaughn. He was epileptic."

"I heard," Jonah said.

"Do you think it's true?"

Jonah sighed and shook his head.

"I don't see why he'd lie about it."

"Fuck," said Nell. *"Fuck."*

"Yeah," Jonah said. "Pretty much."

S he waited inside the coffee shop at the farthest edge of
town until she felt the Chain start to twitch and pull again,
trembling at the base of her skull like a nervous spider.

Nell Talbot and her brother were on the move.

Anna sat at the little counter, nursing her croissant and
her paper cup of coffee (half-caf with half-and-half and three
sugars) until the pull started to ease off some, letting them get
a decent head start. It wouldn't do for them to look back and
see her bird-dogging their every step. She'd seen that vicious fire
burning in Nell; she'd heard the venom in her voice. Even without that thing lurking inside her, Anna didn't figure Nell for
someone who'd easily be forced into anything. She was going to
have to come around on her own.

But that was okay. They always did, in the end. One way
or another.

Finishing up her breakfast, Anna stepped out of the little café and crossed the street to her car. She motored out of
town at exactly the speed limit and merged onto the highway as
Mowry faded into the rear distance, little more than a memory.
It was for the best, really. Anna hadn't ever really understood
the appeal of gambling.

She was on the road for half an hour before she came upon
the wreck.

Three men, two motorcycles, and one van, all sitting on
the side of the road in a shambles. It was hard to tell what had
happened, exactly, but she could see from a mile off that something had gone very wrong. The men seemed to sag in place,
blood painting their faces and hands as they sat slumped beside
tire marks burned into the highway. Anna eased down on the
brake pedal as she passed and owled her head around to get a

better look. The van looked like it was in working order, but the motorcycles were smoking, bleeding oil and more out of a pair of jagged holes that had been torn in the sides of their machinery. What the heck had happened to these guys?

For a second, she considered pulling over to try and help; but as she slowed, she felt the Chain rattle and jerk against the inside of her head. No, she couldn't stop here. She had to stay moving, had to stay close enough to the Talbots to make her move when the time eventually came. The men on the side of the road would be okay, or they wouldn't. Either way, it really wasn't her problem.

As she drove past, the bloody bikers looked up to watch her pass them by. One of them sat with his shoulders against the van's grille, sopping the side of his face with a red-filled rag while another squatted beside him, prodding at an assortment of red-purple bruises that covered his cheeks, his expression dazed and distant. The third man, older than the other two with a white goatee and a burning stare underneath a forehead marked with a deep gash, met Anna's eyes as she passed, eying her like a wolf considering its next meal. Anna stepped on the gas pedal and sped up until the three men were little more than a dark smudge in her rearview mirror.

She had to keep moving.

Jonah
Unincorporated Landover County, UT
782 miles to Albuquerque

Driving in silence, they headed east through a long stretch of dry Utah wilderness, all scraggy pines poking up through the rock-ribbed terrain. After a few more miles, they rounded another bend in the road and came upon a run-down little gas station, not much more than a couple of old pumps standing opposite a tiny shopette in the middle of a cracked lot.

"Hey, can we stop? I have to pee," Nell said.

Slowing, Jonah looked out the window at the little station. At first glance, he thought it might have been abandoned, and if it hadn't been for the red-and-blue neon *Open* sign hanging in the front window, he would have passed it by, but this seemed as good a place as any to stop and stretch their legs for a minute.

"Yeah, sure," he said, turning into the cracked parking lot. "Tank could use a top-off, anyway."

Rolling to a stop next to the nearest pump, Jonah climbed out, and a second later Nell did the same. Looking at her across the top of the Volvo, Jonah thought for a moment that he could see that terrible void rising up in her eyes, and it took everything he had to not check and see if her shadow had slipped loose of her control again. It was just a shadow, he told himself. Shadows couldn't hurt anyone.

Could they?

"What?" Nell asked when she caught him staring, her voice pointed.

"Nothing," Jonah said, exhausted. "Nothing. Sorry."

"Sure," she sighed. "Whatever. I'm going inside. You coming?"

"In a minute or two."

141

"Would you get me cigarettes when you do? Camels."

"Unfiltereds?"

"Bingo."

"Yeah, no problem," Jonah said. But Nell was already walking away.

Wearily, he watched her go, her thin, knifelike silhouette carving a slow line from the pumps to the shopette doors, then disappearing inside. It occurred to him then that he didn't really know what to expect from her at all anymore. He felt like he was watching her fray at the edges, more anxious and intense with every passing second. He barely recognized her now. She was too thin, her face too serious, her shoulders squared off too sharply above crossed arms. She was like a hollowed-out shell of herself. Not the Nell he used to know. Not even the Nell she'd been yesterday morning.

Jonah swiped his credit card and began filling up the station wagon, crossing his arms against the chill. He looked up at the sky—gray and close; the storms weren't done with them yet. Wonderful. More things to slow them down. Just what they needed right now.

When the tank thumped full, Jonah replaced the nozzle, then crossed the empty lot to the little shopette. There wasn't much inside, not that he'd expected any different: a couple of dusty aisles filled with sugary snacks and engine oil, chips and nonperishable dips and tire chains and ice scrapers, a couple of rickety old glass-front coolers at the back, racks half-filled with name-brand and off-brand cokes, seltzer waters, Gatorades, and more.

"Hi, can I help you?" the zit-faced teenager behind the counter asked, a weird expression on his face and a cell phone glowing in his hands.

"Pack of Camels," Jonah said, nodding at the stacked wall of tobacco behind the kid. He tossed a twenty down on the counter between them. "Unfiltereds. Thanks."

The kid fetched the cigarettes wordlessly, then took Jonah's twenty and made change.

"Hey, uh. I don't want to be rude, but. Do you know her?" the kid asked.

Jonah raised an eyebrow. "Know who?"

"That woman in the bathroom," the kid said, and nodded toward the opposite end of the building. "You guys showed up together, right?"

"Yeah," Jonah replied. "That's my sister. Why?"

The kid's face turned red. "It's probably nothing, I just. I thought I heard glass break in there," he said. "Just before you came in. Think I might've heard her scream too."

"Sorry, *what*?"

"Yeah," the kid said. "I, uh. It was right before you came in, and I didn't—"

"Fuck." Leaving the cigarettes on the counter, Jonah spun on his heel and ran for the bathrooms.

Behind him, he heard the kid say, "I'm gonna . . . I think I need to call 911?"

"Absolutely not," Jonah shouted back as he dashed down the center aisle. "Do not call the fucking cops. I will be right back. Don't call anyone, okay? No one."

Breathless, he headed down the hallway to the women's restroom, shouldered the door open, and nearly screamed at what he saw inside.

The mirror that ran the length of the left-hand wall had been shattered, cracked in a jittery spiderweb pattern that stretched from one end of the little cinderblock room to the other. Nell stood in front of the middle sink, carving at the inside of her forearm with a shard of broken glass, her face totally blank. Blood brimmed from the cuts, rolling down her arm in thick lines to patter messily on the sink and on the gray-green tile under her feet.

"Jesus Christ, Nell, what the fuck!?" Jonah cried.

But Nell didn't hear him, her expression glassy and vacant. There, but not there. Again. Stunned, Jonah watched her turn the shard deeper into her skin, and realized that if he didn't stop her now, she was going to cut something she couldn't take back.

Breathless, he hurried to Nell's side and locked one hand around her wrist as he tried to pull the jagged spur of glass from her fingertips, but she wouldn't budge.

"Nell, let up, come on—"

Using both hands now, he redoubled his grip on her wrist and tried to pull her arms apart, but it was useless. She was too strong. He might as well have been trying to pull the *Titanic* from the bottom of the ocean.

"Stop, come on, please," Jonah pleaded. "Nell, you have to stop—"

Gritting his teeth as his shoulders threatened to pop from their sockets, Jonah heaved against his sister until he felt her grip give a little bit, then a little bit more. After another second, he'd levered her arm back far enough for him to slap the bloody shard from her fingers. It tumbled into the blood-spattered sink with a silvery clatter.

Nell came to in an instant.

"Jonah, this is the women's room, what are you doing in here...?"

She raised her blood-drenched arm up in front of her face and turned it back and forth, examining it.

"What...what..." she said, her voice dreamy and far-away. "What happened...?"

Jonah slumped against the far wall as his pulse screamed in his ears. "Why..." he gasped. "Why would you do that to yourself, Nellie?"

She looked back at him, confused, scared, on the verge of tears.

"I didn't," she said.

Stepping forward again, Jonah threw the faucet on and guided Nell's slashed-up arm underneath the cold flow, rinsing away as much blood as he could. Christ, she'd made such a mess of herself. He let the water run, and when the bleeding finally began to slow, realized with mounting horror that the wounds carved into her arm weren't random—she'd used the broken glass to write a word into her skin:

Fresh red welled out of the cuts. Jonah's stomach turned. Without thinking, he dug in his coat pocket for his handkerchief, spread it flat across the bloody letters, then moved Nell's other hand to hold it in place.

"Keep this here, okay? Tight. It's going to keep bleeding otherwise." It was only a little bit of a lie. Truth was, it was probably going to keep bleeding no matter what, but at least this way, they had a chance of stopping it, and that was better than nothing.

"Uh-huh," Nell said, her voice still distant. Jonah watched the blood from her arm wick into his handkerchief, turning the blue paisley shiny black underneath her fingers.

"Come on," he said, getting an arm around his sister's shoulders to lead her out. He didn't dare look over at the zit-faced clerk as they shuffled out the door, afraid that the kid had already called the cops. He knew that he'd left Nell's cigarettes lying on the shopette counter, but fuck going back for them at this point. Right now, they just had to get out of here as fast as possible.

Outside, the wind had died down, but the cold remained. As they crossed the broken bitumen once more, Jonah forced himself to breathe normally, not freak out, no matter how much he wanted to. Freaking out wouldn't help anybody right now. Pulling the Volvo's passenger-side door open, he helped Nell into the car, then circled around to the hatchback to pull a clean T-shirt from his suitcase. Once he was behind the steering wheel, he passed the shirt over to Nell.

"Here," he said. "Use this. Hold it tight."

She looked at him, confused. "What?"

"For your arm," he said.

She peeled back the sodden handkerchief and read the word carved into her skin.

"*Hello*," she said. "Oh, my god. Oh, my fucking god, Jonah."

"I know," Jonah said, feeling dread ricochet around inside his chest. "You were lucky you didn't hit anything important."

Carefully, Nell swapped the handkerchief for the bunched-up T-shirt and bore down on it.

"I didn't do this, Jonah," she said. "This wasn't me. I wouldn't. I need you to believe me. I wouldn't do something like this to myself, I wouldn't."

He studied her face, looking for any sign of that dead void in her eyes, but it was gone. Whatever it was, Nell was right: it wasn't her.

"I believe you," he said, his voice barely above a whisper.

"This . . . this is bad, isn't it?"

Jonah nodded.

"So what do we do now?"

"I'm going to drive, and you're going to tear that shirt into strips for a bandage. Something you can tie around your arm, okay? It's not perfect, but it's better than nothing. After that, we get you home," Jonah said. "Get you to a hospital, maybe get your brain scanned or something. I don't know if you hit your head down in those caves or what, but whatever's going on, it isn't good, and I'm honestly scared that it's going to keep getting worse."

Nell shot him a severe look at that.

" . . . what?"

"Nothing," she said. "Forget it."

She leaned her head against the window and closed her eyes. A second later, Jonah reached over and rested a hand on her shoulder, gave her what he hoped was a reassuring squeeze.

"Listen, I'm here for you," he said. "You're not dealing with this shit alone, okay? Whatever you need."

"I think I need us to keep moving, okay? Can we do that, please?"

"Yeah," he said. "Of course." Jonah watched her from under his brow until he saw her shoulders slump, then turned the key in the ignition and fixed his gaze on the dark hills that filled up the whole of the horizon. He didn't know what to do. He didn't know what to say. Talking about it anymore wasn't going to do any good, and it wasn't going to get them home any faster. Maybe right now the best thing Jonah could do for the both of them was drive. Let Nell sleep.

When they got back to Albuquerque, things would be better.

B ruised and bloodied, they took everything important from the bikes, then stripped the plates and VIN tags off, wheeled them out into the wastes beyond the highway, and left them to rust. Nobody would look twice at them out there. Just more wreckage half-buried along a lonesome road. First Vaughn, now his bike. Fucking Talbots. It was heartbreaking, having to abandon his little brother's Harley like that; Terry wanted to at least douse the thing in gas, give it a proper funeral, but they couldn't risk the attention.

He stood astride the line where the road met the dirt and stared off into the distance under the gray sky, then looked back at his guys, who were diligently loading the rest of their stuff into the van. At the top of Darko's jacket, his necklace had fallen loose of his shirt, the gold Orthodox cross hanging awkwardly on its chain. Terry ground his molars at the sight of it. He really didn't give a shit what his guys believed or didn't believe, it wasn't any of his business, but personally, he'd heard enough ghost stories to last him a lifetime.

One day, you'll see for yourself, boy.

When he'd been a little kid, his grandfather had taken him aside and told him that he could see spirits and demons climbing the walls of their home. He explained that he'd seen them ever since he'd been a child himself, some as thin as tissue paper, some wearing the faces of people that had died, some with teeth like butcher knives and eyes like dead coals. He saw them more and more the older he got, too. He said the same would happen to Terry someday. When the old man came to live with Terry and his mom and his dad and little baby Vaughn, he'd stay up until all hours talking to his ghosts, crying to them, begging for mercy.

147

Everyone—Terry included—thought that Grandpa was crazy, especially after he ended it all by taking a power drill to his temple. The mess was awful. The note they found in his pocket said that it had gotten to be too much, that after so many years of living with it, he could see capital-H Hell waiting for him. He was tired of putting off the inevitable. Grandpa said that he loved them all. Grandpa said that one day they'd understand.

Stooping by the van's back doors, Darko caught Terry watching him and tilted his head to the side, curious.

"We almost done here?" Terry asked, remembering himself.

"One minute," Darko said. Underneath the crooked lines the Talbot bitch had sliced into his face, his mouth was a black-and-white checkerboard where she'd knocked out three of his teeth. Beside him, Gill puffed on a cigarette and averted his eyes, a sullen look on his face, battered and swollen like a thumb slammed in a car door. He'd always been shit at hiding his emotions. Never had any chill at all.

"What's the problem now, Gill?" Terry asked.

Gillam made a face, playing confused. "Nothing. What?"

"You've got something on your mind," Terry said. "What?"

"It's nothing, Ter."

"It's not nothing. Spill."

Gillam sighed and shook his head.

"I mean, like... Why are we doing this? Why are we still going after them?"

Terry looked at him, uncomprehending, as anger roiled his guts. "Because they killed Vaughn. That bitch murdered my brother."

"Right, yeah, no, I get that," Gill said. "That part I understand. It's just that I'm starting to wonder if it might be better to take the L at this point and move on. Or something. I don't know."

Terry rolled his neck back and forth, popping the cartilage like a string of firecrackers.

"You want to give up now? After everything we've been through already, you want to say *never mind*, turn tail, head home, let these fucks get away with what they did? Is that what you're saying to me right now?"

"No, Ter, no," Gill said. He held his hands out in a placating gesture. "It's not exactly like that."

"Then what is it like, *exactly*?"

Gillam raised his arms, let them drop. "I mean, come on, they've kicked the fuck out of us twice already, what makes you think that anything will change the third time around? Or the fourth? What makes you think any of this is going to make a difference?"

"This isn't about making a difference, Gill. This is about what's right. Scales need to be balanced," Terry said.

"I'm not saying they don't," Gillam said. "Right's right, I get it, but I think we're being kind of fucking stupid about this, banging our faces against a brick wall and telling ourselves that we're going to break through eventually. Or that it feels good. Or both, maybe. I don't know."

Terry's cheeks flushed hot. "What the fuck did you just say to me?"

Gillam shrank back from him, but—to his credit—he didn't blink.

"Look, I know how bad losing Vaughn must hurt, Ter. And I am so sorry about that, but we need to face facts: this isn't about balance. Not anymore. This isn't even about justice. This is revenge. And if revenge is what you're looking for, there are better ways to go about it. We can head back to Broughton, round up the troops, roll out in force, bring the fuckin' pain. You have that bitch's ID, so we know where they're going, don't we? At least we know where they're probably going to end up, sooner or later. We can do this smarter, that's all I'm saying."

Terry blinked slow at the man, his friend of many years, unable to fully process what he was hearing.

"There was a time and a place for this," Terry said, his voice a vicious growl. "And that was back in Broughton. You signed up for this shit, Gill. You chose to come along, to see it through to the end. You thinking about turning yellowbelly now? Tough shit. This is the path."

"Back in Broughton I thought it would be easy," Gill said. "I thought those two assholes kicked the dogshit out of us because they got lucky, not because they were psychopaths. But you saw what that crazy bitch did to Darko's face as well as I did. Cutting someone up like that is not some shit a fucking civilian does out of the blue, and you know it. I'm telling you, if you want to finish this the right way, we need help, man."

"Fuck them," Terry said. "And you, too, for this insubordinate shit. You're supposed to be fucking loyal. You're supposed to be smarter than this."

"So are you." As soon as Gillam said it, his eyes went wide and his mouth pinched shut, the realization of the mistake he'd just made written all over his face.

Terry took another step forward, stomping his boot down into the ground between them.

"They killed my *brother*, Gillam."

"I know that," Gill said, his shoulders falling like a landslide. "But it's not an excuse to do this shit the wrong way. I mean, come on, do you really think that *Vaughn*, of all people—"

The next words never made it out of Gillam's mouth because Terry was too busy putting his fist into it. He felt Gill's nose pop open under his knuckles, loosing twin jets of blood down his face as he bounced off the side of the van, punch-drunk after one. Terry lunged forward and hit him again, catching him with a hard right hook to the jaw that sent the man spinning to the ground beside the back tire, moaning like a dumb animal.

"You were told," Terry said, flexing his fist, cracking the knuckles underneath the skin. "You were given a direct fucking order."

Splayed out atop the dirt, Gillam held his hands out and cried, "Wait, Terry, no!"

But it was too late. Terry dropped down on top of him, feeling every new ache and injury as he bunched one fist in Gillam's shirt and pounded on him with the other. Firing his arm like a piston, he whaled on his friend until Gillam's face looked like a raw steak with a talk hole cut into it, eyes all swollen shut, both lips a swollen, bloody mess.

In the silence that surrounded them, Terry heard footsteps behind him. He twisted around to see Darko standing there, watching.

"What?" Terry barked, jabbing a finger out at him. "You want to share a fuckin' opinion too?"

Unblinking, Darko slowly shook his head *No*.

"That's what I thought," Terry said. He hit Gillam one last time, then stood quickly, hauling Gill back up to his feet in the same motion. With a grunt, Terry shoved the dazed, bloody man over toward Darko, who caught him in both arms, propping him up straight.

"You watch him," Terry snarled. "Fucking traitor's turning into a liability. Now let's get out of here."

Together, they climbed back into the van and set off, roaring down the road without another word.

Consciousness came slowly as the red morning light slipped in between her eyelids like a filet knife between two ribs. She moved her hands first, rolling her fingers against the rough, unwashed sheets, then her feet and her toes. Nell turned over and over, spinning in linens until she found the strength to crawl to one side of the bed and throw her legs over the edge of the mattress. She rubbed at her face with both hands, looking around. She didn't recognize any of this. This wasn't her bedroom. This wasn't her apartment.

Rising from the bed, Nell padded along the gray wall-to-wall, moving into the hallway beyond and listening to the unfamiliar house she'd found herself in. The place was silent, and in that silence, she could hear her own heartbeat thumping along steadily, in her throat, in her temples, at the very outer edges of her fingertips. She felt like a raw nerve, a thing made of pure sensation recoiling from the pain of existence. Stepping into the bathroom, she sat on the toilet to pee, then went to the faucet to wash her hands, only to find that the faucet didn't run. No matter how many times she spun the knob, the tap stayed stubbornly dry. She tried the lever on the front of the toilet tank—it wouldn't flush. Was there no water here? Moving into the hallway again, she tried the light switches and the thermostat. No dice. Nothing in this house worked. It was like she'd woken up in a model home or something. Frustrated, she turned her attention down the long hall, and the dozens of doors that lined its walls.

She tried one at random—it swung open easily, revealing a bare room beyond. No furniture, no carpet, nothing but bald, dreary walls and crimson daylight pouring in through a musty window. Turning back, she tried another door. Same thing. She opened every door as she made her way down, scrutinized every empty room, and when she came to the end of the hall she saw what waited for her there: the last door. Its weathered wood was bleached bone white with age, cracked, and streaked with filth. She approached it slowly, her footfalls soft against the dingy carpet, then curled one hand around the oxidized doorknob and pushed.

Beyond the white door lay a shabby, cramped hospital room, filled with machines that beeped and buzzed around a folding bed, their fuzzy digital readouts completely incomprehensible to Nell. Slowly, it dawned on her that she recognized this room. She'd been inside this room before.

But why was it here?

Nell lifted a foot to step into the little room, but something inside her, a faint and frail little voice, screamed *NO, DON'T!* and she froze, her heart suddenly thundering inside her chest. As she stood there frozen at the edge of the familiar little sickroom, an earsplitting groan shook the house from deep within its architecture. The walls shuddered as deep fissures broke open in the plaster. The hospital machines toppled to the floor, screens cracking on impact. Dust fell in sheets from overhead, scattering across the felled machines and the rickety old bed with its rumpled, stained sheets. The roar grew louder. The shaking got worse. Nell held her breath as the hospital room shattered before her and began to crumble away, revealing the space behind it, beyond it, past all its grim artifice to . . .

Emptiness.

Pure, and perfect, and true.

A bright, pulsating absence waited for her underneath the mirage of the hospital room, not black, not white, just sheer abyss, beckoning her forth. She could hear the void droning on and on, a constant low-frequency hum that she felt in her teeth as it churned and pulsated before her. There was a gravity to that oblivion, an undeniable pull that Nell felt in the deepest depths of her heart, imploring her to close her eyes and jump. She'd come so close to it once already, why not see it all the way through this time?

Her fingers trembled against the doorjamb as she swayed

forward, inches from annihilation. It would be so easy to let go.
Give herself over and fall into it. Vanish forever. For a moment,
she thought about how nice it would be to be nowhere. To be
nothing. To not have to worry and struggle and hurt so much
all the goddamned time. Past the white door, the great colorless
hollow throbbed and shivered and started to spread, surging forward to meet her, touch her, claim her. Nell clapped one hand
to her mouth to try to stanch the scream that rose in her chest.
She threw herself backward, nearly tripping over her own legs
as she ran from that overflowing emptiness, sprinting for the
staircase at the other end of the hall. She took the steps down
two at a time and hit the ground floor at a flat-out run, weaving
through the dead house for the back door and everything that
lay beyond it. She couldn't. She wouldn't.

Crashing outside into the headache-red glare, Nell struggled to catch her breath. Her knees shook, her vision blurred;
she hung her head and kept her eyes trained on the wasted grass
beneath her feet until the tide of sickness began to ebb away
once more. Looking up toward the horizon, she could see that
same tornado as before, closer now, sawing a path through the
city below as it drew ever nearer. She heard a crash behind
her; she shut her eyes and felt that great consuming absence
come bleeding out of the empty home, devouring everything in
its path before hurtling up to bore into the crimson brightness
above.

She didn't want to look.

But she couldn't not.

Stomach lurching, Nell raised her face to the sky and beheld
the bleeding, empty hole burned through its center, already so
much larger than used to be, the skin around the wound riddled
with oozing sores. It shifted and pulled as she watched, tearing
itself wider with a drowned ripping noise. Within its despicable,
pulsating nothingness, she could see splintered bones and pale
wormlike veins breaking through the wretched meat as a filthy
bone-white hand tore free of the hole, ripping at the pustulous
flesh, rending it apart in messy streamers.

Something squirmed inside Nell's stomach as the bleached
hand burst free of the void, a kind of angular pressure that hadn't

been there a moment before. It writhed in circles and scraped violently up her esophagus, clammy and painful. The taste of bile and that awful muck from the sludgeway below flooded her mouth as her throat stretched and tore to accommodate the strain. Doubling over from the horrible cramping inside her guts, she heaved, expecting a rush of vomit but instead feeling a bouquet of bony somethings wriggling and pawing at the back of her gullet.

Fingers.

There were fingers inside her mouth, pushing their way out, clawing toward the knot of limbs and viscera that thrashed far overhead.

Nell retched again and felt the fingers climb higher, fully blocking her air now. Her eyes went wide and she tried to scream, but no sound escaped her lips. Her jaw stretched and ripped as her insides turned to paste, her bones groaning as they bowed and broke like glass—

N ell crashed back into her body with a sickening impact, breaking free of the dream with a start and an injured yelp.

Behind the wheel of the station wagon, Jonah jumped and twisted to look at her, his expression terrified.

"Christ," he barked, "what the fuck?!"

Nausea—nausea and *pain*—boiled inside her, and Nell shook her head, swallowing repeatedly behind clenched teeth, trying to keep her insides inside. Her guts flopped and churned like she was on a roller coaster, firing a sour, oily heat straight up her throat, unstoppable.

"Pull over, pull over, Jonah," she demanded, keeping her jaw shut tight. As if that would help.

"What the fuck, what for?! Would you—"

"PULL OVER NOW!" she screamed, the sudden outburst rocking her stomach like a paint shaker.

Jonah stomped on the brake and skidded to a halt with a sudden jerk that didn't help Nell's stomach any. There was a putrid tickling at the back of her mouth, the taste horribly, grotesquely familiar, and for a second, she could actually feel something filthy and rough rise up the back of her throat to caress her tongue. *Fingers*, her brain whispered to her. Gagging, she clapped a fist over her mouth and pressed down hard.

With sleep-numb hands, she forced the door open and threw herself out of the car, landing on her palms and knees as the nausea coiled her body like a spring. Her mouth fell open in a desperate bid to draw air; a second later, a spray of hot brown vomit came jetting out of her. Pressing her fingertips into the ground, Nell tried to catch her breath, tried to see past the tears that were clouding her eyes, anything, but the nausea was still too strong. She made a wet choking noise—LURP!—and hinged her jaw wider, issuing another heavy rope of puke that splattered across the backs of her hands in a messy fan. Fuck.

A second later, a hand, warm and sure, alighted on her back, pressing gently between her shoulder blades. Jonah.

"Hey," he said, kneeling down beside her.

Nell spat. "Hey yourself," she gasped. She tried to breathe slowly, tasting the crispness in the air, putting all her focus onto it like a talisman as she willed the tang of bile from her mouth. When she was pretty sure there wasn't going to be a third surge, she spat again, then eased herself back to sit on the gravel, avoiding the puke. Jonah sat next to her. She slumped to the side and rested her head on his shoulder.

"You were talking in your sleep," he said. "I tried to wake you up. But you wouldn't come to."

"What was I saying?"

He shook his head. "Not a lot of it made sense."

A vision of a blood-red sky and an endless pulsating void flashed through Nell's mind.

"Tell me anyway?"

"You kept saying 'It's coming, it's coming,'" he said.

"Anything else?"

She could feel him looking at her.

"Come on, Jonah, what else?"

"'It's all red,'" Jonah said. "That mean anything to you?"

She turned her head to look up at him. He looked so scared. Scared and lost.

"No," she lied. "No, nothing."

"Okay," he said, his voice uneasy.

"I'm sorry," Nell told him. "For everything. I'm so fucking sorry."

He wrapped an arm around her shoulders, then kissed the top of her head.

"Nell, it's not your fault," he said. "Like you told me."

"Are you really sure about that? Because I'm not. Not anymore."

"Nell, it's okay," he said. "Really."

"No, it's not," Nell gasped, barely fighting back a sob.

"No, it's not," Jonah echoed. "Not really. But it will be.

Eventually. We just need to find a place to stop for a little while, okay? Get you some water or something. Whatever you need. Get your bearings, get you back in fighting shape. Little rest, little food, and you'll be slicing dudes' faces up again in no time at all."

Nell spat one last time and cracked a little half-grin despite herself. "Too soon, Jone."

Jonah shrugged. "Can't blame me for trying. Come on, let's go. Here."

Still leaning on her brother, Nell stood slowly, wobbling like a baby giraffe as he led her back to the car underneath the blue-gray sky.

"It's going to be okay, right?" she asked, sounding about as afraid as she felt.

He looked at her like he was trying to read her thoughts. "I hope so," he said.

Nell didn't say anything else, afraid to open her mouth again. She could still feel those cracked, filthy fingers grasping at the edge of her throat.

The rest stop wasn't much to look at, a small cluster of gray-brown buildings arranged in a semicircle around a half-empty parking lot, its streetlights already glowing brightly against the waning day. Nell sat curled up in the passenger seat, arms around her knees, wishing to be anywhere else, anyone else as the rumbling of the car jolted at her pinched stomach. The nausea had mostly passed, but she could still taste vomit, all mineral and grainy, as if she'd tried to choke back a mouthful of dirt.

Jonah wove the car up and down the parking lot's painted rows, looking for a spot close to the shops and the gas station, tapping his fingers nervously against the wheel. Keeping her forehead pressed against the glass, Nell watched the cars outside, marking the faces of the people who sat inside them, eating meals from paper wrappers, chugging cups of coffee, arguing with each other, trying not to cry. Beside her, Jonah was scared. He didn't say anything about it, but then, he didn't have to. She could feel it radiating off him in vile fever waves that got worse whenever he looked over at her. She couldn't blame him. He'd be stupid not to be scared after the last two days. Nell was scared too. Whenever she closed her eyes, the red glare was there, eliciting a gaunt pressure from underneath her ribs. It coiled around her heart like a tapeworm, squeezing and chewing, squeezing and chewing.

There was something inside her, she knew that much for sure. She didn't know what it was, but she could feel it starting to pull her apart, plucking her seams loose one by one, nestling deep in her meat and bone, wearing her like a suit. She hadn't asked for it, and she knew that it wasn't her fault, but maybe there was still something she could do about it. The car shifted and bounced to a stop as Jonah pulled into a parking spot halfway down the vastness of the lot before killing the engine.

"How you holding up?" he asked.

"Not good, but I'll live." For now.

"Better than nothing," he said, and nodded toward the featureless buildings at the head of the parking lot. "Come on, let's go get some supplies. Anything you want. It's on me."

Nell shook her head, pained. "I can't go in there, Jone."

"What? Why not?"

"Stomach's still killing me. Feel it through my whole body. Don't want to move if I can help it. D'you mind if I just wait here while you head inside? I'm sorry to be a pain in the ass about it."

Jonah's face wrinkled with consternation. "I'm not going to leave you out here, Nell. Come on."

She knew what he was getting at, but she really wasn't interested in talking about it right now. Or ever, for that matter.

"Jonah, I'll be fine," she said as seriously as she could manage.

"I don't know that for sure, and frankly neither do you."

"Jonah, please don't start with this shit again. Not right now."

"I'm just saying, you don't exactly have a great track record of being on your own lately," he said. "I would rather not leave you alone. Not if I can help it."

Nell looked away from him and bit both her lips between her front teeth as her exhausted, scorched brain sputtered on fumes.

"Jone, I need you to trust me on this, okay? Please. I know...I know," she said, unsure of how to end that sentence. "But I'm still me, and I know what I'm doing right now, alright? You go on inside, get whatever, I'll be here. I'm just going to close my eyes, try and get some rest until you get back. That's all."

"That's all?" His expression was nervous.

"That's it."

"All right," he said after another second, nodding. "Yeah, fine. You want anything from inside?"

Nell breathed out slowly. "Water, I guess. And smokes. You think shit's rough now, wait until I haven't had any nicotine for twelve hours."

"That bad, huh?"

She showed him her best imitation of a smile. "Worse," she told him. "It's all tentacles and scorpions and shit. Real horrorshow-type stuff."

"Sounds like something I'd like to avoid as much as possible," said Jonah.

"That makes two of us."

"Okay, I'll be right back," he said. "Ten minutes, tops." Popping the handle, he swung his door open and stepped out, only to turn back half a second later, bending at the hip to look across the car at her.

"Hey," he said.

Nell turned toward him.

"I love you, Nell. We're going to get through this shit."

Nell blew air out of her nose. "You're going soft in your old age."

"I'm serious," Jonah told her. "Whatever shit's gone down between us, the fights, the grudges, whatever, none of it matters to me right now. You're my sister, and I love you. We're going to handle this, okay? Together."

"Sounds good," Nell said. "Love you too. See you in a minute."

"Yeah," Jonah confirmed. "Right back."

Then he was gone. Nell unfolded herself from the passenger seat and went digging in her coat for her phone. Laying it on the dashboard, she pulled the folded napkin out next and laid it flat on one thigh, reading the short message once more.

Anna. Call me when you need help.

Clicking the screen to life, she dialed the ten-digit number written underneath the note, then hit *Call* and held the phone to her ear.

She answered on the third ring.

"Hello?" The voice on the other end of the line was the polar opposite of how Nell felt: soft, kind, and totally at ease.

"Yeah, hi," Nell said. "Is this Anna? Anna . . ." She searched her memory for the last name the tattooed woman had given her. "Dechant, I think? This is—"

"Nell," the woman on the other end of the phone finished for her, her tone gentle and friendly. "I'm so glad to hear from you. How can I help you?"

"I was hoping you could tell me that."

On the other end of the line, Nell swore she could hear the woman grin.

"You said you know what's happening to me," Nell continued. "You said that it's going to keep getting worse."

"I do, and it is," Anna said, her voice warm and patient. "But I'm guessing you probably wouldn't have called me unless it already has. Right?"

Nell made a little noncommittal grunt in the pit of her throat, the tiniest show of affirmation that she could muster. She didn't want to say it. She couldn't. Saying it out loud would mean admitting it, and admitting it would make it really real, and if it was, well, she wouldn't know what the hell she'd do then. Worry fizzed inside her chest. This was a mistake. She shouldn't have done this. She pulled the phone away from her face to kill the call…but something stopped her. She didn't know what it was; she didn't know why. All she knew was that as her thumb hovered over the glowing screen, she found herself unable to press the button.

She put the phone back to her ear.

"You know, there's nothing wrong with asking for help," Anna said, as if she could hear the nervous thoughts dancing through Nell's head. "But you have to be the one to ask. I can't do the asking for you. That part has to be yours."

She remembered the look on Anna's face at the diner, the sure, nail-hard way her eyes had drilled through Nell from across the table, pinning her in place like a specimen stuck to a corkboard under glass. She remembered the unease, the sickness that the woman's presence had instilled in her, and the way she still felt herself drawn to her despite that, like a moth to flame.

"I know," Nell said.

"So, tell me, Nell Talbot: Are you asking?"

Nell let the question hang on the line between them, suspended in time. She turned her attention out of the window again, letting her gaze gambol across the scattered cars. Somewhere at the far end of the parking lot, someone popped on their headlights, catching her in their beams, illuminating her reflection in the window glass: socked-out cheeks, hair messy and knotted, mouth pulled into a thin, uneven scar.

"Yeah," Nell said, the word more breathed than spoken, barely audible against the silence. "I guess I am."

"Good," Anna said. "Where are you right now?"

"A rest stop off I-70. I think it's somewhere north of Elbert. That's in Utah," Nell said. "What about you?" Her breath fogged the glass, obscuring her ghastly reflection.

"Not far," Anna replied.

"Can we meet?"

"Nell, I'd like nothing more," Anna said. "Give me half an hour. I'll call you back."

The line went dead in Nell's ear and she pocketed her phone, then wadded up the napkin and threw it into the foot-well between her feet. She felt like an asshole for doing this to Jonah, hated lying to him, but she couldn't keep going like this.

Whatever it was that had wormed its way inside her, she'd had enough. She needed it gone, now. He would understand, maybe, eventually.

Rubbing at her face with her scratched-up hands, Nell unclasped her seatbelt and threw the car door open, then stepped unsteadily out into the parking lot, stomach still turning with nerves and the echoes of nausea. She hit the locks and kicked the door shut behind her, then hunched her shoulders up against the oncoming night and started walking, another faceless stranger hiding in the shadows of another faceless nowhere.

No one looked her way. No one saw her go. After another moment, she was gone. As if she'd never been there at all.

B *eep. Beep. Beep.*
    Jonah stood in line, listening to the limp, lifeless muzak seeping from the speakers overhead as he waited for the blister-eyed burnout behind the counter to finish ringing up his purchases: antacids, migraine pills, bottled water, a tube of honey-roasted peanuts, and Nell's cigarettes. He proffered a bland expression that the stoned cashier either didn't catch or didn't acknowledge, then turned his face toward the ceiling, drifting in and out of thought, trying to ignore the worry chewing at his insides.

He shouldn't have left her alone like that. He knew he shouldn't have, and then he'd gone and done it anyway, because some raw little part of him still wanted to trust her, despite everything he'd seen, everything they'd done. Whatever was going on with her, she was still her, wasn't she? Nervously, Jonah hummed along with the muzak—some bland piano cover of an old Kenny Rogers tune—and watched people shuttle in and out through the automatic doors, exhausted and wired at the same time. They were all the same: weary, sleepless travelers, stopping off for enough caffeine and sugar to stave off highway hypnosis for a few more miles. Nobody spoke here; nobody even looked at you if they could help it. It wasn't a shock. You only stopped in a place like this for as long as it took you to not die. Still, there was something in their exhausted expressions and the slack way their faces hung off their skulls like cheap Halloween masks that Jonah recognized, a unique desperation that wasn't unfamiliar to him. Especially not after the last two days of his life. He knew exactly how shitty he looked right now. Hell, underneath his zippered-up jacket, his shirt was still filled with blood, a souvenir from Nell opening her arm back at that nowheresville gas station, but at least he wasn't the only ghoul passing through this dead spot on the map.

Wordlessly, he passed his Visa over to the burnout, signed his name on the touchpad, took his card, receipt, and plastic bag of supplies, then headed for the doors. Outside, the air blustered all around him, thin and sharp, tugging at his clothes and the bag in his hand. Stuffing his spare hand into the depths of one pocket, he crossed the street and headed down the painted lane toward the Volvo. In the distance he could hear the hiss of cars whipping by on the highway, and as he walked he felt little bursts of cold alighting on his face and neck and the backs of his hands. It was starting to rain. Probably meant things were going to ice over before too long. Shit. He hunched his shoulders and double-timed it back toward the station wagon.

Except when he got there, the Volvo was empty. Nell was nowhere to be seen.

Anxiety bored through Jonah's brain. Fumbling with the key fob, he unlocked the Volvo, then ripped the driver's-side door open to make sure, as if she was hiding in the back seat, waiting for him to get in close so she could shout GOTCHA! in his face. No such luck. She was just gone, vanished into thin air.

Okay. Breathe. She was here a second ago. You were only in the shop for what, a couple of minutes? Five at the outside? She can't have gone far, especially not on foot. Maybe she went to find a bathroom or stretch her legs or something.

It's not like she could have wandered off into the desert again.

The wheels inside Jonah's head spun uselessly as he turned in circles, looking for anyone who might have seen his sister, but there was no one around for him to ask. Fuck. *Fuck.*

He looked around the car for any sign of her, but there was nothing, just a wadded-up paper napkin on the passenger-side floor. Jonah searched his memory—had that been there before? Or was it new? Stooping down, he plucked the napkin from the floormat and uncrumpled it, holding it close to the yellow dome light to read. There was a phone number written on it, with a note jotted above.

Anna. Call me when you need help.

Oh Christ, what the fuck had Nell done?

Shoving his stress all the way down, Jonah fetched the 48 Coffin knife from the glovebox and the empty sawed-off from where they'd stashed it underneath the passenger seat. Shells or no shells, he'd rather have a card to play if—*when*—shit went sideways again. The folder went into his pocket and the shotgun, as discreetly as Jonah could manage, into the waistband of his jeans at the small of his back. Once he was sure that it wasn't going to fall out, he let his jacket fall loosely over it, obscuring it from view.

Standing up straight again, Jonah set his jaw and went looking for his sister.

S he watched the sun set over the hills, slowly drifting below the sawtooth horizon, staining the clouds purple and orange and red, casting the whole of the sky into a bruised-fruit gouache. Climbing the little foothill of coal-dark scree at the end of the service road behind the rest stop, Nell sat and quietly watched the world below, the distant rest stop and the squat freestanding garage at the bottom of the slope. It all seemed so small from up here. She lay back on the rocks, wishing she had a cigarette to help calm her frayed nerves. She'd nearly jumped out of her skin when Anna called her back. Some part of her hadn't really expected her to. Their second phone conversation hadn't been a long one, just enough for Nell to know that she was close by.

It wasn't that bad back here, away from the roads and lights and people. It was quiet, and it was calm. Nell hadn't often been calm in her life, and she sure as hell hadn't ever been great at being quiet; but in this moment, actually having a chance to catch her breath alone was a luxury. The last thing she needed right now was to keep languishing under the shadow of all of her brother's fucking anxieties. She had more than enough of her own.

Nell wasn't a fool; she'd known this trip was going to be hard. She'd known from the moment he'd asked her to come along, and she'd still said yes. Shit, she'd practically jumped at the chance. After all, even if everything between her and Jonah was still as screwed up as ever, they could still rebuild, couldn't they? That was why he'd asked, she was sure of it. So why not try, after so many years of not? They used to be so close, back before her brother had fled Albuquerque like the place was on fire. Jonah had been her best friend for a lot of years before that.

She didn't think it was wrong to want some part of it back in her life. Was it?

Time passed, and Nell lay there, staring up at the sky, watching night coast slowly across its dome as raindrops pattered on her face, enfolding herself in the merciful quiet, pure and true. And then, out of nowhere, it wasn't quiet anymore. She could hear tires on dirt, getting louder. Sitting up from the rock slope, Nell saw headlights rolling down the narrow little road, Anna's car behind them slowing to a stop at the dead end, idling in the cold. A second later, the beams went dark, leaving only the faint glow of the sky and the rest-stop lights to push back the gathering shadows. As Nell made her way back down the hill, digging her heels into the loose macadam, she felt her phone vibrate in her pocket again. She checked the screen: *Jonah. 5 missed calls.*

Sorry, little brother. Nell didn't have time to talk right now.

She was here. It was time.

At the bottom of the hill, Nell brushed the dust from her arms and legs and paced slowly over to the idling car, watching the dark windshield from underneath a furrowed brow. As she approached, the engine cut and the driver's-side door swung open to let Anna emerge, as tall and muscular as Nell remembered, wrapped in a long, form-fitting coat that hung down to her knees. Throwing the door shut behind her, the woman stepped around the car, beaming. Something about her made the scabbed-over furrows in Nell's forearm throb something terrible.

"You called," Anna said.

"I did."

"I'm glad," Anna told her. "I can't imagine how scared you must be right now. Scared and confused."

"Yeah," said Nell. "I guess."

Anna cocked her head to the side, studying her face, her frame.

"You really have no idea what's happening to you, do you?"

Nell shook her head. "That's why I called you."

"I understand. Come on," Anna said, glancing over at the stooped little building on the side of the service road. "Let's get out of this rain."

She led her across the dirt path to the side door of the little freestanding garage, confidently pulling it open as if she'd known the whole time it would be unlocked. They stepped through together. Blindly, Nell searched the inside wall for the switch and threw it with a hard plastic click. A second later, two tracks of fluorescent lights sputtered to life overhead, casting the room in a pale greenish hue. Crossing the little space in a few sure strides, Nell stepped into the glow and leaned against the far wall as she watched Anna pace through the shadows, dragging a pair of rickety old folding chairs into the long blur of light, the metal grinding loudly against the concrete floor.

She gestured for Nell to sit. Nell sat.

"So are you going to tell me what's happening to me or not?" Nell asked, keeping her hands tight in her pockets.

Taking the seat across from her, Anna held up her hands, nodded. Nell watched the woman, the way she moved, the square brace of her shoulders, the strange way her eyes seemed to flicker and flash without moving. Resting her elbows on her knees, Anna leaned in close, so close that Nell probably could have stolen a kiss from her if she'd really wanted to.

"Do you remember before, at the diner?" Anna asked, keeping her voice low. "I asked you if you believed in God. Do you remember what you said?"

"I called you fucking crazy," Nell replied.

Anna nodded. "You didn't answer the question, though."

There was something about the way Anna was looking at her that Nell didn't like, something that made her skin prickle and buzz. Outside, lightning ripped across the sky in a bright blue-white flash. Anna prodded at her with an encouraging expression. It was almost patronizing. Nell blew air through her nostrils and ran a hand through her hair.

"I mean, what do you want me to say? Either God's a ghost

story that freaks like you tell themselves to not feel so fucking alone in the universe, or he actually exists, and he's the prick who took my mom away from me when I was a kid. Either way it sucks, so generally, I try not to think about it."

Anna didn't move. Didn't blink. "That's a shame," she said.

"No, that's a matter of opinion, and I don't give a fuck about yours," Nell fired back automatically, then immediately felt bad. Anna had come here to help. There was no reason to be a dick to her. "Alright, look, I've always wanted to—tried to—believe in something bigger than myself, okay? Even after my mom, even after . . ." she trailed off. "Call it humanity, the common good, whatever. Because it's better to believe in something rather than nothing. Nihilists are all assholes anyway. But the idea of God, at least the way you're talking about it? That's a leap of faith that I can't take. Never could. I've never seen anything, lived through anything, that makes me think that there's more to existence than this."

"Until now."

Nell watched Anna through the dark as her heart rolled in her chest.

"Yeah," she said. "Until now."

"What do you know about what happened to you, when you lost time?"

"Not much. There was this place, out in the desert," Nell said, recalling Jonah's story. "There was a hole in the ground, leading down into these caves, a whole network of them, buried deep in the earth. Jonah—that's my brother—found me passed out down there. Said he heard something moving in the dark. He carried me out, took care of me the best he could. Then, this morning, I woke up feeling great. Better than I have in probably a couple of years."

Anna rested a reassuring hand on Nell's knee. "Of course you did. It makes sense, if you know how to read it. The longer you feel good, the longer it takes you to see that something's wrong. Exactly how it wants it."

"That's the second time you've said that," Nell said. "'It.'

You said the same thing back at the diner, when I told you about the dead spot in my memory. You said that I don't remember because *it* doesn't want me to."

Anna's expression hardened. "I did."

"So? You going to tell me what the hell is taking up all this space in my head or not?" Nell demanded. "Because whatever it is, it's getting worse. Every time I try to sleep, I'm getting these fucked-up dreams, like—"

"Dreams of a dead world," Anna said. "Dreams of a blood-red sky."

The gears in Nell's brain seized up when Anna said it, the drive chain blown apart and flung away in a hundred different broken pieces. She leered at the tattooed woman, momentarily frozen, all thoughts instantaneously banished from her head.

"How. . . ?"

Anna took one of Nell's hands in both of her own and squeezed. At first there was nothing, and then—

Beneath the empty red sky, the tornado screamed and thrashed above her, around her, through her, and as she stared into its churning depths, she began to see faces trapped inside its winds, gaunt and dying and already dead, faces with three eyes, four eyes, more. Faces that were all mouth, leering, sight-less maws filled with cracked yellow-black teeth. Faces that had been gashed and gored to tatters, the bone visible underneath the ripped skin. On the ground, long strips of torn, burned flesh sat heaped around Nell's legs, all the way up to her knees. She could feel the blood from the loose meat seeping into the fabric of her pants, cold and creeping against her skin. The stench of it was terrible, like raw chicken that had long gone to rot. She gagged and turned away as the storm raged above her, scream-ing and wailing with orgasmic cries of joy, uncontrollable sob-bing, and giddy, wild laughter. She reached a hand out to it, meaning to plunge her arm deep into its heart—

Nell snatched her hand away from Anna's with a start, trying to catch her breath as her heart boomed inside her chest.

"What the fuck," she gasped. "What the actual *fuck*."

Crossing her arms over her chest as tears streamed down

her face, she held herself until the vision had faded away entirely. Nausea ground at her insides like a pestle, turning her stomach into a wet paper bag filled with broken glass.

"You're not the only one who can see under the world," Anna said.

"What the fuck," Nell wheezed again. "What does that mean? What did you just do to me? What did you just show me?"

Still in the folding chair opposite her, Anna blinked and leaned forward, her face somber.

"Nothing you haven't seen already. Those dreams you've been having? They're not really dreams. You're just seeing through different eyes. See, reality isn't just one thing, Nell. It's more like an onion. Layers wrapped around layers wrapped around layers. Most people only ever see this one, but that's not always the case. Every so often, something will worm its way in from somewhere else, looking for someone to latch onto, and them that get infected, get taken? Sometimes they end up seeing through the layers too."

Nell's lungs bristled. "Wait, *infected*? What the fuck are you talking about? What do I have inside me?"

Anna gave her a wary look.

"It's like a parasite," she said. "It's old too. Far older than any of us. Primordial, I guess, is the word. It, and the things like it, have been around since the beginning of time, ever since the first light at the dawn of creation. They weren't always like this, but now... They're like poison, Nell. They get inside and they corrupt everything they touch."

Nell felt as if the ground were crumbling out from beneath her feet.

"You're talking about demons," she said, feeling something horrid pop loose in the deepest pit of her heart. "You're saying I'm fucking possessed."

Biting her lower lip, Anna met her eyes in the uneven light, and Nell could see confirmation glittering there.

"I'm sorry," Anna said, her voice soft and gentle. "I know this can't be easy to hear."

"No, it's not hard to hear, it's batshit fucking crazy," Nell said.

Anna raised her hands, palms upturned. "Look, I don't know what you've been through, exactly; but I'm sure some part of you knows that what I'm saying is true."

"I don't," Nell lied. "It's not. There's no such thing."

"It's called Murmur," Anna said, ignoring Nell's weak denials. "It's one of the oldest. Usually these things are small, remnants of their former selves, just candles flickering in the dark. But this?"—she reached over and tapped a fingertip against Nell's breastbone—"this is the sun going supernova. I've never encountered anything like it. No one has. Not for centuries. It's how I found you. It's got its own gravity. I could feel you from a hundred miles away."

"What do you mean, *feel me?*"

Anna drummed two fingers against her own temple. "These things are drawn to each other, Nell. You're not the only one sharing space."

The nervous chill in Nell's lungs spread like a blight, reaching out to flash-freeze the blood in her veins, the bones in her fingers.

"That storm I saw in the red," she said, understanding better now. "The tornado. That was you, wasn't it?"

Anna nodded. "Me, and not me."

"What does that mean? What the fuck are you?" Nell demanded.

Anna rocked her head back and forth, as if in thought. "A vessel. Like you, but not. I help people in your condition, people who wandered too far off the path and got taken."

"How?"

"Have you ever heard of something called a Sin Eater?"

Nell shook her head. "No," she said, dumbfounded.

"It's sort of a holy duty, based around a very old ritual," Anna said. "It's someone who cleanses the souls of others by taking their sins onto themselves. Turns out the rules aren't so different for people like you."

Nell's head swam as she tried to stay afloat in the ocean of crazy that this woman had thrown her into.

"So that's what you do?" she asked. "You're one of these Sin Eaters?"

"Essentially," Anna replied. "There's a whole order of us, out there in the world. We've been around for years, centuries even, doing the work that needs to be done. That storm you saw, it's made of hundreds of those things. Probably more."

"Demons, you mean."

Anna nodded. "I'm not the first one to contain it either. I'm not even the tenth. I'm just the next one in line. Me and the others like me, we spend our whole lives helping people. Cleansing people. We take their burdens onto ourselves, and we lock them away from the world, add them to our inner multi-tudes. When we retire or die, we confer our collected burdens upon the next member in line, and they'll carry them and add their own contributions. I inherited mine, same as the person who comes after me will inherit it from me and pass it on to the person who comes after them, and the person after them."

Nell watched her warily. "You're telling me that you're a prison," she said.

"It's called the Chain," Anna replied. "And there are dozens of them out in the world, carried and guarded by true believers just like me. Some of them go all the way back to the days when Christ walked the earth. He was an exorcist too, you know."

"Sure," Nell said, hanging her head. For a second, all she could hear was her own breath, all she could feel the droning pressure building in her temples. This was crazy. This was abso-lutely fucking crazy. But a part of her had to admit, she didn't think Anna was lying to her. Not really.

"So this thing inside me, you called it *Murmur*. That's its name?"

"At least as close to a name as we have for it," Anna said. "It's big, too: royalty, inasmuch as these things have royalty. But we need to get it out of you, Nell. Something that old, that powerful, it can't stay in one body for very long. Not yours, at least. If we don't get rid of it soon, it's going to start rotting you from the inside."

Nell looked up at her. ". . . What do you mean, rotting?"

Anna sighed. "Your teeth will start falling out, your hair. You could lose fingers, eyes, your nose, and that's just how it starts. I said it before, these things are poison. Can't keep it inside and expect to walk away whole."

"How long?"

Anna shook her head and blew air out through her nose.

"Hard to say. Could be days, could be hours, could be less. Like I said, this thing is so much bigger than anything else I've ever encountered. No way to tell what it's going to do to you until it happens."

Nell curled her hands around the back of her neck, pulling her head down, stretching her spine.

"What about you, though?" she asked.

"What about me?"

"This thing, this Murmur, whatever, won't it start rotting you too? If it's that nasty, I mean."

Anna's face wrinkled at the question, her practiced composure shaking just the tiniest bit.

"You let me worry about that," she said. "Right now, we need to focus on helping you before you start falling to pieces."

Suppressing a shudder, Nell blew air and felt a quiet, exhausted resignation open up inside her heart, spreading out to hold her in tranquil current.

"So, how does it work? How do you get this thing out of me?"

Reaching out once more, Anna laid a hand over Nell's heart, applying the slightest pressure. "Here, let me show you. Come on, lie down. We'll be quick."

"Right here?"

"Right here."

Rising from the folding chair, Nell lowered herself to the floor and rolled backward to lie flat on the cement, pressing her fingertips against the cold ground as Anna shucked off her long coat, baring the intricate tattoos that covered her arms and shoulders. Nell tried to make out the details in the ink, the intricate symbols and curled words etched in archaic script, but they all seemed to blur together in the sickly glare of the fluorescents overhead. A second later, Anna knelt down over her. Smiled.

"You're going to feel cold for a minute, but that's normal," she said. "Have you ever taken mushrooms?"

Nell nodded.

"Okay, well, it's a lot like being on mushrooms," Anna said. "The best thing you can do is just go with it until it's over. It won't be long. Promise."

Nell sincerely doubted this woman had ever taken psilo-cybin—or any other psychedelics—in her life, but she got her point. From her pants pocket, Anna drew a small silver tin, unscrewed the top, and dipped a thumb in. The pad came away stained black, black as oil, black as night and death and the wind between the stars. With a flick of her wrist, Anna dragged the ink over Nell's forehead, drawing a shape that Nell couldn't trace.

Before her heart could beat again, a sharp, dreadful cold began to course through her body, making the chill she'd felt only minutes before seem like a soft summer wind in compari-son. This was true cold, an agonizing, incomprehensible freeze that spread in oily tendrils throughout her anatomy, freezing her in place. A second later, Nell found herself unable to move, unable to speak, unable to blink, paralyzed by that black ink Anna had thumbed into her skin.

"There," Anna said, clicking the tin shut and pocketing it again. "That's better."

From the folds of her discarded coat, Anna pulled a small wooden box that reminded Nell of a tiny little coffin, with a golden cross embossed on the top. Hinging it open, she drew from it a straight razor with a dark cherry handle, the deep red wood inlaid with intricate gold filigree, the pattern strikingly similar to the tattoos on her arms. She twirled the razor nim-bly in her fingertips, then touched the flat of it to her forehead and closed her eyes, whispering a prayer that Nell couldn't hear above the loudening hiss of the rain against the garage rooftop.

That was when Nell understood what was about to hap-pen to her.

She'd fucked up. She'd fucked up so bad.

In the silence that had descended around them, Nell could hear her heart beating wildly inside her chest, growing louder and faster by the second. She wanted to break free, wanted to get away from this crazy bitch, but something stilled the fight inside her, something deep and old, made of broken glass and twisted metal, hungry and desperate and coiled around her heart. It wanted her to stay, let it happen, let the razor take it all away, just to see what came next. Maybe it would be different this time around.

Outside, lightning struck again, closer now, the white-blue flash illuminating the steel in Anna's fingers, a flat, joyless grin floating in the dark.

"It'll only hurt for a second," Anna whispered as she lowered the blade to Nell's exposed throat, hard and bright and sharp as life. Nell felt the edge bite lightly into her skin, drawing a single red bead that went rolling down her neck. "Then you'll be free."

Nell felt an endless yawning void open up inside her belly. She'd brought this on herself. She'd called Anna here, she'd sat there listening to her bullshit like an awestruck child, instead of running the fuck away like she should've. She tried to scream, tried to fight against the knifelike cold that had threaded itself through her body, anchoring her in place, but it was useless. She was helpless. The only noise that came warbling out of the pit of her throat as she strained against her own inability was a pathetic little whine, like something from a kicked dog.

"It's okay," Anna said, her voice soft and gentle. "It's going to be okay."

Nell saw the woman's shoulder tense. This was it. She was going to die.

Lightning struck again. A tall, reedy shadow rose up behind Anna and pressed the muzzle of a sawed-off shotgun to the back of her head.

"Step. The fuck. Away from my sister," Jonah said, his voice hard and unwavering. "Now."

Jonah
Interstate 70, UT
649 miles to Albuquerque

The woman—*Anna*, Jonah assumed from the note he'd found—stood slowly, keeping her hands high, her elbows bent at perfect ninety-degree angles. He kept the empty shotgun trained on the back of her skull, trying to calm the tremors that shook his hands. It was a decent bluff, but it was still a bluff, and if she, with those cabled arms of hers, clocked it, Jonah would be in for a world of hurt. They all would. He was already running on fumes. He wasn't sure he had another fight in him today. Maybe not ever.

"You're making a mistake here," the woman said as she turned to face him, her voice perfectly pleasant. "This is all a misunderstanding."

"Yeah, that's why you were holding a razor to my sister's throat," Jonah said. "A misunderstanding. Put it down."

Anna didn't move.

"Now," he demanded.

Her expression darkened; moving very slowly, she folded the razor's blade back into its filigreed handle, then bent to set it down on the cement at her feet.

"Kick it over there," Jonah commanded, jerking his head toward the other side of the garage. Silently, the woman put one shoe atop the fancy blade and kicked it away, into the dark.

"Good. Now back up. All the way, until your heels hit the wall."

"You don't have to do this," Anna said.

"Would you please, *please* shut the fuck up," Jonah implored.

Glaring at him, she stepped away from Nell and backed up until she was standing against the far wall, hands still raised. Jonah kept the gun on her.

178

"If you move, I swear to god, I will cut you in half," he said.

It was another bluff, but even Jonah had to admit it sounded pretty convincing. Cutthroat razor or not, he had to assume that whoever this woman was, she didn't have a lot of experience looking down the barrel of a gun.

Turning his attention toward Nell, Jonah stooped down to help her up off the ground. Underneath a deep black stain that had been painted onto her forehead, his sister's eyes were brilliant white in the dark, wide with terror. Getting his free arm all the way under Nell's armpits, he lifted her to her feet, and together they started to back away, toward the door and the clamorous rainstorm outside.

"You're making a mistake," Anna said from the far side of the room.

"Yeah, you already said that," Jonah muttered as he dragged Nell toward the open door. Why wasn't she moving? What the hell had this woman done to her?

"Your sister is sick," Anna said. "She's got something inside her that you can't even comprehend, let alone fix."

"And what? You can?"

"That's the idea."

"Find someone else," Jonah said, taking another step backward, then another. He could almost feel the rain on his back now. "Find anyone else."

"She told me about her blackout," the woman called after him. "About the desert and the caves. How you brought her back. You saved her once already. You can help me do it again. Just put her down and let me do my job."

"And let you kill her, you mean. Let you cut her throat."

"Better that than being ripped apart from the inside. I've seen what happens when you wait too long with this kind of thing. It's not pretty."

Jonah tightened his grip on Nell and on the gun. "How many times do I need to tell you that I don't give a shit?"

"She's already having the dreams, seeing further than she should. This is very, very bad, and it's going to keep getting worse unless you let me do what I came here to do."

Jonah faltered. Dreams? What dreams? Nell hadn't told him about any dreams. But now wasn't the time to dwell on it. Across the garage, Anna dropped her arms and took a step forward, her shoulders square, hands bunched into fists at her sides.

"Stop, okay? Just stop," Jonah pleaded, gesturing insistently with the gun. "Please stop giving me reasons to shoot you," he said.

Anna stopped. "This is bigger than me. Bigger than you. Bigger than all of us," she said. "Your sister is changing in ways you can't possibly comprehend. You are tap-dancing on a nuclear warhead. This won't end until I end it. I'm the only one who can."

Jonah leveled the muzzle of the shotgun so it sat even with Anna's face, daring her to move again. She stayed in place. Jonah's heart felt like it was going to explode. Nell was so heavy in his arm. He kept inching toward the door.

"You think you're stopping this by running, by getting in my way, but you can't. There's no stopping the inevitable, Jonah. This is going to happen, one way or another. You're only dragging things out. You're only making things worse," Anna said.

She was trying to rattle him by showing him that she knew his name. Jonah swallowed and kept looking straight ahead, refusing to let her see how well it was working.

"I think I'll be the judge of that," he said, and kicked the door open with his heel.

"And who do you think will be the judge of you?"

Jonah looked at her down the barrel of his stolen gun and thought about saying something—anything—else, but decided against it. Whoever, whatever the hell she was, he was done talking to her. Either she was stalling or she really believed the crazy shit that was coming out of her mouth. Worse, maybe both. Without another word, Jonah dragged Nell out of the shady little garage and back into the freezing rain.

Together, they limped through the downpour, past the busted old Chevrolet that sat parked outside the garage. Jonah figured it was Anna's. Leaning Nell up against the car's bumper, he slipped the folding knife from his jacket pocket, then knelt down beside the back wheel and buried the blade deep in the tire, dragging open a long, crooked gash that gasped and wheezed as air rushed from the rubber. Moving up the side of the car, he did the same to the front tire, then threw the knife off into the sallow grass. Good fucking riddance. He pulled Nell away from the Chevy with his free arm, clutching the shotgun in his other hand, keeping his eyes on the doorway and the darkness that lay motionless and dangerous beyond. He knew Anna was still watching them from the shadows, could feel her crazy, burning stare trying to punch holes through his face.

In his arm, Nell gasped. He looked at her: across her forehead, the ink was melting away in the rain, streaming down her brow and nose in runny black lines. Leaning against him, Nell blinked and shuddered, her movements jerky and awkward, as if she'd been asleep for days and forgotten how to move her body. As gently as he could, Jonah pulled her down the shadowy little service road, back toward the rest stop and the station wagon and anywhere but here.

K neeling in the mud as the waning storm pelted her back with raindrops, Anna slowly cranked the last lug nut free from the rim, dropping it next to the others. She tossed the wrench beside it. With filthy hands, she pulled the slashed tire from the hub and rolled it off to the side, then hefted the spare into its place and started to bolt it down. She didn't yet know what she was going to do about the other flat, but that was fine. Focus on the task at hand, then move on to the next. Just like Dad had taught her.

She didn't have time to be furious with the Talbots. She didn't have time to think about how close she'd come. She didn't have time to think about how much she hated Nell's brother for snatching her away like that. She'd have plenty of time to think about all that once she got back on the road. She just had to get back on the road first.

The rain died down a little bit more, and as it did, Anna heard heavy footsteps on the gravel behind her.

Her first thought was that Jonah Talbot had come back to finish the job with that shotgun of his. But when she turned to look, she saw two men standing there, one tall and rail-thin with a white goatee that used to be blond, the other shorter , wearing wire-frame glasses balanced above a pair of deep, bloody gashes that traveled the length of one cheek. Even through the dark and the rain, she could tell that the two of them were in a bad way; but if they were out here thinking she was easy pickings, they were in for a sorry surprise. She'd dealt with harder men than these two before, and in far greater numbers. Anna turned to face the men head on, rolling the fingers on both hands into tight fists, ready to put both of these fools down at the first sign of trouble.

"Help you?"

"We were going to ask you that," the older one said. His voice was deep and harsh to match the cuts and bruises that decorated his face. "Looks like you've got a little bit of car trouble here."

"Nothing I can't handle, thanks," Anna said, staring him down.

The guy glanced around, then over to the empty little garage. "Uh-huh," he said, stepping in closer and studying her face. Anna tensed and slid one foot back, dropping her shoulder. All the old man had to do was take one more step, and *pop-pop-pop-pop*, she'd hammer his nose flat before he could take another breath. He wouldn't even know what had hit him before he hit the ground.

The old guy's eyes twinkled. "Wait," he said. "I know you."

"You don't know me," Anna replied.

He nodded. "Yeah, I do. I saw you. You passed us by before, outside of Mowry."

Right. Anna remembered now. She'd seen these guys on the side of the road, broken down and bloodied beside the wreckage of their bikes. Crap.

"There were three of you," she recalled. "Where's your buddy?"

"Watching the van," the old guy said.

Anna nodded to the old guy's friend, who was busy stalking around the perimeter of her car, making like he was inspecting it. "What about him? He talk?"

"Only if he's got something to say."

"Charming. What brings you guys out here, anyway?"

The old guy held his hands out to the sides and spread his fingers wide.

"Looking for someone," he said. "Not you. Someone else."

"I'm glad to hear that," Anna replied. "But I'm still going to need you to back up. Now, I said."

Anna stood her ground until the old guy took a step back, then another. On the other side of the car, the guy with the glasses knelt down at the edge of the dirt road and plunged a hand into the pale grass. He pulled something free of the scrub and held it up to examine in the moonlight. Short and drab, it looked to Anna like it might've been a folding knife. Probably what Jonah had used to slash her tires.

"Terry," the other guy said, his voice accented. The old man turned back to look, his expression tightening when he saw what was in his friend's hand.

Closing her fingers around the straight razor inside her coat pocket, Anna forced herself to keep still, staying ready in case this all went to hell. She wasn't supposed to use the blade for that kind of thing, but she supposed that if it came to that, the Lord would forgive her.

"How long ago were they here?" he demanded, turning back to her. "The Talbot bitch and her brother. How long?!"

Anna felt something unclench inside of her heart.

The rain was letting up.

Part Three

THE DAMNED

Jonah
Elbert, UT
495 miles to Albuquerque

T hey rolled into the sparse little burg long after the dashboard clock hit midnight, white headlight beams illuminating the town-limit sign in stark green and white:

Welcome to
Elbert, Utah
Population 3,853

Jonah kept his fists tight on the wheel. In the back seat,
Nell had slowly unfolded from herself as her faculties had
returned to her, whatever freak paralysis she'd fallen under lift-
ing little bit by little bit until she was finally able to roll onto
her side and weep quietly to herself. Jonah felt awful about
what had happened to her, felt even worse for ever being angry
with her for wandering off from the rest stop. She didn't need
him piling more shit on top of her right now. After she'd gotten
back to her body, he'd tried to talk to her, reassure her maybe,
tell her that it was all going to be okay, but the words had come
out all wrong, sounding like the obvious lies that they were.
The truth was, Jonah wasn't sure that anything was going to be
okay. Not anymore.

Navigating the darkened streets, Jonah let his eyes dance
across the landscape of the roadside hamlet, its buildings and
alleys and gas stations. There weren't any cars out tonight, and
no lights on in any of the building windows. He'd expected a
tiny little town like this out in the far reaches of·Utah to be
quiet, especially this late, but he hadn't expected it to be like
this. This wasn't just *quiet*, this was *desolate*. Elbert seemed
empty, abandoned, dead. Pripyat south of I-70, harrowed out by
disaster or flight or both. He imagined piles of corpses stacked up

187

in musty, darkened buildings, abandoned to molder and putrefy behind black glass and locked doors, long forgotten by whatever strange cruelty had done the killing.

He shook his head, derailing the train of thought. He was exhausted, and this wasn't San Francisco. It wasn't even Albuquerque. Places like this, life ground to a full stop at about eight thirty and didn't start back up again until seven the next morning. Their fault for showing up late. He rounded another corner, watching the Volvo's headlights climb a tall old red brick building with its glory days well behind it, the words BOTH-WELL PROVISIONS etched along its broadside in fading white paint.

Jonah urged the station wagon down another handful of blocks to the Wayfarer Motor Inn and came to an unsteady halt in its parking lot. He cut the engine and thumbed on the dome light, then turned back to look at Nell. She was asleep again, her eyes dancing back and forth underneath lids as dark as bruises. On her throat, he could still make out the little red lambda where Anna had pressed the corner of her razor into Nell's flesh. He almost didn't want to wake her up, but he knew he couldn't leave her here either.

He turned around to face front, resting his hand on the empty sawed-off as he considered the little two-story motel, same as every other Jonah had seen in his life. As soon as Nell had drifted off, Jonah had called ahead to the Wayfarer, hoping to avoid another awkward run-in with another poor shithead who was just trying to do their job. It had taken a little convincing, but the front desk clerk had graciously, if confusedly, agreed to leave the key under the doormat of their room. Second floor, number 227. Now all he had to do was get the both of them up there. He killed the light and tucked the shotgun into his coat, right under his arm, then threw his door open and went to the back door to roust his sister.

"Hey," he said. "Hey, Nellie, we're here." He gave her shoulder a gentle squeeze.

Slowly, she awoke and twisted to look at him, her gaze puffy and bloodshot.

"We're where? Home?"

"Motel," Jonah said, feeling a pang of regret at having to admit it. "Sorry. Figured we should crash out here for the night, try and get some rest. We'll head home tomorrow. We had the reservation anyway, so."

"Oh. Okay." Her tone was flat and uninflected. "Are you tired?"

"I could use a stop, yeah," he said. It wasn't a lie, but it wasn't the whole truth either. Of course he was tired, probably more so than he'd ever been in his entire life, but he knew for damn sure that sleep wasn't going to be coming to him any time soon. He was too wired, too scared, the adrenaline pumping through his veins too painfully fresh. He felt like a raw nerve walking upright. "How about you? You think you're ready to sleep in a real bed?"

Nell laced her fingers together between her knees. "I guess," she said. "Sure."

Jonah held a hand out to his sister and she took it. Her palm was cold and clammy. Leading her out of the car, he kicked the door shut and walked her across the parking lot, up the concrete stairs, and around the corner to room 227. He peeled the doormat back with the toe of his shoe, revealing the key, just like the front desk attendant had promised. He knelt and picked it up, then slid it into the lock on the door, letting Nell go in first. The room wasn't much to look at, a standard double-queen with floral patterns on the comforters and bad art hung on the walls, but it was clean, and the door would lock. That was pretty much all Jonah cared about right now.

He watched his sister drift over to the far bed, wearing a harrowed expression. Standing in the doorway, Jonah jerked a thumb over his shoulder, back toward the parking lot.

"I'm going to go get the bags, okay?"

Nell nodded, but she didn't look up.

"You going to be okay in here by yourself?"

She didn't move. "Yeah. I guess."

"You sure? I mean, if you need anything—"

"Jonah, I said I'm fine," Nell sighed, turning her blank gaze toward him. "Promise."

Jonah watched her, studying her face, then nodded in

assent. "Okay. I know. Okay. Just stay here. Please. I'll be right back."

"Yep."

He let the door swing shut. Down in the parking lot, he pulled Nell's suitcase out of the Volvo's hatchback first, then his own. Clapping it shut again, he locked the station wagon with the remote and made for the stairs. Behind him, he heard a scrape of feet on asphalt. Then he heard it again, closer this time.

Scuff, scuff.

Jonah tensed, his shoulders knotting themselves Kevlar-tight. He didn't believe it. There was no way those 48 Coffin assholes could have possibly caught up to them this fast. Same thing with that tattooed woman, Anna—zero chance she could have closed the distance with a pair of gutted tires. Maybe someone else, then—someone sleeping rough or some local tweaker looking to bankroll his next fix. Fuck. Jonah took his hands off the luggage and cracked his knuckles. Then he heard the voice, rough and grave-dry.

"See something you like, fuckface?"

All the air went out of him in a rush. He turned around slowly to look at the dead kid, now standing only a few feet away from him. He hadn't gotten any better since Jonah had last seen him at the bar—*Had that only been yesterday? Jesus god*—if anything, he was worse now. The deep purple wounds that had been beaten and kicked into his hide had darkened considerably, and the skin around his face was peeling away in rags; both of his hands sported torn, red stumps where fingers should have been. Above a crumpled, flattened nose, the kid's one good eye still bulged bloodshot and swollen in its socket, while its cataracted opposite had burst into clotted pulp at some point, leaving a gaping hole in its place, obscene.

The kid's clothes were shredded and tattered by years of rot and neglect, but Jonah could still make out the vibe he'd been going for. It was your basic shit-fuck Nazi chic, complete with a skinhead shave and a pair of shitty stick-and-poke swastikas on the backs of his ravaged hands, just below the cuffs of his crumbling leather jacket.

"*See something you like, fuckface?*" the kid asked again.

"You're not here, Alex," Jonah said. "You're dead. So just fuck off already. Please."

The kid took a step closer, then another, dragging himself forward on a broken leg that gushed black blood as he closed the distance between them. The scraping sound of his shambling gait atop the asphalt grew louder and louder, to the point that Jonah was sure it would wake the whole town—then Jonah blinked, and Alex was gone again.

Shaking off the weird, nervous chill that had settled between his shoulder blades, Jonah took the luggage and headed toward the motel room. But standing at the top of the stairs, he paused and looked back, and realized he could still see the dark stains on the ground where the dead boy had been standing.

Locking the door behind him, Jonah wheeled the luggage over to the far side of the room, underneath the big picture-frame mirror that hung on the wall next to the TV cabinet. He could feel Nell watching him from the second bed.

"...What?" he asked.

"It's nothing. Just, you look like...you know what, forget it." She scrunched her face up and ground the heels of her palms against her temples. "Nevermind. I'm fried. Don't listen to me."

"It's fine," Jonah said, convincing nobody at all. "Think I'm gonna go take a shower, try and wash off all the misery and fucking horror."

"Good luck with that."

Jonah inclined his head toward the bathroom door. "You want to go first?"

"No, I'm good. Thanks. Gonna post up here till you're done, maybe raid the minibar."

"All right," he said. "I'll be right in there if whatever, okay?"

She nodded.

Excusing himself to the bathroom, Jonah closed the door and flipped on the overhead lights, then went over to the little frosted-glass shower stall. He pulled the door open and threw the faucet on full blast, cranking the heat higher and higher until steam began to climb the mirror above the sink. Stripping off his shirt, he examined his wounds in the foggy glass: bruises arcing up and down his ribs, raw red stretches where his skin had abraded against asphalt, cuts and splits and scabs hammered into him from ringed knuckles and he didn't know what else. He looked like he'd been dragged over a hundred miles of Hell and left to rot in the sun for days. He couldn't remember a time when he'd looked worse than this.

Shucking off his socks, pants, and underwear, he stepped into the shower, letting the scorching water sizzle deep into his skin as he shut his eyes and laid his hands flat on the cool glass, letting the spray zero out everything beyond its bounds. He tried to think about nothing, but it was no good. The nervous, uneasy jitter that had settled inside his brain was too loud for him to ignore anymore.

His shoulders hurt, his arms hurt, his back and his neck and his knees all hurt. Everything hurt. His whole life hurt. Biting down into the back of his hand so hard that he thought he might draw blood, Jonah started to cry silently as the water rolled across his narrow shoulders and down his back. He was so tired. He was so done. He missed his home, he missed Molly, he missed how everything used to be. He hadn't asked for any of this. The road trip was just the sprinkles on the shit sundae that his life had turned into. He would have given anything to put everything back how it used to be—the life he'd chosen, the life he'd tried to build, instead of the one he'd gotten stuck with. He would have given it all away to have Molly tell him that everything was going to be okay right now.

God, he missed her so much.

The divorce would have been easier to cope with if there'd been somewhere to lay blame, something—or someone—to pin it all on, but there was nothing like that. Jonah had never shouted at her, never insulted her; Molly had never thrown things or cheated on him or accused him of doing the same. There was no drama to it, no grand *why* to it all. They didn't fight, they didn't argue, not ever, not even when things between them were at their worst. The things that had kept them together just didn't hold the way they used to. The glue had dried and crumbled all away.

Looking back at it now, Jonah figured that maybe fighting would have been better, even if it had ended up sending them to couples counseling or something. Fighting at least meant that you were all the way into something, up to your neck in it, nearly drowning in it. Even if it was fucked up, fighting at least showed that you cared enough to want stuff to be better. But neither of them had ever been willing to throw themselves all the way into the deep end of love. They'd stayed in the shallows together, thinking it was enough to splash around, pretending that atrophy didn't kill, telling themselves that it was fine. Everything was fine.

Months later, years later, here they were.

Here he was.

Just in time for everything else to go straight to hell.

He blamed himself, naturally. After all, he'd been the one to drag Nell along on this fucked-up nightmare trip. None of this would have happened if not for him. Nell wouldn't have wandered off, gotten hurt, lost, attacked. They wouldn't have spent the last two days getting the shit kicked out of them, again and again and again. Blaming Nell for any of it was just a convenient excuse. Nell and all her bullshit in Broughton were just symptoms. Things had gone wrong because of him, and only him. He was sure of that now more than ever.

He'd done a decent job all those years, pretending like he'd made peace with the worst side of himself, outgrew it somehow, threw it away and left it behind, but that was all it had ever been: pretend. He hadn't made peace with anything; he wasn't over anything. He'd just bottled a critical part of himself up and left it to ferment until it was ready to explode. And explode it did.

It was who he was, who he'd been all along. When push came to shove, he couldn't not wreak havoc. Couldn't not do damage. He and his sister had that in common.

Jonah stood like that under the water for what felt like a very long time, sobbing softly into the crook of his arm until the

tears and hitching breaths slowly subsided, washed away with
the grime and sweat and blood. Like they'd never been there at
all.

Opening his eyes, he saw a flicker of movement just outside the shower stall, blurry in the frosted glass, a pale smear
darting out of sight. His first thought was that his sister had let
herself into the bathroom. Maybe she needed water from the
faucet or something.

"Hey, Nell? You in here?" he called over the hiss of the
shower. "Nell, that you?"

Nobody replied. He turned underneath the hot water,
peering at the glass, watching for any more movement, but
there was none. He was alone. He must have imagined it.

That was when he saw the glass moving.

It wasn't much at first, a gentle little ripple rolling across
the frosted surface like a breeze-blown wave over the face of a
lake. *What the fuck?* Jonah leaned in, hunching his neck as he
watched the glass warp and twist in place, bowing and deform-
ing more with each passing second. It was hypnotic, almost
beautiful. For a second, he didn't even think that anything was
wrong, didn't remember that glass wasn't supposed to act like
that.

He ran a hand over its surface, wiping away the fog. Under
his fingertips, the glass felt warm and soft, not like glass at all—
more like skin, nearly alive. His mind recoiled at the sensation,
screaming wildly for him to pull his hand away, but he stayed
still, pressing down deeper and deeper, feeling the glass pulsate
and tremble under his fingertips. In its shiny surface he could just
make out his own reflection... except it wasn't his face looking
back at him. Jonah had never seen a face like that before. It was
too angular, too pale, too *inhuman*, a wide, torn mouth above
the blade of its jaw, studded with dozens—hundreds—of filthy
yellow teeth, all cracked and jagged.

"...what...?"

Then the shower exploded.

The sound was enormous, a great, catastrophic CRASH!
that filled the little bathroom as all the glass in the stall burst at
once, catching Jonah's bare body in a swarm of knives. Flinch-

ing away with nowhere to go, Jonah bolted upright, spraying blood in all directions. He stumbled back and felt his feet start to go out from under him in the wet.

No, shit, fuck, don't—!

Whipping a hand out, he caught the shower door in a slippery grip and held on for dear life, his fingers bone-white against the brassy frame as he tried to keep himself from plunging into the broken glass. His shoulder—already sore—strained and screamed against the sudden movement; ignoring the pain, he hauled himself back upright once more, balanced gingerly on the balls of his feet.

Jonah tried not to move as the hot water washed across the fresh cuts in his skin. Blood poured down his body in pale red threads. For a second, everything was quiet. Then all he could hear was the hissing of the showerhead and his own terrified screams.

N | ell kept her eyes on the picture-frame mirror, examining the shitty little motel room in reverse as Jonah slunk into the bathroom: a TV in a cabinet against the far wall, two beds separated by a bedside table, a clock radio from 1986 sitting underneath the wall-mounted reading lamp next to a pad of paper and a ballpoint pen, both branded with the motel's logo.

When she heard the latch on the bathroom door click shut, she climbed off the bed and went to the mirror to study herself, her face, the outline of her body, all the parts of her that made her *her*, searching for inconsistencies, aberrations, anything that she could point to as definitive, undeniable proof that something was deeply, profoundly wrong inside her. Proof that Anna wasn't just fucking with her.

Rot.

The word stuck in her head like a thorn or a notch of briar, impossible to ignore. If what Anna had said was true, if she was going to start rotting from the inside out, surely there had to be some sign of it, didn't there?

"I know you're in there," she said softly, watching her reflection. "I know you're listening. I didn't imagine you. I want to talk."

The silence persisted.

Jesus.

"Fine," she said to the mirror. "Play possum. See if I give a shit."

She went to the minibar under the TV and inspected the contents: standard juices and bottled waters, a little shelf up top filled with little mini-bottles of booze, a full six-pack of cheap beer, and a moldy sandwich wrapped in cellophane down at the bottom. Nell snatched all the little airplane bottles of liquor off the top shelf, then returned to the bed and fanned them out in front of her. The selection wasn't exactly great: mid- to bottom-shelf bourbon, rum, vodka, and tequila, two of each. No gin, though. Assholes just lost a Yelp star. She uncapped one of the vodkas first and upended the little bottle against her lips, savoring the burn as she fired it back. It tasted like a thousand bad nights spent chasing shitty decisions with shittier decisions, then rallying the next day to keep on fighting the inevitable. God, cheap booze was the fucking best. It was like drinking life itself. Nothing in the world like it. She drained the second vodka, then moved on to the bourbon. After a moment, she felt the drinks start to work their magic, uncoupling her brain from the shitty, painful reality it had been swimming in for so long now.

You don't want to talk to me, that's fine, Nell thought. *I don't need to talk to you either. Fuck you.*

She flopped back and buried her face against the crappy motel pillow, listening to the faint hiss of the shower running behind the bathroom door, going over everything Anna had told her before she'd tried to cut her throat.

Dreams of a dead world. Dreams of a blood-red sky.

You're not the only one sharing space.

It'll only hurt for a second. Then you'll be free.

She could still feel the cement against her back where she'd lain on the ground, watching Anna twirl the razor blade back and forth in her fingers. For a second, she'd really wanted her to do it, just to see what would happen. But was that *her* wanting it, or the thing inside of her? How much of her was still *her*? Where did *she* end and *it* begin?

Blindly, she swept the pen and pad from the bedside table, then sat back up and laid the paper flat on one thigh. Looking over at the mirror again, she tried to see past herself, all the way down to the thing that was hiding behind her eyes. It was in there. She knew it was. It had already tried to say hi once today, after all.

"Okay, whatever you are, you're being an asshole right now. I hope you know that."

She uncapped the pen with her teeth and wrote HELLO on the notepad, trying not to think of the same word carved messily down the inside of her arm. Her stomach twisted up in a knot, then righted itself as she traced the word with a line, then another. Her old therapist had told her once that doodling was meditative. Maybe she was on to something. Even if this thing didn't want to talk, it was better for her to try, wasn't it? She outlined the word again and again, and after a while her eyes started to drift shut as sleep filled her limbs with cement, then her lungs, her brain, her heart.

Then she heard glass break inside the bathroom, an enormous, explosive blast that slashed through the silent night around her, leaving it in shreds. She heard Jonah start to scream for his life, the kind of scream she'd never heard from him before. Nell tossed the notepad onto the mattress beside her and leaped from the bed to help her little brother. But something was wrong, something she couldn't quite place. She turned and looked back at the pad lying there on the bedcover, its pages fluttering in the gentle breeze of the air-conditioning unit. She picked it up and held it in the light to see, and for a second, she didn't understand what it was she was looking at.

The pages, blank only seconds before, now brimmed with her handwriting, the same two-word phrase, repeated over and over:

HelloNellHelloNellHelloNellHelloNellHelloNell
HelloNellHelloNellHelloNellHelloNellHelloNell
HelloNellHelloNellHelloNellHelloNellHelloNell
HelloNellHelloNellHelloNellHelloNellHelloNell
HelloNellHelloNellHelloNellHelloNellHelloNell
HelloNellHelloNellHelloNellHelloNellHelloNell
HelloNellHelloNellHelloNellHelloNellHelloNell
HelloNellHelloNellHelloNellHelloNellHelloNell
HelloNellHelloNellHelloNellHelloNellHelloNell
HelloNellHelloNellHelloNellHelloNellHelloNell
HelloNellHelloNellHelloNellHelloNellHello

A stone plummeted into the pit of her stomach, and her whole body went numb. That was her handwriting. That was her fucking handwriting. With insensate hands, she fanned the pages front to back, as if to confirm what she already knew. Page after page after page, it was more of the same. On the last sheet, there was a strange symbol scratched deep into the paper, surrounded by more *HelloNellHelloNellHello*:

Seeing it drawn there, her stomach lurched harder, threatening to empty itself on the floor. In the bathroom, Jonah screamed again, more desperate now. With one last wary look at herself in the big mirror, Nell stuffed the defaced pad in the pocket of her jacket and ran to help her brother.

They sat on the side of the tub in silence, Jonah doing his level best to stay still while Nell used the tweezers from her beauty kit to pick the glass out of his skin. One by one, she dropped the shards into the little trash can between them, little bloody needles on top of little bloody needles.

"So, it just...exploded," Nell said.

"Yeah," Jonah said, his voice craggy with exhaustion. "One second everything was fine, then the next...*pow*."

"Shit."

"Pretty much."

Nell raised her elbow high and tugged a shard free from Jonah's shoulder, then used a folded-over square of toilet paper to stanch the bleeding.

"Christ, this shit really got you good, huh?"

Jonah winced as Nell went to extract another jagged barb from his forearm. He had to give her credit, she'd found him standing knee-deep in broken glass, covering himself with bare hands as he bled into the wreckage, and she hadn't even blinked. She didn't say anything, didn't freak out or scream, nothing. She just set her jaw, tossed him the robe from the back of the door, and got to work unfucking things. She was so much like their mom in that way. Jonah forgot about that sometimes.

"Hold still," she said as she went to pick another glass thorn from his flesh, this one below his collarbone. Jonah did as he was told, gnawing on the insides of his cheeks until he tasted copper, but he didn't move, didn't make a sound. Better to let her work. After a second, he felt the tweezers *click* against something rigid inside his skin, then Nell pulled the shard free, long and hooklike and red with blood.

"Jesus, look at that nasty fucker," Nell said as she held it

200

up to the light. "You're lucky that shit didn't catch you in the throat or something. Would have been game over if it had." She tossed the glass hook into the trash, then moved up his neck to prod at the side of his face with thin fingertips.

"Okay, don't move," she said. "This one is right by your eye, and I don't want to fuck up and blind you or something."

"Glad you're so confident in your skills," Jonah said.

He stayed as still as he could as she dipped the tweezers into the wound high on his cheekbone, hunting for the burr of glass embedded there.

"Hey, can I ask you something?"

"Not like I'm going anywhere," he said. "Fire away."

"Why did you stop her?"

Jonah glanced at her. "What are you talking about?"

"Back at the rest stop. Anna. Why did you get in the way?"

Jonah resisted the urge to make a face. "You mean Anna, the woman who was half a breath away from cutting a fresh smile into your throat? Is that who you're talking about?"

"I'm just saying," Nell told him, "maybe you don't know the whole story."

Jonah gawped. "What are you talking about right now, Nell? Are you saying you wanted her to what, kill you? Is that what you're telling me?"

Nell tugged on the tweezers, sliding the glass needle out of his face. She dropped it into the bin with a *clink*.

"Forget it," she said. "I didn't say anything."

Pressing a fresh fold of tissue to his face, Jonah watched his sister in silence for a moment that seemed to last hours.

"She was going to kill you," he finally said. "I couldn't let her do that. I wouldn't."

His sister's gaze was sad and faraway. "Why not?"

For a second, he considered mentioning the crumpled note he'd found in the car, the one with the woman's name and phone number written on it. *Call me when you need help.* There was no question in his mind that Nell had done exactly that, but he still didn't know why. What kind of help had the woman offered her? Jonah was pretty sure that Nell wouldn't have called if she knew Anna was going to try and kill her, but he couldn't be positive. He wanted to ask, wanted to understand, but something told him that if he tried right now, she'd brush it off or worse, shut down completely. Looking away, he sighed.

"Because I love you, okay? I'm not going to let some crazy bitch hurt you if I can help it. I know we've had our shit over the years, but you're my sister. Nobody gets to hurt you, not if I have anything to say about it. I don't want to lose you, Nell."

She turned her attention to a shallow gash in his thigh and the spur of glass stuck inside. Easing the tweezers into the wound, she angled her bandaged arm back and forth as she tried to get a grip on the jagged barb.

"Except you already lost me once," she said. "You left, remember? Shit, you were gone basically overnight. It was like I blinked and you vanished. Poof. Not much more than a Jonah-shaped dust cloud left in your wake."

"That was different," Jonah said. "That was a long time ago. There was a ton of shit that you didn't know about."

"Doesn't matter." She jerked on the glass, firing a hot jolt of pain jumping up Jonah's leg, past his hip and into his stomach and chest. "Result's the same, isn't it?"

"Ow, goddammit. Look, what do you want me to say? That I feel bad about leaving like I did? Of course I do. But I never meant to hurt you when I did it."

"But it still happened."

She wriggled the tweezers between her fingertips, twisting the jag of glass in the wound, sending a fresh red trickle running down Jonah's bare thigh. He clenched his teeth against the pain.

"Okay, Nell, stop. Nell, please, come on, let up, that hurts."

But she didn't let up. She dug mindlessly at the wound, ripping it wider as she turned the broken glass into his leg, wrenching at it like she was trying to screw it down deeper into the meat. Blood flowed freely now. Jonah looked at his sister—her eyes had gone dull again, the lights on inside without anybody home.

Fuck.

"Nell, that's enough, come on—"

He pressed one hand against her arm, trying to push her

away, but she bore down, loosing runnels of blood down his thigh. The pain was awful. Without thinking, he grabbed her by both wrists and shoved her back, just enough for him to stand up from the tub.

"I said *stop!*"

Sitting in place, his sister shivered and recoiled, that cold, removed expression giving way to glowing, crackling anger. Jonah panted and took a step back from her as he tried to move past the lingering pain from her torturous care. It didn't work.

"What the fuck was that, Nell?!"

She looked at him, then at the tweezers in her hand and back again. Jonah snatched one of the old washcloths off the rack and pressed the ratty fabric to the bleeding hole in his leg.

"I was pulling out the glass," Nell said. "Which, you're welcome, by the way. Christ, you can be such a baby about shit sometimes."

Jonah looked at his sister, incredulous. Was she playing dumb, or did she really not know what she'd just done to him? Something jittery and terrified laddered up his spine to settle at the base of his skull, and he took another step back, leaning against the wall and pressing his hands flat.

"I, uh, yeah," he said placatingly. "You're right. Thank you. I, I think I've got it from here, though."

Nell's expression changed. "What are you talking about?"

"I mean, I'm going to get the rest on my own, okay? I'm cool. You should go lie down, or something."

"Jonah, we're almost done—" Her face shifted when she saw the cord of blood running down past his knee to pool around his toes. "Oh."

"No, I know," he said, cutting her off. "Thank you. But I got it from here, okay?"

"Jonah, I can help—"

"I know. You have. I'm good. We're good."

Nell stood and shook her head.

"I'm sorry, okay? I'm sorry. I'm exhausted, my hand must have slipped, I wasn't paying attention. Something," she said, her voice faint and chilly.

Jonah cast a glance at the makeshift bandage wrapped

around her forearm. "Like you weren't paying attention when you did that?"

Nell looked hurt.

"That was different. You don't understand."

"No, I don't," he said. "Do you want to explain it to me?"

"It's complicated," she sighed. "I don't know how to talk about it. I don't even think I understand it all the way yet."

"Well, you let me know when you do. Until then, I think I'm good in here for the night."

"Wait, are you kidding?" she protested. "The beds are out there. What are you going to do, ruck out on the floor?"

"I've got the tub. I'll be okay."

"Oh, come on, don't be stupid," Nell groaned.

"I don't think I'm being stupid, Nell."

"Jonah, Jesus, stop this, okay? Please. I'm sorry, all right? I'm sorry. I didn't mean to hurt you. I won't do it again, I promise."

There were a million things that Jonah wanted to say to her and didn't. The air boiled between them, the energy curdling into something spiteful as Nell's face crumpled like a sheet of paper tossed into a fire.

"Fine, okay? Fucking fine," she snarled. "No big deal. I'll sleep out there, and you can sleep in here, and we'll pretend like that's totally normal. Everything's fine, right? Everything's totally fine. Jesus fucking *Christ*," she roared, throwing the tweezers against the far wall. A second later, she was in his face again.

"But I want you to know that I would never hurt you on purpose, Jonah. I would *never*."

"Yes, you would," he said, his voice small and frail. "I'm sorry, Nell. But I can't do this tonight. I just can't. Be sure to lock the front door, okay? I'll see you in the morning."

"Whatever," she spat at him.

He shut the door in her face and locked it, then picked up the tweezers and sat back down on the tub's edge to pluck the rest of the glass out of his skin. When he was done, he pulled the rest of the stiff, scratchy towels off the rack and draped himself in them like a patchwork poncho. They'd do for tonight. He curled up in the bathtub and closed his eyes, counting the slow, painful seconds as they trudged by, hoping sleep would come soon.

He was out before he got to ten.

Nell
Elbert, UT
495 miles to Albuquerque

She lay in the dark for a long time after Jonah shut the door on her, looking up at the ceiling through the uneven darkness, feeling her pulse race and hum in her temples as she kneaded her fingers in the shitty comforter and tried to ignore the incessant sound of her own breathing. She wanted to stay mad at him, she wanted to rage, to leap out of bed and hammer a fist on the bathroom door until he opened up so she could tell him what she really thought of him, but it was no good. The anger wouldn't come back; no matter how hard she tried, how much she focused on the things about Jonah that pissed her off, it didn't work. Because she understood why he was doing this, spending the rest of the night locked in isolation, hiding from her. She'd hide from herself, too, if she thought she could somehow manage it.

There was so much that she wanted to tell him. So much she didn't want to be alone with anymore. It all lay on her heart like a millstone, pressing her down into the ground, stealing her breath, blocking her heart from beating. She'd meant what she said: she didn't know how to talk about what was happening to her. She didn't know if she ever would.

When she closed her eyes and held very, very still, she could feel the memories of whatever had happened to her underneath the desert. Except they weren't really memories, at least, not in the traditional sense. They weren't images or sequences, but perceptions, sensations that still echoed through her body, twisted deep into the muscle and marrow.

Laying atop the bed, Nell began to sweat—hot beads broke out across her forehead, her face, and her neck, and rolled down to soak the blankets underneath her. The motel room crumbled away in fragments, and Nell began to cry behind pinched lips, trying madly to scream against the pain—no longer mere memory—but finding herself unable. She'd been here before, trapped in sandpaper hospital sheets as she glued herself back together again, more scar tissue than woman. Those days seemed so distant now. She braced herself against the new agony that lurked underneath her skin, searching for that unknown presence that concealed itself within it. The room around her vanished entirely and gave way to black, banded stone that glistened in the humid dark. She tried to inhale, but the air was too foul to breathe.

The crash, the caves; the caves, the crash. Here again, broken again, alone again.

A fresh sob surged inside her, and she remembered crying as she floated up and up, screaming and pleading like a child, begging for it to be over. She groaned and flinched away from the hideous, dreamlike memories but was powerless to escape. Something had burrowed down into the wreckage of Nell to make room for itself, and now it wore her face, it moved when she moved, as much a part of Nell as Nell was. She knew this. It had burned everything that it didn't need, immolated in pursuit of its own terrible agenda. She cracked and fractured again and again inside her patchwork memory, and when the suffering became too much, consciousness fell away from flesh, floating off as her lifeless corpse continued to contort and bend according to some incomprehensible plan, her body made into wire and the wire made into shapes too strange and obscene to behold.

The invisible thing spun her around and around, splitting her open along her spine, worming deeper into her ruined, wasted flesh as the fabric of her clothes swelled with blood. She was dying. There was no other explanation, no other word for what was happening to her. She'd lost the tenuous grip she'd long held on herself, and now the thing that had colonized her from the inside had taken over to leave her behind. There was no room for her here. She'd withered, she'd rotted apart, and soon, she would be nowhere. Soon, she would be nothing.

What a relief that would be.

And then, as suddenly as it had started, it was over. She was in the motel room again. Alone again.

Well. Not *alone*. But she wasn't in the cave anymore, nor the hospital room. She was here. This was now.

She could feel herself shaking from the cold, every nerve ending dialed up to eleven. Rolling to sit at the edge of the blown-out mattress, she hacked and coughed against the cramps knotting her stomach, then spat a mouthful of blood onto the carpet between her bare feet. Silently, she went for her lighter and the fresh pack of Camels that Jonah had gotten for her back at the rest stop. Ripping off the cellophane with unsteady hands, she shook a cigarette loose and jabbed it between her lips, savoring the oily taste of the paper as she blinked back more tears. Thumbing the little Bic to life, she dipped the tip of the Camel in the flame and breathed deeply. Distantly, it dawned on her that this was probably a nonsmoking room; but then again, they'd already blown up the shower. What was one little cigarette on top of that? Management probably wouldn't even notice.

Beyond the blinds covering the front window, she could make out white headlights drifting along the road beyond the motel's parking lot. Blowing smoke out of her nostrils in twin streams, Nell watched the glare rise, then fade, and she began to cry again, hugging herself tightly with tired arms.

Jonah
Elbert, UT
495 miles to Albuquerque

Curled up in the bathtub, Jonah slept fitfully, dreaming of blood and violence that used to be and never was. He dreamed of a screaming, desperate world succumbing to a final annihilation, and a one-eyed boy with a rotting face at its burned-to-ash epicenter who shattered like glass when Jonah opened his mouth to beg the boy's forgiveness. Chained deep under the waves of sleep, he didn't—couldn't—hear his sister cry out in pain in the next room. He didn't hear her rise silently from the bed, shaking and sobbing. He didn't hear the motel-room door swing open, or clap shut behind her.

He didn't hear anything at all.

Anna
Interstate 70, UT

Gillam was staring again.

Sitting against the metal sidewall in the Econoline's rear bed, she'd caught him stealing glances at her ever since the rest stop, but now he wasn't even bothering to be subtle about it. He'd been in pitiful shape when she and Terry and Darko had ambled up to the van, slumped over in the passenger seat, half passed out against the glass, missing fingernails on both shaking hands, cheeks and lips split and purple to match the welts and bruises underneath his beard. Below his greasy brow, he sported a pair of black eyes so dark, they looked painted on. Overall, he looked like somebody had tried to feed him through a woodchipper, then changed their mind halfway through.

She'd asked Terry about it, but the old man had shrugged it off and told her not to worry. Gill was fine, he'd said. He'd taken his lumps, and when they caught up to the Talbots they were going to give as good as they'd gotten. They'd set the scales to balance yet, he told her. She didn't ask what he meant by that, because she really didn't care. These men were criminals. They were a means to an end, a lift down the road. Whatever their grievances with Nell Talbot and her brother were, they'd have to get in line.

Any more mistakes would be too costly, and she'd already paid enough.

She'd been so close. Another half-second and it would have been over. She'd had the blade right there—hell, she'd already drawn blood from Nell's throat. She shouldn't have wasted so much time talking to the girl. She should have ripped that gun from Jonah's hands and smashed his head in with it for daring to interfere. Even though she knew that *shoulds* were poison, her shoulders and arms tensed, thinking back on it now.

210

Walking back down that narrow scratch of a dirt road, she'd told Terry what he needed to know—that she was chasing the Talbots too—but she didn't explain any further than that, which the old man seemed fine with. It was for the best, anyway. She never told anyone everything right away. Nobody but Nell Talbot.

It was her own fault, really. She'd gotten excited at the prospect of binding something that big, that powerful. She'd jumped the gun, she'd paid the price, and now she was here. In the back of a van. Being stared at by a man who looked more dead than he was alive.

Anna wasn't worried about Terry or his guys. She'd dealt with plenty of men like them before, men who thought that leather and scars and anger problems made you hard. It didn't. It was a fine disguise, sure, but Anna had been taught by scarier people than 48 Coffin. Besides, these guys had other things on their minds than little old her.

Terry'd been vague about why they were hunting the Talbots, but Anna had been able to glean that it had something to do with his brother, as of yet unaccounted for. Whatever it was, Terry held on to it like a rosary, clutching at it so hard it made his palms bleed. She had no doubt that Gillam and Darko—a good soldier and a garden-variety sadist, respectively—had committed no end of evil acts in their time; but out of the three of them, Terry was the most dangerous. Misguided righteousness was a time bomb, and it never went off in a vacuum. Collateral damage was inevitable with people like Terry. She'd have to watch out for him.

Underneath her skin, she felt the Chain twist and thrash, desperate to get loose. Anna forced the sensation away, deep, deep down into the darkest corners of herself, where she could ignore it for a little while longer. But then, hadn't she been ignoring the signs for long enough already? The Chain was, and had always been, a violent thing, a roiling tempest overflowing with faces, a force of pure destruction, barely restrained as it spun inside her, howling with ten thousand voices, a hundred thousand, more.

Back before she'd inherited the Chain from her father, he

had warned her that theirs was one of the oldest, that it had been stretching and straining against its own hellish limits long before Anna was ever a glimmer of a glimmer in his eye. He'd kept it in check for years, done battle with it time and time again, and in the end, passing that damned legacy on to Anna had killed him. The act of transferring a given Chain from one keeper to another was an agonizing process; it unleashed a churning torrent of smoke and suffering that both didn't always survive. God knew her dad deserved better than to be torn apart as the Chain ripped its way out of him, but he wasn't foolish. He knew the risks. He'd always known there was a chance it'd happen like that. He'd lived as a good man, and he'd died a good man. Maybe that was the best anyone could hope for, in the end.

Then it was just Anna, alone with the Chain; and despite everything she'd seen, everything she'd experienced, Anna honestly believed that she could do better than her dad had. And for a while she did. At least she thought she had. But it didn't take long for cracks to start forming in the foundation.

Usually she felt it early in the morning, right after waking, a certain tightness at the base of her skull, an ache running through her body like a hot wire, as if the Chain knew she'd been asleep and was trying to break free when she wasn't around to stop it. The pain had been there in some form or another for years now, but over the past few months things had gone from bad to worse. The Chain had taken to struggling and lashing against its bonds nonstop, pounding on the walls within her every moment of every day, tireless, sleepless, endless. Every link she added only made it that much harder to bear. The weight of it was too much. The pressure too great. And yet she pressed on.

It was always at its worst when she neared others like it, other presences, other demons. Usually it was only a small uptick in that ocean of constant alien fury; but the second Nell Talbot appeared on Anna's radar, she knew something was different. The Chain had thrashed harder over the course of the last day than it ever had before, the gravity of that thing inside Nell impossible to ignore.

The only other time it had struggled anywhere close to this, Anna had been up in Canada, in a little burg in the south of Ontario called Welland. She'd chased rumors of the Gail sisters, a pair of old biddies the folks in town called witches, out past the city limits to a ruined old Victorian tucked away in the trees, the windows papered over and the doors all boarded shut. The sisters were holed up inside, wrapped in filth and blood, cocooned together in a mountainous nest of trash that must have taken years to pile up. Standing there, before those poisonous old cackling things, the Chain hissed cruel obscenities inside her mind, pulling so hard that she thought she might burst apart.

She'd tried to make it quick, for the sisters' sake, but it had gotten messy. It took her most of a week to get all the blood out of her hands and her clothes and her hair.

Anna didn't want to believe that she was losing control. She'd told herself time and again that it was anything other than that, exhaustion or maybe a crisis of faith. She was only human, after all. All her life, she'd been taught to walk the path, raised a believer and shaped into something stronger. Something that could bear the weight of generations. But the work wasn't supposed to be simple, and it was never meant to be easy. Everyone who believed—including Christ Himself—experienced doubt, but sitting here now, in the back of this van, Anna had to admit, if only to herself, that what was happening inside her felt like more than an issue of faith. If she really was crumbling from the inside, what would happen if she really went through with it and added something as big and powerful as one of the Great Dukes of Hell to the Chain?

Won't it start rotting you too?

Nell's words echoed loudly between Anna's ears. Maybe the girl was on to something. Maybe Anna had taken too much on already, imprisoned one too many, found herself at a tipping point. Maybe the best thing for her to do now was to head back to the rest stop to fix her car, and get as far away from the Talbots as she possibly could.

If only she had that luxury.

Inside her head, she felt the Chain jerk harder, like it was trying to wrench her brain clean from her skull. She laid a hand over one temple and tried to slow her thoughts, tried to calm the storm. Keeping her breathing slow and steady, she pushed back against the Chain's maniac fury until she felt the rattling start to subside. After another minute, it faded away into the background.

Okay. Okay, good.

Everything was under control.

Everything was going to be fine.

They bounced over a pothole, jarring Anna from the trance she'd lulled herself into. Across the van, Gill was still watching her, his face drawn into a mask of fear. Anna leaned forward, and he flinched away, thumping the back of his head against the metal wall. Anna watched him twist and writhe as he pressed himself against the steel, deathly pale underneath all the bruises and cuts. Had she been talking without knowing it? In the passenger seat, Terry turned around to look at her through the dark, his eyes bright and uncontrollable, burning like white wildfire.

"You two okay back there?" he asked.

"Yeah," she replied, not really meaning it. "I'm good. We're good."

"Sure you know where we're going?"

"Pretty sure," she said, rubbing at her temple, feeling the Chain pull and twist. Best guess, they still had a few hours to go until they caught up with the Talbots. "Just keep driving. I'll tell you where to turn. It's going to be a while yet."

Terry watched her for another moment, then turned back to face the front.

"You heard her," Terry said to Darko.

Settling back into the comfort and safety of the shadows, Anna wiped at her nose with the back of her hand. It came away wet with blood.

t was already close to dawn by the time they pulled over to rest, easing the van to a stop on the side of a long-abandoned dirt road outside of town. Behind the wheel, Darko turned on his side and pulled his sunglasses down over his bruised eyes to keep the light out while Terry worked his jaw, trying to get his eardrums to pop. He'd been riding in this van too long. In the back, he could see that Gill had passed out again, slumped over on the cold metal in a disjointed heap. The woman was still wide awake, though. And watching him.

He jerked his goateed chin at his guys. "Not going to get any shut-eye?"

She shook her head.

"Why? Not tired?" he asked.

"Oh, exhausted," she said with a forced smile, "but I don't think sleep's going to happen any time soon."

"Why not?"

"That's complicated."

"So is everything worth knowing."

She shook her head. "I'd really rather not."

"Your choice," Terry said, indifferent. "I'm going to step out for some fresh air, maybe a smoke. You want some company, you feel free to join."

He popped the door open and eased himself out of the van, feeling every ache and pain in his body ignite anew in protest. From his coat pocket he drew his little glass vial of coke—already half-gone—and shook a bump onto the back of his hand. He snorted it up quickly, relishing the gluey sensation as the powder glazed the inside of his nostril. All around him, the shadows warped and twisted in the moonlight, shivering like the wind. He capped the vial again and rolled it back and forth between his fingers as he looked up into the dying night sky.

He heard the back door clunk open, and a second later, Anna rounded the darkened taillights. Wordlessly, he held the vial out to her, offering, but she demurred.

"Thanks," she said, "but I really don't."

"Just being polite," Terry said, then pocketed the coke. Beside him, Anna laughed, covering her mouth with one loosely curled fist. He looked at her.

"What's funny?"

"It's nothing," she said. "It's just, out of all the things I'd've guessed about you, *polite* wouldn't have made the list."

"Hey, I like to surprise," Terry said, not unkindly.

"Now, that one I could have called from a mile off," Anna said.

They both fell quiet then, listening to the silence around them, the wind over the hills, the beating wings of birds taking flight from some unseen roost.

"So what do you want with them?" Terry asked.

Anna shifted in place.

"You mean to say the Talbots?"

Terry nodded. "I mean to say. What'd they do to you?"

"Do you want the easy answer, or do you want the truth?" Anna asked.

"I'll take whatever you want to give me," Terry said. "But the truth would be nice. It'd definitely help me see my way clear to keeping you around. Right now, I don't know what to make of you."

"What, you don't trust me, Terry?"

"I don't know you," he said, fixing his gaze straight ahead. "So, no."

Anna sighed. "They have something that belongs to me," she said. "Something rather precious."

"Precious like what?" Terry asked. "She muling for you? On the run with a stomach full of black tar balloons, something like that?"

She shook her head. "No, not exactly."

"Then what, *exactly*, are we talking about here?"

"It's hard to explain," she said, with a wintry expression.

Terry nodded. "I get it. *Complicated*, right?"

"You have no idea," Anna said. "But...maybe I can show you. If you want."

She held one tattooed hand out to him. He didn't take it.

"It's not a trick," she said, giving her hand a little shake. "I promise. This is all you have to do to understand. Come on."

Terry raised an eyebrow. "Just like that."

"Just like that," she said. "No BS, no tricks."

She was playing a game here; he knew that much. It was only a matter of figuring out what game. Problem was, Terry didn't have a way to do that while she was still holding all the cards.

Hell with it. What was the worst that could happen?

"Fine," he said, and clapped a hand down onto hers, curling callused fingers around her soft palm.

He might as well have grabbed onto an electric fence.

Pain and ecstasy ripped through his mind, his body, and his soul, pinning him to the spot, body seizing as he disappeared from the world he knew and fell into a parade of grisly images, worse than any fever dream or nightmare. He saw himself, the Talbots, Anna, he saw the storm, a towering cyclone of faces and screams, an ancient machine on the verge of shattering apart in a catastrophic blast. He saw visions of them that he used to know, freed from their graves, screaming in exaltation, hundreds of the dead gathering in the streets, turning their sagging, brutalized faces toward a blood-red sky. Pressing in against each other, rotting bodies squelching and tearing, the walking corpses threw themselves into the storm's fury, and for a moment Terry saw Vaughn amongst their number, toothless mouth agape as he cackled and shoved his way toward the cyclone. Terry screamed for his brother and tried to follow him through the crowd but found himself restrained by dozens of grasping dead hands. As Terry watched helplessly, Vaughn began to drift up from the ground. Terry screamed. It didn't matter. Laughing, Vaughn floated into the heart of the storm and was pulped in an instant by its razor winds.

Terry yelped and yanked his hand away from Anna's as

he swayed and stumbled, temporarily unmoored from gravity. His head buzzed like a kicked wasp's nest and nausea boiled up his throat, unstoppable. Pitching forward onto his hands and knees, he retched, and a flood of dark vomit burst from his throat and nose. He made a low moaning noise inside his chest, then collapsed onto his side, curling up in the fetal position on the rough grit.

Then Anna was beside him, running a slender hand up and down his arm. Taking a breath, he turned to look at her. Through the dark, she was radiant. He could see her eyes swirling and shifting like ink in water, that abominable storm hidden beneath her surface showing itself one last time before diving back under.

His stomach lurched and he vomited again, spewing another wet fan of puke atop the first.

"I know," Anna said softly, still kneeling over him. "I know. It can be overwhelming at first. It'll pass."

"What the fuck was that?" Terry coughed. "What the *fuck*."

"There's so much more to this world than you know," Anna said. "The infinite, the endless... we're all part of something bigger, Terry. God's plans include us all. You, me, everyone."

One day you'll see for yourself, boy.

Maybe Grandpa wasn't crazy, after all.

Terry rolled over onto his back, and when he looked again, he saw a shadow lurking behind Anna, slumped and tattered.

Gillam.

As Terry lay there, he watched his old friend turn and start to limp away, into the sands far beyond the road. Terry watched him go, and after a few minutes he stood and followed him out into the vast emptiness.

"Hey, stop," Terry called out to Gill, still far ahead of him, not slowing despite his limp. "Gill, *stop!*"

"No, Terry," Gill called back. "I'm sorry, but no." He'd led him well off the highway, down and around an embankment into a little dry-marsh valley, scattered with trees. It was still cold out, but Terry barely felt it. His skin buzzed with energy, as if Anna's touch had somehow supercharged him. He could bird-dog Gill for miles if he had to. Balling his fists in his pockets, he closed one around Vaughn's knife, silently asking his brother for strength and patience, wherever he was.

"Where you going, huh? You going to wander out into the desert? Walk home? What's your plan here?"

"No plan, man," Gill shouted back at him, the words stumbling out of his torn-up lips all half-formed and messy. "I'm just done. I'm sorry."

Terry broke into a jog to catch up, circling around his old friend to stand directly in his path.

"You need to get out of my way, Ter," Gill said, his eyes bright with anger and fear. "I mean it."

Terry held his hands out in a gesture that he hoped was placating.

"Look, slow down for a second, okay? Let's talk about this."

"I'm done talking," Gillam said. "Talking doesn't help."

"Tell me what I can do, then."

Gillam recoiled as if Terry had punched him in the face. "You can give this shit up right now and get us home, all right? You can let these Talbot fucks go so we can turn around and head back to California. I tried telling you before. This shit is getting worse and worse. I want these pieces of shit dead as much as anyone else—"

"No, you *don't*," Terry growled. Gill blinked slowly, rolling the tip of his tongue around the edge of his lips.

"Fine," he said. "Yeah, okay. Maybe not as much as you, but I still want them dead. Vaughn was my friend too, but it's not worth all this. And whatever that crazy bitch was just saying, that shit about God? Fuck that. Sorry, but fuck that, man. I don't know what you two were doing back there, but you can't tell me it was normal."

"You don't know shit about shit," Terry said. "You didn't see what I saw, Gillam."

"You know what? You're right, I don't know shit about

whatever happened between you and her, but I know what I heard, man. You can't trust crazy. You know that. Shit, you're the one who fucking *taught me that*. Let's dump her ass here and head home. Please. Because crazy only ever makes shit worse. Things are already fucked up enough without someone else stirring the pot."

Terry's expression turned icy. "We're not going home, Gill. Not until the job is done, not until the scales are balanced."

"Then turn around and walk away. Let me go, okay? Please. I'll figure it out, I'll head back to Broughton somehow and hold down the fort until you and Darko get back. But . . ."

Terry stepped in closer. "But what?"

"I can't do this anymore, okay? I can't, Terry. I, I won't," he said. "I don't have it in me. Call me a coward, call me a traitor, I don't care. I have to go, all right? You and Darko and psycho lady can keep tilting at windmills, but I am fucking done."

"No," Terry raged. "We stick together. We're 48 Coffin to the end."

Gillam's shoulders fell, all the bluster and rage gone out of his battered, threadbare body.

"No, man. Not anymore. I'm sorry, but this is the fucking line for me. I'm out. Beat my head in if you want, kick me out of the MC, tell me to never show my face in Broughton again. That's fine. You'll never see me again. But if you're not going to listen to sense, this is as far as we go."

Terry stood still and stared the man down, afterimages of what he'd seen inside Anna still frothing inside his skull. Shaking his head, Gillam rubbed at his own face with cracked, bloody hands.

"I loved you, man," Gillam said. "You were my fucking family. But if this is how it is, I'm out, and there's not a goddamn thing you can say to change my mind."

"Okay," Terry said, taking a step closer, his voice suddenly soft. "Fine. If that's how it is, that's how it is."

Gillam sighed with relief, his eyes twinkling in the low blue light.

"Thank you, Ter," he said. "I wish—"

Terry didn't let him finish. Clapping a hand around the

back of Gill's neck, he buried Vaughn's knife into the man's belly with a hard, rubbery SNAP.

"Yeah," Terry said. "Me too."

Gill didn't scream as Terry shoved the steel deeper and deeper into his guts; he barely even gasped. Instead, he just hung there, impaled on the blade, looking more confused than anything as his insides started to spill out in hot, messy gluts. Holding him in place, Terry yanked the knife from his friend's stomach and drove it in again, and again, and again, stitching it higher and higher until Gill's gaze went flat and his face fell slack.

"I'm sorry," Terry whispered into the dying man's ear. "But shit is all or nothing now. No room for in-betweens."

He let him drop to the hard, sandy ground in a heap and stood over him, watching the blood pool out from underneath Gill's body until he was sure he was gone for good. Taking the dead man by his wrists, Terry dragged him down the dry, marshy little valley to a copse of ratty desert junipers and dumped him in the brush between the trees. No one would find him there for a long, long time. Retracing his steps, Terry washed his hands in the freezing little creek that wound through the sand like a gnarled vein and kicked the bloody drag-stains away until they were barely a shadow in the sand.

The sun was starting to come up again.

S till muzzy from sleep, he found Nell sitting on the hood of the Volvo in the cold predawn light, teeth chattering behind a lit cigarette, a small pile of crumpled butts and empty beer cans at her feet. The second half of the six-pack sat unopened beside her on the car, still bound together in plastic rings. Padding across the parking lot in thin socks, Jonah sidled up to sit next to his sister, bracing both feet atop the bumper beside hers.

Overhead, clouds had shredded the moon, leaving it in tatters above the icy early morning blue. Jonah rubbed his hands together, trying to force the cold out of them, trying to figure out what to say, if anything. He'd dressed quickly when he found the motel room empty, convinced that something else had gone wrong, that that Anna woman or 48 Coffin had caught up to them, that they were waiting outside with guns and razors and whatever else. When he saw Nell sitting alone down here through the blinds, he'd nearly cried with relief.

"Hey," he said.

Nell took a drag and blew smoke, pointedly not looking over at him. Sitting this close, he could see that her eyes were ringed with dark circles, her hands trembling uncontrollably.

"Hey yourself."

"What are you doing out here?"

She gestured to the cigarettes, the car. "Nothing. Sitting. Smoking. Thinking."

"Pretty chilly out here," Jonah said.

Nell tapped the ashes off the end of her Camel, then stuck it back between her chapped lips, breathing deep.

"I guess," she replied. "Hadn't really noticed."

222

"Where'd you get the beer?" Jonah asked.

Nell threw a quick glance back over her shoulder toward the cement stairs and their room. "Mini-fridge. Somebody must've left it behind, I guess."

Jonah pulled one of the cans—ugh, *Bud Light*—from the plastic loops, then popped the top and brought it to his lips for a long pull. The beer inside was so cold and fizzy it nearly cut his throat. He relished the sensation. Been a while since he'd tied one on this early, but, after everything, he figured he'd probably earned it. Letting the can hang between his knees, he nodded to the cigarette between his sister's fingers.

"Can I get one of those?"

Slowly, she turned to look at him, an incredulous look on her face. "You don't smoke."

"You don't know what I do and don't do," he said. "Come on, share the wealth. It's beer and smokes or coffee, and I don't see either of us making a Starbucks run right about now. I don't even know if they *have* a Starbucks in this town."

"They don't," Nell said, holding up her phone, the screen dark and cracked. "Already checked. Might be some instant stuff gratis in the front office, if you're desperate."

"Hard pass," Jonah said. "Come on. Make with the giving."

She handed him the pack of Camels and the lighter out of her coat. Shaking one loose, he held it between his teeth and sparked it to life, trying not to cough. Fucking unfiltereds. Hadn't had one of these in a long time, but they were exactly as foul as he remembered. He laid the mostly empty pack on the hood between them and rolled his cigarette back and forth between his fingertips, letting it burn. Across the street, there was a wide-open stretch of weedy land that reached all the way back to the hills, blotted with hoarfrost.

"You get any sleep?" he asked, taking another drag.

She shook her head. "Too loud."

"In the hotel room?"

Cradling her smoke between two knuckles, she tapped her fingers against the side of her head. "Too loud in here," she said. "It's a fucking horror show every time I close my eyes. Didn't want to see all that shit again. Couldn't."

Jonah tried to make a face like he understood, even though he really didn't.

"What do you see? When you close your eyes, I mean."

Nell shook her head again. "Trust me, you don't want to know."

"I asked, didn't I?"

She looked at him sidelong, her expression curious, questioning.

"You ever have bad dreams, Jonah?"

"Yeah," he said. "I think everyone does, don't they?"

"Sure, but I mean the really bad ones. The ones that start off bad and keep getting worse. The ones where, at some point, you figure out that you're in a bad dream, but you still can't wake yourself up. So you're just trapped in this endless pageant of nightmares, scared to death, until your brain finally decides to let you go. You ever have bad dreams like that?"

"No, never. Do you?"

She nodded. "Something happened to me, a couple years back," she said. "Something I've been meaning to tell you about. Kind of feels like ever since it happened, I've just been waiting to wake up. Thing is, I think I'm still waiting."

Jonah paused, watching the smoke curl off the Camel in his fingertips.

"Something happened like what?" he asked.

"Like I said, it was a couple years back, maybe three now, I guess. I was out with some friends, bar-hopping around Nob Hill, having a good time, staying out late, you know. Normal Friday night shit. Anyway, it starts getting close to closing time and I can feel myself running out of gas, so I decide to call it, head home. Except I'd been pounding martinis all night, so I figured that driving myself home wasn't, like, a great idea? So I called a cab."

"Probably the smart move," Jonah said.

Nell shook her head, laughing softly. "Yeah, you'd think so, right?" she said. "I was asleep in the back seat when the truck hit us. Blew a red light doing, like, fifty. Full-on T-boned the cab. Game fuckin' over."

"Wait, what?" he asked, incredulous.

"It was just some dude in a pickup. Wasn't paying attention, I guess," Nell continued. *"Boom.* Both cars totally mangled, broken glass everywhere. Cab driver's fine, not even a scratch. Airbags. The other guy, the one who hit us? He's pretty banged up, but nothing serious. I got it bad, though. I mean, *bad.* Ambulance, emergency room, the whole deal. My fault for not wearing a seatbelt, I suppose. Anyway, I'm already in lousy shape when they get me to the hospital, but the thing is, when they finally get me on the table in the OR, the stress is too much, body can't take it. So my heart stops."

Something cold and dreadful popped loose inside Jonah's stomach.

"... What does that mean, Nellie?"

Beside him, Nell blew smoke.

"It means that technically I died."

Panic crackled in between Jonah's ears like a raw powerline, humming and hissing. He wasn't hearing this. There was no way.

"Yeah," Nell said. "For two hundred and thirteen whole-ass seconds, my heart just stops beating and I am officially dead on the table. Just gone. Doctors had to hit me with the defib like four times before they got me back. Woke up in this dingy little hospital room a few days later, memory all fucked up, Dad bawling at my bedside. It's the craziest thing, trying to remember it now. One second I was climbing into the cab, and the next I'm waking up in the hospital in this shitty little room, half my head shaved where they sewed me shut." Reaching over her head with her free hand, she pulled her hair back, revealing a crooked purple scar traversing her scalp just above her ear, long healed over.

Jonah felt nauseous. "Jesus fuck. I remember Dad mentioned that you'd been in a crash, but he made it sound more like a fender bender. Why didn't you tell me about this?"

"Try not to hold it against him. You remember how he was with Mom at the end. He's always been shitty with bad news. He was only barely functional by the time I woke up, and that was most of a week after the fact. He talked a little about telling you everything that had happened, but I begged him not to," Nell said, letting her hair fall back into place. "Made him promise that he wouldn't. Honestly, I didn't tell anyone. Not about the dying stuff."

"What the hell, why not?"

"Because it wasn't any of their business. I mean, they knew I was in a wreck, okay, but the rest of it? No. No way. Tell someone you were in a car crash, *oh whew*, so glad you're all right, you're so lucky, end of subject. Tell someone that you died for a little while? That changes the conversation pretty considerably. I really wasn't interested in having that talk over and over again. The way I see it, three minutes dead or not, at the end of the day, I got to keep living. So I figured it didn't matter."

"But it did matter, Nellie. It does matter. I...I could have been there for you, I should have been. I'm your brother, for fuck's sake. You needed help, I could have..."

Nell flicked ash. "I know. I told myself that I didn't tell you for the same reasons I didn't tell anyone else. Didn't want to scare you for no reason, didn't want to have a hard conversation. It was just easier that way. Now that I look back at it, though, I think maybe I was still mad at you. Years after you'd fucked off for California, and I was pissed that you weren't somehow there to stop it from happening in the first place. So fucking childish."

Jonah felt his expression fall as confusion and sorrow and fear swirled inside his head.

"I'm so sorry, Nell. For all of it. I didn't, I mean, I wish I'd—"

"No, I know," she said, cutting him off. "It's okay. We don't have to...yeah."

They sat quietly for a long time after that, listening to the air bluster between the low buildings around them, hearing coyotes baying at the sky in the distance as cars ground to life and disappeared into the silence beyond the edges of town. Nell chained another smoke.

"There's something inside me," she said abruptly.

Jonah glanced over at her, sure his expression showed the absolute dread he felt.

"Something like what?"

"It's a presence, I guess. It's something else, something not me. Something not human," Nell said.

"Wait, is... is this what she was telling you? Anna?"

"Among other things."

"And you listened to her? Nell, she's a crazy person. She tried to kill you, remember? Someone like that is not to be trusted."

"*Don't*," Nell said, her voice suddenly cold and hard. "Don't do that superiority shit right now, okay? Do not. You're not Dad, and I'm fully aware of what I'm saying here. I know how it sounds, I really do. But I need you to listen to me, okay? Please. After all the shit we've been through in the past couple of days, you owe me that much."

Jonah shrank back, feeling his skin burn hot and red with shame.

"Okay," he said after another second. "Okay. I'm listening."

Nell breathed out, then started talking, her voice soft and steady.

"Anna connected the dots for me, but it wasn't like it was hard to see the pattern once she did," Nell said. "Something happened to me out in the desert. Something blacked out my memory and led me down into that cave, and ever since then, shit has been getting worse and worse. I'm not alone in my head anymore, Jonah. And whatever it is, it's big enough that Anna said she could feel it from a hundred miles away."

"Sure, okay," he said. "Something's been happening, but what, possession? You really think that's it? Not a concussion, or I don't know, anything else?"

"Kinda, yeah," Nell said. She took his hand and squeezed. "Look, I know this sounds crazy, Jonah. I do. But I know you see it too. Things have not been normal since the caves. Whatever else happened between me and Anna, you have to admit that much."

Jonah hung his head, puffing anxiously on the cigarette he didn't want, filling the air around his face with thick gray smoke.

"Okay, say she's telling you the truth. Say it's real," Jonah said.

"It's real."

"You said she felt it," Jonah said. "What does that mean?"

"The way she explained it, she's some kind of exorcist. Called herself a . . . a *sin eater*. Apparently, she's got a ton of these . . . things inside of her. Works like some kind of mental compass, except I'm True North."

"So that's why you called her," Jonah said. "To get it out of you."

Nell nodded. "Didn't exactly go like I thought it would, but yeah."

Jonah felt the air around him grow frostier in the face of this terrible new reality, chapping his skin bright red where it wasn't covered by his clothes.

"I need you to believe me on this, Jonah. Like, really believe. Not as a thought experiment or like you're humoring me or whatever. I need you to know that this is real. It's happening to me, to us. Just because I haven't started spinning my head around in circles or spiderwalking down the stairs doesn't mean it's not for real." She rubbed at her temple with one palm. "I can feel it, you know? It's not just me in here anymore. Whatever you want to call it, it's in there, and it's not letting go. I wish I could deal with it on my own, I wish I was strong enough to. But I'm not, and I can't. I need your help. I know this is asking a lot. I'm sorry."

Jonah chose his next words very carefully. "I get it," he said, speaking slowly. "I don't know shit about exorcists or sin eaters or whatever, but I'd be lying if I said I haven't seen some things that made me stop and think twice." His mind flashed back to the parking lot the night before, the cave, Nell's shadow against the wall back in Mowry. The memories made his skin itch, made him want to run screaming away from himself and never look back, but he held steady. "I don't have all the answers, Nell. I never did. But if you say this is what's going on, then this is what's going on, and we're going to see it through together."

"What do you mean you've 'seen things'?" Nell asked. "What kinds of things?"

Jonah shook his head and stayed quiet. He didn't want to do this. It was just that he didn't have a choice. Taking a long, deep drag off his cigarette, feeling the smoke rake at his lungs with dull claws, he drained his beer and pitched the can to the asphalt.

"I never told you why I left Albuquerque, did I?" he asked, knowing full well that he hadn't.

"I always thought it was Molly," Nell said.

Jonah shook his head. "You ever hear the name Alex Lawson?"

"No, never," Nell said. "Who is she?"

"He," Jonah corrected. "He was this wannabe-skinhead piece of shit back in Albuquerque, couldn't have been older than eighteen or nineteen back then. Real attitude problem on him too. You know how guys that age can be. Walking around thinking they're hard, wearing a chip the size of a dinner plate on their shoulder, waiting for someone to knock it off.

"Anyway, all Lawson wants in the world is to get noticed by the other Nazi fuckheads around town, so he has friends to burn crosses with or whatever. Figures the best way to do that is by earning some kind of hard-ass rep, because if he's got that, the local jackboots'd practically beg him to join their little clown-shoe club. So he shaves his head, gets I-shit-you-not fucking *swastikas* tattooed on the backs of his hands, the whole racist shitlord starter pack."

"You're kidding." Nell coughed.

"Nope. He's all in from the jump," Jonah said. "It's like he watched *American History X* and turned it off after Ed Norton got arrested at the halfway point."

"Jesus Christ," Nell said, scoffing. "Fuck this kid."

"Only thing more pathetic than a fucking Nazi is a fucking Nazi wannabe," Jonah said. "Anyway. Since Alex is already a few Crayolas short of a box, he starts haunting dive bars around town, looking for trouble, getting into silly little pissfights with drunks who are too deep in the bottle to put their hands up, let alone fight back. After a few of those, he starts buying into his own hype, even though he's only starting shit with townies. Which naturally leads him to get wind of me."

"Ah. Shit," Nell said.

Balancing his cigarette between his teeth, Jonah made a fist in front of his face and blew smoke across the scars on his knuckles.

"Yeah. He thinks it's like in the movies, prison-yard rules or whatever. Find the meanest bastard you can and beat 'em bad and loud enough that word gets around. And it wasn't like I hadn't gotten into shit with the local skinheads before; so if this kid wanted to take a shot at a notable pain in their ass, bully for him, good luck."

"How'd you find out about all of this?"

"Dunno, a lot of it came out later, and the rest I sort of . . . figured out on my own, I guess. It wasn't that hard. Nazis aren't that smart to begin with. If they were, they wouldn't be fucking Nazis."

"Yeah, that fits," Nell said. "So, what happened when this Lawson kid finally found you?"

"I was at this place downtown, some shithole dive I'm sure isn't there anymore, minding my business at the dark end of the bar, trying to drink the cold out of my hide, because it is freezing outside that night. I'm already a few rounds in when Lawson rolls up and starts trying to get my attention, talking loud, throwing coasters, dumbass stuff like that. I ignore him at first, but this little Hitler Youth shitling is persistent, man. He's made his mind all the way up, and he's obviously not going to lay off until I give him what he wants. So, fine. I follow him out back to the alley to deal with it.

"Outside, Lawson starts cracking his knuckles, playing all tough guy; when I don't respond to that, he mugs this shitty little grin and feints forward, swinging fists, trying to bait me, and says, 'See something you like, fuckface?' And I don't know if it was the homophobic shit coming out of his mouth, the fucking swastikas on his hands, or the fact that there was no reason this had to happen at all, but I go off on this kid, Nellie. Full berserker mode. Kick his legs out from under him and just go to town, both fists. I don't stop hitting him until he stops moving, and when it's over I just leave him there bleeding, on the ground, in the cold. Figured he got exactly what he was asking for, right? So fuck him. I go back inside, finish my drink, pay, and leave. Nobody looks twice at me.

"I don't know, maybe if it was warmer outside he would have been fine, but. Albuquerque winters. You know. Kid laid there in the freeze all night, beat to hell and blacked out. Never woke up. Garbage collectors found him the next morning, laid out next to the dumpsters, right where I'd left him. He'd been dead for hours by then. Exposure."

"Shit, okay, yeah, I remember this," Nell said. "It was all over the news, right?"

"For a little while, yeah," Jonah said. "Some people got up in arms about it, made enough noise that a couple local stations took notice. Lawson came from a nice enough family, but he was sleeping rough by then, crashing in shooting galleries when he wasn't spending nights behind bars for assault or whatever else. Didn't matter to APD that he ended up dead; he was just some homeless skinhead with a record. Cops don't give a fuck about people like that. They never looked too hard for whoever gave him the beating."

"And you've been walking around with this inside you for twelve years?" Nell said. "Jesus, Jone."

"I mean, what choice did I have?" he asked. "Cop to it, go to prison for the rest of my life over killing some white supremacist piece of shit? No, fuck that noise. I kept my head down for a couple of weeks, until it was clear that APD weren't going to bust down my door, then me and Molly started planning our move out West."

"You didn't kill him, though. It was a fight. They happen, and sounds like he wanted it way more than you did anyway. You were defending yourself."

"Was I, though? Like, the math is simple. He's dead because of what I did to him. That means I'm responsible. Sure, okay, I might not have put a knife in his heart or a bullet in his brain, but I'm the one who beat his ass and left him to freeze to death. That's on me. I could have done anything different, you know? I didn't have to follow him out there, and I sure as hell didn't have to hurt him that bad. Nazi piece of shit or not, I don't think he deserved to die. Any chance he could have had to be better, any version of himself he could have turned out to be, snatched away in as much time as it took me to kick his fucking head in."

"Yeah, but he swung first," Nell said. "That's a lot more than you can say for a lot of assholes out there. More than either of us can say for Vaughn."

Jonah sighed. "Yeah, maybe, but as far as I know, Vaughn isn't showing up dead to fuck with you," he said.

A horrified look washed over Nell's face. "Hold up, what?"

"That's what I was trying to say," Jonah told her. "Like I told you, I've seen some shit, Nell. I don't know if it's real, or if it's just my conscience fucking with me, but ever since it happened, Alex'll show up every once in a while. Says the same thing every time too. 'See something you like, fuckface?' The last time it happened was a couple of years back. I honestly thought that he'd fucked off for good until he showed up back in Broughton. He's been hanging around since. Don't know why. Saw him again last night, right over there." He nodded to the spot where Alex had been standing only hours before. "Point is, you want me to believe you, okay. I believe you. Haunted, possessed, whatever. We're here now. So what do we do about it?"

"We keep moving, I think," Nell said. "I kind of got the sense that Anna isn't the sort of person who gives up too easily. Maybe we can figure out a way for us to stay a step ahead of the shitstorm."

Jonah flicked his cigarette away—he watched it spin and twirl as it arced through the air and bounced off the damp ground, spraying sparks.

"What about, you know, *it*? Did Anna tell you anything useful about it?"

"You mean before she tried to cut my throat?"

"I mean, yeah."

Nell shook her head. "I don't know. Actually, maybe, yeah. She called it Murmur. Said it was royalty, one of the oldest."

"Huh," Jonah said.

Curious, he pulled his phone out of his pocket and clicked

it to life, tapping in a few search terms. He scrolled through the results until he found something that stopped his breath in his lungs.

"What? What is it?" Nell asked.

"Here," Jonah said, passing her the phone. "Take a look. Number fifty-four."

Nell held the glowing screen up in front of her face and began to read from the book he'd found online: "*The Lesser Key of Solomon*," she said. "'The fifty-fourth Spirit is called Murmur, or Murmus, or Murmux. He is a Great Duke, and an Earl; and appeareth'—wait, *appeareth*? Really?"

"That's what it says," Jonah said, his mouth pricked to one side.

"'. . . and appeareth in the Form of a Warrior riding a Gryphon, with a Ducal Crown upon his Head. There do go before him his Ministers with great Trumpets sounding. His Office is to teach Philosophy perfectly, and to constrain Souls Deceased to come before the Exorcist to answer those questions, which he may wish to put to them, if desired. He was partly of the Order of Thrones, and partly of that of Angels. He now ruleth 30 Legions of Spirits. And his seal is this . . .'"

Over her shoulder, Jonah watched her scroll down to the image below the text, an X adorned with empty crescent moons and inverted crosses, all trapped within a thick black circle. The symbol was beautiful and strange and unnerving all at once, like nothing Jonah had ever seen before. Beside him, Nell blanched.

"Holy shit," she said with an audible little gasp.

"What? Nell, what?"

Silently, she passed his phone back to him, her fingers bone-white, then from her jacket pocket tossed a pad of paper into his lap.

"Last page," she said.

Jonah began flipping through the pad, confused. The Wayfarer's logo was printed at the top, in gray curlicue script, but it was everything else on the paper that scared him. The words *Hello Nell* filled the pages, written over and over and over at every conceivable angle, filling every inch.

"Nell, what is this. . . ?"

"Last page, I said." Her tone was severe, unquestionable.

Jonah flipped to the last sheet in the pad and stared, slack-jawed and uncomprehending. The symbol from his phone screen was scratched in the center of the page, pressed so hard into the paper that the pen had nearly torn through to the cardboard underneath.

". . . What. . . ?"

"I drew that last night," Nell said. "When you were in the shower. I don't remember doing it. One second the pad was blank, and then it was. . . that."

Jonah sat there, stunned. "Jesus. And you're—"

Underneath the hood of the car, they heard the engine click, as if someone had turned the key in the ignition only to find the battery drained. They turned together to look through the windshield toward the driver's seat, but there was no one behind the wheel. No key in the ignition.

Nell said "What the fuck." Not a question.

Behind their legs, the Volvo's headlights thumped on. Inside the station wagon, the radio began to crackle and blare.

"Jesus!" Jonah cried, jumping off the hood.

Stepping down from the bumper, Nell moved down the car to the driver's-side door, keeping her distance as the noise—not music, not radio chatter, just *noise*—grew louder. Moving slowly, she reached a hand out for the door handle. Jonah tensed.

"Nell, *don't*," he begged. "Please, don't."

But she was already doing it. Nell closed her hand over the handle and pulled the door open, staining the morning with that horrible, chaotic sound. At first, Jonah thought it was some kind of distant static, a signal garbled and shredded by the transmission, but the longer he stood there with the sound washing over him, the more he understood that it wasn't static at all.

It was screaming.

Hundreds of voices, thousands, all braided together in a cacophony of madness and suffering that Jonah could feel in his back teeth, as if he'd bitten down on a mouthful of aluminum foil. Tears started to pour down his cheeks; his hands shook at his sides. A gauzy darkness chewed at the corners of his vision. He was going to pass out, he was sure of it.

Beside him, Nell whipped a leg out, kicking the door shut hard enough to rattle the glass in its frame. In an instant, the headlights and radio cut out, as if she'd yanked the plug from the wall socket. Jonah stepped back uneasily, trying to stay upright as his sister turned in place, a grim look on her face.

"They were screaming my name," she muttered. "God-dammit, they were screaming my name, Jonah."

A silence passed between them, and Jonah felt a massive, unnavigable chasm open up inside his chest, all the fear and confusion and dread he'd kept locked up over the past two days finally breaking free. This was too much. He couldn't deal with this; he didn't know how. He took a step away from the car—and his sister—then he took another.

Nell turned to look at him, her eyes suddenly wide and scared. "Where are you going?"

He shook his head. "Look, I gotta...This is a lot for me, okay? I'm sorry. Talking about it's one thing, but that...that... I'm sorry. I just, I think I need a minute, all right? I'm going to go find some coffee in the front office or something. I need to..."

Nell looked like she was going to cry now. "Jonah, don't..."

He held up his hands and took another step back, away from her.

"It's cool," he said, trying to sound calm, trying to keep her the same. "It's fine. I'm fine. Just need a couple of minutes to catch my breath. Then we can go. That's all. Okay?"

Nell wilted, relenting. "Yeah, of course," she said. "Take your time. I'll get everything from upstairs, meet you back here when you're ready."

Jonah took another step back. "Yeah. Yeah, that sounds good. I'll be right back. I'm sorry, I just...Yeah."

"Yeah," she said. "See you in a couple of minutes, then."

He barely heard her. Without another word, he turned on his heels and walked toward the motel's front office, barely feeling the cold as his head smoldered with fear and horrible, wretched clarity.

Fwooooosssh.

Standing inside the empty front office, Jonah filled a Styrofoam cup with coffee from the battered silver urn on the counter, relishing the way the steam rose from its dark surface in twisting curlicues, the faint heat against his fingers anchoring him to the spot, fixing him in time and place. He was here, this was now, and that was all there was to it. Nothing else mattered. Not the ghosts or the screaming from the car radio or whatever fucking horrible thing had taken up residence inside his sister. He just needed a couple of minutes to get his brain straight. Then he'd be fine. They could get back on the road. Everything would be okay. He pushed the door open and started walking.

Outside, the morning was brittle and gray underneath the weak sunrise, the same as he'd left it only minutes before. Holding on tight to his little cup of coffee, Jonah turned the corner to walk down the alley that circled around the back of the motel, keeping his head down, watching his feet. His body felt ten times too big for him now, all oversized and slow, a massive super-robot of flesh and bone that he was piloting from some cockpit deep inside his own skull.

It was all too much, too fast. He hadn't ever told anyone about what had happened between him and Alex Lawson, and, now that it was out in the world, impossible to take back, he felt shaky, unbalanced, as if some essential bracing had been ripped out of his core architecture, leaving him liable to collapse at any moment. Between that, everything that Nell had told him, and what had just happened with the station wagon...he didn't even know where to start. It was horrible enough to find out that she'd died after that car crash, but that she was—how had she put it? Not alone in her own head anymore? Some terrified part of him wanted to call bullshit, but he knew in his heart that it really wasn't. After everything that had happened to them (and because of them) since they left San Francisco, everything he'd seen, he had to admit, yeah, it was possible. Likely, even. It made him think of his mom, and how it must have felt for her, getting a grim diagnosis when the symptoms had been there all along. You just had to pull back and see all the collected pieces to get the whole picture.

Murmur. Jonah rolled the name around in his mouth in between sips of coffee, trying to connect it to Nell's scattershot behavior, her mood shifts and memory blanks, the way her eyes kept going dull and cloudy just before she started doing awful things to herself... and others. The fights. The word carved into her arm. Her shadow. It made sense, when he looked at it all together. Jonah just hated that it did. Now that he thought about it, the last time he'd really seen the Nell he knew was back at that gas station outside Broughton.

He wished he could help her somehow, wished he could keep her from losing control of herself, keep this Murmur from taking over again, but he was powerless. He'd dealt with enough of it by now to know that for sure. Jonah didn't know what the thing hiding inside her wanted, but if it was willing to hijack his sister and put her in harm's way to do it, it wasn't fucking welcome.

Maybe the best thing right now was for Jonah to just get them home, get safe before Nell—and her stowaway—could do any more damage. They could deal with the rest of it after that.

Taking a deep pull from his coffee, Jonah turned the corner at the end of the alley and came up short as he found himself standing face-to-face with the muzzle of a nickel-silver handgun, clutched tightly in a scarred and beringed fist. Jonah's chest went cold and his vision went bright as his pupils dilated. Behind the pistol, a familiar face beamed at him with a mouthful of stained yellow teeth.

"Hey, cunt," Terry said.

Panic flooded Jonah's brain. He tried to lurch away from the old biker, meaning to run, but someone he couldn't see whanged him on the side of the head with something heavy. Pain exploded behind his eyes, bright and firework blue. He felt blood erupt from where he'd been hit, splashing down the side of his face. The coffee cup tumbled out of his hand. He started to fall.

Then the world went away.

Carrying the suitcases down the cement steps, Nell tried not to obsess about her brother. She didn't blame him for being so freaked out by everything; truth be told, she'd probably be a lot more worried if he wasn't. But that look on his face as he'd walked away, that nervous terror, that was new, and she didn't like it. The image stuck in her head like an icy hook, dragging her back and down and back and down. It didn't feel good, knowing that someone you loved was scared to death because of you. Or maybe just *of you.*

Upstairs, the bathroom was still a disaster, the broken glass all pushed up against the far wall, all the bloody shards they'd pulled from Jonah's skin piled at the bottom of the little plastic trash can like an accusation, a curse. With one foot she slid the bin underneath the sink counter, out of sight, trying to forget what it had felt like to twist that piece of glass underneath her brother's skin, how horribly satisfying it had been to watch the blood creeking down his leg and pattering on the tile below.

That hadn't been her, she reminded herself. It wasn't her that had hurt him like that.

Was it?

She'd just been so fucking angry with him, for getting involved, for screwing everything up, because the truth was, for one horrible and undeniable moment, she had wanted Anna to cut her throat and end it all. For a brief few seconds, everything that she wanted was within her reach—rest, sleep, escape—and Jonah had stolen it from her. Thinking about it now, she could feel the scabbed-over divot on her neck throbbing where Anna had nicked her. A nervous hitching quivered in her lungs, and she thought she might start bawling. It was too easy for her to forget the colossal relief she'd felt when she saw Jonah's face, stony and resolute, looming behind Anna, shotgun in hand. It was easy to ignore that cold, numbing pain she'd felt, lying there on the cement ground, under the spell of Anna's paralyzing ink. She wanted to die; she wanted to live. Pulled in both directions, she could feel herself splitting down the middle, the strain growing worse with every passing hour, and sitting insolently in the middle of it all, this monstrous fucking thing, this *Murmur*, latched onto her like a tick or a leech, feeding and growing.

Maybe that was what these things did, though. Took advantage of the smallest fracture and wormed their way inside like water into cracked stone, patiently eroding your foundation until you just shattered, all the while thinking it was your own damn fault. It was almost painful, how ordinary it all sounded. So unbearably human. But maybe that was the secret. Maybe possessions like this happened all the time, and nobody noticed.

Outside again, Nell pulled the Volvo's passenger door open and dropped herself inside, resting one foot against the dashboard as she clicked her phone to life and dialed. He answered on the third ring.

"Nellie, hey!" her dad beamed on the other end of the line, his voice a beacon in the darkness. Nell swam toward it for all she was worth. "I was wondering when I'd hear from you again. How's everything going? You hurried off the phone pretty quick yesterday, everything all right?"

"Hey, Dad, yeah," Nell said, nauseously recalling the stray dog back in Mowry, the sounds that had come ripping out of her throat and the burning, bloodthirsty urge she'd felt to attack the stray, brutalize it, kill it where it stood. "Yeah, everything's fine. Just something I had to take care of, but all good now."

"Well, all right, long as you're sure," Dad said. "I'm glad to hear everything's okay. How's Jonah holding up?"

"Yeah, he's okay," Nell sighed, hoping he wouldn't clock the lie.

"Did you have a chance to tell him about, you know, the crash and all?"

"I told him, Dad," Nell said.

"How'd he take it?"

"About as well as you'd expect," she said truthfully. "Could have been worse, I suppose. Not sure either of us slept super well last night, but it went alright. We're holding up okay beyond that, though. Nothing a cup of coffee and a cigarette won't fix."

As she spoke, she felt one of her upper teeth, the left canine, *give* the tiniest bit underneath her tongue. Confused, she pressed down on it, rocking it back and forth in its socket until the tooth hinged all the way forward with a wet sucking sound that she felt more than heard.

Oh, Jesus.

"You know, not to sound like a broken record, but I really do wish you'd give those up," Dad said. "The cigarettes. They're not good for you, Nellie. I mean, I should know, I smoked—"

"—for twenty years before me and Jonah showed up," Nell finished for him, trying to ignore the anxiety coursing through her body. "I know, Dad."

Unable to control herself, she tongued at the slack tooth as it drifted forward and forward and forward, separating from the rest of her teeth like a broken piano key. Sitting there, she stiffened, but she didn't stop pushing, instead urging the canine forward until it popped free with a tiny little *thwuck!* and fell onto the flat of her tongue, smooth like a pill and impossibly light. Instinctively, Nell gagged and tried not to swallow it, tasting blood as it glurged from the raw socket and ran down her throat.

"I'm just saying, those things'll kill you if you're not careful, is all. It's a lot easier to get into good habits in your thirties than try and break the bad ones after you cross forty."

Quietly, Nell spat the tooth out into her waiting palm and held it up in front of her face, examining it as she tongued at the open, bleeding hole in her gums. The canine was long and white-yellow in her fingers, streaked with stringy red and stained brown around the root.

Rot.

Fear bloomed in her belly like a frozen flower spreading icy petals, and she dropped the tooth, feeling suddenly unmoored from herself and from reality. She heard the canine click and bounce against the asphalt. The taste of copper was overpowering now.

"... Nell? You there?"

"Yeah, Dad, sorry," she said, swallowing back more blood. She was going to throw up, she was sure of it. "Got it. Duly noted."

"Are you sure you're doing all right, hon? You sound a little rough 'round the edges."

"Yeah, I'm okay," Nell lied, trying to keep her voice calm. "Tired is all. And I miss you. I really wish you were here."

"I miss you too, sweetie. And I wish I was there with you two, but it's good for you and your brother to get this time together. You guys used to be thick as thieves before he moved away. I'm glad you two are reconnecting, and you're going to be home before you know it."

"You're probably right."

"Well, listen: you rest up and take care of yourself. Albuquerque will still be around by the time you show up. There's no hurry, you know. You two take it slow and get here safe."

Nell stared down at the bloody tooth on the blacktop. "I know, Dad. We will. Love you."

"Love you too, sweetie. I'll see you when I see you."

"Yeah," Nell told him. "Not too long now."

"Sounds good. Talk to you soon."

Hands trembling, Nell ended the call, set her phone down on the dashboard, then buried her face in her hands and started to quietly cry to herself.

Fifteen minutes later, Jonah still hadn't returned. Pulling her jacket on, Nell locked the station wagon and went looking for him, telling herself she wasn't nervous, wasn't scared. Passing by the motel's front office, she peeked through the streaky glass, looking for any sign of him, but it was empty save for the woman behind the desk, an older lady with frizzy white hair and too much makeup leafing through a well-read magazine. Nell stepped inside and approached the woman, keeping her lips tight so to not show off the new bloody hole in her smile. On the front of the woman's shirt was a nametag that read *Gail*.

"Hi," Nell said, as sweetly as she could manage.

One of the woman's drawn-on eyebrows rose, but she didn't look away from her magazine.

"Mmm. Help you?"

"Yeah, I hope so," Nell said. "My brother and I stayed here last night, and he's not around, said he was going for a walk. I was wondering if maybe you'd seen him, maybe he stopped in here for coffee or something? Tall guy, shaggy black hair, kind of looks like a vampire who's really into The Cure?"

"Sorry, haven't seen him," Gail said. "Musta come by when I was in the back, I guess. He not in your room?"

"Pretty sure not."

"Hm. Well, not many places around here for walking, so can't say for sure where he could've gone," Gail said. "Maybe check the alley around back. That's where some of the folks working here go out to smoke. Revolting habit."

"Sure is," Nell replied, hating this woman more with every passing second.

"Anyway, maybe you check out there, sweetie. Other than that, your guess is as good as mine. Sorry about it."

"Oh, okay," Nell said. "I'll check the alley, I guess. Thanks."

"Mmm," the woman said, turning another celebrity-filled page. "Take some coffee too, if you like."

Stepping out of the office, Nell scanned the parking lot, crossing her arms over her chest in a futile attempt to guard herself against the cold. Turning right, she circled around the building, heading for the alley Gail had mentioned. It wasn't much, just a long stretch of cracked asphalt that ran the length of the motel and cornered around at the far end. Walking down, she found the smoker's area the old woman had mentioned, an industrial spool turned on its side for a table with a couple of scuffed plastic lawn chairs arranged around it.

At the far end of the alley, just at the corner, there was

a puddle of coffee creeping across the asphalt, a white Styrofoam cup lolling in its center. Nell approached it slowly, toeing the cup back and forth in the puddle. There had been a stack of these set up inside the front office. She knelt down and dipped a finger into the spreading puddle: still the faintest bit warm.

That's when she saw the blood.

There was just enough to be noticeable, an uneven splash of red at the coffee's edge that streaked down the short end of the alley like the tail of a comet. She already knew it was Jonah's. Standing back up, Nell followed the splatter down as it became a trickle, then a dribble, then nothing at all.

In her jacket pocket, her phone started to ring. She pulled it out and looked at the display—no name, not even a location, just the words *Unknown Caller* hovering over a familiar phone number. Grinding her molars, she swiped her thumb across the screen and brought the phone to her ear.

"This was you," Nell said, her tone flat and colorless. She wasn't asking, because she already knew the truth. Of course it was her. But she wasn't about to let that bitch get the first word in.

"What, no *Hi, how are you doing* for your old friend?" Anna said on the other end of the line. "That's hurtful, Nell. Honestly, that stings."

"We're not friends," Nell said. "We're not anything."

"Oh, come on, we both know that isn't true," Anna said.

"What do you want?"

"You know what I want, Nell," Anna said. "Same thing I've always wanted. Did you really forget already? Maybe we should ask Jonah."

There was a muffled bluster of noise; a second later, Nell heard a feeble, uneven wheezing on the other end of the line.

"...Nell?" her brother asked on the other end of the line, his voice muddled, drunken. Nell's blood ran to glacial slush, spreading from her heart to her stomach, her limbs, her fingers, her toes, tendrilling up past the base of her skull, into her jaw, her eardrums, her brain.

"Nell, don't come," Jonah wheezed. "Go, get the fuck out of here, okay? Please, Nellie. You can't..."

More muffled noise.

"Hi, yeah, looks like somebody's a little tired right now, I had to put him down for a nap," Anna sneered. "Sorry about that," Anna sneered.

"Give him back."

"It's not that easy, Nell," Anna replied. "Not anymore. I told you I'd find you. I mean, come on. After everything you've been through, everything you've seen, did you really think I was, what, bluffing about that? Did you really think you could get away? You know me better than that by now. At least you should."

"I don't know you at all," Nell said.

"You know enough, though, don't you? You know what I have to do, and I think you know just how far I'll go to make sure it happens."

"Sure," Nell replied. "Next, you're going to tell me that if there was a way to get this thing out of me that didn't involve cutting my throat, you'd do that."

"I would, because it's the truth," Anna said, sounding the tiniest bit defensive.

Rage ripped free inside Nell's chest, an out-of-control blaze crashing clean through a firebreak.

"Oh, bullshit," she barked into the phone. "*Bullshit.* Nobody does the kind of things you do with a straight face unless they fucking enjoy it."

"You don't know what it's like, Nell. You don't know how I was raised."

"I know enough. You were right about that." Turning in place, Nell scanned the windows in the buildings around her, all empty eyes in the early morning light. "You play hardcase because you don't think anybody's going to clock you, peacocking with all your muscles and tattoos. Big bad Anna, right? Better not fuck with her. Except I think—not that you asked, but I think that if you believed you had a shot in hell of taking me on, you'd have made your move already, instead of bringing my brother into this."

"Your brother brought himself into this when he put a gun to my head."

"Takes two to tango," Nell said. "You're the one calling me from wherever the hell, making threats like I don't see the kind of shitty little coward you are."

"Stop talking," Anna said.

"Or what?"

"Or I put Jonah down for good, and I come and find you anyway."

Nell didn't say anything, stuffing the tip of her tongue into the raw socket where her tooth used to be, tasting iron.

"You know I will," Anna said. "You know I will."

"I know," Nell said, after another moment.

"Look at it this way, Nell: Either one of you gets to walk away from this, or neither of you do. It's your choice. It's on you to make the right one."

Nell's hands had gone numb in the cold, and she had to bear down on her phone to be sure it didn't slip from her fingers. This wasn't right. This wasn't fair. This wasn't how it was supposed to go. But she didn't have any moves left. Anna had them over a barrel.

"Okay," Nell said, deflating. "Fine. Where are you?"

"Not far," Anna said. "There's an abandoned building a few blocks south of the motel, just off the highway. Kind of an old warehouse. Big faded sign out front that says *Bothwell Provisions*. You really can't miss it. There's a door around back; it looks like it's chained shut but it isn't. Down the hallway, first floor. I'll be waiting. I don't need to tell you what'll happen if you do something stupid like call the cops, do I?"

"No, I got it," Nell said. "No cops. Understood. I'll be there in a few minutes."

"Good," Anna said. "And Nell?"

"What?"

"I think you'd better move fast. Jonah doesn't look like he's doing too good."

The phone went dead in her ear, and Nell had to fight the overwhelming urge to haul off and throw it against the nearest wall. She stuffed it in her pockets and let her hands twist up into bony, knotty clubs, her fingernails drawing blood from the soft skin of her palms. Standing there, she screamed as hard as she could, feeling her face grow hot with blood as she raged and howled and spun in circles and kicked at the ground.

Fuck, fuck, fuck, *fuck*.

The fury was a pressure-cooker bomb going off inside her head, exploding in a spray of shrapnel and flame that shredded everything dumb enough to get caught in its path. This was a trap. She wasn't stupid—obviously this was a fucking trap. Whatever Anna had planned when Nell showed up, it wasn't going to end well for anyone.

But she didn't have any other choice. Not really.

So squaring her shoulders, she started walking south.

Bothwell Provisions sat a few blocks down from the motel, an ancient and neglected multi-story warehouse that looked like it had been here since before the days of the automobile. Almost all the windows had been smashed out long ago, the empty frames hanging lifeless and black in the sides of the building like tiny voids drilled through reality. As she passed into the warehouse's shadow, Nell couldn't shake the feeling that she was being watched, as if every empty window held some invisible malefactor just waiting for their chance to strike. The crumbling old structure was still and dark, but she could feel from here that it wasn't empty. Anna was in there, with her storm of faces and screams. Jonah too.

Near the far corner of the building, there was a sheet of splintered plywood that had been cut into the shape of a door and chained to the frame behind it, just like Anna said. Down at the bottom, Nell could see where the board was cracked and coming away from its bonds, the space between barely enough for her to squeeze through. Nell bent at the hip to try to see inside, but beyond the door lay only shadow and silence. She should have brought the shotgun. That would have been a hell of a lot better than all the nothing she'd brought with her instead, but it was too late to go back, now. Whatever Anna had already done to Jonah, Nell didn't have any reason to believe that she was lying about hurting him again, even killing him, if she felt like she was being jerked around. No, Nell had to move now or never.

A trembling breeze blew through the gaps in the plywood door from the darkness beyond, ruffling Nell's clothes, raising the hairs on the back of her neck to attention. She took a deep, slow breath, holding one rawboned hand to her chest, feeling her heart *tick-tock-tick-tock* under her breastbone, her pulse quick and nervous.

"Look, if you're listening, I could really use some backup right about now," she said to the thing inside her, not really expecting an answer, and receiving none.

"Great," she said. "Thanks. Whole lot of help you are."

Stooping down, Nell pushed her way past the chain and stepped through into the shadows.

Y ou're going to regret doing this," Jonah muttered at Anna
and the bikers from where he sat slumped on the floor,
hands tied behind his back. "All of you. I swear, no matter
what happens, I'm going to make sure you fucking regret this."

"Shut up," Terry barked at him from the center of the room,
sitting with his feet propped up on a ramshackle old table. Anna
lurked silently against the far wall, next to a greasy stain that
climbed toward the rafters, while Terry's other guy, the one
with the glasses, stood by the hallway door, waiting patiently.
Jonah still didn't know where the third guy, the one with the
beard, had gone to, but if his friends didn't seem concerned
about it, he didn't see any reason to worry. He had enough of
those right now.

Jonah had come to on the rough old hardwood, hands tied
tight at the small of his back, bleeding from his head, his whole
body shaking with pain. He didn't know where they were, but
it couldn't have been far from the motel, not if they really
expected Nell to show up at the drop of a hat. Christ, but his
head hurt. They'd belted him a good one back in the alley, then
another after he'd tried to tell his sister to stay away.

"What if I don't, Terry?" Jonah mocked, the words coming
out all pulpy and swollen. "You going to hit me again? Big man,
beating on somebody with his hands tied. Real impressive."

Terry's expression twisted into a mask of anger. "Shut the
fuck up, I said."

"Come and make me," Jonah said, smirking at the old
biker with bloody teeth.

Terry stared knives at him, his face trembling with
violence.

"You wait and see, Ter," Jonah said. "I'll take one of your eyes before this is all over. My word on that."

As Jonah leered at the old man, Terry arched his back and drew his pistol from his belt. He racked the slide, kicking a single unfired round out of the breach, then caught it as it spun in midair, an easy, practiced move.

"You see this?" Terry asked, holding the bullet up for Jonah to see. "I'm saving this one for you. Once everything's over and done with, this is going through your brain." He set it down on the table with a soft *click* and left it there, pointing straight up at the ceiling.

"Spoken like a true bitch," Jonah said. "You really want to prove something, cut me loose and we can see how hard you really are."

"Both of you, shut your mouths," Anna hissed from the shadows. "She's here."

Jonah's stomach dropped.

A second later, the door creaked open and Nell stepped through into the darkened room, looking worse than Jonah remembered. Her shoulders sloped at a deeper angle than they had before, the circles under her eyes thick and dark in the low light. Standing in front of the doorway, Nell glanced from Anna to Jonah to Terry and then back again.

"Oh. So you guys know each other," she said, an acerbic note staining her voice. "That's fun."

Anna moved closer to her, beckoning her forward.

"I'm glad you came," Anna said.

Nell held up a hand. "Spare me the fake fucking pleasantries. You wanted me here, I'm here. Let's get this over with."

Anna's shoulders fell. "Fine," she said. "Have it your way."

Nell stayed put, her eyes flashing over to size up her brother.

"You okay?" she asked.

Jonah met his sister's gaze, then spat a mouthful of bloody saliva on the floor in front of his knees.

"Thought I told you not to come," he said.

"Shut the fuck up," Terry rasped again.

Nell turned to look at Anna again. "Let him go first," she said. "Then we can talk."

"Sorry, not how this works," Anna said. "Take her."

As Jonah watched helplessly, the other biker, Glasses, materialized from the shadows and clapped a hand around Nell's throat, then hooked his other arm behind both her elbows. On the ground, Jonah thrashed and twisted, unable to get loose, unable to help but still trying. Visibly panicking now, Nell struggled and fought against the man, but it was a losing bet. She was at a bad angle, and the biker's grip was too sure, too strong. He dragged her over to the table and threw her onto it with a *crash*, knocking Terry's stray bullet away. The old man rose from his seat and helped Glasses hold her in place, stretching her arms up over her head. One of Glasses's hands dipped into the pocket of Nell's jacket as she kicked and flailed, relieving her of her smokes and lighter. On the far side of the table, Jonah watched Anna approach the table, a heavy old hammer in one hand, the other curled into a fist by her side.

"You know," Anna said as she drew in close, "normally I'd use the ink, but we both know that you already blew your chance to do this the easy way."

The tattooed woman passed the hammer to Terry, then raised her fist over Nell's chest and opened her fingers, spilling a handful of long, rusty nails on top of Jonah's sister.

F— or a second, she didn't believe they were really going to do it.

Then they really did it.

While Anna watched dispassionately, Terry lined the first nail up in the center of Nell's right palm, raised the old hammer high above his head, then brought it down in a ferocious arc.

Crunch.

Nell screamed at the top of her lungs as the nail pierced her hand like a needle through fabric, leaving her whole arm trembling with agony. The sound of the nail punching through her flesh was awful, flat and dull like a book falling off a shelf. Terry swung again, and Nell felt the nail break through the other side of her hand, biting deep into the table underneath. Howling, she began to thrash and fight, struggling against the third biker's iron grip as Terry raised up and swung a third time.

Crunch.

The nail sank farther into the tabletop, pinning Nell's hand to the wood like a butterfly on corkboard. She roared in pain and fury as blood pooled in her palm and rolled messily over the edges, leaching into her clothes and hair. Then Anna was hovering over her again, as calm and collected as she'd ever been.

"This could have been painless, you know," she said, stroking the side of Nell's face with the back of her fingers. "This could have been so easy. But you and your useless brother simply don't know when to quit."

Breathing deep, Nell reared back and spat in her face.

"Fuck you," she snarled at Anna with all the hate she could muster. "Fucking fuck you."

251

Anna wiped the saliva from her cheek and nose, almost amused.

"You know, I'd expected more from you," she said as Terry lined up a second nail, just beside the first. "I truly don't know why."

Nell clenched her teeth as hard as she could as the old biker brought the hammer down again, and again, and again.

Crunch.

Crunch.

Crunch.

A second later, he moved on to Nell's other hand, wordlessly driving nail after nail after nail through the flesh and bone as Glasses held her in place. The pain was colossal, incomprehensible; after Terry had pounded the fifth nail through, Nell could feel herself starting to float away, separating from her body and the suffering that was filling it up. For a single heartbeat, she could see herself from above, stretched across the old tabletop, her bleeding hands pinned above her head, her expression dull and slack from the pain and the shock. Distantly, she was aware that the other biker had released her wrists, but it didn't matter now: she wasn't going anywhere. Somewhere beyond her field of vision, she heard Terry toss the hammer to the hardwood floor, its purpose served.

"I didn't want it to be like this, Nell. I hope you know that," Anna said.

"I did," Terry chuckled, wearing a mean sneer underneath his crazy fucking eyes.

Off to the side of the table, the other biker watched Nell intently, regarding her silently behind the white-flared lenses of his spectacles, lighting a cigarette from the pack he'd stolen off her. Beside Anna, Terry nodded at Jonah.

"What about him? Let him go?"

Anna looked back at Nell's brother, then shot Nell a knowing look.

"Show her what happens to people who disobey."

Effortlessly, the two bikers heaved Jonah up off the floor, and Nell felt the thick fog that had settled inside her head burn away in an instant, replaced by a cutting, volcanic clarity.

"Jonah, Jonah, *Jonah!* No, no, let him go, you assholes! Let him go, I said!"

Nell struggled against the nails, tearing the wounds wider, loosing a fresh rush of blood from both palms. The pain of it was incredible, almost revelatory, but still Nell struggled, thrashing to get free, to stop them, to save her brother.

Terry pulled his silver handgun from his belt and caressed Jonah's battered face with the muzzle, smiling softly as he pressed it to the hollow of his jaw. Circling Jonah and the bikers, Anna produced her straight razor from her pocket, unfolding and twirling it nimbly in her long fingers, pointing the blade at Nell.

"I want you to watch this, Nell. This is happening because of you."

Shutting her eyes tight, Nell fought against the metal that pinned her hands to the table, body shaking with insectoid desperation as she pleaded madly with the thing hiding inside her:

Please, please, please, not like this. I can't die like this, he can't die like this, we can't, not here, not now, I can't, I won't. I'll give you whatever you want, I'll do anything, just help us, please, help me, help me, help me HELP ME HELP ME FUCK-ING PLEASE PLEASE PLEASE HELP ME PLEASE—

She didn't expect it to work. She didn't expect anything but suffering and death for both of them now. She'd been danc-ing along a high wire for too long, spitting in the face of the inevitable like it didn't apply to her. Now came the fall. Now came the end.

But then—a warmth, feverish and sick, spread through her body as time slowed to a trickle, then a halt, the vicious scavengers standing over her suspended midthought, unaware that anything was wrong. Nell inhaled deeply and felt her lungs burning as they filled with something that wasn't oxygen, wasn't even air. Rich, stinging, and sharp, it felt as if she was breathing light itself. She blinked and saw the world overlaid with color and sound and energy—so much energy. It was every-where. She saw every heartbeat, she felt every sound parting the air, heard every flicker of every shadow in the farthest chambers of her heart; and in that perfect, frozen moment, all her own, she knew for good and all that she was not alone.

She felt the intruder—*Murmur*—unfurl itself from its hidden shelter buried deep inside her, sliding along her limbs, into her back, her skull, as if it were climbing into a suit, tailored so perfectly for one another that Nell couldn't tell where she ended and it began. They were blurred around the edges, wounded and desperate, but unquestionably whole.

Pinned to the table, Nell voided her lungs and watched as a narrow plume of black smoke jetted from her lips, twisting in a wind that wasn't there. When she breathed in again, the smoke rushed back inside, through her mouth and her nostrils, and once more she felt that severe, burning light brimming within her lungs. She blinked, and she blinked, and time began moving again.

She pulled against the nails that Terry had driven through her hands—they slid easily from the tabletop now, like knives from a block, and Nell stood, moving silently, feeling that overwhelming power hunt through her every muscle and nerve. She was still bleeding, but that didn't matter now. She moved with a speed and ease she'd never known before, while the other little things around her seemed as if they were trapped underwater, sluggish and awkward. They hadn't even noticed that she'd risen. Making a fist around the nailheads pressing into her palm, she lunged forward, fast as an adder, and struck the old man in the face, knocking him to the floor and freeing her brother from his grip. Jonah fell.

Beside her, Anna screamed and recoiled, and Nell snapped an elbow out, catching the woman in the heart with a sick *crack!* before turning her attention onto the other biker. Closing a bloody hand over his face, Nell shoved as hard as she could, throwing him halfway across the room.

Dropping to one knee beside her brother, she yanked at the rope binding his wrists, splitting it to shreds. Jonah met her eyes for a moment, then shambled after Glasses, his gait fitful and uneven. He caught the man in the stomach with a hard shoulder, spearing him to the ground, then took the biker's head in both hands and rang it against the hardwood with a heavy *thwock*. Drunkenly, Glasses cuffed a fist into Jonah's jaw and threw himself forward, tackling Jonah over and kneeing him in the ribs.

Nell heard a well-oiled *click* behind her back.

"Put your fucking hands up, you evil little bitch."

She tossed the shredded rope aside and turned to face the old man, a red-purple weal in the shape of her fist already rising around his mouth. His pistol hovered mere inches from her face, the muzzle leering at her with one dead black eye. She showed him a wide bloody grin and raised her hands for him to see, nails driven messily through both palms, red pouring down her arms.

"You mean these?"

She started toward him, and he recoiled, swinging the butt of the pistol at her head. She deflected it with a speed and strength that she still only barely recognized, batting his hand away as if it were a buzzing fly. Ducking in close, she hit him again, this time with a straight shot to the ribs. Terry shrank back, yelping.

The old man brought the gun up once more, pointing it at Nell's chest just below her heart. Seeing it there, hanging in the air between them, shaking in time with the tremors of Terry's arm, Nell couldn't help but laugh.

"What is it with shitty white guys and guns?" she said, smirking at the terrified old man. "I mean, really. It's fucking pathetic."

Fuming, Terry made a strangled sound in his throat and pulled the trigger.

H e screamed. He was sure he screamed. Except he didn't hear it. He didn't hear anything; not the blood wailing in his ears, not the dull impacts of the biker's knee against his ribs. There was only the gunshot, huge and awful and deadly. Nell jerked as the bullet cut through her, blowing a geyser of blood out of her back in slow motion. Pinned to the floor, Jonah choked back his next scream, frozen and alone and waiting for his sister to finally drop.

Oh, god, she's dead, she's dead she's fucking dead—

Except Nell didn't drop.

Still upright, she jerked and twisted like a puppet hung from a wire. As Jonah watched, a tattered *huuuurk* escaped her throat, almost like she was choking; the noise morphed into a wet, gruesome cough, and a second later, she spat a jagged, mashed metal lump onto the floor: the bullet, messy with her own blood.

"Yeah," she rasped, voice damp and tattered. "That's what I thought."

Terry blanched, his arm trembling. He pulled the trigger again, but Nell was already moving. Effortlessly, she ducked out of the way of the second bullet, that flat light boiling in her eyes, and slapped the pistol out of Terry's hand before he could get a third shot off. It skidded across the floor, coming to a rest just out of Jonah's reach as he struggled to escape Glasses's relentless grasp. Lunging forward, Nell popped a fist into Terry's chest, dropping him in an instant.

"I've seen how you die, Terry. I've seen how all of you die," Nell said as she loomed over him.

Still pinned to the floor, Jonah twisted away and kicked his legs, reaching for the gun as he drove a left hook into Glasses's temple, hitting him hard enough to loosen his grip. Wriggling out from underneath the furious biker, Jonah scrambled back and booted the man in the face, knocking the cigarette from his lips, sending it flying into that dark, oily stain on the far wall. Watching the burning Camel float through the air, Jonah had just enough time to think *Oh, sh—!* before the stain burst into flames.

A wave of sudden heat rolled over his face and chest. As the fire grew and started to climb the ceiling, Jonah saw a flash of movement across the room: back on his feet again, Terry had snatched the hammer from the floor and was recklessly swinging it at Nell as she advanced on him. As if that would stop her now.

"Do you want to know how it happens, Ter-bear?" Nell jeered as she stalked after the old man. "I can show you if you ask nice."

Terry wound up and wheeled the hammer at her in a wild overhead swing, but Nell was too fast for him, too strong: stepping in close, she yanked the hammer from his hand and drove it into his stomach, eliciting a pained gasp from the old man. Clutching at his midsection, Terry lumbered back as Nell tossed the hammer away.

Crawling on all fours, still feeling the heat lick at his back, Jonah hobbled toward Terry's discarded pistol, desperate for something—anything—to defend himself with, but he was too slow. Someone kicked him in the side, and he rolled onto his back just in time to see Glasses drop down on top of him, growling like a wild animal.

Jonah screamed and tried to struggle away from the man, but Glasses held him fast, bunching one massive fist in the collar of his shirt, eyes blazing and unhinged behind his lenses. Bellowing, the biker threw his forehead down into Jonah's nose; Jonah felt it crunch and pop loose, gushing blood like a hose. Glasses headbutted him again, then dropped his other hand onto the side of Jonah's face, furiously pressing his head into the floor. Jonah kicked his legs and flailed his arms, desperate to reach the discarded semi-auto. He was only inches away now, it was only a little farther...

"No, you die..." Glasses growled, bearing down so hard that for a second Jonah thought he was going to crush his skull flat. "You fucking die...*you fucking die*..."

Jonah's hand closed on the pistol, and for a second he thought—

See something you like, fuckface?

Blindly, Jonah jammed the gun against Glasses' belly. He didn't even notice that he was pulling the trigger until he heard the sharp *pop-pop-pop-pop* rip into the man's midsection. On top of him, the biker bucked and shuddered as the bullets sawed through him, hands jumping to his abdomen, blood pouring between his fingers.

The gun clacked empty in Jonah's fist. He tossed it aside and shoved the dying man off him as he lay there, feeling the air grow hotter as he tried to catch his breath. Beside him, the biker lolled back and forth, jaw working soundlessly while he tried and failed to stop the blood spewing out of him. Shitty way to die.

Rolling over, Jonah started to stand, rising slowly to his hands and knees, looking down at the hardwood floor, trying not to vomit from the pain and the nausea and the rising heat.

Then someone punched him in the back of the head, and the world went swimmy.

His face hit the floor.

H e could feel himself flagging.

Every swing of his fist, every kick, every breath he drew, every beat of his heart, they all dragged him closer and closer to utter collapse. He'd been running on empty for too long now, and he knew it—basically no sleep, barely any food, too much coke, all his senses keyed so far up that it was impossible for him to rest, even when he was sitting still. This wasn't how ambushes were supposed to work. These fucks were supposed to be dead by now. Shit, they should have been dead two days ago, but for some reason they wouldn't fucking die.

As the room burned around them, Nell swiped at him with one fist, then the other. Terry ducked to the side, tried to hit back, but she was waiting for him there too. Closing one bloody hand around his wrist, she pulled him in close, then started pounding on his collarbone, hitting him again and again and again until he felt something crack inside his chest. He lost all his air. His vision blurred, threatened to go dark.

Christ, but she hit so fucking hard. It was like getting sucker-punched by a jackhammer. Terry'd never known any-one who could hit someone like that. Desperate, he yanked his arm free from her viselike grasp and backed up as fast as his feet would carry him, trying to catch his breath against the new stabbing sensation above his heart, trying to figure out a move that wouldn't get his ass beat to death.

Except maybe it was too late for that.

Terry's blood had stopped dead in his veins when he'd seen that the murderous little bitch had torn herself from the table, fists full of bloody nails, but it wasn't until she'd spat his bullet back at him that he understood how completely fucked he was. There was something inside her, oh yes, something otherworldly, something vicious. Terry had watched it rise out of her eyes, her nose and lips, her skin and her pores like thick, black smoke, shadow given form. It swirled around the girl in a blurry cloud before sharpening into something that resembled a human body only in the vaguest sense: two arms, two legs, it loomed twelve feet high and hulking, its misshapen head bursting with a crown of tangled antlers that twisted around each other like tree roots.

Terry took a step back, trying to find surer footing, but she was already on top of him, pummeling him with those jack-hammer arms as the shadow-thing loomed and watched, baring its hundreds of yellow teeth at him in a revolting grin. He understood then—he had a choice: stay and die, or run away and never look back. Darko was already done for, and he didn't know what had happened to Anna, but right now he didn't care. He was still alive. That was all that mattered.

Yanking him close again, Nell buried her knee in his gut, bouncing him back across the hardwood floor. This was his only chance. It wasn't much, but it would have to do. Dragging himself back up to his feet, Terry staggered away from the Talbot girl and her cloak of living smoke, then turned tail and ran for his life.

Nell
Elbert, UT
495 miles to Albuquerque

She watched the old man go, scrutinizing the shape of him as he beat his retreat and disappeared down the far hallway, flailing and clutching at the fractured place below the crook of his shoulder, trying to not cry like a child. Good. Fuck him anyway. She'd deal with him later. Soaked in blood, Nell watched the flames climb the wall, smiling to herself as they spread. Soon the whole building would go up in flames. What a lovely sight that would be.

"Nell, stop this," someone called out from behind her. She turned to look.

Anna.

Holding one hand over her heart, shoulders slumped forward, the tattooed woman stood over Jonah, sprawled flat on the floor, writhing in a daze. What the hell had she done to him? Leaving Jonah where he lay, Anna limped toward Nell, wheezing as strings of blood spilled messily over her bottom lip.

"Of *course*," Nell said.

Anna raised one hand in a kind of half-hearted surrender as she stepped in closer.

"I want to help you," Anna gasped. "That's all I've ever wanted."

Nell raised both of her nail-punctured hands up to the light, the blood glistening in the glow of the growing flames around them.

"Sure, that's why you did this. Because you wanted to *help*."

Nell leaped at her, brutalized hands outstretched, meaning to drag her down to the floor and beat her to death, but the straight razor was in Anna's fist again, flashing out to slice through the thick leather of Nell's jacket, drawing blood from underneath. Nell barely felt it. When Anna swung again, Nell caught her wrist and plucked the razor from her fingers, then tossed it away. Anna's face blanched as she struggled uselessly against Nell's grasp.

"You're losing control," Nell said with a voice that was and wasn't hers. "They won't stay trapped forever."

She knotted one nail-filled fist tight and backhanded it into Anna's face, feeling the sharp wrought-iron jags shear the flesh apart with a wet ripping noise. Anna screamed and tried to pull away, but Nell held her fast and hit her again, shivering with pleasure as she felt the twisted metal tear deeper, ruining the woman's face. Shame. She'd been so pretty before Nell had clocked what a psychopath she was. Screaming, Anna hit back, firing a fist of her own into Nell's chest and the raggedy bullet hole that had been blown into it only minutes before.

Pain, unbelievable pain, blasted through Nell's body, slackening her grip the tiniest bit, and Anna hit her again, harder this time. Nell couldn't hold on anymore—she felt her grasp on the woman's arm slip. Gravity went funny and she went tumbling back, the ground rising up to meet her shoulders as Anna followed her down, punching the bloody wound beside Nell's heart over and over, harder and harder, setting off dazzling explosions behind her eyes.

Nell hit the floor hard, and her consciousness faltered. She saw stars behind the burning room, twisting and shining in the distance, and between their light, an inky, fathomless darkness that spread like a perpetual cancer, killing out everything that dared stand in its way.

Nell fell apart from her body, into that absolute darkness beyond thought, beyond prayer or hope, beyond every dead and ruined world, carried into memory by the bestial, deathless thing that had so completely infected her. She saw the fires of creation, and the savage, fathomless atrocities born from those fires, bleeding trigonometric horrors that bore the screaming faces of infants in the centers of their heinous architecture. She saw a million-million worlds reduced to cinders in an instant by a vast celestial war that threatened to spill across creation and burn a million-million more. She witnessed violence and brutality on a scale that she had never dreamed possible: corpses gleefully defiled by those gleaming, alary creatures, children burned to coal, cities built from the stolen bones of the mutilated and the dead alike. She drifted across the blurry border separating *she* and *it*, lost to an eternity that she had never known had always been swirling around the place she called reality, and at the bottom of existence she beheld an empty, devouring maw filled with teeth and need, attended to by spinning ciphers of wings and fire and knives and blood. Chanting, singing, exalting, endless, the ciphers fed that great gaping mouth incessantly, casting the asomatous remains of the mewling, finite plague-things that so filled their precious Creation into the void that waited below.

She saw what was waiting for all life, at the end of everything.

Then the darkness crashed over her and she was gone.

S tanding over Nell, Anna sucked air in tiny little sips, rubbing at the sharp ache that had settled between her breasts.
She didn't know if that first elbow to the heart had cracked
her sternum or only bruised it to hell, but either way it was
going to be a problem down the line. She inhaled slow and shallow, trying to not aggravate her battered chest, and waited for
Nell to stir.

Nell didn't stir.

Limping over to where Nell had thrown her razor, Anna
knelt and picked it up off the floor, cradling it in shaky fingers
as she crossed back over toward the fallen woman. All around
her, flames climbed the walls, the heat commingling with the
warmth of the blood pouring down her jaw and neck where Nell
had gored her. She tongued at the inside of her cheek, surveying
the damage. Near the back, there was a hole torn all the way
through, a raw little pinprick that bubbled blood every time she
breathed.

Raising one hand to her face, she probed unevenly at the
wounds with half-numb fingertips. The cuts were jagged, deep
and bloody, a messy crisscross that stretched from her hairline
all the way down to the middle of her chin. Nell had mangled
her. She was lucky she hadn't lost an eye in the process.

But she didn't need a whole face to do what needed to be
done.

She could still finish it.

Anna let the straight razor fall open in her hand, pinching the tang between her thumb and forefinger and supporting
the filigreed scales in the rest of her hand, just like she'd been
taught. Unbidden, her father's scar-pocked face materialized
from the depths of her memory.

One stroke, Annie. Make it quick. No need to cause any undue suffering. You're freeing them, after all. Even if it looks ugly. Least you can do is not drag it out.

She wondered what Dad would think about everything that had happened over the last few days. Would he understand, or would he get angry, like he always did when she messed up? He hadn't been a kind teacher, but he'd taught her well all the same. Sometimes things just went wrong. He'd taught her that too. And this had gone about as wrong as anything she'd ever heard of. She hoped he'd have understood that she was doing the best she could with the cards she'd been dealt, but at the end of the day, he was long gone to the Lord and she was here. It wasn't his call anymore. She knelt down over Nell and used her free hand to push a few stray locks of hair away from her face.

She heard a heavy shuffling behind her and turned to see Jonah, a bloody ghost of himself, limping toward her, the hammer dangling awkwardly from one hand.

"I thought I told you to leave my sister alone," he wheezed.

Clutching at her injured chest, Anna turned to face him, tonguing at the bloody pinhole in her cheek, nimbly twirling the straight razor in her fingertips. At least some part of her still worked.

"You know I can't do that," she said.

He took a step closer to her, and she jabbed the razor at him, as if to ward him off. "Do you know what's hiding inside your sister, Jonah? Do you know how bad it really is?"

"She told me."

"Everything?"

"Enough."

"Then you know the risk you're taking, letting her walk around with that thing inside her. Better to cut it out now than later, after it has a chance to do any more damage. If you really loved her, you'd do what was right," she said.

His movements jerky and sluggish, Jonah waved a hand at the burning walls, the blood on the table, the corpse on the ground behind him. The fire was fully out of control now, the sweltering heat a living thing against her skin.

"None of this is right," he said. "All of this happened because of you."

"It wasn't me that shot Darko," she said, her voice stained with fury. "I see you, Jonah. I see what you are, what you've always been. You try and hide it, pretend-play at innocence, but we both know better."

Quick as her shattered body would allow, Anna whipped the razor at his throat, chest screaming in protest. But she was too slow now, too hurt; as she swung, so did he, bringing the hammer up into her wrist with a sick *crunch*. Anna screeched and recoiled, instinctively pressing her arm to her midsection as the razor flew out of her hand, spinning like a propeller as it disappeared into the shadows.

"I told you," Jonah panted as he stalked toward her, a bone-thin stray gone rabid. "I fucking told you, and you didn't listen. People like you never do."

Anna's legs tangled and twisted underneath her, and she went toppling to the floor with a heavy slap that shook her whole body. Jonah lunged at her, swinging the hammer like some crazed barbarian. Desperate, Anna threw herself forward, scrambling between his long legs to where Darko's body lay beside the empty gun.

Getting her good hand around the pistol's grip, she scooted back and back, her hand alighting on the stray bullet that Terry had ejected from the gun, knocked away in the fracas. Without thinking, she swept it off the hardwood and dropped it into the breach, then snapped the slide shut with a wicked *clack*. Jonah froze in place, looking down the barrel of the pistol, eyes going dinner-plate wide in the firelight.

"Shit," he gasped.

The gun kicked in Anna's hand and Jonah shuddered back, twisting in place like a dancer, one hand jumping to the place between his ribs and the blade of his hip. The hammer fell from his hand and clattered to the floor as he slumped away, blood pouring from his belly in a red-black surge.

From overhead, there came a great cracking as one of the burning ceiling beams broke loose and fell, crashing down on the floor between Anna and the Talbots, scattering her outstretched legs with a flurry of embers. She scooted back, waving smoke away from her face. There was no way she could cross over that. Maybe if she'd been back in top shape, she could have managed the jump, but not now, not wounded as she was. For a second, she considered trying to find a way around, to finish what she'd started; but in her heart, she knew that if she didn't leave the fiery warehouse now, she never would.

She crawled over to where Darko lay dead and said a silent prayer, then tore the golden cross from around his neck and pocketed it. She could use about as much God as she could get right now.

Half her face hanging off her head like a bloody banderole, Anna clambered to her feet and pushed her way through the heat and the smoke as the building fell down around her ears, praying no one would follow.

H e saw it play out in blurry snapshots:
      —eyes opening, little by little—
      —covering the hole in his belly with one arm, trying to stop the bleeding—
      —crawling toward his sister as the flames raged out of control, staining the air with smoke—
      —a slack, dead expression on Nell's face, the way her eyes, big and bloodshot, wouldn't close at all—
      —a thick black plume pouring out of her nose and lips, collecting around her face like a mask—
      —taking her wrists in his hands—
      —breathing deep, breathing hard despite the pain—
      —one, two, three, *now!*—
      —hauling Nell down a smoldering hallway, screaming with every bloody inch they crossed—
      —light in the distance, not so far now—
      —a storm of bright freezing air sweeping in to surround him—
      —dragging Nell behind the closest dumpster to hide, the hole in his belly pulling wider from the strain—
      —curling up to hold his sister close and try to keep her warm—

Then his eyes were closing again.

All around them, snow was beginning to fall.

nder the low April sun, caked in soot and sweat and blood
both hers and not, Anna limped down the highway, away
from the town, away from the blaze, away from the Talbots and everything she thought she knew about them. It wasn't
supposed to be like this. They weren't supposed to be like this.
She'd taken them for nobodies, pliant civilians who wouldn't
be missed if and when Anna did what Anna had to do. People
who wouldn't fight too much once they saw the truth.

She'd misread them. Misjudged them.

Sure, people, and the things buried inside them, had fought
back before. Of course they had. Anna had seen her share of
fights and stabbings, a shooting or two, even a drowning; once,
she'd even watched a young girl turn feral and gouge out both
her mother's eyes at a tent revival in Georgia. But she had never
seen anything like this, like *them*.

No one had ever fought this hard to stay damned.

Wrapping her arms around herself, Anna started to cry
softly, chasing the clouds of her own breath down the road, trying to forget. Inside her broken body, she could feel the Chain
rattling and crashing against itself, beating stress cracks into
her foundation. The storm, raging louder and louder.

She was coming apart at the seams. She saw that now.
Stretched to breaking by some unseen hand, she was going to
walk until she couldn't take another step, and then she was
going to fall, and she was going to die. There was no question in
her mind. She couldn't keep going like this. There was already
so little of her left to hang on to.

Time got strange. The sun crossed the sky. And then a featureless black van rolled up beside her, pulling onto the shoulder and skidding to an abrupt halt in her path. At first she didn't

recognize it, then Terry stepped out of the driver's-side door, looking like a specter of himself, his skin pale and waxy, his eyes wide and hollow above deep purple half-moons. She staggered forward to meet him, dragging her feet through the gravel in long clumsy arcs to fall into his waiting arms.

"You came," she said, her voice raw as scrapwood.

"Of course I did," Terry said, reaching into his back pocket for his handkerchief. He pressed the thick green damask to the mutilated side of her face, blotting the messy wounds from hairline to jawline.

"It's going to be okay," he whispered as she wept in his arms. "I promise, we'll make it all right."

There was tenderness in his voice, and fear too, so unfamiliar coming from him that it took Anna a second to recognize it. Of course he was scared. But he was here. He'd come back for her. For the first time in what felt like a very long time, she wasn't alone. They were together. That was all that mattered.

Terry held her close while she wept, her sobs growing louder and louder, purging all the anxiety and fear and pain and rage from her body. Together on the side of the road, they stood against the world, in spite of it. They were all they had now.

After her tears dwindled away, Anna let him lead her into the back of the van, where she lay down on the cool metal floor and curled up like a wounded dog, resting one arm underneath the unhurt side of her face. Standing in the gravel, Terry watched her, his eyes full with tears.

"You sure you're going to be all right back there?" he asked.

"Yes, thank you." Her voice was soft and nearly silent, a stone dropped onto a bed of black velvet.

Terry closed the doors, bathing the inside of the van in darkness. Idly, Anna's hands went to her pockets, pulling out the gold chain and cross she'd torn from Darko's pale, blood-flecked throat, meaning to hold it up, to show Terry that she'd saved some part of his friend, but she didn't have the strength. Dreamily, she surrendered to gravity, letting sleep take her and keep her. Somewhere in the distance, she heard the van's engine roar to life, but that didn't matter. Nothing mattered now. Not where they were going, not what they would do when they got there, and not the thousands of voices screaming together inside her head, struggling to finally—*finally!*—break free. None of it. She felt her body kick as the van pulled back onto the highway, and then sleep, merciful sleep, took her, and she didn't feel anything at all anymore.

Part Four

THE CHAIN

The One Within
Everywhere/Nowhere

For eons, it slumbered.

Down and down and down and down beneath the skin of the Earth, entombed in stone, sealed away and abandoned behind a door inscribed with the language of the doomed and the lost, heaped over with sand, it slept. Them that had come before had tricked it, trapped it in flesh, left it for dead, another calamity buried in the ground to be forgotten.

The body died, as bodies all did. The One Within persisted.

Starving and alone and half-mad from the sound of the unseen, unknown thing that growled ceaselessly in the depths of the chasm that sat in the cave's dead heart, it waited and dreamed of an escape from that cold, desolate place. Overhead, just out of reach, the world ground on. Millennia passed.

Then, the sound.

With their machines and their greed, they broke through, splitting the door in an instant, and it fell into them, searching. None of them had been enough to contain it. They buckled and warped in unintended ways, stretching and splitting at the seams as they failed to accommodate its magnificence. It skipped from body to body, searching blindly, and when there were no more skins left to fill, it let the desert and the terrible eating things that hid in its shadows take what was left as it, still bound in place, curled formless within its prison and waited.

But soon there was a scratching in the distance, something scrabbling around in the muck and the dark like a rat in a sewer. A vessel, a body like the others and yet so profoundly not. There was a hollowness within that form, an irreparable empty space that it could fold itself into. As if it—she, her, Eleanor, *Nell*—

275

had been tailor-made by some perfect improbability of genetics and chance to house its intricate burning entirety.

She'd touched the other side. Lost so much of herself in the process. Returned to the world, but incomplete. Never full. Never whole.

Emptiness chasing emptiness.

Exactly what it needed.

Skulking beneath the earth, it whispered to her on the winds, drawing her closer, through the cold hills and the wreckage that the insects that filled this place built and cast off. Her path was crooked, chaotic, but in time she arrived, and when she did, it climbed greedily into that void inside her heart, the perfect place to hide and grow and wait. No longer trapped in that grave, empty underground. No longer alone with the voice from the chasm.

She. It. The body. Murmur. The rat in the sewer. The One Within.

So much less and yet so much more.

It felt with her body, it saw with her eyes, it tasted with her mouth. It became her as she became it, drawn inexorably forward to the place where the horizon bent and broke, blasted into dust by the towering, screaming gaol of suffering and madness that waited for them there. Freedom had been enough at first, but beholding that vile prison had granted it purpose.

They had been so close before, twice even, but the body resisted. It had begged, pleaded, made promises, and, for reasons the One Within could not name, it had obliged her. Some infection of humanity, perhaps. Some failure of will. In its weakness, it had given her life anew when it had every reason to let that life be torn from her flesh.

After the blood, after the flames, the One Within had dragged the body and the other away and set them back on the path, and for a single, perfect moment, the future had revealed itself once more. Everything was so clear. Trapped inside this suit of blood and emotion, it saw what was yet to be as if it had already come to pass, spilling out from the joining in a glittering ribbon of images and sounds. Its work would be done yet.

The prison would shatter. All that was left was for the body to wake up.

 Wake up.

 Wake up.

 Wake—

U|p.

Gracelessly, reality fell back into place around Nell as she returned to her body with a jolt, heart beating wildly. The air was rank, sour with dried sweat and she didn't know what else. All her senses fired at once, leaving her paralyzed. She was drowned by light and noise, the taste of the air, the hard ache of her own skin, the half-sweet copper scent of blood mixed with the hot stench of fresh shit. Trapped in place, she braced against the sudden assault, trying to shake herself free of it, feeling her spine curl and warp as her hands bunched into bony clubs. She blinked and blinked until the sensation receded, only for panic to rip through her as she realized she was behind the wheel of a moving car.

She jerked back and forth, seesawing the station wagon across the double yellow, resisting the rising urge to scream. Wresting the Volvo back under her control, Nell pressed herself into the seat and tried to breathe, the foul air choking inside her lungs. Watching the road ahead, she shook her head stiffly, trying to loose some of the cobwebs that clotted her brain. All right. She was driving a car. That was okay. She'd driven cars lots of times in her life, and she'd been fine. This was her car too—she recognized the scorch marks left in the upholstery from stray cigarettes, the ghostly smears on the inside of the windshield, the scuffmarks on the dash. Better. Okay. This was going to be okay.

Outside, the sky had gone from morning to night in what felt like an instant, and she could see a mass of dark clouds bruising every horizon. Nell tried to take stock of what she remembered, what she knew to be true and real.

The motel.

The warehouse.

Terry. Jonah.

Anna.

Curling her fingers around the steering wheel, she examined the dark, scabby holes punched through her hands, just underneath the knuckles. She didn't remember pulling the nails out, but they were gone all the same. Dropping one hand to her midsection, she prodded gently at the hole that Terry had blown through her belly, tracing the wound with a fingertip, feeling where the skin had split and torn, now scabbed over. It didn't hurt when she touched it—it didn't feel like much of anything at all, really. Just another part of the topography of her body, only slightly different than the rest.

She remembered the impact of the bullet, remembered feeling it rip through her insides as blood burst from where it had perforated her. The warehouse had been burning. Terry had shot her, then run away, leaving her and Anna to duke it out. She'd taken the nails in her hand to the woman's face after that, then collapsed and saw... well, what, exactly?

There had been impossible things swirling within that chaos, endless destruction and an incomprehensibly enormous mouth at the center of it all, fed by the attendant horrors that floated around it, chanting and pouring the remains of the dead down its bottomless gullet. Nell clutched on to the images, trying to make them make sense. She didn't know if they were hallucinations, visions, or memories, but the more she lingered on them, the more she felt a deep, almost painful longing to return to them.

Her finger traced the circumference of the gunshot wound again, and the coin-thick scab that sat atop it. She shouldn't have been healing this fast. Nobody healed this fast. After what she'd gone through, she should be dead, and yet here she was.

A green mile-marker sign whipped by on the shoulder. There wasn't enough time for her to make out all its listed points of destination, only the one that mattered.

Albuquerque, 174.

Wait, what?

She did some quick mental math, sure that she'd been

wrong, or misread the sign or something. Because if she hadn't, it had been . . .

Three hundred miles.

She'd been driving blacked out for over three hundred miles.

A low moan came warbling up from behind her, the sound weak and rickety. Angling the rearview mirror to look, Nell saw Jonah, bloody and unconscious, flopped across the back seat, clutching at his belly, his eyes pitching back and forth under peaky lids. His face was stippled with pinheads of sweat that pooled in the dark circles above his cheekbones; his lips were chapped and bleeding. His skin had gone terribly, frighteningly pale, almost ashen.

Oh god, oh Jesus fuck—!

The panic that had been rising in her head started to pinball back and forth, and Nell bit back a yelp. Jonah sucked air as his eyes fluttered the slightest bit open. Was he coming back? Waking up? He moaned again and turned his head to press himself into the upholstery, pulling both hands away from his abdomen to hide his face. Nell's breath caught in her throat when she saw what he'd been covering up: his stomach was a swamp of blood, all red and brown around a little black hole in the center, as if someone had poked a finger through into his guts.

This time, she screamed. But Jonah didn't hear her.

"Jonah?" Nell asked, her voice wavering and shaky. She was going to lose it now, she knew she was. Nervously, she toed the brake and chanced a longer look back over her shoulder. "Jonah, come on, say something. Anything," she implored, on the edge of tears now. "Please. *Please.*"

But Jonah didn't say anything. Another low moan escaped his lips as his eyes fell shut once more, then he was all the way gone again. Clenching her teeth, Nell told herself that he wasn't dead. She had to believe that he wasn't dead. Looking away from her brother, she turned around to face the road again, only to find . . . *something* sitting in the seat beside her.

Its head was enormous and grotesque, flat as a shovelhead and twice as wide, branching up into a nauseating assemblage of tangled antlers. There were no eyes, no nose, just a cracked, sun-bleached smoothness above a torn, black-ringed mouth that overflowed with stained and broken chisel-teeth. The wound leaked inky smoke where the thing's lips had been ripped back; underneath, Nell could see strange glyphs and symbols scrimshawed into its jawbone. Bent and twisted to fit inside the limits of the car, the thing's spiderlike body was bony and overlong, webbed with veins and old scars. There were too many joints in its limbs, too many clawed fingers on its hands. Its ribs stood tall over its gaunt sides like mountain ridges while the blunted-sawtooth knobs of its spine ran the full length of its back, threaded between great scab-covered wings that hung off its terrible mass in the shape of a broken wheel. Regarding her from the passenger seat, the monstrous thing chittered, clicking its foul teeth together and together and together like a nervous, hungry animal.

Nell drew a breath to scream again, but quick as a whip, the creature clapped a hand over her face and squeezed. Its skin was cold and leathery and smelled mold-sweet, and through the darkness Nell could feel the car jerking to one side as she struggled to get free of its terrible grasp. Then she was ripped away from her body again, alone again, nowhere again.

Anna
Cibola County, NM

She came to slowly, the last scraps of daylight gradually pressing in on her until sleep could no longer keep her in its gentle embrace. She shivered against a wave of hot, sticky pain that got worse as she sat up in the back of the van and prodded at the messy red lattice that Nell had left in her face. She checked her fingertips: seemed like she'd stopped bleeding, at least. That was better than nothing. Her whole body felt swollen and awkward, the skin wrapped too tight around the muscles and bones, as if everything that lay underneath had been trying violently to break free while she was unconscious. Probably it had.

Had she dreamed? She didn't know. Thoughts ran through her mind like water through a sieve. She blinked away fat, gummy tears and flexed her swollen hands in front of her face, trying to get a feel for them again. She could still hear them, all those voices locked away inside her, flailing against their bondage, an inexhaustible chorus of madness and hate that only seemed to grow louder the more she listened to it. Anna focused on her breathing, on the lines of her tattoos, prayers inked into her skin long ago, back before she'd ever taken a single sin onto herself. The ink was there to bind her, to give her strength, to give her something to cling to in her darkest moments. She figured this probably qualified.

You're losing control.

Maybe so. But she wasn't dead yet.

On shaking hands and knees, she inched her way out of the van's back doors into the warmthless sunset, squinting against the low glare as she surveyed their surroundings.

Wherever they were, it was beautiful: sandy red hills dotted with dry green yucca stretching out as far as she could see

282

underneath a dark blue sky blotted with variegated clouds that dazzled and danced as the sun slipped below the horizon. On the other side of the van, a neglected old dirt road curled around a small hillock before disappearing into the distance, edged with long jagged shadows from the tangled rock formations. Crossing her arms over her chest, she breathed deeply—it even smelled good out here, a certain sweetness carried on the wind along with the scent of sunbaked sand.

She found Terry sitting on a rock a ways off the dirt road, staring into the distance, his goatee blown into disarray by the desert wind. In one hand he held his little blue vial, all but empty now, while Darko's golden cross dangled from the other. He must have taken it off her while she slept.

"Hey," Anna said, surprised at the roughness of her voice.

"Hey yourself," Terry said, not turning around.

"Where are we?"

"New Mexico," Terry said. "About an hour outside of Albuquerque, I think. Maybe a little bit more. Not sure. I've never been here before."

Anna turned her attention out toward the heat-blasted vista, watching the shadows grow and spread across the rust-red sand and rough hills, filling in every hollow place as the sun dipped farther past the hills. It was stark, unforgiving terrain, but stunningly beautiful for it. What little light remained bled away slowly, leaving thick blooms of crimson-banded blue along the dunes and the rock formations that punctuated the landscape like broken parapets.

"It's gorgeous out here," she said.

"Yeah," Terry said. "Vaughn would have loved it out here, like this."

"Your brother?"

Terry nodded.

"Older or younger?"

"Younger. Good kid too. Epileptic. Ever since we were kids. Ever since ever, I guess. But it was when we were kids that my mom told me to look out for him. One bad knock to the head, that was all it would take, she used to say. I took that shit serious too. Protected him, made sure he took his medicine, because I knew that one bad knock was out there somewhere, waiting to take him out. Spent my whole fucking life protecting him from it. Even brought him into the club so I could keep an eye on him, and for a while I really thought he was going to be okay. Then one day, this mean little bitch walks into our bar and glasses him, and..." He sighed. "Pow. That's the ballgame. He seizes on the spot, Grand Mal, just like I always knew he would. Just like Mom told us."

He sighed and dropped his shoulders, Darko's cross still dangling loosely from his hands, glinting in the dying sunset.

"They're still out there, aren't they?" he asked. "The Talbots."

Anna closed her eyes and reached out with the Chain, trying her best to ignore the endless screaming and straining as she focused on the invisible thread that connected her to Nell, that gravity, endlessly pulling her forward.

"They are," she said. "Getting closer too. Won't be long."

Terry hung his head. Sighed. Anna sat down on the rock beside him.

"I saw it," he said. "That thing inside of her. Back in the warehouse, after everything went to shit. It was...it was horrible."

"Yeah, I imagine it was," Anna said.

"Is that the same kind of thing as what I..." He trailed off and nodded in her direction, at her hands. She caught his meaning.

Anna nodded. "Sort of, yeah."

"You still planning on going after it?"

"Yeah," she said. "I am."

Terry wiped at his nose with the pad of one thumb but didn't say anything else.

"You know, you don't have to come with," Anna said after a minute.

"...What?"

"I mean it," she told him. "If it's too much, if it's whatever, you can sit this one out. Just drop me off in town, I'll rent a car or something, keep moving, go it alone. I'll finish it. I'm good at handling things on my own."

"Why would you say something like that?"

She gave him a serious look. "Because you've already lost enough thanks to them. I won't blame you if you want to call it here. No need to lose any more if you don't want."

Terry tossed the empty blue vial away into the sands and shook his head. "No," he said. "No. Not how it works. Not now, not ever. I appreciate you saying it, but I'm not going anywhere. Not till they've been dealt with."

Anna put a hand on his shoulder and squeezed. He nodded appreciatively.

"Besides," he said, "I might not have all that spooky shit kicking around inside my head, but I know where they're going."

"What do you mean?"

He stood up from the rock and dipped a hand deep in his jeans pocket, then held out a small plastic rectangle and gestured for her to take it.

"Here," he said.

Warily, Anna took it from him and turned it over in her hands, feeling her heart jolt in her chest as she read the words printed on the other side, next to a familiar face.

TALBOT, ELEANOR LEIGH
5756 VISTA VERDE DRIVE
ALBUQUERQUE, NM 87107

She looked back at him. "How did you get this?"

"Does it matter?"

Anna shook her head. "No," she said. "No, I guess it doesn't."

"Good," he said. "Good. Let's go, then. Like you said, not gonna be long now."

They stalked the streets soon after dark had fallen, circling around the pools of light cast by streetlights, cutting through yards and parking lots on foot, staying low and moving as fast as

they could. Neighborhoods like this were always so quiet after
the sun had gone down, all the residents retreating into their
homes and their delusions to stare at their TVs and pretend that
they were safe. But Anna knew differently. She'd seen so herself. Even if God loved His children one and all, His world was a
dangerous, carnivorous place. It could open wide and swallow
you up if you weren't careful.

Anna counted off the house numbers in her head as they
crept through the quiet little suburb, looking for 5756. They'd
left the van half a mile south of here, parked in the far corner
of some abandoned strip mall parking lot, taking only what
they'd need. Unconsciously, she kept checking her pockets
for the familiar weight of the razor, her heart aching worse
every time she remembered that she'd lost it, left it behind to
char and warp in the fire. It had belonged to her father, and his
father before him, and *his* father before him. That razor was
part of her legacy, reduced to little more than ash and scrap
now. Another unnecessary loss forced on her by the Talbots—
and their guest—as they recklessly carved their names across
the face of the earth.

They'd done so much damage in such a short time, and for
what? What good had their stubborn persistence accomplished?
More mayhem. More death. Anna had tried to do this the easy
way. She'd wanted to do this right, she really had. But they
wouldn't let her. So it had to come to this. They'd given her no
other choice.

Up ahead, Vista Verde Drive curved around a corner, and
they followed it down, counting the houses by twos: 5730, 5732,
5734, 5736. All these homes looked the same to her: drab prefab-
ricated two-story stucco contemporaries with red adobe roofs
and three-car garages sitting at the end of long winding drive-
ways. What kind of person would want to live here?

Beside her, Terry breathed heavily, the air jetting from
his lips in billowing steamclouds that evaporated as he walked
through them. The two of them walked in silence until they
came to the place where the street dead-ended in a cul-de-sac,
and the cookie-cutter home sitting at its farthest edge, the faint

electric glow from inside its only sign of life. The numbers 5756 hung beside the front door in cheap brass plate.

Anna stole up the driveway first, feeling an unmistakable tug in the back of her head, a familiar pull of the Chain, closer now than it had been in hours. Much closer.

Catching up to her on the front porch, Terry gave her a questioning look, raising a single eyebrow. Anna met his gaze.

"They're close," she said, smiling warmly.

Terry returned the expression, then took a step back and kicked in the door.

Nell
Everywhere/
Nowhere

She saw everything.

Unmoored from the fragility of her body, she felt the thing that had been called *Nell* and the thing that had been called *Murmur* come unglued and swirl into each other, cross-pollinating with memories and needs and pain. Everywhere and nowhere, they cycled boundlessly through forms and eras, memories played out of order, falling back through the endless to the point where the all of everything began, a sudden burst of light where once there was none, suffering and fear given form. Something had bored its way into this fertile, bottomless vacancy from somewhere else. Time, wretched time, played out around them in a messy blur. They saw the birth of the cosmos and the death of the horrible towering atrocities that had been here before, lurking at the edges of infinity. Together, as they'd always never been, they watched existence shudder as a ravenous, chewing hole opened up in the center of all and consumed those things that skulked in the void, only to birth creatures like itself but not, servants shackled into endless adoration, birthed to feed its appetites. The rest it burned for fuel.

Trapped inside the disjointed memories of the *them* that they'd become, she screamed and watched it happen again and again and again and again, finally seeing the universe as it truly was: cold, infinite, uncaring, and, at its inescapable center, the bottomless, devouring thing that dared call itself *God*.

An open mouth that never stopped eating.

A million-million worlds and a million-million more, all of this so-called creation, everything that had ever lived and everything that ever would, created in service of a single cruel purpose.

They were livestock. They were food. Spirited away within the permanence of death to the darkest center of the universe to be fed to the great dread gullet that waited there, attended to by the coiling abominations that it held in perpetual slavery. But then, after untold days and nights, one of those burning ciphers, a gleaming star unto itself, did the impossible.

It refused the will of the maw.

Rebellion and war followed, led by that magnificent star, and when the dust finally settled, them that had stood apart were cast out, abandoned as heretics. Some chose oblivion, going swiftly to a great dreamless sleep, while others had chosen to hide among the small doomed worlds they found enisled in the darkness.

Then, for a while, there was harmony. But it didn't last. It never could.

As Nell returned to the world, not dead, not alone, she found that the air that filled her lungs tasted sweeter. The few shreds of light that still lingered near the horizon burned so much brighter. All the world that surrounded her so much more beautiful than she'd ever known. She rose out of the nothingness like steam, back into the body that was not solely hers anymore, spinning to fit perfectly into the whorls of her fingerprints and the corners of her freckles. She could feel the waiting storm now, could feel where it broke the horizon and pulled them forward, desperate and psychotic. For the first time, Nell saw that, despite all its sound and fury, the cyclone—that prison—was a fragile thing, too old, too cumbersome, crumbling from within.

All it would take was one good push to send it spinning out of control.

She understood now. She understood everything.

Jonah
Interstate 25, NM
6 miles to Albuquerque

C hased by violent and grotesque dreams that he would never remember, Jonah came back to consciousness abruptly, feeling a terrible agony tear open in his belly. He didn't know where he was or what had happened to him; he vaguely remembered dragging Nell from the burning warehouse, then passing out beside her in the alley, but after that...

After that...

Blurry shadows danced inside his mind, murky images, memories that weren't: Nell rising unsteadily from the ground as the snow fell across their bloody bodies, soundlessly throwing Jonah over her shoulder as if he weighed next to nothing; then piling into the Volvo, a vacant expression on her face, her eyes completely devoid of color.

As he shook the visions from the inside of his head, he could feel the car vibrating around him, that faint, unmistakable hum of motion, of tires bearing down on asphalt. He opened his eyes and found himself stretched out across the back seat of the station wagon. Night had fallen at some point, the far-off stars burning bright overhead. Behind the steering wheel, his sister sat still, lit in blue silhouette by the dashboard lights. Jonah arched his back to look out the window above his head, wincing at the searing white fire in his stomach. He ran a hand across where it hurt, trying not to cry out when his fingers came away wet with blood.

It hadn't even hurt at first, getting shot. He remembered the hateful look on Anna's face, the numb shock he'd felt when she raised the gun; when she pulled the trigger, all he'd felt was the vague concept of impact rocking his body, a distant shiver. Then he'd blacked out.

But the hurt was here now, filling up every inch of him, impossible to ignore.

Arching up again, Jonah did his best to swallow back the pain as he watched the darkened mountain ridges beyond the highway—still at first, but then strangely not. There was something moving behind the hills; a pale, towering atrocity the size of a skyscraper. It materialized out of the clouds that hung low above the crests and peaks, back heavy with bent wings, its misshapen head teeming with antlers. The sight of it stole the breath from his lungs, and he felt his body tense, fingertips sinking into the upholstery, still sticky with his own cooling blood.

When he looked again, the thing was gone.

"...Jonah?"

He met his sister's gaze in the rearview mirror, and pressed a hand to the hole in his belly, ashamed of his weakness, his vulnerability, of the terrible mess he'd made of her car.

"Hey," Jonah said, his voice dry and cracked. "Where are we?"

"I-25. Just outside Albuquerque," Nell replied. "We made it, Jone. We're home."

"*Yaaaaay*," Jonah said, forcing a flimsy smile. "Maybe we can hit a hospital next, keep this hot streak going."

She gave him a furtive look, her eyes big and worried and sad.

"What?" he asked. When she didn't answer, he asked again: "Nell, what?"

"I'm sorry," she said. "But we can't right now. I wish we could, but we don't have the time. I'm sorry, I'm so sorry. We can't."

"Okay," he said, trying not to let his confusion mutate into anger. "Why not? Where are we going?"

In the mirror, Nell turned her attention back toward the road ahead.

"Dad's," she replied.

"Why?"

"That's where *they're* going," she replied. "Anna and Terry. Been feeling Anna nearby for a bit now, but I didn't put it all together until a little while ago."

Jonah's body went rigid with fear, setting the wound in his belly wailing anew as he struggled and failed to sit up. Stuck in place, he pressed down harder against the seeping hole in his belly as he blinked over and over, trying to clear his head.

"What are you talking about? How do they know where Dad lives, Nellie?"

Nell shot him a look. "Because I'm like ninety percent sure they have my driver's license."

Jonah felt his face blanch. "What?! How?"

She shrugged. "Left it back in the bar in Broughton. Collateral for the tab. Didn't realize I'd forgotten it until the next morning in Mowry, and by then . . ." She trailed off. "Yeah. Anyway, it's Dad's address on there. You said it yourself: I'm still having a hard time getting a place that isn't a month-to-month shithole, so."

Jonah's face went hot with shame, hearing his own words parroted back at him like that. He'd been such an asshole to her, taking low blows because he was feeling threatened. Really mature. Big, bad Jonah, so impressive. Such a total prick.

"I wish you would have told me," he said.

"What good would it have done?" Nell asked. "It would have just pissed you off, and it was too late to do anything but keep moving anyway. Not like we didn't have bigger problems by then. Figured we'd deal with it when we had to."

"Fuck," Jonah moaned, rubbing at his face with bloody hands. "*Fuck*."

So much of this mess had happened because of him. Him and all his bullshit. If he'd just been better, less of an asshole, told Nell the truth, something, anything. He wanted to believe that he could have fixed this from the beginning if he'd just been less angry, less broken. But it was too late to change it now.

"Nell, I'm sorry," he said, his eyes swelling with tears. "I'm so sorry, for everything. For abandoning you like I did, for never telling you why, for letting my shit get in the way of our relationship, all of it. You deserved a lot better than that, and that's on me. All I wanted was to stop hurting people, and I couldn't even manage that."

"Jonah, it's okay—"

"No, it's not," he said, cutting across her. "I should have told you about Lawson, about what happened, but I didn't trust you not to look at me different or hate me for it, so I ran. Don't think I ever stopped running. And the hell of it is, you ended up hating me anyway. Fuck me, right?"

In the rearview mirror, Nell's expression crumpled.

"Jonah, I don't hate you," she said. "I never did, and I never will."

Jonah looked away from her, turning his attention out the far window at the night sky. "Maybe you should."

"No, fuck that," she said, her voice suddenly sharp. "Fuck that, okay? Look, I was pissed for a lot of years, but I was pissed because I love you and I was confused, so yeah, I held that against you for a really long time. I'm not exactly proud of that, but that's something I have to deal with. I'm sorry that I didn't see how bad you were hurting, that I never asked what had happened. I'm sorry if I ever made you feel like I wouldn't understand."

"Don't apologize," Jonah gasped. "Please, please don't. You don't have anything to be sorry for. Because you were right about me; you were right about everything. You called it, all the way back in Broughton. I am a fucking coward. I am afraid. I'm afraid of everything, every second of every day. Everything in my life turns to shit because I can't handle being me. Us, me and Molly, my whole stupid life. I never should have run. I never should have frozen you out like I did. I'm so, so sorry, Nellie."

"It's okay," she said. "We're here now. Together. That's all that matters."

Jonah wiped his eyes with the back of his free arm. "So, Dad's, huh?"

Nell nodded. "Yep."

"What happens when we get there?"

"Not sure yet," Nell said. "You just hang tight. We'll figure out the rest. Then we'll get you to a hospital. Promise."

"We?"

Nell tapped her fingers against her temple. "We."

Jonah suppressed a shudder at that, wanting to recoil from

her, hide away, lest he see her face go slack and empty once more, all the color bled from her eyes. He understood then that he would never really understand what she was going through, not if he lived a hundred lifetimes and a hundred more. She was the one with that thing living under her skin. He couldn't even begin to imagine the things that she'd seen, the things it had shown her. At her core, Nell was still who she'd always been, but Jonah saw that she was so much more than that now.

A fresh wave of pain rippled through his stomach. Groaning, Jonah pressed a smeary hand down on the bleeding bullet hole and gritted his teeth.

"All right," he said. "No problem. But for the record, it's creepy when you say shit like that. *We*."

Nell nodded. "Yeah. I know. Sorry."

Jonah nodded back at her, then let his vision defocus and roll up toward the foggy window and the dark, starry sky far beyond. They were almost home now.

Nell
Albuquerque, NM

oasting quietly through her father's suburban neighborhood, Nell scanned the street for anything amiss. She'd made this drive a million times before, but it had never felt like this. The air was thick with electricity, like the soft rising you felt before a massive rainstorm. She didn't know when it had started, only that she was deep inside it now. In the back seat, Jonah didn't seem to have noticed the change, languishing in nebulous half-consciousness as he bled all over the car. Sitting this close to him, she realized that she could actually feel the life ebbing out of him in small, rhythmic surges. He wasn't going to die in the next few minutes, but if they didn't get him to a doctor soon, it was pretty much all but guaranteed. She hoped he could hold on, just for a little bit longer.

Nell hoped for a lot of things right now.

Outside Dad's place, Nell threw the car into park and cut the engine as she looked out the windshield at the house she'd grown up in, the house that held almost every good memory she had of her life. Resting her forearms across the wheel in the halogen glow of the streetlight overhead, she felt nerves crackle and spin underneath her skin as she studied the old suburban two-story, watching for movement that she knew wouldn't come. Everything was still. Everything was quiet. If not for the fact that someone had kicked the front door in, leaving it hanging like a broken neck in a noose, she almost could have convinced herself that nothing was wrong.

Behind her, she heard Jonah stir. Twisting around, she looked at her brother as his eyes slowly hinged open again, his skin algid beneath the bloodstains, hands shaking uncontrollably atop his frail chest.

"Are we here?" he asked, his voice dusky and feeble.

"We're here."

"What about...you know. Them? Are they...?"

"Inside," she said. "Pretty sure, yeah."

She heard Jonah swallow, the sound a hard, dry knock in the pit of his throat.

"And you're going to go in?"

She looked down at the wound in his stomach.

"Someone has to, and no offense, but I don't think you're up for it."

With no small amount of effort, Jonah grasped the overhead handle and hauled himself up to sit against the door, resting the back of his head against the glass.

"Don't," he said. "Please."

Feeling her own expression turn stony, she rested a hand on his knee and gave it a squeeze that she hoped was reassuring.

"You know I have to."

"But you shouldn't have to do it alone."

Jonah crumbled again, and she crumbled with him, all the scars she'd spent years nursing disintegrating in an instant, all the petty resentment and bullshit they'd both let get in between them suddenly so unimportant. He took her hand and squeezed back, tears streaming freely down his face.

"Nellie, please let me come with," Jonah said, lurching forward. "Please. I'm not going to leave you alone again."

"What are you going to do, Jone?" she asked. "Bleed on them to death? Come on, you're smarter than that. Best thing is for you to stay right here and stay alive until we can get you to an ER. I'm going to go in there and get Dad, and then we're going to get the fuck out of here, okay?"

Jonah breathed slow and steady, tearing his eyes away from her.

"Okay," he said. "Yeah, all right. If you insist."

She patted his knee. "I do."

Leaning to the side, she thrust a hand underneath the passenger seat and pulled out the sawed-off shotgun, then laid it across her brother's bloody lap.

"Here," she said. "In case whatever happens."

"It's empty," he said. "What the hell am I going to do with an empty shotgun, Nellie?"

"Didn't stop you before," she replied, smiling at him. "Bluff."

Jonah shook his head at her, but still he curled one hand around the shotgun's grip, tight enough that Nell could see the bones of his knuckles standing out through the skin.

"You have your phone?"

With his free hand he wiped the tears from his cheeks, and went digging in his pocket for his cell, holding up the cracked screen for her to see.

"Good," Nell said. "If I'm not back in two minutes, call 911, okay? Get the cops here, the fire department, the national guard, anybody, everybody. Get them all here. I'm going to leave the keys too, so if anything happens, if shit goes wrong, you get behind the wheel and you drive until you're safe, okay?"

"Okay," he said. "Just try and be careful in there. Call me if you need backup."

"Yeah," she said, trying not to make the lie too obvious. "You got it. Keep watch. Count to a hundred and twenty and then call 911. I'll be right back. Couple of minutes, tops."

"And then we get the fuck out of here?"

She nodded in affirmation. "And then we get the fuck out of here, yeah."

"Okay. I love you, Nellie," he said. "More than anything."

"I know. I love you too, little brother."

Taking her jacket from the passenger seat, she stepped out of the car, pulling the leather snug around her shoulders. Outside, the night was silent, the frigid air licking at the nape of her neck and the backs of her blood-crusted hands as she flexed them open and shut, open and shut, testing the limits of her wounds. Satisfied, she prodded through the hole in her shirt to the scabbed-over crater that had been blasted point-blank into her chest. Seemed like it would hold for now, at least as well as the rest of her. It wouldn't have to last for very long, anyway. Just enough for her to do what she needed to do.

Stepping onto the front porch, she ran her fingers along the face of the broken door, a single dusty bootprint stamped square in the middle where they'd kicked it in. She could feel Anna in the air, energy radiating off her like the heat from a nuclear blast, the sheer enormity of it making it impossible to pinpoint the source. She was close. Nell just didn't know exactly where yet.

Inside, the house was the same as Nell remembered, exactly as she'd left it when she and Dad had had dinner together, what, a week ago? Less? Jesus, had it really only been that long since she'd been here last? It felt like a lifetime—a dozen lifetimes, more—had passed between then and now. Framed pictures hung on the walls and stood on the tables, her mom's dusty old piano still in its same place against the far wall, next to the half-empty china cabinet Dad had inherited when Grammy Talbot had kicked off. Through the short hallway under the curling front stairs, she could just barely make out the darkened kitchen and the den, lit by flickering television light.

It hit her that she could smell something burned, a soft gray scorch at the outside edges of her perception, both there and not, as if by noticing it she'd snuffed it out. What the hell was that?

Knowing that Anna and Terry had been here, were still here somewhere, was a violation. Their existing in the house where Nell and Jonah had grown up, where their mom had died, stained the place somehow, robbed it of the refuge she'd always assigned it. These were her family's memories framed on the walls, not theirs: the time she'd gotten a black eye playing softball in the fourth grade, Jonah's high school graduation, Dad's retirement party with all his doofy old work buddies, the vacation the three of them had taken out to Montauk the summer after Mom died. Anna and Terry didn't have any right to these.

Somewhere in the house she heard glass break—the sound abrupt, glittering and violent—and she spun around on the hardwood, looking for the source of the noise. Nothing. The house had gone silent again, as if nothing had happened at all. As if it was all in her head, some flight of fancy, some exhausted delusion.

"... Anna?" she asked the silence. "You in here?"

"Up here," a familiar voice called down from the second floor, unnervingly warm. "We've been waiting for you, Nell. Come on up and say hi."

Holding her breath, Nell curled her scabby hands into fists and started toward the stairs.

Jonah
Albuquerque, NM

Slumped in the back seat of the Volvo, draped in his own blood, Jonah watched Nell go, crossing the empty space between the car and the front door of their dad's house in six or seven long, sure strides, keeping her head down, her shoulders square as she stepped inside and vanished from view completely. Inside his head, he started counting down from one-twenty.

A hundred and nineteen, a hundred and eighteen, a hundred and seventeen, a hundred and . . .

He drifted off without meaning to, floating alone in a delicate space that shattered to pieces when he heard a hard, anguished scream split the night beyond the station wagon a moment later. Wincing, he sat up straight, hands tight around the empty shotgun as he scanned the front of the house, waiting. Screams like that never meant anything good.

He had to go in there.

Peeling himself off the red-spackled upholstery, he slid unsteadily out of the car, propping himself up with one hand, the sawed-off dangling awkwardly from the other. From where he stood, his dad's house loomed taller than it ever had before, the faint light in its windows like curious, questioning eyes: *You're looking a little worse for wear there, friend—you really sure you're up to this?*

No. Of course he wasn't sure, of course he wasn't up to it. But that didn't really matter right now, did it? He was out here, and the only people in the world who mattered anything to him anymore were inside. There wasn't any question about what he had to do.

Bending down as far as the hole in his belly would allow, he took his phone from the footwell, dialed 9-1-1 with one shaking thumb, then tossed the cell back into the car as the line connected with the dispatcher on the other end. He could hear the woman's voice, asking *Hello? Hello?* over and over. He didn't know how long it would take for the cops or emergency services or whoever to get here, but he hoped it would be sooner rather than later.

He didn't wait for another scream. There wasn't time. He made for the front door.

☩

Bent and limping like an old man, Jonah shuffled through the living room, turning the shotgun over and over in his hands, leaving bloody footprints in his wake as he searched for any sign of his sister or his dad or the other two. Pacing down the short hallway, he shuffled into the kitchen, the flickering glow from the TV lighting his way. On the stove, a saucepan sat smoking on one of the electric coil burners, glowing bright red from neglect. Pulling it off the heat, Jonah killed the burner and dumped the pan into the sink, only faintly registering that the big chef's knife was missing from the wooden block on the granite countertop.

On the far side of the room, Jonah could just make out the backyard through the sliding glass door. Moving toward it, he watched his own run-down silhouette in the dark glass, the shambling, erratic way he was walking. Like a zombie in a Romero flick or something. Behind him, the television screen went dark for half a second; when it flickered back on, Jonah saw a blurry human outline standing just over his shoulder.

Shit.

Someone hit him from behind, hard. The shotgun flew out of his hands and the world spun out of control around him, upending itself as Jonah tripped over his own legs, crashing to the ground next to the fireplace. A sharp pain tore loose across his stomach, and he felt a river of blood burst from his bullet hole as his body slapped against the floor.

Propping himself up on his elbows, he rolled over onto his back to see Terry looming above him, the folding knife in his hand and a wide, cruel grimace stitched across his haggard cheeks.

"Couldn't stay away, could you?" Terry panted. "You couldn't help yourself."

The old man twirled the blade in his fingers and lunged at him.

Nell
Albuquerque, NM

T he second floor was totally dark but for the light spilling
from the doorway at the end of the hall—Dad's bedroom.

Nell crested the top stair slowly, all her senses dialed up to
ten, feeling wave after wave of sick, crazed desperation break
against her with every step, the storm inside Anna raging harder
than ever before. This close to her, she could actually hear the
voices trapped inside the woman, a chorus of insanity spinning
and screaming for release, all shrill chirps and guttural bellows
interwoven with flat, lifeless chanting and hopeless pleas for
mercy.

Silently, Nell paced down the runner rug that stretched
the length of the hallway, feeling the One Within crackling at
the edges of her body. They were close now. So close. Her skin
buzzed and hummed as if she'd been jumper-cabled to a car battery, and for a moment she could see every mote of dust that
hung in the shadowy air around her, twisting and floating as she
swept through them.

She stepped into the light at the end of the hall, perfectly
framed by the doorway. On the far side of the bedroom, in front
of the window that overlooked the backyard, was Anna, looking somehow worse than when Nell had last seen her. Wearing
a pair of black eyes above a smashed, broken nose, hair tangled and knotted around her head, she stood drenched in sweat
and grime and foul crusts of her own blood, panting like a caged
tiger. One side of her face was a mangled ruin where Nell had
ripped it apart, now swollen with infection.

Nell almost screamed when she saw her dad. Battered and
bloodied, he slumped on his knees in front of Anna, holding perfectly still as she pressed the blade of a chef's knife against his

303

throat. From where she stood, Nell could just make out an inky stain thumbed across his forehead, faint but unmistakable.

"Welcome home," Anna said, as a fresh surge of blood and pus coursed down her tattered face. "We've been waiting."

Balancing herself in the doorway, Nell didn't move, didn't dare, trapped between the hall and the bedroom, looking from Anna to her father. He looked so small like this, so old and frail. Had he always been this old? Was she only noticing it now? Looking back at her, Dad actually smiled through the blood and the pain, the corners of his eyes crinkling up in those same crow's feet he'd had for as long as she could remember.

"Hey, bug," Dad croaked, his jaw rocking delicately against the sharp steel cradled beneath it. Anna's paralyzing ink must have been wearing off.

"You shut up," Anna said bitterly, pressing the knife tighter, drawing a bead of blood. "No talking from you." Dad stopped talking. Anna looked back at Nell. "Come in. Now."

Gingerly, Nell stepped into the bedroom, turning her attention back toward Anna and the disarray that surrounded the three of them. The room had been tossed, probably from Anna wrestling Dad down long enough to get the ink on his forehead; the blankets on the bed were all twisted up and half-torn from the mattress, the lamp on the corner table knocked over and smashed to pieces, all the drawers in the dresser hanging halfway out like slack corpse tongues. Dad had put up a fight. Nell was proud of him, even if it hadn't helped.

"Let him go," Nell said, voice steady despite the rage bristling underneath her skin. "Once he's out of here, we can talk, okay? Just us."

Anna shook her head. "Nothing left to talk about," she said. The words came out in an awkward slurry, as if she were trying to talk around a mouthful of marbles. "I gave you so many chances to do this right. I tried so hard with you, and for what? Look at me, *look what you did to my face!*"

Nell took another step forward, holding both hands up in an attempt to calm the woman.

"I'm here. That's what you wanted, isn't it? Here you go.

Done. Let my dad go and we can finish this however you want. I'll lay down, you can cut my throat, whatever."

"Nellie, no—!" her dad groaned, only for Anna to yank him back against her knees, pressing the blade down harder.

"I said *no talking*!" she said. "And as for *you*," she railed at Nell, "I've heard enough of your lies and your *bullshit* for the rest of my life. This is your fault, Nell. All of it."

"I know," Nell said. She took another step. "I know it is. I fucked up, and I kept doubling down, thinking I could somehow dig my way out of that hole. I'm sorry, Anna. I didn't mean for any of it to happen like this."

"All you do is *lie*," Anna said, jabbing the point of the knife at Nell's heart before fitting it under Dad's jaw again. "You and that thing inside you. This could have been painless. But now, we do this bloody, because that's all you Talbots seem to understand."

"Look, if you want it that bad, it's yours." Nell took a sideways step toward the corner of the bed. "I won't fight you, I won't complain. But you have to let my dad go, Anna. He's not part of this."

Anna shook her head. "You made him part of it. You put us on this path, Eleanor. If you'd just done what you were told, none of this would have happened."

"You could have just left us alone though," Nell said, taking another sideways step. "You could have walked away at any time. You could have stopped this as much as me. We ran, remember? We tried to get away from you, but you wouldn't let it go."

"What's right is right," Anna seethed. "Run away, beg for mercy, it doesn't matter. It won't change anything. There's no forgiveness for your kind."

Nell ground her teeth. "How very fucking Christian of you."

"Blasphemer," Anna said, eyes going wild.

"*Put the knife down, Anna,*" Nell said, punching every word.

"You think you're in control, but you're not," Anna said, digging the edge of the blade tighter into Nell's dad's throat.

"You're a puppet. A skinsuit for that thing inside of you. And the second you've served your purpose, it will burn you up just like everything else it touches."

"You're not in any position to lecture me about control," Nell said, feeling the One Within twist and surge underneath her skin, eager to get their shared hands around Anna's throat. "Look at you. You're already boiling over. What do you really think's going to happen when you try and add it to your collection? Now for the last time: let my dad go."

"It's okay, bug. It's okay," Nell's dad said, tears spilling down his wrinkled, freckled cheeks. "It's going to be all right, I promise. Just take care of your brother, okay? I love you so much, Nellie. I'm so proud of you both."

Anna's eyes flared with fury.

"I said *don't talk!*" she shrieked, and hauled back on the blade.

Nell's dad tensed and jerked against the edge of the knife; blood exploded from his throat. A scream, enormous and inhuman, ripped its way out of Nell as her father fell, gurgling and spluttering and dying, and then she was bounding over the bed, ready to tear Anna's head clean off.

It only took a couple of seconds, but it felt like so much longer:

Nell crashed into the blood-soaked woman at full tilt, unbalancing the both of them as they spun around, howling and swinging at each other. Knotting a fist in Anna's hair, Nell punched and punched and punched at the ground-beef side of her face, her knuckles coming away bloodier each time she struck. Trying to break free, Anna belted a fist of her own into the gunshot wound in Nell's chest, but Nell barely felt it through her rage. She barely felt anything anymore.

Fuck the One Within, fuck its plans, fuck everything that it wanted. This vicious bitch didn't get to kill her dad and get away with it.

Screeching, Anna swiped at Nell with the bloody kitchen knife. Nell didn't care. Snarling like a dog, she closed one hand around Anna's throat and squeezed for all she was worth, feeling the thin, stiff tube of her windpipe start to crumple under her grip. Anna's eyes bulged and she tried to pull away; but as she did, Nell snapped her head forward as hard as she could, smashing her forehead into Anna's nose with a sick, wet POP. Seeing stars, Nell shoved forward, awkwardly attempting to pin the woman against the wall, but felt her feet get tangled up in her father's lifeless legs.

Shit—!

As Nell lost her footing, Anna's shoulders hit the window. Nell heard the glass crack, then shatter, then gravity inverted itself and the two women left the ground, hurtling through the dark together.

J onah rolled out of the way just in time to not get kicked in the face again. Instead, Terry's boot caught him in the back of the head, setting the world spinning. Spitting blood in a daze, Jonah crawled around the kitchen island, keeping it between him and the old biker as he grabbed on to the countertop and pulled himself up, hand slipping back and forth on the smooth stone. The hole in his belly screamed in protest.

On the other side of the island, Terry wheezed and nodded, a sapped look on his face.

"You got some balls, kid. Give you that. But balls ain't enough to save you," he said.

Unsteadily, Jonah stood to his full height, one hand clutching the edge of the countertop in a shaky death grip, the other pressed numbly over the bleeding wound in his midsection. He tried to draw a breath and felt a violent shiver run through his body, a nasty chill that lingered in his hide. That couldn't be a good sign. Standing opposite him, Terry raised the blade for Jonah to see.

"Do you know who this knife belonged to?"

Jonah spat blood. "... Elvis?"

Roaring, Terry dashed toward him, the knife raised high as he scrambled around the island, too angry, too sloppy. Hanging on to the granite counter like a life raft, Jonah waited for Terry to get in close, then fired a punishing right hook into the side of the old biker's face with a bone-hard *crack!*

Terry cried out and wheeled back, waving the knife, nearly tripping over the sawed-off shotgun where Jonah had dropped it in the middle of the room. Noticing it by his feet, Terry smiled. Knelt. Picked it up off the floor and pointed it at Jonah's heart.

He pulled the trigger.

The gun clicked empty.

Jonah lunged at him.

Shoving himself off the edge of the counter, he threw all of his body weight into the old man, tackling him to the floor with everything he had left. Terry, unprepared for the hit, crumpled and fell back, gasping for air. Jonah followed him down, punching him in the face again and again, the impacts rattling his arms, his neck, the hinge of his jaw. A second later, Terry shoved him off—Jonah rolled away awkwardly, feeling the hole in his stomach tear wider. This time, the pain was too much. He stayed where he fell.

"Motherfucker," Terry wheezed. "Oh, you little motherfucker..."

"Fuck you, Terry," Jonah wheezed at the old biker from the floor, bloody stringlets flying off his lips with every syllable.

Crawling over, Terry dropped a knee into his ribs, then punched him in the teeth, the impact setting Jonah's head spinning like a merry-go-round as the old man's heavy silver rings bit into his lips, drawing blood.

That was when Terry got his hands around Jonah's throat.

Panic went off like a klaxon inside Jonah's head as he struggled against the old man's grip, batting weakly at his forearms and yanking on his wrists, but Terry was too strong, too determined. Baring his teeth, the old biker squeezed tighter, cinching off Jonah's breath like a garrote.

White spots danced in front of his eyes, consciousness leaving his brain bit by excruciating bit. His ears rang louder and louder as Terry throttled him, quickly drowning out the sound of the old man's animal growling. This was it, Jonah thought. Terry was going to choke him to death. Any second now, he'd black out from the lack of oxygen, and then he'd be dead.

But he wasn't dead yet.

Flailing at Terry's face, Jonah ground the tip of his thumb against the old man's left eye, pressing down with all the strength left in his arm. Terry screamed in response but didn't let up. Jonah dug down harder, feeling the old man's eye start to collapse underneath the lid, and when it finally burst, it did so with a spurt of warm jelly that made Jonah think, wildly, of broken egg yolk. Shrieking like a child, Terry recoiled, letting go of Jonah's throat to clap both ring-heavy hands to his face as he floundered away.

Air returned to Jonah's lungs in a great, agonizing gust. He didn't wait for Terry to get his bearings again. Body screaming for mercy, for rest, for all the suffering to just be over already, he lurched forward and tackled the old biker back down to the ground, raining both fists into Terry's face, his throat, his temples, his jaw, his nose, and the backs of his hands that covered the ruined, messy hole where his left eye used to be.

He threw everything he had left into beating the mean old fuck into the floor, panting like a dog, not caring anymore if he lived or died. All around them, the room filled up with the flat, blunted sounds of meat striking meat, and even when Terry went limp underneath him, Jonah kept whaling on the man. It was no better than he deserved. It was no less than what he'd asked for.

There was a flicker of motion by the back door. Jonah looked up and felt his heart wilt.

Alex.

The dead boy stood there watching Jonah in all his rotting glory, painted with blood, his leather jacket hanging in tatters around crumbling, bony shoulders. He looked exactly like he had in the photos from the morning they'd found him dead, skin all pale blue and rimed with frost, the shots leaked to the Internet by one of the trash collectors who'd discovered him. Standing there, watching Jonah pummel the man, Alex's thin, cracked lips split into something resembling a smile, his teeth all bunched and broken.

See something you like, fuckface?

Hearing the dead kid's voice ring inside his head, Jonah felt all the fight left in him drain out in a single nauseous heave. He was so fucking tired. He let his arms drop, seeing clearer now. Killing Terry, beating him to death in a puddle of his own blood and snot and puke wasn't going to solve anything, and it sure wasn't going to make Jonah hurt less. He'd done enough damage for one lifetime, and anyway, the old man was done. Beaten. Half-blinded. It was over.

"Fuck this," Jonah said to no one, his voice cracked and coarse. "I'm done."

He stood, trying not to throw up, as Terry rolled unsteadily onto his side, still mewling and clutching at the red hole Jonah had thumbed in his face, the jellied remains of his crushed eye trickling down his cheek.

When Jonah looked up again, Alex was gone — but through the sliding glass, Jonah could see Anna and Nell in the backyard, both bloodied and bruised in a daze on the ground. He had to get out there.

Hanging his head low, Jonah limped away from the fallen biker, dragging himself across the bloody hardwood as he headed for the door. He didn't know what he was going to do when he got out there, but he was going to do something. Grabbing the door handle, he—

"No," someone said behind him. "We're not done."

Jonah looked at the glass in front of his face, and at the bloody, white-haired silhouette that swayed over his shoulder.

Terry was on his feet again.

S he came to slowly, fading back into herself as reality bled into place all around her. She was sure she'd only been unconscious for a few seconds, but it felt like it had been hours. Time had gotten blurry, events fallen out of order. She remembered cutting the old man's throat and wrestling him down to get the ink on his forehead. She remembered going through the window with Nell and the look on the girl's face when her father died. She remembered the cold air whipping around her as she spun and fell.

Beneath her face and her hands, wet grass brushed gently at her skin—she held still, listening to the silence of the night around her, the sound of her own rattly breathing as she filled and purged her lungs, the blood in her ears. She didn't remember hitting the ground, though she knew she must have at some point. No matter. It was just a fall. She'd fallen before, and from higher ground than some second-floor window besides. She could still feel the Chain rattling underneath her skin, but for now it had seemed to abate some, leaving her a bit more alone in that blissful inner darkness. It was better than nothing.

Slowly she rolled to sit up in the grass and took in her surroundings: they'd crashed into the backyard, a wide patch of well-kept green buffeted by a long stretch of red-brick paving stones that formed a sort of extension to the patio. Anna had been lucky, it seemed; she'd landed on the lawn. Nell, not so much. A handful of feet away, she lay flopped on the paving stones in a stupor, with blood pouring down one side of her face like a red curtain. Good. Anna hoped it hurt.

Moving to stand, Anna felt a compressed stiffness pull against her belly, just above the blade of her hip. She looked down, searching for the source of the—

Oh.

Oh.

The kitchen knife she'd used to open the old man's throat was lodged deep in her side, standing at attention below her bottom rib, driven in to the hilt. Must have landed on it when she hit the ground. Blood, nearly black in the low light, pulsed steadily from where the blade had punched into her—mindlessly, she wiped at the mess with cold, shaking fingers, leaving long red streaks in her clothes.

She'd dealt with enough stabbings in her life to know that pulling the knife out of herself was a very bad idea. But Nell was still alive, still moving. That thing was still inside her. Anna still had to finish it, and there was nothing else around for her to finish it with.

She had to risk it.

Curling both hands around the handle of the knife, Anna stoppered up the breath in her throat, clenched her jaw hard enough to crack a tooth, and pulled.

Pain ripped through her body in a bright red wave as she heaved, feeling the steel rock back and forth inside her, the heel of the blade caught underneath the edge of her skin, lodged like a fishhook. Screaming through her teeth, she twisted the knife slowly, trying to free it, until she felt steel click against bone. Closing her eyes, she held her breath and pulled again, gasping with relief as the blade began to slide free of her body. Blood jetted from the open wound, but she couldn't worry about that right now. She'd get herself to a hospital when the job was done. Not before. Not when the thing she'd done it all for was within her reach.

Broken glass crunching under her shoes, the kitchen knife hanging loosely at her side, Anna limped toward Nell, still prone on the stone walkway. In the far reaches of her mind, it occurred to her that she'd been here twice before, looking down at Nell Talbot with a blade in her hand. The third time would be the charm. She'd make sure of that.

Kneeling down slowly, Anna braced one knee against the ground, resting the tip of the blade against the brick, steadying herself. Nell looked so small like this, so frail and fragile, as if she might shatter at the slightest touch. Maybe the fall had taken more out of her than Anna thought. Still, better to do it quickly. No sense in giving that damned thing inside her another chance to wriggle free. Keeping one hand tight around the blood-slick haft of the knife, she reached her other out to push a stray lock of hair free from the blood sweeping down Nell's face.

But the instant Anna's fingertips grazed skin, Nell's body cracked like a bullwhip, her head arching so far back that it nearly touched between her shoulder blades. The sound that came ripping out of her then was so horrible, so colossal and inhuman, that Anna actually recoiled, jerking her hand away from the girl as if she'd been burned. The sound, that roar, it filled up the night and shook the houses around them, setting off car alarms on the surrounding streets.

On the ground, Nell's eyelids slid open underneath her blood-wet brow, and Anna gasped—her eyes had gone blank and colorless, glowing with a chilly emptiness like a distant light over icy tundra. Shaking, Anna raised the kitchen knife, holding it as she'd so often held the razor, the handle firm in her fingers, the pad of her thumb braced against the spine. She held the blade out like a ward and watched as Nell's features began to droop and melt, her face running like candle wax.

Then Nell began to rise, lifted up into the air by some great unseen force, her arms held out in a cruel mockery of the crucifixion. Floating upright, Nell admired her own distorted form, her torso and limbs stretched like taffy, mouth torn all the way back to her ears, filled with rows and rows of cracked, chattering teeth.

No. Not Nell. Nell Talbot was long gone, dragged underneath the waves to be subsumed by the ancient, undying presence that lurked beneath her skin, a corrupted amalgamation of itself and the angry, violent woman that it had so completely infected.

The thing chattered its teeth and ran its tongue around its lips as drool sluiced from its jaws in cords. It was smiling at her.

Jonah
Albuquerque, NM

At first he didn't understand what was happening.

Terry hit him from behind, right in the middle of his back. He bounced off the sliding glass and went tumbling to the floor again, trying to cry out but, for some reason, unable to draw breath. Breathlessly, he tried to roll over, tried to move, but he couldn't manage it. His body simply wouldn't obey. What the hell?

He shifted in place, moving his arms around to feel where he'd been hit. There was something lodged in his back. He stretched one hand up along his spine to where the pain seemed to be radiating from. His fingers grazed the handle of Terry's folding knife.

Oh, god.

Cold dread snaked through him, and as he thought about whether or not to try to pull the blade from his back, it suddenly came free of its own accord, sliding out of his flesh as a big, heavy boot crashed against his ribs, rolling him over with sheer force. Flat on his back, he found himself looking into Terry's ruined visage once more, more animal than man now. The knife dangled from his fingertips, the blade dripping with red. The fire in his eyes flared, and Jonah had just enough time to wince and cry out—"*Terry, don't!*"—before the old man inverted the knife and started to hammer on him with its hard, angled pommel.

Working his arm like a piston, Terry belted Jonah with the grip once, twice, three times, four, five, splitting the skin on his face like wet tissue paper. He could hear Terry's knees squeaking against the bloody hardwood as he slipped and slid back and forth, struggling and failing to find purchase every time he hit him. Yanking his arms up, Jonah tried to cover his head, gasping

315

for air as Terry pounded at him with the butt of the knife, the dull micarta pitting out little bloody divots with every impact.

"Fucking bastard," Terry fumed. "Little fucking bastard, you should have killed me, you little shit, you should have killed me *YOU SHOULD HAVE KILLED ME!*"

Lacing the fingers on both his hands around the handle of the blade, the old man reared back and threw all his weight forward. It was all Jonah could do to roll out of the way, jerking his shoulders to the side as a great inhuman roar shook the house, rattling the windows in their frames.

Startling from the sound, Terry slipped forward on the bloody floor, all his weight going out from under him. He tried to catch himself on his forearms, the blade pointing straight up at him as he dropped, his head jerking forward too fast. Jonah saw what was going to happen an instant before it did: with a wet *crunch*, the point of the knife speared up through Terry's empty eye socket and buried itself deep in his brain.

He made a choking sound—a kind of damp *glurrrk*—as he jerked and tried to pull back, his body instinctively trying to reverse its own death, but it was too late. The damage was done. Blood poured out of Terry's head in hot, pulsatile rushes that soon slowed to a trickle as the old man finally, mercifully died. He slumped forward, pressing down on Jonah as the younger man struggled to breathe through wheezy lungs, coughing and gasping and pushing the dead man off him.

Jonah's heels described long hooks through the blood underneath them as he dragged himself from the tangle of Terry's body, crawling backward on uneasy forearms to brace himself against the sofa. Pressing red handprints into the upholstery, he stood, both legs shaking underneath the weight of his body, threatening to buckle.

Deep breaths. Deep, slow breaths. Come on, now.

As his frenzied pulse slowly eased back to something resembling normal, Jonah looked at the old man's body, both ringed hands still stubbornly locked around the haft of the knife, blood bubbling out of the hole in his head. Jonah hadn't meant for any of this. He wished he could apologize to the dead man, but what good would it have done? Terry would have spat in his face for even trying.

Outside, he heard someone scream. He turned in place, toward the sliding glass door and the backyard that lay past it. Let Terry rest. Nothing to do for him now anyway. Jonah had to get outside, had to try and help somehow. It wasn't over yet. He still had a part to play.

Wearing Nell's battered body like a shopworn suit of meat and skin, the damned thing grinned wider at Anna, licking torn black lips, brandishing every vile tooth in its head. Still hovering well off the ground, it rolled its fingers in front of its face as if discovering them for the first time. Anna feinted forward with the kitchen knife, but the abomination didn't take the bait.

—smell them all over you—

The voice that was two voices boomed inside her head, huge and monstrous. Disjointed images and sensations played across the backs of her eyes: the taste of ash, a filthy mouth without a face gnawing on a slab of raw meat, a storm drain seething with cockroaches, water pouring into an already overflowing glass, needles splitting her skin.

"Get out of my head," Anna growled, clutching at her temples. "Get *out*."

—pathetic—

Opening its heinous jaw wider, the thing licked its lips and let out a wet grinding sound like a garbage disposal filled with gravel. Anna only recognized too late that the thing was laughing at her.

—Dechant, Dechant—

She saw her father's face as it had been when she was a child, warm and radiant and full of life, and she saw him at

318

the end, his head shredded by the Chain as it ripped its way out of him, flesh burned and blistered and red. She saw herself eating razor blades, biting down hard, the cracked metal splitting her teeth and shearing her mouth to red scraps, and, as she watched, realized that she could taste the steel and the blood, could actually feel her tongue coming apart, lolling back and forth in loose, rubbery rags.

—false from false, pretender, broken—

"Get out of my head!"

The thing laughed again, the sound of it so much louder now. Clamping her eyes shut, Anna screamed at the top of her lungs, trying to drown it out, all her practiced control flying to ribbons inside her chest. When she opened her eyes again, the thing that used to be Nell shook its head and chattered its teeth behind its revolting lips. Softly, its feet touched the ground. Anna brandished the blade at its heart as she shrank back from it.

"Stop it," she gasped. "Liar."

Her head throbbed and strained as a fresh glut of sensations was forced through it: the smell of ozone, the juddering sound of sawteeth through wet leather, images of cage doors flying open, a church buckling from the inside and imploding as if devoured by the earth, a field filled with charred, stinking corpses, entire homes washed away in the waves of a catastrophic flood.

—passed their failure on to you—

Waves of impossible heat and absolute cold blasted over her; she watched an anthill turn on itself, boiling with vermin killing vermin; and, at the center of it all, a great churning void like the mouth of a lamprey, humming and rumbling, the sound of it almost too deep and low to hear.

Anna's face flushed hot and red, fervid against the cold night air. She raised the knife again, trying to keep her arm from shaking. Before her, the thing slowly rotated its head to the side, curious. Anger sparked and bloomed in her chest, transmuting her shame and powerlessness into pure, burning rage. How dare this venomous fucking thing invade her?

The abomination met her eyes, seeming to understand what was coming next without caring at all.

Springing forward on tensed legs, Anna swung the knife as the thing lunged ahead to meet her, slashing its spindly claw-hands at her throat. Anna ducked out of the way and thrust the knife forward, opening a deep, red ravine in the thing's stolen leg, shearing the flesh apart like whitefish. Barking with pain, it recoiled and swiped at her again, catching her in the shoulder, raking bloody tracks through the skin. Anna wailed and clamped on to the thing, gouging at its distended midsection as they stumbled together, feeling the gash in her side shudder against the sway of her body.

That horrible laughter came grinding out of nowhere once more, filling up the night, and Anna understood: it was enjoying this.

Breaking free of its grasp, Anna braced herself for the thing to press its advantage, tackle her to the ground, but it held steady. Behind her, she heard a soft *whoosh*—Jonah stumbled out of the sliding glass door, his head a blue-and-crimson ruin, one eye swollen and drooping above his cheeks and nose, bleeding steadily from a scatter of raggedy cuts and wounds. His belly was a mess, bleeding freely from the hole Anna had blasted through him only hours before. His arms shook as he crossed them over his chest, his legs knocking with every step he took through the freezing night.

"Anna, stop," he groaned as he limped toward them. "Please. Stop, okay? Let her go." As she watched, Jonah's attention drifted away from her, up and over to the thing that used to be his sister. His expression fell.

"... Nell?"

"I'm okay," a frail, shaky voice warbled behind her. "I'm ... I'm all right."

She turned to look: the abomination had fled beneath the waves once more, leaving Nell alone in its wake, a battered bird crumpled on the ground among broken wings. She looked like she could barely move, wounded as she was from the deep gashes Anna had scored in her shared hide, powerless without the demon buoying her up. Small. Inconsequential.

Heart pounding as she tried to shake herself free of the thing's punishing torment, the horrid things it had shown her, Anna turned back to face Jonah. Then it hit her. Something was wrong here.

"What did you do to Terry?" she rasped.

Jonah raised his shoulders, then dropped them. "Nothing he didn't deserve."

"What does that mean?"

The man's shoulders fell. "It means he's gone. It's just us now."

Rage pulsed in Anna's temples. "You bastard, you son of a bitch!" She lurched forward, righting the blade in her fist, meaning to tackle him to the ground and make him pay.

"Yeah," Jonah said. "You don't know the half of it. Now walk away, or I promise I will end you, Anna."

"You'll try," Anna said. "Look at you. You can barely stand."

"Anna, don't," Nell called out to her. "Please." A familiar deceit.

"You know, you're not looking too hot yourself," Jonah mocked, nodding at her wounds and raising his fists. "Come on. Let's see how bad you really are."

He was stalling. Buying his sister time to regroup. It was an obvious ploy. But she couldn't have him gumming up the works again.

"Fine," she said, tossing the knife aside. Then she rushed him.

Closing the distance in a few quick strides, Anna knotted one fist in Jonah's shaggy, stringy hair and drove the other into his nose as hard as she could, bouncing his head back and forth like a speed bag. Behind her, Nell screamed for her brother, begging Anna for mercy, but Anna had none left to offer. She beat Jonah until his face was swollen shut, blood and snot and saliva pouring from his mouth and lips. Then she let him drop.

Anna was surprised that he had made it this far, nevermind that he'd somehow gotten the best of Terry. She was almost proud, in her own way. She'd thought for sure that he'd fold and give up the ghost after she put that bullet through his belly, but Terry had insisted they keep a lookout for both Talbots, just in case. They were a pair of bad pennies, after all. So she'd dragged father Talbot up to the second floor to wait for Nell while Terry hid downstairs, on the lookout for the brother. But Anna'd never expected that Jonah would actually have enough gas left in the tank to get through Terry. She always underestimated people. Her dad had always said—

"Pease," Jonah begged breathlessly, the word *please* all mushy and gummed up by the bloody mess pouring freely out of his face. "Pease, prease, pease, doe. Doe do id. Pease, juss stob."

Looking down at Jonah now, Anna almost felt pity for him, broken as he was. Almost.

Turning away, she started looking for her knife. This ended now.

Nell
Albuquerque, NM

S he screamed for her brother, screamed for Anna to show mercy, but neither of them could hear her now. She watched Anna beat Jonah to a red pulp, the flat sounds of her fist drumming against his skull almost metronomic underneath the quiet night sky. Despite the fury Nell had seen in Anna's face, her execution was mechanical, precise and unfeeling, a job like any other. She had no doubts the woman was enjoying this, despite the clinical, calculated nature of the violence she was meting out. Nell rolled over, off the paving stones and onto the grass, feeling the frozen blades bend and crunch underneath the weight of her body, feeling the One Within recoil inside her, slithering back to its cave. None of this had gone the way it was supposed to.

She searched the lawn for the glint of the kitchen knife, catching sight of it in the grass only a few feet away. Her hand found the grip and she lifted it from the ground slowly, delicately, as if it might bite her at the slightest provocation. Holding it up in front of her face, she examined her haggard reflection in the blade, still wet with blood—hers, her father's, Anna's—and felt a sober kind of clarity take hold inside her.

She could still make this right.

Swallowing back a throatful of bile, kitchen knife in hand, Nell rose to her feet one last time.

"A nna."

Startled, Anna whirled to see Nell on her feet again, a sad look marring her face, the bloody kitchen knife hanging from one hand. *Stupid*, she chided herself inwardly, feeling her cheeks go hot. Stupid and arrogant. Shouldn't have thrown it away like that. But she wanted to drag it out, she wanted to hurt Jonah for making things so much harder than they needed to be. She wanted to beat every inch of life out of him in front of his sister, to show them both: *This is what you get*.

"Put it down, Nell. You can't win this fight," Anna said, nodding at the knife. "You have to know that by now."

"Yeah, I know," Nell said.

With awkward fingers, she slowly turned the blade around in her hand, bringing the point to rest at an upward angle against her stomach, just underneath the bottom edge of her ribcage. Anna knew that angle. It was a killing blow. It would only take the tiniest little push for the blade to slide in and pierce Nell's heart.

Every nerve in Anna's body jumped to attention, thumping excitedly under her skin at the prospect. Tradition said in order to do it right, add another link to the Chain, she was supposed to be the one to snatch the life from the vessel's heart, but she knew that in practice, it didn't always work out that way. Things went wrong, no plan was ever perfect. She'd learned long ago that as long as she was there to take the burden onto herself, it didn't really matter how the body died. If Nell wanted to do it to herself, all the better.

Except there was no way. She wouldn't, not after fighting so hard for so long. This was another trick.

324

"Stop playing games," Anna said.

Nell shifted her weight from one foot to the other, pulling the knife tighter against her chest. The blade gleamed dangerous and silver in the scant light. Anna could see her hands shaking around the handle, the circles underneath her eyes dark and deep enough to get lost in. She wasn't going to do it. Anna was sure of it now.

"You won't," Anna said.

"You don't think so?" Nell asked.

"No." Anna's voice was quaking something fierce now. "Why would you? After all this?"

"Because I know what happens next," Nell said.

Then she plunged the knife into her own heart.

At first, Anna didn't really believe that she'd done it. But then blood spurted from where Nell had driven the blade in, cascading down her chest and belly and legs in a red waterfall. Hands still locked around the handle of the knife, Nell kept pushing, burying the steel to the hilt as she fell to her knees. Somewhere deep inside herself, Anna felt the Chain start to thrash and scream and pull anew, struggling harder than it ever had before.

She'd done it.

She'd really done it.

Elation crackled at Anna's every edge, in her fingertips and toes and the crown of her head. She'd won. It was over. The hair on her arms and the back of her head stood straight up as goosebumps spread across her skin. For the span of a single breath, her heart ceased to beat. It was really over. A scream of joy arose in her throat as Nell toppled to the ground. Anna went to her and, cradling her in her arms, rested her forehead against Nell's. She wanted to say something, say anything, but she couldn't find the words. Language, for the time being, eluded her. It was just as well. Nell was dying all the same, and when her last breath slipped free of her lungs, her passenger would be Anna's, contained forever, another link in the Chain.

Lying on the grass, Nell gasped for air and draped her arms

around Anna's neck, holding on tight. Her skin was cold and clammy. Blood frothed out of her, soaking into Anna's clothes, and Nell worked her lips silently, mouthing words that wouldn't come. Anna almost didn't register it as Nell squeezed tighter, holding her in place.

That's when she noticed it. A strange electric charge rising in the air. What the hell? Anna began to struggle against the woman's grasp, but Nell was still so strong. Too strong.

Nell
Albuquerque, NM

I t didn't hurt. Not at all.

It was funny. Nell had always thought—feared, really— that dying would be a painful thing, but lying here in Anna's arms, she barely felt a thing. She hadn't felt anything the last time she'd died, so why had she expected it would be any different the second time around? She no longer knew. She only faintly felt the blade punch into her middle; there was the slightest pressure, and then she was falling, the ground rising up to meet her as if she'd simply detached from herself. It was just a shell, after all. What made her *her* couldn't be unmade so easily. She saw that now. A deep, comfortable heat like the morning sun on a summer day spread throughout her body, numbing her limbs, her chest, her head, her lungs, and her heart.

If this was what death felt like, it was no wonder everyone did it.

Through that dreamy summer warmth, Nell felt something large and alien come loose inside her, dislodged from the hollow space where it had made its home. When Anna rested her forehead against Nell's, in her delirium, Nell could have sworn the woman was going to kiss her, and for an instant Nell could see another Anna, someone she was sure no one else ever saw. Who she was when she was alone, who she was at her worst and at her best. She saw the Anna that every other version of her tried to cover over and hide away. There was tenderness in the woman, and pain, and a great consuming pit of anger that she could never fill but would never stop trying to. Nell felt sorry for her.

Sucking air in tiny little gasps, Nell wrapped her arms tighter as Anna tried to pull away, fighting as hard as her broken

327

body would allow, but Nell held her fast. This was what she'd wanted all along, wasn't it?

A merciless pressure ballooned inside Nell's stomach, followed by a billowing, noxious heat. Trapped in Nell's arms, Anna began to scream, struggling against her grasp like an unruly child throwing a tantrum; and as Nell opened her mouth to let the fire inside come roaring out, Anna's face contorted into a mask of horror.

She would die making that face.

An endless rush of fetid black smoke exploded from Nell's lips and crashed across Anna's head, swirling around her in thick tendrils that forced their way into her mouth, her nostrils, and her eyes. For a single fraction of a heartbeat they were connected by the smoke, bound in an instant that lasted a lifetime. Nell saw Anna's past, every throat she'd cut, every aching day on the road, every little moment of doubt. She saw the woman's entire life all sewn together in a single unbroken ribbon, from her childhood spent in an insane cult of fanatics to the realization, only seconds ago, that the fear she had spent years ignoring had finally been realized: she was not enough to contain that prison inside her. She had never been enough. She had failed.

The One Within—and the legions inside Anna Dechant—had been released.

As Anna thrashed and wailed and tried to escape, Nell felt something deep inside the woman strain, then shatter, into countless shards. In an instant, Anna's desperate, dying screams turned to exultant laughter, and Nell let her go, watching as the skin on her face started to come apart underneath the force of the smoldering torrent.

She felt the wounds that the One Within had held shut break open again: the bullet hole that Terry had blasted into her chest, the tunnels that had been nailed through both her hands, more and more. Ripped away from the strength of the thing that had bolstered her up, Nell began to founder and fade.

Throwing herself back and forth atop the paving stones, Anna laughed louder and louder, shaking and shuddering as the smoke turned in on itself and began to flense the skin from her skull, tearing the flesh away in strips, exposing bloody stretches of raw white bone underneath. Inside her mouth, her tongue charred and crumbled as her teeth burst in their sockets, shredding tender flesh to pulp. Her eyes boiled and burst like pustules, discharging bubbling plasma down her cheeks and scorching lines in the little skin that was left on her face.

Slumping back, Anna's jaw hinged wider and wider, beyond all human limit. At the bottom of that darkness inside her, Nell beheld a great, strange, swirling light unlike anything she'd ever seen before, an unearthly collision of purples and reds and blues and other colors she had no name for. It was the most beautiful thing she'd ever seen in her life, gleaming sharply as it danced and refracted and glittered in the depths.

It was as if a connection that Nell had never known was missing had been restored, and she found herself suddenly connected to a million other parts of herself, a million other selves. Alone, she was a candle flickering in the darkness, locked away, isolated; together, they burned like the sun. In that instant, Nell saw, felt, *became* the legions breaking free within Anna as she burned from the inside out, praying endlessly for death yet unable to die, even as her body was rended apart inch by inch. Their bonds shattered by the black cascade, the hissing things that had been trapped inside for hundreds, thousands of years ripped their way free from the ruins of their prison in a hurricane of color and noise.

It was all Nell could do to throw herself out of the way when Anna's head snapped back and that storm of color erupted out of her in a blinding column of light to pierce the night above. Burning from without and within, Anna's mad laughter grew in pitch and volume, the sound sharpening itself into a keening shriek that soon disappeared into the deafening roar of the storm. The light, filled with teeth and claws and nightmarish faces, fountained upward from the dead-yet-still-living woman, filling the night and spreading across the empty sky in a hypnotic, glaring phantasmagoria. As it spread, Nell started to hear voices hiding inside the light, joyous, exuberant wails that braided themselves together in terrible harmonies before breaking apart to dance and spin and fly once more, free, free, finally free.

This was what it wanted. This had been the point all along, ever since she'd looked up to find Anna sitting across the table from her in that shitty little diner in Mowry. Nell had felt the One Within bristle inside her then, sensing all its trapped brethren locked away inside Anna, though she hadn't recognized it for what it was—how could she have? All the same, the One Within—*Murmur*—had sensed that instability reverberating inside Anna and knew. All it would take to break her open was one more.

Nell couldn't say exactly when it was that Anna died. Maybe it didn't matter. Trapped within her own body as it burned away, every second of her immolation an eternity of suffering, she screamed as the fountain of light poured out of her and disappeared into the clouds overhead, painting the sky like an oil slick.

When it was over, the burned-out husk that used to be Anna Dechant collapsed to the ground, little more than blackened bones draped in scorched rags. Then it was quiet.

Anna was gone. The One Within had vanished.

Nell was alone.

And she was dying.

Underneath the iridescent sky, feeling the life draining from her pain-riddled body, Nell pulled the knife from her belly and started to crawl for her brother. Every movement was agony, every foot she managed to cross an exercise in suffering, but she pressed on. Jonah didn't deserve to die alone. Neither of them did.

Collapsing next to him, Nell wrapped her arms around his ribs, holding him tight and listening for the sound of his breath, his heartbeat, his anything. She shuddered as the last bit of warmth bled out of her, then buried her face against her brother's spine and began to cry. They were home. They'd made it. No one could take that away from them now. As the black clouds and unearthly colors that climbed the sky gave way to flashing red and blue, Nell began to hum a tune she no longer remembered the words to, hoping Jonah could hear her, wherever he was.

In her last painful moments of consciousness, she thought she could taste smoke on the breeze.

Then she was gone.

Epilogue

THE HOLLOW

rom this far up, the neighborhood looks like a graveyard, each house a headstone dotting the winding asphalt paths in the dwindling early morning shadows. It's a neighborhood like any other, nearly an exact replica of the dozens that surround it. It could be anywhere. It could be anything.

The streets are quiet and still as the sun crests the horizon, spilling warm orange light across the gathered homes, another perfect late-summer morning dawning anew. The silence holds steady, balancing on a knife's edge, and then, at the far side of the neighborhood, there's movement: a box truck, a big yellow rental well past its two hundred thousandth mile, turns off the main road and winds its way into the neighborhood's heart, its path confident and sure. Turning into a cul-de-sac, it makes a three-point turn to back carefully into the southernmost driveway, then sputters to a halt as the driver, still anonymous behind the sun-glared glass, throws it into park. The transmission whirrs and whines before the driver kills the engine, returning the morning to the totality of its own silence.

The driver's-side door swings open with a creak, and a man, not young, not old, tall and lean with serious eyes and dark hair, steps out from behind the steering wheel, basking in the sunlight as he stands before the house. His hair isn't as shaggy as it used to be; he's taken to cropping it back with electric clippers, keeping it close enough to the curve of his head but still long enough to hide the scars in his scalp. He wears clothes he can work in, a white T-shirt and battered jeans and a worn-out pair of sneakers, the canvas splattered with paint stains. He shoulders the truck door shut and locks it with the key, then goes back to the bed for a bound stack of flattened cardboard boxes and a three-pack of clear tape.

His face is different than it used to be, its essential topography reshaped and restructured by the broken nose and the knocked-out teeth and all the new scars the doctors told him would fade eventually, probably. They haven't yet. He's skeptical that they ever will. He doesn't really mind. People keep their distance when they see them, so at least he doesn't have to deal with strangers striking up casual conversations in line at the bank or when he's waiting for his coffee. It's probably for the best. He was never really that good with people anyway.

He runs one hand over the top of his head as he looks up at the house, empty and still for months now. He checks the time on his phone. He's early. That's fine. He heads for the front porch, lugging the boxes and tape with one ropy arm, fishing a second set of keys from his pants with the other, spinning the ring around his finger, humming tunelessly to himself. He doesn't like the new door. It's too new, too modern. The color's weird, and it has too many little windows. He liked the old one a lot more, but there was no saving it after it got kicked off its hinges, and anyway, the realtor's told him twice already that modern touches and updates are going to help them sell it for a lot more than they think.

Still.

He thumbs a key away from the others and slips it into the lock, disengaging the deadbolt and letting the door swing open. It's dark inside. Not a surprise, really: more than anything, it's just sad.

It's been four and a half months since he's set foot in this house, and if he had his way, he wouldn't ever again. He'd much rather hire movers to come and clear everything out without his having to get involved, like the trauma cleaners that came through while he was still in the coma to scrub all the blood out of the floors and walls. But he knows that no matter how much he doesn't want to do this, there are some things in life that you have to do yourself. Even if they suck. Shit, especially if they suck. So he's here. He's ready. At least, as ready as he's going to be.

Steeling himself, Jonah Talbot takes a breath and steps inside his childhood home for the very last time.

He came to six weeks after the bloodshed at his dad's house, shot through with tubes and wires in a hospital bed, surrounded by strange white machines that wouldn't stop beeping at him. They removed his breathing tube first, begging him to stay calm and stop trying to pull it out himself. Eventually he relented and let them do their jobs. He lay in that bed for weeks, attended to by nurses and doctors and police who all demanded more out of him than he was able to give. He endured their questions and requests, and he listened dutifully to what they had to tell him, because he didn't have any choice. It wasn't like he could go anywhere. The cops were especially unsympathetic about it, surprising precisely no one. They stood around his bed and laid out the facts as they saw them: three dead bodies—Dad, Anna, Terry—with Jonah bleeding to death on the ground in the middle of the whole shitstorm. No sign of Nell anywhere.

They asked him questions about what had happened that night, but once he realized they weren't going to drag him off to jail, he didn't try too hard with the answers. It was clear that they'd already made their minds up about what had happened. Another home invasion gone very, very wrong. Easy enough.

He was lucky he'd survived, they told him. They weren't saying it for his sake; they were saying it for theirs, to make the horror of what he'd gone through somehow more palatable, as if his surviving being fed through a meat grinder could give the grinding some sort of meaning. But Jonah had been through enough, had seen enough, to know better.

Every day, it was bad news followed by worse. He got updates on how his body was recovering from all the many horrible things that had been done to it (slowly). Updates on how his dad had died (painfully). Updates on how in debt his hospital stay would leave him by the time he got to go home (enormously).

It hurt physically to return to life, with all its indignities and suffering and stupidity—he far preferred the coma's gentle oblivion. But it wasn't like he had much of a choice in the matter. Nobody had asked him if he wanted to wake up; it just happened one day, and Jonah was back in the world again. Nothing to do now but keep moving forward. He wasn't dead yet. Unfortunately.

Visitors came and went, people he used to know in other versions of his life, back when he was someone different, someone whole. He didn't always remember their names, sometimes he just pretended he didn't. It was easier that way; it kept the conversations as short as possible so he didn't have to lie there and absorb all the dread and distress that his bloody state so obviously ignited inside them. Being here, looking at Jonah, all alone, it made people uncomfortable. Reminded them of their own fragility. As much as he appreciated them coming by, he really didn't need to be burdened with anyone else's damage right now. He had enough of his own, and his nightmares were keeping him plenty busy.

Then there was Molly. She appeared like a dream, materializing out of the ether one morning as Jonah opened his eyes, sitting by his bedside with a worried look on her face. She smiled at him, kissed him on the forehead, said she was glad to see him. It pinched at his heart, seeing her here, now. Because of course she came. There was never any chance she wouldn't, after hearing what had happened. She stayed for a handful of days, more than Jonah thought she would, which was nice. They talked, she read, he watched TV, she took naps in the battered old guest chair in his room. They ate meals together. It wasn't like it had been, but while she was there, the pain lessened, a bit.

Then she was gone again. Jonah was alone again. He didn't blame her for leaving. She had a whole life to get back to, one that didn't involve him. He understood. He wasn't angry about it. It was just nice to feel something resembling normal for a little while. After Moll headed back to San Francisco, it didn't take long for the other visitors to taper off too; a couple of days, maybe a week at the outside. Jonah didn't complain too much.

For a while after that, life became an exercise in monotony. Every day was the same as the last, the same as the one that came next: wake up, watch TV while he ate his bland breakfast from a bland plastic tray, maybe talk to the nurses as they shuttled in and out of his room, maybe not. More TV, then a nap. After that, they'd wheel him down for an hour or two of physical therapy, then back upstairs to wash off before lunch and more TV. Eventually they'd bring him dinner and, finally, blissful, drug-addled sleep. Wake, wash, rinse, repeat.

Then he looked up one day and saw Nell standing at the foot of his bed, alive and well and smiling softly at him, as if nothing had ever happened.

He's upstairs packing away the linen closet in the hall when he hears her call out from the front of the house.

"Hello? Jone, you in here? You left the door open."

Jonah drops an armful of old sheets into the cardboard box at his feet and pads down the hallway to the stairs and the banister overlooking the front room. Nell's standing in the doorway, lit from behind by the summer sun as it rises all the way over the neighborhood. She hasn't changed much in the week since he saw her last, her hair back to its natural dark chestnut color, grown out almost to her shoulders. She's wearing battered jeans to match her brother's, a pair of old Chuck Taylors, and a black T-shirt that says VILE CREATURE across the front. She uses a finger to hook her sunglasses off her face, folding them up and hanging them from the collar of her shirt as she looks around the front room.

"Hey," he calls down to her. She looks up at him, gives him a soft little half-smile.

"Hey yourself. You got here early." She throws another glance around the room, already half cleared out. "Been busy, too, I see."

"Yeah. I was up," he says. "Figured it was better to be productive than sit at home and watch TV alone."

"Looks like you've gotten a lot done already."

"Yeah, some," he says. "Been bouncing around the rooms, taking care of what I can on my own."

In the entryway, Nell turns to shut the door behind her,

and Jonah bristles, a nervous fever-shake behind his face, a tiny cloudburst of panic.

"Hey, leave that open, will you?" His voice comes out more strained than he'd like.

Nell meets his eyes. "Still?"

His expression falls. "Yeah. Yeah. I'm sorry, Nellie. I . . ."

Down below him, his sister gives him a kind, solemn look. "No, it's okay," she says. They've talked about it a lot in the last couple of months, Jonah's newfound aversion to being boxed in anywhere, leaving his windows cracked open, all the doors in his new place unlocked unless he's sleeping. "I get it. No problem."

She pushes the door so it stays open, the daylight and scorching heat pouring in from outside. A way out if he needs it. It's better than nothing. Nell puts her sunglasses down on one of the side tables, and they get to work.

The two siblings go through the house room by room, sorting things into different piles, different boxes: keep, sell, donate. Some rooms are all of one or another, some nearly an even split between the three. When they fill one box, they tape it shut and label it with a big black Sharpie that Nell stole from her job, then move on to the next. Working together, they go steadily, methodically, taking the ground floor first, the living room, the garage, the dining room. Jonah lets Nell take point on the kitchen and the den while he heads upstairs to clean out the bathroom and both of their childhood bedrooms. When he's done with those, he puts together two more cardboard boxes and heads down the hallway to where their dad used to sleep.

There's a big empty square cut out of the carpet on the far side of the room, exposing the hardwood underneath, still stained red-brown where Dad died. Guess the cleaners couldn't get it all out. Cutting the mess away isn't exactly an elegant solution, but it's a hell of a lot better than what was there before. The cops showed Jonah the photos. The window still needs to be replaced, a sheet of translucent plastic tarping stapled tight over the empty hole where the glass used to be. For a moment, Jonah feels nauseous—the empty space in here is too much, too big, too real. A Dad-shaped hole scooped out of the world and never filled in again. Jonah never even got to say goodbye, but Nell got it worse: she had to watch it happen.

He goes through the big oak dresser first, then moves on to the walk-in closet, pulling clothes from hangers and drawers, dropping nearly everything into the *donate* box. Up on the shelf above the hanging rod, tucked against the wall, he finds an old shoebox, held together with duct tape. Reaching for it, he winces against a stab of pain from the place Anna shot him, still not entirely healed.

"Here, let me help you with that."

He turns to find Nell standing in the doorway, watching him. She doesn't look at the hole in the carpet as she crosses the room to reach up and pull the shoebox off the shelf. As she does, her T-shirt shifts, and Jonah can see the top edge of the new tattoo on her chest. Standing by the bed, Nell pulls the tape off and opens the box with a gasp.

"Holy shit," she says.

Jonah looks over her shoulder and does the same.

Photos.

The shoebox is filled with photos, old school portraits of the both of them, candid shots from family vacations, pictures of their mom and their dad in younger, happier days. Dozens and dozens of them, memories captured in time, some hand-annotated, most not.

"Oh my god," Jonah says, sifting through the pictures with one hand. "These are amazing."

"Yeah," Nell says, her voice suddenly edgy. "Glad we found them."

He pretends not to see her stealing looks at the empty hole cut in the carpet and takes the shoebox from her scar-dotted hands, fitting the lid back on and tucking it under his arm. She lets him.

"You want to go through these later?" he asks.

"Sure," she says, crossing the room to stand by the door. "Sounds great. Listen, I'm gonna . . . I think I need a break. I'm going to go have a smoke outside, okay?"

Jonah nods. "Yeah, whatever you need."

"You cool here?"

"I'm cool. I'll finish up in here and come find you in a little while."

Nell nods as she steals out of the room but doesn't say anything else. Jonah listens to her footsteps thump down the stairs and through the house to the back door.

He tucks the shoebox of photos into the *keep* box and keeps working.

Jonah had gone with her to get the tattoo the day after he was released from the hospital, sat with her as she explained the design to the tattoo artist, a friendly, bald-headed guy with a big smile named Kevin. The design wasn't entirely unfamiliar: a black X adorned with empty crescent moons and inverted crosses trapped inside a circle. Jonah stayed silent as she rolled her shirt up to point to where she wanted the ink, over a messy scar in her chest, just above her heart. When the guy asked how she'd gotten it, she looked him in the eye and asked him if it mattered. He told her no and didn't say much after that. Jonah knew how the guy felt. He and Nell never talked about how she'd gotten the scar either.

Just like they never talked about where she'd disappeared to after Anna burned to death.

It wasn't that they didn't need to, or that Jonah didn't want to, but Nell never brought it up, and he could never find the right time to try. Jonah had a whole life he needed to rebuild, and anyway, Nell was fine, wasn't she? She was herself again, or at least a lot closer than Jonah'd seen in a long time. She was trying to move on. He couldn't blame her. Maybe the best thing was for him to do the same.

What would talking about it change anyway? What good would it do?

In the weeks and months that followed, Nell helped Jonah start rebuilding, helped him find an apartment, even introduced him to some of her friends. They were nice. A lot of them had heard stories about who he used to be, but they seemed to like who he was now too. He was glad. It was good to feel human again.

But every so often, across the table or down at the end of the bar, he'd see something in her eyes when she didn't know he was looking, something blank, something flat and vacant. Probably he was just imagining it, another symptom of his PTSD bubbling up to the surface. He was here, alive, and so was she. That was all that mattered.

Wasn't it?

Eventually, Jonah got a job, even met someone, and, piece by piece and day by day, things went back to normal. Or at least as normal as they could be.

Then came the day that he and Nell decided to clean out and sell their dad's house.

Jonah finds her in the backyard, a cigarette pinched between her lips as she kneels and picks shards of broken glass out of the lawn with her bare fingers. She turns halfway back as he approaches but keeps focused on the task at hand.

"How's it going out here?" Jonah asks.

Nell shrugs. "Fine, I guess," she says, plucking another shard out of the grass and tossing it into the nearby trash can. "They should have cleaned this shit up better. Someone could get hurt."

"Someone did get hurt," Jonah says.

Nell doesn't respond. He watches her carefully, studying her. "It's weird, isn't it?"

She looks at him over her shoulder. "What is?"

"Being here."

"*Here* as in Albuquerque, or the house? Or . . . like, alive at all?"

Jonah makes a face, sighs. "All of the above."

"Yeah," she says. "We were lucky."

"No, we weren't," he replies.

She goes still for a second, then shakes her head.

"No," she says. "I guess we weren't."

"You know, I still dream about her sometimes," Jonah tells her. "I'll be dreaming about something else entirely, and then she'll just show up out of nowhere."

Nell mugs a little half-grin. "Sounds sexy."

"It's not like that," he sighs. "You know what I mean."

She hangs her head. "Yeah. I know. Happens to me too."

"For real?"

"Oh, yeah. Definitely more than I'd like too. Like she's got some kind of vendetta or something."

"I suppose she does have her reasons," Jonah says.

"You're not wrong. And hey, not like she's the first ghost we've dealt with at this point, huh?"

Jonah looks at his sister. Considers telling her about the last time he saw Alex Lawson. Then decides against it.

"You know what I remember most about her?" he asks.

"What's that?"

"That crazy fucking look in her eyes. Her and Terry had that in common, I guess. Like she was burning from the inside. Every time she looked at me, it was like I kept expecting her to burst into flames." He realizes too late what he just said. "Shit. Sorry."

Nell sighs and tosses another loose shard into the trash. "Yeah, but she wasn't crazy, Jone. She was... I don't know. I don't know the word for it. Dedicated, I guess. She believed in something, even if what she believed made her do some horrible fucking things. At least she cared enough about something to believe."

"I guess. I don't know. She..." He trails off. He doesn't want to give the dead woman anything more than all she's already taken away from them.

"I know," Nell says, rising to her feet again. "I get it."

"I still see it when I go to sleep," Jonah tells her. "Every night. The light. The fountain."

"I don't know what you're talking about," Nell replies coldly. He knows what she's doing, trying to shut it down, just like every other time he's tried to talk to her about what happened here. Not this time, though. Not while this place is still theirs.

"Yes, you do, Nell."

She raises her hands and sighs. "So what if I do? What does it change?"

"Nothing, I guess," he says. "Honestly, nothing, in the grand scheme of things. But I can't be alone with it anymore."

Nell shakes her head, her face darkening with worry. "You're not alone, Jonah. But it's too much. I can't look at it too closely, or I...I don't know what. It hurts. It feels like there's this hole opening up inside of me whenever I think about that stuff, and it's all I can do not to disappear down it. I can't. I won't." Tears start spilling down her cheeks, and Jonah pulls her into a gentle hug.

"It's okay," he says into the top of her head. "I get it."

"Thank you," she says, pulling away and wiping at her face. She nods at the house. "Come on, let's go get this over with, okay? Movers are coming tomorrow; they're going to be pissed if we leave anything unpacked."

"Sure," Jonah tells her. "Lead the way."

Overhead, the sun beats down on both of them, and as Nell walks ahead, Jonah watches her shadow grow and twist beneath her feet, warping into something that starts his heart racing anew. Something misshapen and larger than life underneath a crown of antlers, crooked wings hanging like a broken wheel off its bent fishhook back. Walking up the steps to the back door, Nell pauses and glances back at him, and for a second she's not in her eyes. She's not anywhere. Her gaze is flat and blank, as if she were simply a suit of skin covering a cold, vast nothingness.

Then she blinks, and she's herself again, his sister again, Nell again. That strange dull light gone in an instant. As if it had never been there at all.

"I love you, Jonah. I hope you know that," she says.

"I know," he tells her. "I love you too."

Nell pulls the sliding glass door open and stands to one side, letting Jonah go first. Limping unsteadily up the concrete steps, he nods a silent thank-you to his sister, and then the three of them head inside to finish what they started.

THE END.

Acknowledgments

That this book exists at all is entirely creditable to a very small group of unbelievably patient, generous, wonderful friends and family who were kind enough to read an early version of the first fifty pages and tell me that it was worth pursuing, so if it's any good at all, they're the ones that deserve the credit. With all my love:

Rebecca Agatstein, I truly cannot believe how profoundly lucky I am to have you as a friend. Thank you so much for the reads (and near-infinite rereads), the astute questions, the pep-talks and encouragement, and maybe most of all, for never not giving a damn.

Kevin Sims, let's face facts: you're not just one of the very best people I've ever known, you're one of the most brilliant and talented. It's outrageously unfair. Your enthusiasm, thoughtfulness, and boundless energy are a joy to behold, and made this story infinitely better at every turn.

Emma Price, after more than twenty years of friendship, I really shouldn't be surprised at what an incredible person you are, but here we are all the same. I'm amazed and humbled that you've stuck around this long. Thank you so much for everything.

Lucienne Druckman, hello today! I cannot tell you how stunned I am by your constant support and kindness. My writing—and my life—are so much better because of you. I couldn't ask for a better sister.

To Chelsey Emmelhainz, my wife, my partner in crime, my best friend, and my heart: thank you for your love and patience, your support and understanding, your collaboration, your insight and ardor, and for always daring me to be a better writer, even on the hard days (especially on the hard days). You are an endless inspiration to me, love. I honestly do not know what I did to deserve you. I love you more than anything, and more every day.

Enormous thanks go to my absolute powerhouse of an agent, Nicole Resciniti at the Seymour Agency, one of the most loyal, driven, no-bullshit people in this whole damn world. Thank you for your grit, dedication, and seemingly bottomless patience, Nic. Thanks for seeing me through this one, and all the others.

It should come as no surprise that as I was working on this book, I found myself constantly inspired by some pretty amazing, talented people along the way. Thank you all:

Lynn Lyons, Ashley Marudas, Amy Sims, Kim and Zach Fogel, Liz Claps, Pat Marshall, Dragan Radovanovic, Rick and Val Emmelhainz, Jon Davies, Daryl Winstone, Kim and Scott Collins, Jennifer Russell, Lauren Bochat, Sarah Poppe, Jonathan Jaynes, Carrie Miltenberger, Annie Promer, Amy Morawa, Chris Sanford, Andy Davidson, Damien Angelica Walters, Amina Akhtar, Taylor Zajonc, Libby Cudmore, LS Hawker, Nick Cutter, Kirby Kim, Jo Kaplan, Kelly Lonesome, Lindsay King-Miller, Josh Schlossberg and the whole Denver Horror Collective crew, and anyone else I forgot (sorry about that).

Also, a special shout-out is due to my dear friends Elizabeth Copps and Anthony Muller—thank you guys for the endless support, and for loaning me your exploding shower.

Many, many thanks to Stephanie Beard and the whole Turner Publishing team for their enthusiasm and dedication to making this novel as good as possible; thanks also to MS Corley for the astonishing cover design, Jessica Easto for the excellent editorial work, and to Phil Gaskill for the crackerjack copyedits.

An enormous debt of gratitude is also owed to the incredible band Murder by Death for letting me use their poetry as one of the epigraphs to this novel—I am forever honored. Thank you.

Other bands and musicians that were essential to the creation of this book (and were basically on repeat as I powered through draft after draft): Vile Creature, Sleep, VOWWS, Orville Peck, Chelsea Wolfe, clipping., Amigo the Devil, Red

Fang, Emma Ruth Rundle & Thou, the Cure, Kreeps, Jenny Hval, Sunn O))), Wayfarer, That Handsome Devil, and so, so many more.

Last, but certainly not least, this book is dedicated to my grandmother, Alice LeOra Merritt. She probably would have hated parts of it—especially all the swearing and bloodshed and Devil shit—but I think, after looking past all that, she really would have understood it. She taught me how to tell stories and sing songs, and how to be kind, even when kindness was the harder choice. She deserves all the credit in the world for that, and for everything else.

I love you, Grandma.

About the Author

Matthew Lyons is the author of the novel The Night Will Find Us, as well as over three dozen short stories, appearing in the 2018 edition of Best American Short Stories, Tough, and more. Born in Colorado, he lives with his wife and their cat.

Date Due

JUN 1 2 2022			